THE BAD BOY'S HEART

BLAIR HOLDEN

THE BAD BOY'S HEART

Published by Blair Holden

Always for my Shortcake army, you all made this a reality.
And for my best friend, A. for loving Jess and being my favourite fangirl

The Bad Boy's Heart

By Blair Holden

PART 1

CHAPTER ONE
I've Started Developing a Cannibalistic Hatred for Redheads

Here's the thing about time: it doesn't give a shit about you. It doesn't care whether you've been shattered and broken beyond repair. It doesn't care that you're grieving for a loss so immense that your heart literally aches every time you breathe. Nope, time doesn't care. It keeps on moving, never just staying still. You might want it to remain unmoving, everlasting, but that doesn't work out, does it? Time doesn't care that you aren't ready to move on. It doesn't care that you don't want to pick yourself up to do things just because the hour requires it.

It doesn't care that you're in so much pain that your body's become numb. All it does is keep on ticking and asking you to move along with it.

So I do.

Eventually, that is.

***

One Week Later

The bed and I have become really good friends this past week. We've never left each other's side, if you're curious. This is the week where we were all going to go on a road trip. Megan, Alex, Beth, Travis, me, and…him.

Now I've destroyed it for them.

I told everyone to go without me. That I just needed some time to get my head sorted. I wanted them to believe that I was okay but then, these people are the ones who actually care. Everyone saw right through me and they canceled the trip. What's worse is that Megan and Alex end up fighting over me. That's the tricky bit about dating within your group of friends. When breakups happen, loyalties come into question, and people get put in spots they don't want to.

The word *breakup* teeters across my consciousness but I push it aside, as always. The tears that come usually by this point are threatening to make an appearance again, and I am sick of crying. This is not the person I want to be. I don't want to be the girl who hasn't gotten out of bed in a week. I don't want to be the one who pushes away everyone who cares for her. I don't want to cause my friends to ruin their relationships. I don't want to hurt this bad over a guy.

But I am exactly that girl.

When Cole came back into my life, I promised myself that I wouldn't let a guy become my whole world again. The decision was more about Jay than it was about Cole, Jay's stepbrother and the guy who I'd pined over for longer than necessary. I never questioned the strong hold he had over my emotions. I didn't think he would crush them the way he did. So, I fell, and I fell so damn hard. But he's gone now, and I'm still that stupid girl who feels too much.

Pulling the quilt over my head, I squeeze my eyes shut and pray for some sleep. When I'm asleep, nothing bad happens, but then as soon as I wake up, the pain is there and it's stronger than ever.

***

Two Weeks Later

I'm told he comes to see me every day. Every day they send him back. Beth says the first day, Travis gave him a black eye, and things could have gotten a lot worse if she hadn't stopped my brother. She also tells me that he didn't fight back at all, that he just stood there and let Travis do whatever damage he pleased. That causes a pinprick-like feeling to get through to my heart. The numbness is still dominating every other sensation, but that particular image in my head causes me to feel something. I push it away immediately. I don't care.

What Beth doesn't know is that I see him leaving every single day. He slams the door like he wants me to know that he's going away. That's when I make the effort to leave my bed and take a peek from my window. Every day he stands on the same spot for approximately ten seconds before walking away. Once, in the very beginning, I saw him fall to his knees as his body shook with silent sobs. That almost—almost—broke my resolve, but then I remembered the pain. The pain he caused and how he could cause it again.

It was enough to make me hide.

So now I have to pretend that I don't care. But I'm lying to them and, most importantly, I'm lying to myself. The fact is that I hate myself for even thinking about him. He sure as hell hadn't been thinking about me when he…

No.

I'm not going to think about it. I've thought about it and I've thought about it again, but I'm done. I need to put this behind me. I have to put this behind. I can't put my life on hold for him. Everyone says that teenage love is the kind you get over, that it's never as serious as you make it up in your head. Being this depressed over a relationship that might not have had a long shelf life seems naïve and stupid, right?

But I can't help but disagree. What Cole and I had felt more, much more. It felt like more the rest-of-my-life kind of thing than puppy love.

Note the use of the past tense.

Now, hear that sound? Yeah, that's the sound of my heart cracking open once again.

This is also the week that Jay starts coming by more and more. I think he's finally started to gain some insight toward how I feel, well, insight and some tact. To his credit, he doesn't look absolutely disgusted when he finds me in my bed, looking like a homeless person. I haven't showered in a few days, so I can only imagine how I look and, well, my pajamas aren't exactly from Victoria's Secret. His eyes do widen for a nanosecond, but he quickly composes himself and takes a seat on the armchair to my left. I'm watching *Supernatural* since all I'm ever in the mood for now is blood and gore.

We sit in silence for a few seconds before he speaks up. If he mentions Cole's name or even remotely begins to talk about what happened, I'll get Travis to kick him out. Simple.

But he surprises me. "So, which season is this? I stopped watching it like a year ago."

The Stone brothers never fail to shatter expectations, do they?

***

Three Weeks Later

A breakup is good for at least a couple of things. When you're trying to get over heartache and the constant, painful memories that hound you every second, you tend to find distractions. I desperately needed such distractions, so I put myself to work. Finals were here and I'd been studying my butt off. Normally when you're this devastated and dead to the world, studying would be the last thing you'd want to do, right?

Wrong.

I study, and I study harder than I ever have. I think even Megan's starting to freak out a bit, and she's the one who's all prepped and ready for finals three months in advance. Yet she can't sleep during the entire week that they take place. Parking herself outside the library, she lives on coffee until she's sure she won't get anything less than an A+.

And I'm taking it to a new level, so please feel free to question my sanity.

Sleeping makes me dream, and I wake up drenched in sweat in the aftermath of those. They're always similar. Erica and he, kissing, tangled bodies and lots of touching. Usually there are tears rolling down my cheeks when I get up, so I've given up on the entire concept of an eight-hour sleep. Now I take naps, lasting two or three hours, maximum.

The rest of the time, I study.

And by the time the first final is a week away, I'm ready to fall to my knees, because I'm going to have to see him.

***

One Month Later

Present Day

"Yes, Mom. I'll let her know. No, I can't promise anything…you need to listen…okay, fine. I'll try. Love you, too, bye."

Travis sighs as he plops down onto a stool at the kitchen counter. He looks tired and weary. It makes me feel horribly guilty. Not only does he have to deal with a girlfriend who's overcoming her mother's death, he has me, his psychotic, emotionally unstable sister. And let's not even mention our parents.

But at least I'm feeling…something. It's better than the haze of self-pity that's been surrounding me for the past month. A month, it's been a whole, entire month of me hiding out in my room and recovering, as I call it. But now it's time to get up and stop being so pathetic; that's what my mother said once when she called. She doesn't know the dirty details, but she knows about the breakup and my moping, as she calls it.

I haven't talked to her since.

She has no right whatsoever to tell me how I need to live my life. She's out there, living off her parents and doing god knows what with men half her age. She hasn't checked up on either Travis or me in what seems like months, and now, all of a sudden, she wants to be my mom again.

It's not really that big of a surprise. My dad finally got some sense knocked into him and filed for divorce. He says he doesn't care about the social repercussions but that he's ashamed of the mockery he and my mom have made of the "institution of marriage." Mom hasn't signed the papers, though, but Dad's already starting seeing someone, his secretary at that. Thankfully, she isn't young enough that people would mistake her for an adopted new sister, but she's young enough.

And Mom feels threatened.

Right now, she's trying to convince Travis to convince me to spend summer break with her.

As if my life isn't miserable enough.

"You should tell her that I'm not going to go."

"I would, if that would get her off my back, but it won't. She'll keep trying just because she doesn't want you to be around Daphne."

"What's she worried about? It's not like Daphne and I are going to be braiding each other's hair anytime soon. It's too awkward between us."

"Try telling her that."

I let the conversation go and can practically see the disappointment in Travis's eyes. It kills me to know that I'm the reason behind his pain, but there's only so much I can do. I got out of bed, I worked my butt off for my finals, and I'm going to school today. But that still doesn't mask the obvious changes he sees in me. I laugh a little less, talk a little less, and something inside me just feels…dead. Everything requires effort. Smiling hurts more than is worth the effort, and it's becoming increasingly hard to be the person I used to be.

"I'm so nervous, I'm going to puke. What if I forget everything I crammed for yesterday?"

Beth is in panic mode and it's understandable. School hasn't exactly been her priority the past couple of months, and she's fallen a little behind. We've tried helping her as much as we can, and, in all honesty, she's got no reason to be afraid, but she is. I watch as my brother calms her down. I watch as their love for each other shines so brightly in their eyes. I should be happy for them; that's what a good sister and friend would do. Instead, I'm staggered by the feeling of loss that courses through me.

I'm so distracted that I don't even notice it happening. The knife I've been using to prep some fruit for a quick smoothie misses the orange and goes right to the skin of my wrist, slashing across it. At first, I don't feel the pain—nothing at all. I just notice the blood pouring out of it, my eyes stuck on the red fluid and my feet glued to the floor.

It's only when I start to feel really light-headed that I cry out in pain. This catches the attention of the two people who really shouldn't have to deal with my mess. Travis hurries across, catching me before I face-plant onto the kitchen floor.

"Shit. Shit, what happened, Tess?"

My heart's hammering away; I feel so dizzy. I just want to close my eyes and fight the nausea. There's so much blood. It's trickling down my arm, it's on the kitchen floor, and it's soaking up my brother's white T-shirt.

"Get the goddamn first aid kit!" Travis shouts at a stunned Beth, who forces herself to move. I hear the thumping of her feet as she runs up the stairs to the bathroom. My vision starts to blur. Travis sinks us both to the ground and cradles me in his lap. It feels like I'm six again, the time when I scratched my knee badly against the neighbor's rosebush and Travis took care of me.

"Hold on, Tess. I'm going to make sure you're okay." He breathes heavily, applying pressure on the pulse point at my elbow. He's trying to stop the blood flow, but there's so much of it. The knife must have really gone deep.

Why can't I stop messing up?

There's no point trying to fight the darkness that begins to enclose my vision. It's the blood loss, and I know I'm seriously messed up when I thank my horrible knife skills for giving me a break from reality.

***

"Has she been eating?"

"I…I try to make sure she has at least three meals a day, but she just picks at her food. She says her appetite is gone, and eating too much makes her sick."

"Well, that would explain what happened today. She's weak, and I can see that she's lost weight. You add that amount of blood loss to it, and this was bound to happen."

I know the woman's voice. It's eerily familiar, but it's annoying that I can't place her face. Consciousness tugs me toward it, but my mind fights it. I don't want to get up; this right here is good. I'm surrounded by silence and it's oh so peaceful. All the noise that's constantly buzzing around my brain and making me…feel things is gone.

"What do I do? She's been pushing herself so hard for the finals, like she's possessed. She isn't sleeping, she doesn't talk to me, it's like she's here but not really…"

"Present. It feels like the person they've become is just a shell of what they used to be. And, Cole's the same."

I flinch inwardly. People know better than to say his name in front of me. I want to tell the woman to go away, but at the same time, I'm curious. She's talking about him; she knows how he's doing. I want to know if he's in as much pain as I am.

"Mrs. Stone, I appreciate the fact that you made a house call for my sister, but don't bring him up again. He did this to her. She won't tell me what exactly happened, but he's the reason she's so…broken. No offense, but I don't give a damn about what's wrong with him."

I shiver. It's Cassandra. Does she hate me? Does she think I'm responsible for hurting both her sons? Any other mother would blame me for tearing her family apart. Yet she's here and she's helping me. And Travis is being inexcusably rude to her.

My mother would have a heart attack. Such a pity she isn't here.

I keep my eyes shut, wanting to listen to the rest of their conversation.

"Mom." There's a new voice. It doesn't take me long to figure out who it belongs to. Only two people would call Cassandra mom, and, thankfully, it's not the person I'd rather not see for the rest of my life.

"They're paging you from the hospital. I think there's an emergency," Jay says softly. They're all talking in hushed whispers like they're afraid of waking me up. It's kind of funny that after all my insistence on not being treated as someone made of glass, I go ahead and slash my wrist.

Unintentionally, that is.

Cassandra sighs. "I should go, but make sure she has plenty of fluids when she gets up. And rest, she needs to rest, and just try to make her happy. The better she feels on the inside, the more it'll reflect on the outside. Get her out of the house once she's better, do anything to get her to move on." She chokes at the last word, and I hear the clicking of her heels as they come toward me.

"Get better soon, sweet girl." Her signature scent of Chanel No. 5 surrounds me, and I almost break down. Cassandra is the closest I've gotten to a motherly figure recently, and all I want is to hug her, ask her to take the pain away. She kisses me on the forehead, sweeping my hair to the side.

"Call me if you need anything. Jason knows how to re-dress the wound; he can tell you everything you need to know about that. But remember what I said, make her feel happy."

Is that even possible?

***

I slip in and out of sleep. When I wake up for a few short minutes, Beth gives me my pain killers and a huge glass of freshly squeezed OJ.

Before I know it, I am asleep again. Given that I haven't slept more than three hours a day during the past two weeks, it is a welcome reprieve. Due to the medication, my sleep remains dreamless, for the most part.

Until I am woken up by my worst nightmare.

"I just need to see her once; that's it. I need to make sure she's okay."

"I can't…if someone found out that I'd even let you in…Cole, they'll never forgive me."

Megan. I recognize Megan's voice. When did she get here? She usually visits in the morning, and we study together while I try not to ask her about him through Alex. She pretends, too, like she isn't dying to tell me things I may or may not be ready to hear.

It's an incredibly healthy partnership.

But right now, right this very second, I want to throttle her, wring her neck with that red hair of hers. After all, I've started developing a cannibalistic hatred for redheads.

My breathing starts to quicken; my heart starts to race. He's here. He's so close, right outside my door. I'm hearing his voice a month after I started deleting all his voice mails and leaving his texts unread. I cannot find it in myself to delete those, always promising myself to read them when I'm ready.

I'm so not ready.

And he's just a few feet away from me.

I swear, I don't breathe as I listen in on their conversation.

"She's sleeping, right? I'll go in and be right out. Travis won't know. I'll leave before they get back."

Make him go away, Megan. You can do this. Please don't let him in. I won't be able to take it. It's taken me so long to put the pieces back together, if only tentatively. I might break apart at the sight of his face.

"I shouldn't be doing this…Alex shouldn't have told you. You hurt her, you hurt her so much, and now you expect me to just forget that and let you be with her. You haven't seen what she's been like…" Her voice breaks off. She sounds close to tears, and again the guilt comes back to haunt me. How bad have I been for the last four weeks? How did I not see that I'd been hurting the people who love me? And then I feel anger, anger all directed toward him because he ruined everything. Just when I'd started to think that my life had changed for the best, he went ahead and swept the rug from beneath my feet.

Why does he even care now?

"I love her, Megan. I love her so damn much. Don't you think it's killing me to know that I hurt her? You think I'm doing any better? I have to see her…I just need to see that she's okay."

"She's not okay!" Megan cries out, but lowers her tone before continuing. "She's not okay, and I don't know if she ever will be. You were everything to her. I don't know what you've done, but whatever it is, you cut her deep."

"And I'll regret it for the rest of my life. I've lost the girl who was supposed to be my forever. I'm in hell, Megan; just give me this."

Don't listen to him—he's lying. If he loved me as much as he says he does, he wouldn't have shattered me like this. A tear slips down my cheek, and it's followed by another. Everything I've done to patch myself up goes to waste. And it's like I'm bleeding from every single pore on my skin, there's so much pain.

"Fine. Go see her, but you only have five minutes. I don't know how long Beth's therapy sessions take, but Travis will want to be back soon. She's asleep; don't do anything to wake her up. Your mom said she needs to rest."

Shit.

I think I die for about the time it takes my brain to spring into action.

But then I decide that I won't throw a tantrum and that I need to stop acting too affected. People break up all the time. Men cheat; that's what they do. It's up to me now to decide whether I want to spend the rest of my life mourning the loss, or whether I should put it all behind me.

It would be so much easier if I still didn't love him so much.

I turn onto my side, my back toward the door. I bury my head into the pillow, hoping my tear-streaked face isn't visible. Then I try relaxing my body so that it's somewhat believable that I'm asleep. Thankfully, there's a blanket covering most of me so that he won't be able to see just how stiff I've become and how shallow my breathing is.

The door creaks open.

Thump. Thump. Thump.

Can he hear how loud my heart's beating?

Footsteps. I'll probably never forget the sound of his boots. It used to comfort me, at one point. I always associated it with him, my safe place. Now there's just hurt and pain and then some more of it.

Then my senses are swarmed by his scent, the citrusy, woodsy smell that defines him. I hadn't realized how much I craved it until now. I'm torn between screaming accusations at him, hitting him, and begging him to lie down beside me and hold me in his arms. How weak does that make me sound, huh?

The bed shifts, the mattress dipping beneath his weight.

The bandaged hand is toward him, and the moment he gingerly touches my wrist with the back of his hand, I nearly jolt out of bed. It takes every ounce of willpower to just lie there. Anger simmers just beneath the surface because I like his touch too much. But then there's relief that he's here. He's really here.

"I'm so sorry," he whispers. His voice quivers, his body shakes, and once again it's a testament of my will that I don't react.

He's quiet for a while, but then I feel wetness on my arm and it's followed by more. It's when I hear his breath catch that I realize that he's crying.

Oh God.

He can't! He can't do this! He doesn't get to cry. He isn't allowed to make me hurt for him. He's supposed to leave me alone and let me forget that he ever existed. I can't feel this for him. Please stop; please don't do this to me.

"You know I'll always love you. So, I'll wait; if you ever decide to come back to me, I'll be there."

He presses his lips to my hairline in the softest of kisses. It's barely there, but I feel it to the tips of my toes.

Then he’s gone, and I’m left broken all over again.

CHAPTER TWO
I Currently Have the Self-Worth of an Amoeba

"So, is it true you tried to kill yourself because Cole broke up with you?"

I stare at the door of my locker, observing the rusted metal and the paint that never stops chipping. It looks strong, sturdy, even if it's aged. If I were to bash my head in repeatedly, it would cause some sort of damage, right? I might even talk the school nurse into giving me a, "She's crazy; never let her enter the building again pass." But then again, if I calculated how many times in my life the "what ifs" actually came true, the math could probably be done on a single hand.

Oblivious to my suicidal thoughts, Stacie, an ex-Nicole minion, continues her probing. Inwardly, I curse myself for not ditching the bandage when I could. If it's not bad enough that I currently have the self-worth of an amoeba, of course, to these people it would look like I slashed my wrists courtesy of a broken heart. Apparently, our breakup has created quite the hype and caused conspiracy theories to spin out of control.

The first one I squashed was that I was pregnant. To someone who'd always been fat, being told that you looked like you could possibly be carrying another human being inside you when you're not is like a blow to the head—with a fifty-pound sledgehammer.

I turn to face the tiny blonde who's still wearing her cheerleading uniform even though there are no games left to cheer for or any tournaments to practice for. She's the kind of person who perhaps lets this uniform define her; without it, she'd be lost. The cheerleader, that's what she'll always be.

Opening my mouth to give an explanation I've already given more times than I can count today, I'm stopped before I manage to get the words out.

"Shouldn't you be more worried about your boyfriend nailing Melissa in the girl's bathroom, Stacie?"

You'd think it would be Beth being this brutally defensive of me, but I'm blown away when I see Nicole towering over a flushing Stacie.

Huh. People never cease to amaze you, do they?

Stacie struggles to find words, sputtering and choking on half-formed responses. Finally, when she thinks she's got something good enough to throw in Nicole's face, a malicious grin spreads across her face. It turns her otherwise good-girl, angelic features vixen-like.

"What is this? The 'dumped by the Stone brother solidarity club'? Isn't that sweet," she sneers, gesturing between the two of us, "two ex-bfs brought together because their boyfriends didn't think they were good enough? How darn sweet."

Whereas I'm horribly embarrassed and want to be anywhere but here, Nicole is eerily calm and composed. Instead she gives Stacie a look that'd have the strongest of men cowering in their boots. I would know. I've been subjected to the look more times than I can count.

"Well, at least we had the pleasure of enjoying their fine, fine bodies for however long it lasted. Last I heard, neither would touch you with a ten-foot-pole. What exactly was it that you got tested for at the health clinic last month?"

Ouch.

I'm so glad I'm not Stacie. Poor girl, she looks like she would be relieved if Armageddon arrived right here, right now. Oh well, she had it coming. I'm pretty sure she's one of the strongest proponents of the "Tessa tried to off herself" brigade.

"You're such a bitch! I'm glad Jay broke up with your sorry ass." Stacie's face is turning a rather garish shade of purple at an alarming rate. I'm afraid she might have a stroke; Nicole needs to back off, but the poor girl is giving her one too many excuses. She's going to get pulverized. That sorry excuse of a retaliation is just more ammunition for someone with the skills of Nicole.

"At least we had monogamy, honey. I don't know how I'd feel about my boyfriend being more active than a stud horse."

She shoots, she scores. The round goes to Nicole Andrea Bishop; actually, wait, she wins the whole freaking championship. Someone give her the gaudy gold belt now. I look at Stacie and am actually scared for her. She needs to run, run right now before she suffers a nervous breakdown. Smart girl that she isn't but decides to be, she huffs and shoots us both a death glare and stomps away. I think she might need a therapist after this.

I turn to Nicole, who's still watching her latest victim stomp away and try to figure out her latest angle. Why on earth would she stand up for me? Is it because Cole and I are no longer together? Does she think she finally has a shot with him now? Is she going to use me again?

I really, truly don't know; besides, both my brain and heart aren't ready for going into that. Who knows what twisted scheme Nicole's working on now? What I do, however, know is that from now onward, I need to focus on the positives in my life. It's been a month of moping, and while I'm yet to recover from the devastation that is my poor heart, I'm done hurting the people around me. Time to man up, Tessa.

"Thanks?" I say to her and she simply shrugs in response.

"I always wanted to say all that to her. It was even more fun than I expected."

Leaning against my locker, I study her. "Do you spend your days trying to figure out how to hurt people?"

Facing me, she crosses her arms over her chest and raises an eyebrow. "Is that how you normally thank people who help you out?"

I huff out, "I never asked for your help. And it's not like I don't remember that; that was me seven months ago."

She whistles lowly. "Well then, next time when I see one of them going at you, I'll just leave you to the sharks."

Feeling bad about being mean to her, I stop her as she's walking away, "I'm sorry. You were just trying to help, but I don't really agree with your method."

"Too soon?"

"Too soon," I agree and she nods.

"But can I ask you something?" Here it comes. She's going to ask me about the breakup. Then she's going to ask if Cole's available and if, in the shadow of our newly formed truce, she could steal him as smoothly as she's done in the past.

Honestly, I might have a love-hate, mostly hate, relationship with the guy right now, but I'd rather have my hair catch fire than see them together, or even entertain the idea.

Preparing to bring my claws out, I practically snap at her, "What?"

"I get it that you're really affected by whatever happened with Cole, but Tessa, what the hell are you doing to yourself? You're mopey and letting people walk all over you. I mean, if you had the nerve to stand up to me, the rest of these shitholes should be a walk in the park. When are you going to get a grip and control what's happening?"

I'm rendered speechless. After people tiptoeing around me for so long, never testing my emotional stability, Nicole's words are like a bucket of ice-cold water. I'm thrown for a loop, nothing coming to mind as to what could be the right answer. I don't know how to answer her.

It's because she's right. I'm doing it again, being weak and a pushover. The only difference is that now it's not Nicole who's bullying me, it's my feelings and my stupid, pathetic, blackened heart. All it wants to do is retreat into my shell and whine and cry. It's what I used to do before Cole, and now I'm doing it because of him. Oh boy, have I come a twisted full circle.

"Think about what I just said. Don't let one bad relationship experience knock you down. If you go back to being who you were at the start of the year, then everything he's done for you becomes pointless."

I know who she's referring to, but it's not the argument I want to hear. I don't owe Cole anything, not anymore. But she's right about one thing—I can't go back to being who I was. That would just make every life-changing experience I've had this year a waste of time, and nothing's worth doing that.

"Is she bothering you?"

Jay, bless him, has been trying his best to act like my knight in shining armor. No one dares ask offending questions when he's around, so he's taken the role of my bodyguard this finals week. Most importantly, it wards off Cole and buys me some time while I get myself ready to talk to him.

It's only because I need some closure; that's it.

Though the look on his face when he sees Jay around me is kinda like a kick to the stomach. He looks hurt, but he has no right to do so. He doesn't get to act hurt and be the victim here. But Jay doesn't seem fazed and is really insistent on being well…anywhere where I am. I can't be bothered to talk to him about it. He shows up at all the inappropriate times; this one would be a prime example.

"Don't get your panties in a bunch, Stone; I am capable of having a civil conversation."

It's weird that she refers to him as Stone, and it makes my heart ache.

"Not with her, you aren't. She doesn't need your shit right now."

I roll my eyes. "Jay, it's okay. She was just helping out. I had a little run-in with Stacie Dixon and she stepped in."

Jay narrows his eyes at her, but Nicole doesn't flinch. It's really strange to see them like this and an even more awkward position to be in. I have no idea what their post-breakup relationship is like. From what I've heard, they avoid each other at any cost, so it's not the easiest thing to be in the middle of their showdown.

"Stay away from her. You've done enough damage as it is; don't bother being her friend now."

"Hey!" I want to hit him over the head for being so insensitive, but my words fall on deaf ears. Nicole's raring and ready to have a go at him.

"And you haven't? God, do you know what you did to her? You're as much to blame as I am! Stop acting so high and mighty, Jason. You always knew what I did or why I did it."

I don't wait to hear his response and leave them to hash it all out. If the hatred that's radiating from the two of them for each other is any indication of how they feel, then it's a miracle that their relationship survived as long as it did. Maybe all relationships are meant to be doomed. Every single one I've witnessed in my life is an example of it, the biggest being my parents.

I shudder at the thought of one day ending up like them and go to take my last final and that is calculus. If that doesn't bring you down, then I don't know what does. Oh wait, I have the perfect answer to the question.

It's the person who has sat next to him during every single exam this week.

When I reach the classroom, I ignore Cole and sit at my desk, making a big show of digging my pencils and pens out from my tote. He always tries to catch my eye, but I religiously try not to and am pretty good at it. I usually end up finishing my exam early and leave early, and he doesn't have the opportunity to corner me after class.

Except today.

It's calculus, and despite all my hard studying, math is not a monster I can defeat. By the end of the first hour, I'm pulling at my hair and resisting the urge to just get up and leave. Megan's tutored me and helped me catch up with any classes I'd zoned out in, but this is beyond saving. I struggle until I'm certain I'll get a B- and then start packing up my stuff. Today I finish at the same time as everyone, so my usually evasive technique fails me.

Megan and Beth are taking an exam for another class right now, so there's no one I could've had stand guard. This is exactly why, as I'm briskly walking away, Cole catches up with me.

I could pretend that I haven't been staring at him this week. I could pretend that it doesn't give me any satisfaction when I notice how tired and haggard he looks all the time. The circles under his eyes tell me he hasn't been sleeping. He's lost weight, his hair's longer, and he no longer bothers to shave daily. Even today, there must be a five-day stubble on his face.

He still looks good, the bastard.

Not that I care.

"Wait, hey, wait!"

Gritting my teeth, I force myself to slow down. That would be the mature thing to do, right? I can't avoid him forever. We live in the same neighborhood, for Christ's sakes. I need to handle this like a grown-up. Even if what I want to do most involves a train track and some really sturdy rope.

The worst part is that it's not him I want to subject to a painful, writhing death. It's her, the girl who came and wrecked my whole world.

I don't know if I can even hate him.

Walking slowly till I get to my car, I lean against it and wait for him to get to me. It looks like he's been running or had the breath knocked out of him. I notice how unhealthy the pallor of his skin is. He looks terrible but in a…cute, tortured, starving-artist kind of way.

My conflicted emotions about him are so healthy…not.

My heart's racing wildly, and it reaches the point of bursting out of my chest by the time Cole nears me. We haven't been this close in weeks. Not since he came to my room that one time, but he doesn't know that I know. This, right here, is the first time we both know we're going to talk and that it's going to be important.

I'm not sure I'm ready.

***

"Hey," he breathes out, his voice hoarse.

I feel the pull immediately, that intense emotional connection that

I've always had with him. It's there, thickening the tension between us. I'm genuinely at a loss for words or actions. It's not like I've read up on the protocol for dealing with cheating boyfriends, or ex-boyfriend? I don't know. I'm so confused, and he's making it worse by being all up in my space. When he's at a distance, I can store away all the memories and feelings. There's only this dull ache somewhere in the back of my mind. I've trained myself to ignore it, but I can't do that now. It's all coming back. Him, her. Him with her, and the past month, everything's playing like a film reel inside my head.

And all he has to say is "hey."

"What do you want from me?"

He looks crestfallen that those are the first words he hears from me. I sound harsh, but not overly emotional. The goal is to tell him that he can't be a part of my life anymore, and nor can I be a part of his. We need to let each other go. There's too much pain in the past, and if I ever go through something like that again, I won't make it out of there alive.

"Tessie, please just..."

"Don't. No one calls me that anymore, so just don't."

He exhales and runs his hand through his hair; the familiar sight makes my eyes sting.

"I deserve that—I do. But can we...can we try to fix this? I...I just wanted to check up on you. How's the wrist?"

His eyes dart to my bandaged hand. It makes me so glad I'm having the damn bandage removed tomorrow, but it'll leave a scar. Good, that way I'll always have a reminder of when I was at my lowest. It'll remind me to never get that way again, especially not over a guy.

"It's okay."

"Congratulations about Brown; I always knew you'd get in."

Oh right, that. I got into the one university I'd always wanted to get into, the only one I'd applied to, stupidly enough, and I'd received the acceptance a few days ago. I kind of resent him for the fact that I wasn't as happy as I should have been. He took that away from me. Regardless, at least that's some good news.

"Thanks."

He struggles to make conversation, and I stick to overly economical replies. It's painful being here with him when all I want is to scream and shout at him, hit him. I don't know what he's doing by making us both go through with this.

So, I ask.

"Why are you here? Why are you asking all these questions that don't even matter?"

He sighs and shoves his hands into his pockets. "I miss you; I really miss you. I still love you, even if I don't deserve you. I needed to see you, hear your voice. I'm—"

"If you care about me at all, then do me a favor." I look him right in the eyes as I prepare to deliver the final blow.

"Anything, ask me anything."

"Leave me alone. We're done; you did what you had to do. I watched my parents cheat on each other; I saw my brother get shattered over what Jenny did to him. I can't be like that; I can't be them. So, you need to back off before we make things worse."

His lips turn into a straight line; his eyes blaze with fury. "What we have is nothing like your parents or what happened with Travis. You know I love you; you know I would never hurt you on purpose. If you never believe anything I ever say again, then just believe that."

Heart pounding, I will myself to not become weak. "You're right about one thing. I'm never going to believe anything you say ever again. You think it's just what you did that's the problem here? Are you forgetting what you said to me? How you ridiculed me? All this time you've been telling me to respect myself, but you never learned to respect me. In your head, I'm still that pathetic girl who's obsessed with your brother. You never got over that, and I did everything to prove you wrong. Do you see how big of a hypocrite you are? You did everything you were afraid I would do."

There—damage done. I've said all that I've been venting into a diary these days. But while it felt good on paper, it feels absolutely horrible now. The blood drains from Cole's face; he looks sickly pale and like he's just been struck with something heavy. His eyes become glossy, oh god.

I need to get out of here before I say or do something else. He doesn't try to stop me when I get into the car and leave. As I drive away, I see him in the parking lot, right where I left him. But he isn't standing anymore. He's on his knees and his body is shaking violently.

What have I done?

***

Summer break starts with the girls and me planning a road trip. We're all going our separate ways in the fall, but for now we can stick together and enjoy what's left of our time together. But we've promised to not lose touch. Weekly phone calls and Skype dates have been sworn upon, so we're good on that front. Frankly, I'm not worried; I know I'll have these two girls as my friends for a lifetime.

I'm coming back from yet another day of packing up things in Beth's old house. I pull into my driveway, only to see an unfamiliar car there and someone sitting at the doorstep of the house. It's a guy, judging from the body shape, but his face is hidden since he's clasped his hands at the back of his head and is staring down at the ground. I squint to get a clearer vision because although I would not like to be murdered in my own house, I'm guessing an ax murderer wouldn't be driving a Mercedes.

He looks up when I get out of the car, shutting the door loudly enough to demand attention. I'm wise enough not to approach a stranger directly, but when I see his face, I realize that he isn't a stranger at all. He's much worse, and he reminds me of a time I'd rather not be reminded of.

Getting up, he dusts off his jeans. "Hi."

Rooted to the spot, I try not looking too hostile, but it's impossible. He shouldn't be here, even if that's only because I'm being grossly immature about the whole thing.

"Lan, w-what are you doing here?"

He chuckles nervously. "Can we at least go inside the house first?"

The manners ingrained in me by my country-club mother make me kick myself. Of course, I should invite him in regardless of the fact that he's Cole's best friend. So what? That doesn't make him the enemy or something. It's the same as with Alex. I can't blame him for what his friend did.

"I'm sorry; please come in."

Unlocking the door, I let us both in and grab some sodas to make up for my earlier lack of manners. He's made himself home at a stool by the kitchen island and is studying the house.

"Nice place."

"Thanks, it's my parents'," I say dryly, popping the top off my Diet Coke and taking the seat opposite him.

"Rich kid problems, I get it. Been there, rebelled against that."

I nod, and then an uncomfortable silence follows. We're both concentrating heavily on the pattern on the countertop. Finally taking a deep breath, I repeat my earlier question. "What are you doing here?"

"You know the answer to that." He studies my face carefully, probably waiting for a violent reaction of some sort.

But I remind myself of the need to be mature about this, even if I want to run away screaming.

"What if I don't want to talk?"

"You should. What I have to say is important."

"But I don't have to listen."

"It would be better if you did, Tessa, please."

"Better for whom?"

"Everyone. You, Cole, your family and friends who have to see the two of you like this."

It stings that he's brought up the ripple effect of our breakup and reminded me of how selfishly I acted. Beth lost her mother, for God's sake, and even she didn't go into a downward spiral as badly as I did. I should be ashamed of myself; I am ashamed of myself.

So, I listen to what he has to say.

"What has Cole told you about Erica?"

Hearing her name creates a sort of inferno inside me. I picture her with her red hair, her whole innocent act, and the way her eyes followed Cole's every move. The more I've thought about her recently, the more I've realized that she probably came with the plan to ruin my life already formed inside her devious mind.

"That she's a man-stealing witch, and that's the PG version."

He laughs. "No, seriously, do you know anything else about her?"

"They mentioned that their parents are friends, that they've been friends for a long time. She told me a bit about her parents, grandparents. I think that's all."

"But you could see how attached she was to Cole, couldn't you?"

"I think that would've been obvious to anyone within a two-mile radius. She looked at him like…I don't know, like she worshipped the ground he walked on or something."

"But Cole doesn't see that, does he? He just sees her as this…"

I complete the sentence for him. "Like his buddy who just happens to be a girl. He buys the whole can-do-no-wrong act. It's disturbing, actually."

He sighs as if he sympathizes and understands exactly how I feel. "You're right, but I've talked to him about it, and I think he finally gets it that Erica's not just a friend."

"Well, that's brilliant, but it's too late."

"No, it's not. There's something else you need to hear, Tessa, and it could change everything. I know more about Erica than you might think…I wish I didn't, but I do."

Confused as all hell, I ask him, "You're scaring me. What are you trying to say?"

"I'm saying that I dated her last summer. I stayed at the beach house, and so did Jameson and Seth. Cole invited us, and we all thought it'd be this guys' summer, but then she showed up. I didn't notice anything weird at first, but I should have. She was hot and staying in the same place. I was attracted to her, and we started going out. I didn't realize until later that she used me to make Cole jealous."

My heart starts pounding; he sounds like he's going to deliver a much harsher blow now.

"She would find ways to bring him up during our dates. She'd ask questions about him, about you…it was weird, but I pushed it off. When he was around, she'd start feeling me up just to get a reaction. When she didn't get any, she'd get mad and lock herself in her room for hours. Cole never noticed any of this. He even got into a fight with me because he thought I wasn't treating her right. We got over it eventually, and I haven't talked to or seen Erica since I left that summer."

"Oh. My. God," I gasp. She's psychotic, she's obsessed, and she finally got what she wanted.

"It's a lot to take in, I know, but you need to know something about her, Tessa. The thing about Erica, Tess, is that…it's that she's a compulsive liar."

I'm going to pass out, that's what's going to happen here. I can't breathe, and apparently Lan's not finished talking.

"I don't believe what you do. I don't think Cole did anything with her. I talked to the guy that night; he was trashed out of his mind. She could've told him anything the next day and he would've agreed. Because that's what he does. He blames himself for screwing things up, even when it isn't his fault. Come on, Tessa, do you really believe Cole would do that to you?"

Would he?

Did he?

Holy Shit.

"But you said…you just said that he was drunk, really drunk. I…I remember Cole saying he'd been drinking a little, and that would mean he might have had too much to drink when he…"

"I drove up to give him a ride back into town, Tessa. I was there; I saw the tequila and the whisky and the vodka. I also noticed that …Erica wasn't hung over at all. Cole, on the other hand, well, it's lucky he didn't die from alcohol poisoning."

"So, what are you trying to tell me?"

"I'm telling you that Erica probably fed him shit. That what he thinks happened probably didn't. Drunk or not, he wouldn't touch a girl that's not you. Trust me, I know him

CHAPTER THREE
I Burst Like the Freaking Fort Peck Dam

"Don't look at me like that."

"Like what?"

"Like you want to wring me by the neck and feed me to flesh-eating turtles. Beth!"

"I don't want to do those things to you, okay, fine, maybe not the second one."

I'm lying on my stomach, on my bed observing my two best friends and witnessing a very surreal, *Freaky Friday*-like moment. Is soul switching possible? If so, then it's definitely what happened to Megan and Beth. I should ask them if they had Chinese food recently, but I don't really want to poke that particular bear right now.

How do I approach this gently?

"Guys, would you stop pacing? I'm getting a headache here."

Their banter immediately stops, and a guilty expression crosses their faces. I'm sick of everyone treating me like I'm made of freaking glass and looking at me like I'll crack any second. We were doing fine a minute ago; they were discussing the latest development in my love life like the morning news. Then I had to open my big mouth, and suddenly everyone's on alert to dial 911—wonderful.

"Sorry, we were just…" Megan stuttered and mentally, I smacked myself around.

"I understand and I'm sorry; I shouldn't have snapped at you guys like that but just…just sit down and stop threatening to violently kill each other."

That got rid of the tension. But it wasn't the only problem, by far. The two of them settle down and it begins again. I've just told them about Lan's visit to me yesterday, and it's caused some strong reactions. It's also obviously that at some point I told them about what happened at the beach house, what Cole did, and everything up to the point where I basically crushed him with my words in the parking lot. They weren't happy. I had to barricade the door to prevent Beth from stabbing Cole. Hey, he hurt me, but I still want the guy alive and breathing.

Now, however, after what Lan told me about Erica and her history with Cole, I'm all kinds of confused, and my best friends aren't helping. They're like the devil and angel on either side of my shoulders, making me question everything.

Beth, the always practical and pragmatic no-nonsense kind of girl, has told me to go with my gut and not immediately give up on Cole. I want to believe her, accept what she has to say to me and go with it more than anything else right now.

But then there's Megan.

"Don't you think it's just a little convenient? He just happened to be so drunk that he couldn't remember what he did? And doesn't it seem unrealistic that he'd confess to you when he was hazy about the details? Why would he throw away everything for what could be a misunderstanding?"

Megan voiced all the questions I didn't want to ask.

I sigh as they start arguing again. I don't know; I absolutely don't know what to do or whom to trust. The only person that could give me some answers is also the person I want to feed to the three-headed dog in *Harry Potter*.

Yeah, it's better if Erica and I don't ever cross paths again.

"Tessa, think of it this way—you have nothing to lose. If you just talk to Cole…ask him what he really remembers about that night, then maybe…maybe you could finally have some closure. That's the worst-case scenario; you could move on." Beth sighs, plopping down on the bed beside me.

My brother has made her quite the optimist; I want to puke. The words *move on* swirl inside me, twisting my heart and causing all kinds of visions to flash in my head. Me with someone else, Cole with someone else, and eventually we'd become strangers.

It'd be like I never met him. We'd be dismissed as the doomed high school couple people knew would never make it into the real world. One more casualty of puppy love—the thought breaks my heart.

"And what if Lan's wrong?" I whisper. "What if something did happen? I can't go through that again."

"That's why we need to think this through." Megan is our voice of reason right now, and I'm clinging to her. She joins us on the bed too, leaning against the headboard. "Don't rush into it; you could just be setting yourself up for disappointment."

That's what I feared most.

***

"Hey."

I smile widely at my brother, who hands me a cup of coffee. He's all dressed up wearing a button-down shirt and slacks. He's even managed to tame his hair, which is quite a big feat for someone in our crazy clan. Looking at Travis, I can't be more thankful for how far he's come. If he were in the same headspace he'd been in last year, Travis wouldn't have known that I'm graduating today, let alone dress up for the occasion.

But now? He'd been up and going even before I got a chance to wake up, and he treated me to his special Kit Kat pancakes.

"Yeah?"

"Where'd you go?" he asks, his lips tilting up in amusement.

"I just feel happy. We've never had the best parents, but right now I feel like I have all the family I'll ever need."

To my utter embarrassment, my eyes begin to tear up, while Travis's eyes reveal panic. Remember the thing about fragile glass? Well, you're witnessing yet another effect of it. Quickly I wipe away the tears from my face, sniff, and let out a mortified chuckle. "I'm sorry; I didn't really mean to be such a girl."

Travis doesn't say anything; he just hugs me close and kisses the top of my head.

"You know I'm really proud of you, right?" he says when he lets me go.

I snort, "Yeah, right. You literally had to watch me like a hawk the past month while I moped around. I just…I blocked you out; I blocked everyone and everything out. How could you be proud of someone like that?"

"Do you think after everything I put you through the last two years, I would be in any position to judge you? Tess…I…" he struggles to get the words out, and I hurt for him and all the guilt he carries. "I abandoned you when you needed me the most. If anything, you should hate me but you don't. You still look at me like…"

"Like you're my hero." I leave no room for an argument. "You're the only person in this family who's never made me feel like I wasn't enough. I wasn't enough for Mom to stay or even attend my graduation," a bitter laugh leaves my mouth, "Dad's only coming because the school requires him to be there. With parents like that, no wonder we turned out the way we did. But you make things better; you always did."

I wasn't wrong when I noticed how Travis's eyes glistened and this time I hug him, holding my brother a little tighter because he's been there for me in a way no brother should have to. He's gone above and beyond what's asked of an older brother and I appreciate that so much today. Whatever this day brings and no matter how much my life changes, I know that Travis will always be watching out for me.

***

We are waiting for the ceremony to begin, teetering around the gym while the parents and other guests sit down. Without even noticing that I'm doing it, my eyes keep darting around the space looking for a certain someone.

I haven't seen him since the parking lot incident. I skipped prom and heard that he did, too, even though he was voted prom king. Lauren, the cheerleading captain, had been crowned prom queen. When Cole didn't show up, they gave the crown to Jay, who was the runner-up.

I can only imagine what that did to Jay's "always second best" complex. Poor guy.

But now, right here, it's inevitable. I will see him eventually, and the new information that I hold has me all kinds of twisted and knotted. I don't know what I'm feeling. A part of me wants to see him, is craving his presence, but another is dreading looking into those soulful blue eyes and seeing the hurt behind them.

Let's just call me bipolar and get it over with.

"Looking good, O'Connell." Lan has his arm looped around my waist and kisses my cheek before I even know what's happening. I place a hand on his chest and create some space between us. Clearly, they don't teach you the meaning of personal space in military school.

Cole has the same problem.

My friends watch him with gaping mouths as I stutter, "W-what are you doing?"

"I'm telling you that you look beautiful because my best friend obviously can't." He grins.

He's being charming! How am I supposed to react to that and why…I whirl around looking for Cole; he must be close by. I don't see anyone from the Stone family, though, and they're a hard bunch to miss, given their striking looks. Disappointment courses through me, and it's a feeling I'm becoming very well acquainted with.

Shaking my head, I introduce him to Megan and Beth and, being the perfect picture of social etiquette, they immediately bombard him with questions and, well, accusations, courtesy of Megan. We slip out inconspicuously and head to the empty courtyard toward the back of the school. The ceremony won't start for another thirty minutes, and we won't be needed until the last ten. Maybe that time will help us all make sense of what's happening.

"Do you really believe what you told her? You think nothing happened between Cole and what's-her-face?" Beth asks Lan as the four of us sit on the steps.

He doesn't even think about his answer for a second. "Absolutely. I know that girl; she's one hundred and ten percent of crazy locked inside that pint-sized body. She showed up knowing what she wanted to do and she did it…successfully. But you can't let her walk her crazy ass into the sunset, Tessa."

Confusion and even more of it sweeps through me, making my head ache. I don't respond to him and instead let my pair of angel and devil battle it out.

"But no one's that drunk that they just believe whatever they're told. Something must have happened, something Cole was very aware of."

Thank you, Megan.

"She could've gotten him drunk to the point that he wouldn't have the sense to know what he was doing. Trust me on this; I've been there, and it can happen. Everyone's heard of a drunken girl being taken advantage of; why can't it happen to a guy? Say they did kiss and maybe did something more, Cole didn't do it intentionally."

Nicely put, Beth.

I groan and rub my temples. There's no point arguing and hypothesizing when we all know that the only way to get to the truth is to talk to Cole and Erica.

I hate how I just thought of their names together; it sounds wrong.

"You know what you have to do, Tessa." Lan tries to calm us down. "Talk to him; ask him to find out what really happened. He won't lie to you; you already know that. The guy thought he'd done something wrong and he blabbed it all out to you without even checking if the story was straight. There's nothing he won't tell you."

I think about what everyone's said as we all head up to get our caps and gowns. I'm near my best friends since our last names are literally in alphabetic order, but that also places me near the Stones. First Cole, followed by Jay. I see Jay first, since he's headed right toward me with a big smile on his face. For the second time today, I'm hugged against my will. What I wouldn't give to live in a world where people didn't touch you unless you specifically asked them to.

"Can you believe we're graduating?" He grins, and I can see why he still has legions of girls falling all over him. He's the perfect all-American nice guy, the guy you want to marry, the guy your parents want you to marry. I can now see clearly why I'd thought that he was the love of my life. For me, Jay had represented perfection, something I could never attain. He was everything I thought I needed to have the perfect life. But then I met someone who taught me that it was okay to not be perfect and to accept and love the imperfections of others.

Jay isn't perfect to me anymore, but I've accepted him, flaws and all. We're…friends now, and it's nothing like before. I don't have any feelings for him anymore, not like the ones I have for his brother. I'm not constantly starstruck and dazed when he's around, and we can actually talk about things without fear of his girlfriend.

"I counted the seconds to the day, Jason; I couldn't be happier," I say, my voice laced with wariness. His enthusiasm is tiring; I need to bring him over to the dark side.

He tilts his head to the side, his smile getting a little less bright. "How're you holding up? Have you seen him?"

The *him* in question rolls in lazily just as I'm about to tell Jay no. My reaction to Cole is immediate and uncontrollable. Pounding heart? Check. Clammy hands? Affirmative. Ball the size of Texas choking my throat? Definitely.

He hasn't seen me yet, and I'm hidden by Jay's looming frame. I duck around him, just as Cole nears us to grab his cap and gown and stumbles a little on his feet. It's then that I notice how disheveled he looks; still devastatingly gorgeous, but it's obvious that nothing's changed since I last saw him. He's still not sleeping, still not eating right, and at this very moment…

"You have got to be kidding me. Are you drunk, man?"

Alex voices my exact thoughts, and the school secretary's eyes become as wide as saucers. The gown she's handing him is now quickly thrust at him as she scurries toward the next student. I would laugh at how scared she seems, but any humor dies when I see the state Cole is in. He is, in fact, drunk, and hopelessly so. Everyone's staring at him, and the muttering starts. He walks around clumsily for a while, high-fiving random people and letting girls paw at him. My vision turns hazy, and the amount of anger I feel is not normal. After what happened the last time he got drunk, I'd think he would be more careful with his actions, but that doesn't seem to be the case. He's still doing the same old shit that got us here in the first place.

"We should get him out of here," I hear Jay say, and I watch as Alex and Lan try to talk him into leaving. But it's too late, and I know why they're in such a hurry to get Cole out. His eyes meet mine and then dart to Jay.

Oh Crud.

If he looked terrible before, well, he looks worse now. His face pales, and an undeniable hurt flashes in his eyes. I know where his mind's going; he can't help it. I hate the thoughts running through his head, and his expression mirrors them. He's looking at me like I betrayed him…like I broke his heart.

Hilarious.

"Don't," I tell Jay, "He's gotten the wrong idea about us. He'll want to pick a fight with you. Let them take care of him."

He listens to me, but there's a strange look on his face, almost hurt. I don't have it in me to figure it out. There's enough trouble in my life due to one Stone brother; I don't want to bring in another one. Cole manages to tear his eyes away from us long enough to pay attention to Alex and Lan, and whatever they say to him must have made sense since he nods and walks out the door with them. I can only hope that they manage to sober him up in time. His father would not be happy if he looks the way he does right now while getting his diploma.

***

The ceremony thankfully goes off without a hitch, and Megan gives the perfect valedictorian speech, which has the parents in tears. Travis cheers embarrassingly loud for both me and Beth, which makes me love him even more. There's no commotion when both Cole and Jay get their diplomas, and I finally let out the breath I'd been holding for so long. But the tension between them is obvious. I keep glancing to where the family stands. Cassandra looks stressed as her sons are locked in yet another stare-off. The Stones are hosting the first graduation party of the summer, and the only one I'll attend before leaving for the road trip.

I have to go; my dad's making me. I don't want to, but I will go.

"Hey, do you want to get out of here?" My brother watches me with ever-present concern. He notices that I'm outright staring at the Stones; maybe he's waiting for a meltdown. No, I'm not at that stage yet, but I still need to leave. I can't see him like this anymore. His sadness is tearing me apart, especially when I know that I could make it go away.

He hasn't looked at me once since he saw me with Jay. I know he's angry, but there's only so much I can do to convince him that I feel nothing for Jay anymore, not in the romantic way. His harsh words from the trip constantly haunt me and make me feel that he'll never get over the stupid crush I had. Maybe that's why we'll never work as a couple. Our combined insecurities are a recipe for disaster.

"Yes, please," I tell him and avoid looking at the once-happy family.

That's me, ladies and gentlemen, Tessa O'Connell—the destructor of happiness.

***

I go home and change, deciding on a simple, empire-waist, little white dress with a cutout back for the party. My mother's left me a voice mail with congratulatory wishes, but there's more gushing about the new man in her life. Mom has gone ahead and found herself a man with more money than most developing countries, Patrick McQueen, a Wall Street heavyweight. She is of course thrilled with her new relationship and never hesitates to tell me all about it. I feel the urge to throw up. My dad's meeting us at the party and will no doubt want to talk to me about staying with Mom for the summer, but I'd rather gouge my own eyes out.

"Ready to go?" Beth asks as she comes to sit on my bed. She looks amazing in her cobalt-blue, knee-length dress, but not only that, she looks happy. We were all worried that the day would be difficult for her, knowing that her mother wouldn't be there to watch her graduate. But she seems to be handling it really well, and I know Travis has a huge role in that. He's been so attentive today, to both of us. I almost feel bad for him, having to deal with two emotionally unstable teenage girls in his life. Almost, because I'm selfish enough to know that I'd crumble away into a pile of self-pity if he weren't there to support me.

"Is that a trick question?" I ask her, applying the final coat of mascara to my lashes.

"It's going to be okay, you know. Yeah, it could be awkward as hell, but maybe this is what you need to do. You've avoided him long enough."

I swivel in my chair and frown at her. "Your optimism and practicality is killing me here."

She smirks. "Blame your brother; he's brainwashing me. I can't handle all the feels."

"Did you just use *feels* in a sentence?"

She shrugs. "I'm a changed woman; kill me."

We burst out laughing, and that's how Travis finds us ten minutes later. By the time we make the five-minute walk to the Stones', the butterflies are back in my stomach. They're not your typical pretty little ones, either, these are mutant butterflies, mammoth ones. Travis and Beth flank me as we go around to the backyard where there's a BBQ set up, and Sheriff Stone is working the grill. I see most of my classmates and their parents, but my eyes don't find the person I want to see the most.

Alex and Megan join us shortly, and even Alex has no idea where Cole is; apparently, he disappeared after the ceremony. I'm starting to freak out a bit, and there's a bad feeling in the pit of my stomach. The more time that passes without Cole being here, the worse the feeling gets. I try to catch Cassandra's eye, but she's too hassled handling her guests, though I can tell that she's worried, too. She keeps on checking her phone every five minutes, calling someone and hanging up when they don't answer. I find myself doing the same.

But neither of us can get a hold of him.

I don't know why I'm panicking. He might just be getting drunk again somewhere, but that theory is vaporized when Lan calls us an hour into the party, telling us that he's checked every place that he thinks Cole could be and that he can't find him anywhere. I start hyperventilating at the idea of his car stuck in a ditch somewhere. He could be anywhere right now, possibly hurt and definitely alone.

"Don't panic, Tessa; we don't know anything yet." My friends and brother are huddled around me as we try to hide from everyone else. The people outside don't have any idea that I'm having a panic attack, and I'd like it to stay that way.

"But we can't find him! He's not answering his phone, and he was so mad when he left…he could've done something incredibly stupid." I quickly wipe away a tear with my wrist. Now is not the time to lose it. The only thing I can think of is what my last words to Cole were…when I left him in the parking lot. Oh God.

"That doesn't have to mean that something bad has happened to him. You can't think like that." Megan's voice is shaking as she says that, so it's not quite reassuring. I can see the panic in her boyfriend's eyes. Even he knows that something's wrong with his best friend.

"What are waiting here for, then? Why can't we leave and find him? I—"

I never get to finish my sentence; there's a loud crash from where the party's held. All of us immediately jump to our feet, and I'm out the door in what seems like a second. My heart's racing furiously, and it has due cause when I see the scene before me.

My first reaction is to exhale in relief. He's okay; he's here and he's okay. My second reaction is fury when I see the state he's in, nearly unconscious and barely able to keep his eyes open. He's leaning heavily on Jay while his parents try to get him to talk. The crash was caused by what appears to be him colliding with a table laden with pitchers and bowls of punch.

That's not what makes me angry. It's the redhead who's standing with the family, sobbing hysterically as she tries to explain what happened. My blood boils as she hugs Cassandra, babbling on and on about something I can't make out.

"Is that…" Megan gasps.

"Yeah, that's her."

"Let me at the bitch; she won't walk out of here alive." Beth sneers, moving forward, but Travis restrains her, and I'm glad he does—I don't have enough good sense right now.

"What the hell did the crazy chick do now?" Lan groans from beside me.

My feet cannot move. My brain's screaming at them, but they refuse to do anything but remain firmly planted on the ground. I watch as they take Cole inside the house, and immediately everyone starts whispering, probably once again coming up with conspiracy theories about the people who've fed them the entire day. The last thing the family needs is these people making up stories. So, I ignore the redheaded elephant in the room and get to work.

"Ask everyone to leave; the party's over."

I push everyone away and head into the house. Sheriff Stone and Cassandra are sitting at the dining table, both looking obviously stressed. They look up when I enter, and I watch them have a silent conversation.

"Tessa, honey, we know that you two aren't together anymore, but could you…" Cassandra's eyes tear up midsentence, and my heart breaks. Just like my family and friends witnessed my meltdown, Cole's family must have seen his, too. I now know how much that can hurt the people around you, and clearly, it's hurting Cole's family.

"I'd like to talk to him."

The sheriff gets up and does something completely out of character. He hugs me, and it's as awkward as can be, yet strangely comforting. "Help him, Tessa; just help him."

I rush up the stairs to his room, blinking tears away. I'm in such a hurry that I ignore the loud voices coming from Jay's room. He's arguing with her. She's still here, in extremely close proximity to me, and if weren't for Cole, I would definitely let my fists have a conversation with her.

He's passed out on his bed when I enter, but the irregular rise and fall of his chest tells me that he isn't asleep. If he realizes that someone else is in the room, he doesn't show it. I cross the distance to him silently and sit at the edge of his bed. One look at him and my heart breaks all over again. His cheeks look sunken, his face lifeless and devoid of color. There are purple-colored bruises beneath his eyes, and his jaw is scruffy; no matter how many times I see him like this, it still rips my heart into two.

"Hey," I whisper and immediately feel him tense.

He's definitely awake.

"You don't have to talk to me; just listen to what I have to say, okay?"

No answer, but he squeezes his eyes shut even more.

"This isn't you. Whatever happened between us…well, it happened, and I can't change that. I spent a month wallowing, and it got me nowhere. All it did was hurt the people around me. We can't do that to them just because of how messed up things between us are. Drinking like this, not caring how much it's killing your parents…Cole, you are not this person. Please stop, I can't…"

My sobs don't allow me to complete the speech I had planned. One minute I'm lecturing him and trying to remember what the school nurse told us about underage drinking, and the next minute, I burst like the freaking Fort Peck Dam. Any sound that then comes out of my mouth is like something akin to a dying cat.

In a split second, Cole is up and has his arms around me. I clutch his shoulders and cry into his shirt, which reeks of booze. He rubs up and down my back, trying to calm me down, but all I can think about is how bad he looked when Jay carried him in.

"Please don't cry, Tessie, please." His voice is raspy from lack of use, and it makes me cry even harder.

Everything is so different between us. It's like all those little things that made us *us* have died a painful, merciless death. And it's all the fault of a person who is within killing distance.

I wonder if the sheriff will vouch for me if I commit manslaughter in his house.

"You can't do that anymore! You nearly killed me today; don't disappear like that, ever, and promise me you'll stop drinking so much." I hit his shoulder, and it's so familiar and easy that I want to wring his neck for destroying what we once had.

"You care?" His voice is gruff. "I thought you decided you wanted nothing to do with me."

The pain in his voice basically claws my heart out of my ribcage, leaving a bloody, tattered mess behind. "Cole, do you have any idea how much you hurt me?" My voice is a little louder than a whisper. "You broke my heart. The least you could do is expect that I would hate your guts."

He winces.

"Do you? Do you still hate my guts?"

Sighing, I look into his eyes and see the hope brimming in them. It's like everything depends on what I choose to say next. No pressure or anything.

"I'm confused. On one hand, I've had the time to think about it and realize that maybe both of us made a lot of mistakes that day. It was a whole chain of catastrophes waiting to happen. On the other hand…there's her, and she's here. You brought her here, and I don't know what to think anymore."

"But you're not outright saying that you hate me?"

I groan. "Did that seem like the only important part? Tell me you'll do better; tell me you won't drink."

"You want me to get sober?"

"Yes!" I say exasperatedly, throwing my hands up in frustration.

"Then give me another chance."

I stare open-mouthed at him, watching some of his old spark and determination return. It's like magic, how he immediately starts looking better. But, dear lord in heaven, is he trying to negotiate our relationship here?

"Excuse me? We are not making a deal here! We're talking about you cutting your life short by becoming a raging alcoholic and…and I won't let you do that!"

"So, trust me again, let me prove to you that I made a mistake, and I'll spend the rest of my life making it up to you."

"She's in your freaking house, and she brought you home! What kind of an idiot do you take me for?" I nearly scream at him, getting up from the bed and pushing myself against a wall.

"It's not what you think!" He struggles to get up, and it looks like he feels dizzy. Groaning, he falls back into his bed. "Lan told me about what he said to you; he told me about Erica…"

"Did he tell you that she's crazy and spends her free time sacrificing animals at the shrine she's dedicated to you?" I huff and Cole seriously looks at me like I'm deranged.

Great, make *me* the lunatic here.

"I found out about her…problems, and I left to see her, ask her about what really happened that day. It was weird that she was staying in town, but I didn't make a big deal out of it. When I went to her hotel, she started crying and getting all grabby. Apparently, she's had a change of heart and doesn't want to lose me as a friend."

"That's bull crap and you know it."

"I do now. I tried asking her to tell me everything about the night. I was stupid back when I accepted her explanation that day. It just felt like I'd done something wrong, and when I asked her to tell me the truth, she just broke down. She became hysterical, and I didn't know what do to."

"You send her to the asylum where her people are; that's what you do."

"Yeah, well, in this case, I had some tequila in hand, and I thought she needed to loosen up a little. Probably should've gone to see her when I had more alcohol in my body than water."

"But how did she end up being the one who brought you home?"

That's when he looks at me sheepishly. "I might have finished my first bottle before she even had a shot."

I want to ram his head into the wall repeatedly. "Did you learn nothing from what happened last time? Do you realize the things she could've done to you? I…I don't get you!"

"Well, what was I supposed to do? Jay was all over you at graduation today, and you wouldn't even look at me. I wasn't thinking straight."

"Oh, great, it's that excuse again. You never think straight, do you? Even after everything that's happened, you say it like it's my fault. Jay is my friend, Cole, my friend. Unlike you, I know where to draw the line with them."

That's a low blow, but he deserves it.

"I'm sorry; I know I should stop bringing him up, but it hurts, okay? I hate seeing him with you."

"Well, then imagine what it felt like to see you with Erica, today and that day, too. And you acted like I was being paranoid. Then you go ahead and do the thing I feared most. I was right, Cole; I was right and you, on the other hand, don't have any proof to base your insecurities on."

"I told you that I will apologize to you every day for the rest of my life for what I said, for what I did. Just please, don't leave me. I love you, Tessie; damn it, I can't lose you. Not when I just got you."

I slump down to the ground and practice my breathing. It would be really easy to say yes, to tell him that I would give him a second chance. It would be even easier to believe that Erica somehow tricked us all. But would that make me a fool? The fact is that I love him, and I'll always love him. Remember what they say about your first love? Well, they're right; you'll never forget that person, even if you get premature dementia. I know that Cole is engraved onto my heart and in my memories forever.

So, is it worth my pride and trust issues to suffer that kind of a loss?

"I'm leaving with Megan and Beth tomorrow, you know? I won't be back for a while, and even when I do come back, I'll be off to college. How do we even…"

"What if I tell you that I applied to Brown, too?"

I gasp and check to see if he's joking. My heart's doing these weird flip-flops, and I'm tingling all over. What the…

"B-but Duke. You were going to Duke; you had scouts come to the games and everything. How…why?"

"I applied before everything blew up. It was always the plan, Tessie; Duke was never an option. I managed to get an athletic scholarship there, a better one, actually."

"And now you assume that we're…Cole, there's so much wrong with this situation. It's like we're sweeping all our problems under a rug and just deciding to move on."

"Then let's not do that. Let's talk about it; let's figure out what to do next together. We always planned a summer road trip, all of us. Let me come with you."

My head starts to spin at the possibility. Yes, we'd made plans, and the boys were included in them. But after what went down, those plans changed drastically. The whole dynamic was disturbed, and bringing boyfriends wasn't an option.

"It would be so awkward." I breathe. "Can you imagine how weird things would be between us?"

I couldn't believe we were even having this conversation.

"C'mere."

Hesitantly, I walk toward him on the bed and sit close. He gingerly touches my cheeks, his thumb grazing my bottom lip. It feels like heaven, especially considering how long it's been since we were like this.

"We can go back to who we were; maybe we could even come out of this stronger. Don't give up on us so easily, baby."

"But Erica…I can't…how do I deal with that?"

He sighs, shoulders sagging in defeat. "I don't know what I can do about that except apologize and maybe try to remember what happened that night. I know something's off…the way she's acting now. If it helps, I won't try to come on to you until I'm sure of what happened."

"Do you seriously want to come with me? I'll probably be very mean to you at times."

The corner of his mouth lifts in a small smile. "I wouldn't expect anything less. I'm willing to risk castration as long as I'm around you."

How do you say no words as sweet as that?

CHAPTER FOUR
Screw Lemon Sherbet, Ice Cream Is the Magic Word

"Hey."

Everybody talks about that feeling when you tilt a chair too far back. You know that split-second fall in the pit of your stomach that is a culmination of all your nerves? Yes, well, the feeling of someone addressing my butt as I lean in to the trunk of my car is somewhat similar.

Dear Butt talker, you are responsible for what I do next.

With a yelp, I whip around and nearly jam my elbow into Cole's eye. He has the good sense to back away before I injure him seriously. Glaring at him, I try not to show how badly my pulse is racing just knowing that he's here. Nope, I'd sooner sentence myself to the grave than give him that kind of satisfaction.

"Is it that difficult to wait until I turn around to scare the living daylights out of me?"

He grins sheepishly, "Well, I didn't mind the view, but I thought you wouldn't want me appreciating your…"

I turn red almost immediately. "Whoa there, Stone, boundaries."

He immediately becomes somber, and I kick myself for feeling bad about it. It's not like I promised him that we could go back to what we were. There's still an ocean worth of issues between us, and for him to fall so easily back into our old pattern is unnerving. We're not on equal footing here, not by a long shot. But, as I open my mouth to lecture him on our situation, I'm reminded of why he's going with us on the trip. I'm doing this for his family, for him. There's no one who understands better what alcohol can do to both a person and a family. Travis sought it after everything that went on at college and with his ex. For nearly two years, he was almost nonexistent. I couldn't see Cole going down the same path. So, if I have to suck it up and risk my heart getting broken all over again, then so be it.

He shoves his hands into his pockets and kicks a pebble, almost like a child. "Sorry. Sometimes when you look at me like that, it's easy to forget what things are like now."

I blink a couple of times and then tear my eyes away from him. Breathing raggedly, I stumble away from him and let his words wash all over me. How do I look at him? Do I still look at him like he's the center of my universe, or, well, if we're being honest, like he is my entire universe? The feelings are so instilled in me and feel so second nature that they might possibly be pouring out of me without me even realizing.

Wonderful, just so damn wonderful.

I clear my throat and point to the duffel bag slung on his shoulder. "You want to put that in the trunk?"

He nods and proceeds to do so, along with dragging all my luggage to the car with ease, and, let me tell you, my suitcase may or may not weigh as much as a baby elephant. I try resisting the temptation to watch his muscles flex as he does the heavy lifting, but my eyes are glued to him and he knows it. There's a smirk forming on his face, the sneaky little douche nozzle.

"Well, if he keeps that up, I'm not sure you'll be able to keep your hands off of him for long."

I jump at the sound of Beth's voice. She's standing over my shoulder, studying Cole's movements as closely as I was. Does she not have a boyfriend, a boyfriend who's my brother?

"I don't know what you're talking about."

"I'm talking about how you were looking at Cole like you wanted to rip the clothes right off him."

"You're wrong," I say flippantly and push past her to go inside the house. Travis is staying here since he needs to catch up on his online college courses in order to go back to "real" school in the fall. I did the groceries, and there are enough frozen meals in the fridge to save him from starving to death, but I need to check. Dad doesn't come home a lot, just checks in once or twice during the week, and my mother is too busy going through a midlife crisis to care. Beth's going with us, which means that my brother will be on his own for a while.

It scares me.

"All I'm saying is that if you want to try being in a relationship with him again, you shouldn't hold yourself back."

Beth follows me into the kitchen as I check the fridge and the pantry. Once I'm sure that Travis won't go without food for at least a year, I turn to her.

"I'm not holding myself back. It's not even about Erica anymore, Beth. I get it, I understand mistakes, and I think I've come to terms with it and know why he did what he did, but…"

"But what? Why can't you just give him a second chance? Don't you think he deserves at least that? The guy changed your world and that, too, for the better. He made you so happy. Isn't that worth anything?"

Of course it is. She's right; he did change my world and made everything better. But what she doesn't realize is that there's something so terrifying about loving a person like that. Because when you do fall for them, you fall with your entire entirety. Every single fiber of you is addicted to simply the presence of them; you would do anything for them, even stay when you know they could tear you apart with the flick of a wrist.

That's what the most terrifying part is. It's knowing that someone has that kind of power over you and jumping headfirst into the relationship anyway. The month I spent away from him, drowning in my misery and not caring about anything but my own broken heart, isn't something I ever look forward to doing again. But something tells me that if Cole and I were to get back together, there would always, always be something that could send both of us spiraling back to what we just went through. The crux of it all is that I am a big, fat coward and don't want to do anything to fix that.

***

We both watch Cole from the kitchen window as he leans against my Jeep and stares into the distance. He looks better already than the last time I saw him, but the guilt is gnawing at my insides. He has a different idea of what could happen between us than I do. What I want is to end the summer and go to college unscathed, but something tells me he won't allow that. He's following me to the same college, for Christ's sake. Does that sound like someone willing to let go?

An arm comes across my shoulder, and Travis squeezes me to his side. "She can do whatever she wants, no pressure, Tess."

He must have come from the back entrance, having gone out earlier to run some errands. I sink into him and nod into his shoulder. "Thank you," I whisper.

"I've talked to him. He knows not to expect anything and just see where things go. You don't have to feel obligated to go back into a relationship with him. That's not the way to fix your problems."

I breathe a sigh of relief, thanking my lucky stars that I won't have to have that conversation with Cole now. Times like these make me grateful that my brother can be so dang protective. It helps when I choose to be a wuss, so you won't hear me complaining.

Soon it's time to leave. Our first stop is New York, where a friend of the family has an empty apartment for the summer. It's only a three-and-a-half-hour drive, so we leave relatively late. I've been to New York before with my family, but it's always been those stuffy trips with ritzy hotels and ten p.m. bedtimes. Obviously, I'm excited, especially knowing that I'll be in the city that never sleeps, without my parents and, more importantly, with my best friends.

And Cole.

Alex is coming along, too, so it's no longer a girls-only trip. We invited Lan, too, but he said he'd meet us in the city rather than drive all the way there. Actually, what he specifically said was that he couldn't stand being around that kind of sexual tension. I'd nearly died of embarrassment when his eyes narrowed between Cole and me, a smug grin on his face.

We have lunch at Rusty's before leaving for the road. It's Megan and Alex, Beth and Travis, and lastly Cole and me squeezed into a rounded booth. Since my brother isn't coming with us, I'm subjected to watching him and Beth stare at each other longingly, and you can clearly see that they'd rather be somewhere else, doing something that would traumatize me for life.

No, thank you.

Cole has been strategically sitting next to me, and I can feel the heat of his thigh, searing into mine even though he isn't touching me. He's leaning forward in his seat, joking with Alex about something, but what that does is give me a first-row kind of view of his lips. Darn it; he really is testing my patience. But I'm glad that he's out and about, that he no longer looks like death and reeks of a bottle of Jack. If him being happy and well means that I'll have to stab myself in the eye to avoid molesting him, then so be it.

I'm jerked back into reality when I see that everyone's finished their food and that Beth is leaving with Alex and Megan. Wait a second; someone needs to hit pause right now.

"I thought you were driving up with me?" And then my heart sinks because I know that look in her eye. It's also not that difficult to figure out what she's up to when my brother starts glaring at her.

She's playing cupid.

"Oh, I thought I'd drive with these two." She points toward the sheepish-looking couple standing near the exit to the diner. "No offense, but that monster Jeep of yours scares me."

She loves my car. She named my car Joplin, for crying out loud.

"But you can't leave me alone!"

I can feel Cole's stare, and I don't want to hurt his feelings by saying that I don't want to be alone with him. But that's the truth; I can't handle three hours in an enclosed space with him. But apparently everyone else has made up their minds.

"Look, if it's a problem, then I'll go home…you don't have to do this, Tessie." Cole gets up from the table and stands in front of me, blocking everyone else from view. His shoulders have sagged and he looks dejected; the hurt in his eyes is back. I've done it again, and it makes me feel two feet tall.

"No…I'm sorry. That didn't come out right. Don't go."

"Are you sure? If you're not comfortable…"

"I'm sure," I interject quickly, "I want you to come with me."

That's the most honest I've been with myself for a long time.

Once the tension has melted away, we all get in our cars to leave. Travis hugs me and gives me "the talk." The embarrassing moments in my life seem to be never-ending, and by the end of our conversation, I'm left like I'm having sunstroke, well, at least my face does. Honestly, no girl should have to listen to her brother talk about protection and unplanned pregnancies. Now I can't even look at Cole without…without picturing what Travis just put inside my head. He also warns me that he may check in unannounced if I don't call him twice a day and that he "knows people," so he will find out if I participate in my own version of girls gone wild.

Super, now I have to worry about him being in the mafia.

It's around two in the afternoon by the time Alex's car with Megan and Beth in it drives away and I'm left in my own Jeep with shaking hands clasped on the steering wheel. Suddenly, I'm all nerves and can't even look at the guy sitting next to me, let alone drive. This is such an awkward situation, and the way I'm handling it is even worse.

"Do you want me to drive?" Cole asks softly, and no sooner has he said the words than I get rid of my seat belt and jump out of the car, answering his question. If I were to drive in the state I'm in, I'm sure we'd end up wrapped around a tree. That's how shaken I am, but it's not that unusual. You put Cole anywhere near me and I'll be reduced to a quivering mess, and that still hasn't changed.

After the initial awkwardness wears off and we pull out of the town limits, Cole and I fall into a companionable silence. Everything's going absolutely okay, until the radio decides that the universe cannot possibly be happy with things being relatively normal for me. As the notes of Edwin McCain's "I'll Be" start, we both tense. He doesn't change the station or turn the radio off, and nor do I.

We listen to the song play on and on.

It's kind of masochistic of us, really, but who cares.

"Do you remember how nervous you were that day?" he asks, chuckling.

"I had every right to be! You and I dancing would've normally meant me landing flat on my butt and you laughing at me."

"It was a good day," he says softly and then looks at me with sadness in his eyes.

Of course it was. It was the best day ever, not because I won a stupid tiara but because the next day everything changed.

"It was," I agree and then return to looking out the window.

But now I can't get the stupid song out of my head. I can't get rid of the memories of that day, the image of us dancing, and all the feelings and emotions that swirled inside me that day, the day that made me see how this boy was changing my life as I knew it.

And look at us now. It crushes me to see how different we are now than we were then.

He must have been having the same thoughts since he says, "You know I want you back, right?" His voice is gruff; his fingers clutch the steering wheel tightly. "Maybe Travis is right; maybe this is a pity trip for you, but for me, it's another chance. I intend do to whatever it takes."

My breath catches. His intensity is so overwhelming, and sometimes it's so easy to forget everything, to forget the reasons behind why we're here right now. Because all I want to do in this very moment is to crawl toward his lap and kiss the life out of him.

When I finally find my voice, I tell him, "It's not a pity trip, and I'd appreciate it if you would tell me about these talks that you seem to have with Travis all the time. Maybe then…maybe if you told me more than just assuming things, we wouldn't be in this position."

He sighs, and then after a few long moments, I distinctly hear him say "fuck it."

"I told you before that I came to see you before I left for military school, right?"

I nod and he takes a deep breath. "I also told you that Travis and I had some words; he didn't let me see you, but he told me he'd tell you that I'd been there. He told me that he would tell you how sorry I was about everything."

But Travis hadn't done that.

Before I'd disregarded it because of what had happened with Travis later on, but the issues with school and Jenny took place nearly two years later, and I could no longer use that as a reasonable excuse. The truth is that my brother did a shitty thing; now it's just time to know why.

"Before I left, I was into some pretty bad stuff. I'm not that person anymore, but back then, it wasn't so simple. You hated me; I had started to hate my brother and my dad…let's just say he didn't like me much, either. So, I got involved with things that I should've stayed miles away from."

"What…what things?"

He takes another deep breath. "There was a lot, but the worst part was the drugs. You saw me these last few weeks, right? You saw how bad it got? It was so much worse back then, and I was barely fourteen."

Fourteen…just a kid. What the hell had he been into, and who would give drugs to someone his age?

"One of Travis's friends from the baseball team sold the drugs to me and a bunch of other kids. Travis found me one day with a needle in my arm."

I gasp, and Cole cringes at my reaction. "I nearly OD'ed that day; there were too many things in my system, but he…he took care of it. I couldn't go to the hospital because Cassandra would find out, and Travis had the kind of pull that would get a nursing student to pump my stomach or whatever. I don't remember a lot of it, but when it was over, I knew I had to go away and get clean."

"Military school," I whisper.

"Yeah, I told my dad parts of the story I just told you but not everything. He made the decision, and I didn't fight him on it. But I wanted to do one last thing before leaving. I guess your brother didn't want someone like me to be part of your life back then…maybe even now."

I have no idea what to say to him, nothing at all. It's a lot to take in, but what I feel the most strongly is sadness for the lost boy he used to be. He'd been in pain, and he'd turned to the wrong source to help fix that. I had a big part to play in that, even though the idea seemed laughable to me. An overweight, awkward girl with absolutely no social skills or a social life was the reason why the most loved bad boy of the town nearly took his own life. A few months ago and I would not have believed that, but now I do.

"Say something, Tessie…anything. I know you won't look at me like you used to. Maybe you're disgusted by me; maybe you hate me. Tell me what you're feeling," he rasps.

"I could never hate you or be disgusted by you; that's not possible, not for me. What am I thinking? I'm thinking about how we manage to hurt each other so much without knowing that we're doing it. I mean for two people who claim to love each other, we sure do enough damage, don't we?"

He smiles sadly. "Who said love was easy?"

"Don't go all cliché on me now, Stone, not now." I shake my head.

It's a lot to take in, and the conversation we just had isn't really the road trip kind, but if it takes being in the middle of nowhere with a two-hour drive in front of us to get us to spill our guts, then I'll take it. There's so much more I want to know, so much that I want to ask, but this confession is enough for now. I'm done trying to make him miserable and in turn making myself feel miserable. We deserve a break.

"So, college, huh? Are we really doing this?"

He grins and shakes his head at my not-so-subtle change of subject. "If you'll have me, then I'll follow you anywhere," he declares theatrically, and I slap his arm.

"You'll follow me, and those sorority girls will put a price on my head. Shouldn't you try to sow your wild oats in college?" I say playfully but realize that I've said the wrong thing when his expression hardens.

"I have tunnel vision when it comes to you, so no, I don't care about anyone else."

"So, you want to go to college…"

"With a girlfriend, yeah, that's what I want. Do you want to be single?"

His eyes bore into mine, and I'm half afraid that he'll crash into something, but the road's mostly empty with only a few cars lagging far behind.

"We still have so much to talk about…you can't ask me that now." My voice comes out all breathy and ruins the impact I was going for, one where I actually have a stance.

"It's a simple question. Do you want to date other people, Tessie?"

"No," I say softly, feeling my cheeks flush.

He uses his free hand to tip my chin up so that I'm looking at him. "Good, because I really wouldn't like getting jailed for manslaughter my freshman year."

"And about what you said before, us talking. Well, I plan to do that. I'm not hiding anything from you now. If it helps us get back to what we were, then you can ask me whatever the hell you want, baby."

***

It's not long before we enter New York City and a kind of excited energy thrums through me. I'm here, and now I'm in a good place with Cole. A weight has been lifted off my shoulders, and there are things I'm fairly certain of. I still am madly in love with him, more so than ever. He needs me to take away his past and his insecurities as much as I needed him to do the same for me in the past. I also know that we have problems, a certain redhead being the biggest of them all. But he said we'll talk, and I know he won't lie to me. He didn't lie when he first told me about what had happened with him and Erica, even when he wasn't sure of it himself, so my trust in him is now unwavering.

But I'm still cautious; we still can't jump headfirst into a relationship. Baby steps, that's what we need, because the wounds are still fresh, and we're both a bit fragile right now.

"Hey," Cole says, bringing me out of my thoughts. "How about we get some ice cream before we join the others?" He grins, and I can't help myself.

Screw lemon sherbet; ice cream is the magic word.

I remove the seat belt and watch as his eyes widen when I lean toward him and kiss his cheek. He breathes raggedly when I move back and wink at him.

"That would be perfect."

And when we walk into Serendipity later, I try not to overanalyze the workings of the universe.

But sometimes the universe does tend to throw some love my

way, and when Cole gently brushes his hand against mine as we walk together, I beg the very same universe for some courage and then take his hand in mine.

The smile that then comes on his face weakens my knees, and I know that this boy will be my undoing. I welcome it, of course, because I know there's no one else for me.

CHAPTER FIVE
My Life, A Congregation of Life's Cruelest Clichés

My eyes take in the gleaming surfaces of the penthouse, and I think that this definitely isn't your typical rite-of-passage road trip. We're supposed to be staying in dingy motels, driving for days, and staying alive on dubious roadside diner food. If you ask me, that's what I would have preferred, but instead I find myself in an apartment that takes up the entire fifteenth floor of the impressive and opulent building on the Upper West Side. It figures, though, that this is where my friends and I'll be staying for a couple of days since my dad took it upon himself to make the arrangements. Maybe I'll get lucky and find more destitute surroundings on our next stop.

"Whose place did you say this was?" Cole asks as he takes a look around.

"Whoever's it is, I'm sending them a thank-you basket. Have you guys seen the size of the hot tub?" Beth walks out of the room she and I will be sharing, grinning like an idiot. She's been dying to get me alone ever since Cole and I got here, which would be about an hour later than them, because we stayed out and just walked around the city before driving back to the apartment.

"He's a friend of my dad's, and he and his family are touring Europe, so they won't be back for a while." I answer Cole's question and then narrow my eyes at my best friend, who's still looking at me smugly. Maybe it's because Cole's standing so close to me and I'm not running away from him a mile a minute.

"Dude, have you checked out—"

Alex and Megan walk out from their shared room and Cole dryly completes his sentence. "—the hot tub? I already heard."

I wonder why everyone's so excited about a hot tub in the middle of summer. It's a hot tub, ergo, meant for the colder months. If I didn't know any better…

"We've got to try it tonight; don't worry, Tessa, I packed your bikini," Beth says in a singsong voice before disappearing into our room. Lucky for her, I don't instantly go after her with a butcher knife, because Cole started choking the minute she said *bikini*. She couldn't be more obvious about what she's trying to do if she held out the wedding rings right this moment. We need to have a talk; I glare at her retreating back.

"So," I enthusiastically clasp my hands together facing Cole, who seems to have calmed down a bit. "What do you guys want to do first?" I start rattling off a bunch of options, but everyone's in the mood to shower, eat, and then go out. So, we agree and retreat to our rooms. Beth's on the phone with Travis and lost in her own world.

Thinking about Travis confuses me, especially after the revelation in the car. I don't know if I should be angry at him for hiding something so important, or grateful that he saved Cole's life. Whichever it is, I'll need to talk to him soon.

***

Showering helps put my feelings into perspective. The car ride helped us make progress and cleared a lot of misunderstandings, but we're still fragile. Sometimes when you have a history of the most important people in your life backstabbing you, trust becomes a novelty. I know that I need to man up and deal with the fact that Cole made a mistake. Something may or may not have happened with Erica, but he did put himself in a compromising position, and he's sorry enough about that. I've been as cruel as I could and did my best to resist what we have, but sometimes you can't fight enough.

The girls and I help each other find outfits since it's going to get dark outside soon, and everyone plans on finding a club where they'll believe that I'm twenty-one. I'm guessing it'll be easier to find Ryan Gosling wandering the streets shirtless, looking for a rebound. Though you never can tell with this city; anything's possible.

This might explain why Megan and Beth are trying to stuff my body into a handkerchief; at least that's what I think it is by the look of it. They like to call it a little black dress; I agreed to disagree. If it takes me dressing like a hooker to finally get my friends to have some fun, then so be it. God knows, I've done nothing but be a depressed and emotional time bomb the last month and a half. My skin is buffed, polished, and plucked. Fake tanners and my legs have come to be on a first-name basis, along with our new best friend, the bronzer. Beth does my makeup eerily similar to her own, going heavy on the eyeliner and eye shadow. My hair is curled and left in big, bouncy waves, falling over my shoulders. I've managed to stuff my feet into a pair of Beth's spiky black high heels and begin to wobble around the room.

Standing in front of a full-length mirror, I acknowledge the effort my friends have made. Cliché as it sounds, I hardly recognize the girl staring back at me. She looks…different, to say the least, prettier. Vain as it sounds, I like the way I look after being tweaked. There's a certain kind of confidence that comes with this look. I've always been someone who's never quite been comfortable in her own skin, but the material changes finally make me feel like I could be someone who a guy like Cole could be with for the long haul.

And someone who doesn't lose out to people like Erica.

It's a petty thought, but, hey, if I look like it, then I have to act the part—bring on Diva Tessa.

"So? What's the verdict?" Beth asks as she's trying to tie up her combat boots. She's wearing a black shimmering playsuit and carrying it with a confidence that is quite foreign to me. Her apprehension gives way to a relieved and satisfied smile when she catches the awestruck look on my face. She knows she's done it; she's given me some of my confidence back. It's what I need for a night out with Cole. Who knew I'd fit the cliché, give a girl the right shoes and she can rule the world? Then again, sometimes it feels like one could call my life a congregation of life's cruelest clichés.

If the alliteration fits…

"Cole definitely isn't prepared for what's about to hit him." Megan grins smugly as she curls her own hair. She's come around and strongly back to cheerleading for Team Cole. I think Alex had a lot to do with it, but she's definitely been more supportive, and I could use that in truckloads.

We walk out of the room to a gawking Alex. His lips part and mouth hangs open as he takes us in, in all our club-attire glory. But when his eyes come to rest on Megan, we know there's no looking away. She's rocking her deep-plum, body-con dress, so he's a lost cause. I look around for any sign of Cole but am horribly disappointed when I see a Post-it Note stuck to the fridge. It's his handwriting, and when I get closer, the now extremely offensive piece of yellow paper is telling me that Cole will meet us at the club. Apparently, he has to see some friends who were seemingly more important than spending time with the rest of us.

I try to ignore the hurt and laugh at the rather anticlimactic end to my efforts to blow my sort-of-boyfriend's mind. Now that I think about it, it does put the feminist movement to shame. Dressing up for my man? What decade is this, the 1950s?

Scoffing, I pull myself back together and turn to Beth, who's chewing her lip nervously over my shoulder.

"So how drunk are we going to get tonight?"

***

We end up at a club called Nova where Alex's cousin works. It's convenient enough because we get to skip the line and no asks us for

IDs. Inside, it's exactly like what one would expect a club to look like. What's glaringly obvious is that we're not in a small town anymore. The girls and I sit in the bar section of the club, which has a direct view of the dance floor, and order our drinks. I let Beth make that decision since some cheap beer and wine is the extent of my alcohol knowledge and consumption. Honestly, she could possibly kill me from alcohol poisoning and I wouldn't really know that it's happening. In fact, I rather like the idea of some good old tequila, or maybe some vodka; whisky has a nice ring to it, too, and I've always been intrigued by the idea of scotch. I'm distracted, and it's annoying. I want to get lost in the music, dance with my girlfriends, get drunk and wake up with the hangover from hell, but I can't. My eyes are glued to the entrance.

Where is he?

Weren't we supposed to be using this time to move past our problems and get closer, to try to solve our problems and put them behind us? So, then where is he, and what's so important that he would bail on me like this?

Knocking back the burning, bitter liquid in my glass like a seasoned pro, I grab my friends' hands and drag them to the dance floor. The music is loud, reverberating through me and breaking through the hurt and the apprehension. I love the song that's playing, and it gets easy to lose myself in it and let my body take over. We laugh and move our hips, pretending to be seductresses but ending up cracking up, making people roll their eyes in our direction. After a few songs, Alex comes up to Megan, and we lose them to the crowd.

Beth and I go to the bathroom to freshen up, and when she gets back, she drunk-dials my brother, against my better judgment. Travis is smart enough not to be expecting us to paint fingernails or be braiding each other's hair at midnight, but he also isn't going to be particularly pleased by the fact that his little sister and his girlfriend are, well…busy getting sloshed.

I shrug and let her go to her death, returning to the floor. Travis can be handled in the morning, and you don't just let a Beyoncé song go by without dancing. Pretty soon I'm lost in a world of my own, eyes closed and thoughts of a dark-haired boy shoved into the darkest corners of my mind. I feel the constant heat of bodies behind me. Strangers dancing nearby but not quite crossing the invisible boundaries that define club etiquette. But then, after a while, there are strong hands at my waist, pulling me back, and the feel of someone rocking their hips against mine. In my inebriated state, it feels nice. His hands never stray, just gripping my sides firmly, and there's no grinding. We just roll our hips in synchronization, and it's completely innocent.

I don't feel the urge to see the man's face because as long as I don't, I can pretend he's anyone I want him to be. Besides, it feels good to be noticed, to have someone pay you that kind of attention and give you such closeness. Everything doesn't feel like a wasted opportunity right now.

"Get your hands off her." The warning uttered in a low, threatening voice forces me to open my eyes and push aside the encompassing drunken haze. Goose bumps break out over my skin, and the hair at the back of my neck stands up. He's here. God, he's here, and he's pissed off. He made me wait for him for hours, and now, when I'm a sweaty mess, with my makeup melting beneath the lights and my legs sore from dancing in high heels, he has the nerve to show up and be angry.

"What's your problem, man?" The shaggy-haired blond guy I've been dancing with asks Cole. And yes, that's exactly what I want to know, too. I turn toward Cole, who is standing there in a plain gray T-shirt and jeans, looking all brooding and sexy.

"Yeah, what's your problem, man?"

I emphasize my point by poking his chest repeatedly. He doesn't acknowledge my question but simply narrows his eyes at me. He then steps toward my new friend a bit threateningly and subjects him to a look so fierce that it would have reduced lesser and, well, relatively not as drunk, men to puddles on the floor.

"My problem is that you had your hands all over my girl, and if you don't step away from her in five seconds, I'm going to have bigger problems."

The poor guy's eyes widen, and his Adam's apple bobs nervously as he takes in Cole, who is both heavier and taller than him. He then looks at me and must decide that I'm probably not worth the hospital trip, since he scurries away from me faster than I can feel the insult.

But now I'm mad.

Who the hell does Cole think he is? How dare he go all alpha male on me when he's the one who hurt me? Again.

"You didn't have to do that!" I glower at him and he clenches his jaw, nostrils flaring. He's got that look about him, the one that tells me that he might have been drinking. He isn't drunk yet but is on the verge of it. His senses have dulled enough, and his emotions are heightened, but he's aware of them, of everything.

"What?" He scowls at me. "Was I interrupting something? I sat there and watched that fucker grope you. And I let him do it. I let him do it, because I thought that that's what I deserved. I deserved watching another guy's hands all over you, but that doesn't mean that I'm going to let that happen."

People are watching us. I can feel their weighty glances, but at this point, I can't be bothered to care. This is the most passion and honesty I've had from Cole for a long time. He's so busy treating me with kid gloves that he's forgotten that I want this from him, too, this raw and brutal vulnerability.

"That's not what you deserve," I tell him softly. "Why would you do that? Why did you let me pretend that the random stranger I was dancing with was you? Because that's all I wanted; I wanted you here with me. Not him, just you."

His eyes become glassy and then his gaze heats up, warming me to my core. He yanks at my wrist, drawing me away from the pulsating crowd. I catch the worried glances of our friends and give them a reassuring smile. Cole doesn't scare me; when I'm with him, I'm the safest I've ever been.

He's on a one-man mission to get us alone, and I can sense his urgency. So, when he pushes me against the wall of an empty corridor, I'm prepared. He leans against me, pressing his forehead to mine.

"You make me crazy," he breathes.

"Ditto."

His lip twitches and his mouth curves into a smile. "I would say I'm sorry for acting like a jackass out there, but I won't."

"And I should be mad at you for being such a caveman, but I'm not."

"It turned you on, didn't it?" He grins, and it's scary how easily and effortlessly we go back to being us. The questions still linger at the back of my mind, but I now know that there's a good enough explanation for everything. I don't doubt him like I would have; the world isn't crashing down around me. We're just…us.

"Shut up!" I laugh and smack his shoulder.

"It did, didn't it?" he says, sounding smug and way too happy teasing me.

I huff out loudly, "Even if it did, you just ruined the moment." I pretend to be annoyed.

"Oh yeah? We're going to have to fix that, then." The heated gaze is back, and my breath hitches.

"Oh My…"

He brings up his hands to my face, his fingers trailing over every feature. My lips, nose, eyes, chin, and even the sensitive spot behind my ear burn where his fingers trail. His touch lingers, almost worshipping. "I've missed this," he breathes, and my eyes close on their own accord, a contented sigh escaping me.

"Me, too," I breathe as he drags his knuckles down my neck, over my collarbone, and nearly down the front of my dress.

"I like the dress," he whispers in my ear, and I gasp as his teeth lightly scrape against the skin of my throat. "But so did every other guy out there. I wanted to kill them all." He continues driving me crazy with his gentle ministrations.

"You're feeling particularly murderous tonight." I feel him smile against the crook of my neck.

"It's all your fault; apparently, you like the idea of me in prison." He nuzzles his nose against me.

"I…I don't." Honestly, I've lost my train of thought; who could blame me? When Cole Stone's doing such magical things to you, coherence or presence of mind isn't really much of an issue.

He kisses all over my face and I'm lost, utterly and completely lost to him and what he's doing to me.

"Tessa?" he rasps as he moves my hair to one side, exposing my bare shoulder and then kissing it.

"Hmm?" I mutter distractedly. He needs to talk less and do more of whatever he's doing.

"Can I take you home? Because we need to talk, and I don't know if I can…I'm losing any semblance of control here, and I'd rather not do this in the dirty doorway of a club."

Whoa.

What do you say to that?

I have questions, a lot of them. We do need to talk about a lot of things, and he's still being a bit evasive, but we have all the time in the world. Right now, though, I pull away, only to nod once, and then it's all a frantic rush to just be alone. To be Cole and Tessa, and, if it were possible to die from anticipation, then I would.

CHAPTER SIX
Stop Being So Sweet and Shirtless

I don't think I've ever seen Cole move faster than when he's tugging at my arm and walking us both out of the club. Palpable excitement bubbles though my chest, and any effect that the alcohol may have had on me is quickly disappearing. Cole Stone is definitely more intoxicating. He keeps shooting glances back at me, like he thinks I'm going to vanish at any given second, but I smile at him reassuringly, basically telling him that this girl isn't going anywhere. It's funny how my feelings for him are always all over the place. I can go from hating him immensely to loving him with just as much extremity in a matter of seconds. That's definitely not going to be the tagline of a functional relationship, but, hey, to each his own.

Outside it's a warm summer night, and there are still lines of people waiting to get inside the club. A few, okay a lot of them whistle and yell not-so-polite things at me as we pass them by. Cole glares at the source of each and every, er, comment, and they pipe down pretty quickly. Scowling, he spins and asks me, "Couldn't you wear a coat or something?"

I should be offended at such a caveman mentality, and a small part of me is. It's not my fault that men are such constant horn dogs, and I shouldn't have to cover up in order to save myself from their perverse looks, but that's a battle I'll fight another day. Right now, I can't help but laugh at how adorable he looks.

"You want me to wear a coat, in this temperature? Seriously?"

"It's either that or I'm going to have to go knock that guy's teeth out," he yells at someone who had apparently been checking out my backside. All of a sudden, I start laughing and laughing hysterically. It's all so ridiculous, men leering over me. If they'd seen me a couple of years ago, I'm pretty sure they would have reacted differently. The fact that guys would find me sexually attractive is baffling on its own, and having a boyfriend like Cole threaten them away is even more mind-numbing.

"What's so funny?" Cole pouts as he pulls me to his side, wrapping his arm around my shoulders. God, I love it when he's all possessive. I try to stop laughing, but the side effects of alcohol linger, making the situation funnier than it actually is. Clutching my sides, I lean into Cole and stifle my laughter into his shirt.

"It's just…" I gasp, still feeling a bit hysterical, "this time last year I was in bed in my Scooby pajamas, gorging on chocolate therapy, hoping Jay would notice me. It's just funny how different everything is now."

His entire body stiffens, and I'm pretty sure mentioning Jay was a big mistake. But he recovers quickly, squeezing me tightly and kissing the top of my head. "It's a new summer, baby, we'll make plenty of new memories, and none of them will involve my deadbeat brother."

I melt into him, kissing the spot over his heart, and close my eyes while he hails a cab. Everything is already so much better. It's miraculous how much of a difference it makes being with and without him. It's not healthy, that kind of dependency on a person, and I've suffered the consequence of being so addicted to him. The wounds are still fresh, the memories still traumatic, and a wiser person would be cautious before plunging headfirst into a relationship, but that person's not me. I'm tired of being cautious, of holding myself back when I know that the kind of happiness Cole brings me can't be matched by anything else. The small voice at the back of my mind nags me, though, reminding me that the heartache Cole brings is unparalleled, too. I give that voice a proverbial middle finger.

When we finally manage to get a cab, Cole literally has to drag me inside, I feel that tired, but everything changes once we get in an enclosed space. As Cole tells the driver the address to the penthouse, the excitement and thrill from the club comes rushing back. The tension between us is palpable, especially when Cole captures my hand with his and then places them both on my thigh. He grins at me mischievously before using his thumb to trace circles on the bare skin that the bottom of my dress doesn't quite reach. My breath hitches and I sneak a look at the cabbie. He seems oblivious to the fact that I'm losing my mind over some innocent caressing. But then as Cole's fingers begin to move higher, I realize that it's not so innocent and that he's enjoying my squirming. I swat his hands away and try discreetly nodding toward the driver. He grins and leans in as if he's going to kiss me, and my heart nearly barrels through my chest. He still hasn't kissed me on the lips, and I don't know how I feel about it happening in the back seat of a New York City taxi with a cab driver who has now started glancing warily in our direction from the front mirror. But just as I prepare myself to say screw it and kiss the life out of Cole, the man is question changes direction and places his lips next to my ear.

"We can't have an audience for what I'm planning, Tessie." He kisses the sensitive spot beneath my ear and then moves away, casually resting against his seat like he hasn't just unhinged me to the core.

Jerk.

I narrow my eyes at him and then turn my head stubbornly in the opposite direction, watching the city pass by us in blurred images. I hear him chuckle, but he doesn't attempt to touch me again and I'm glad. Being so on edge, if he made another move, I would self-destruct if he didn't go through with it. And everything feels more, more vivid, more consuming. Maybe it's the wait; maybe it's the fact that it's been so long since we've been together like this and known that it might lead to something bigger. There's no ax hanging over our heads, no guilt or distrust on either side. A weight feels like it's been lifted, and the freedom that comes with it makes this moment so much sweeter.

As we get dropped off and pay the cab driver, who looks relieved to get rid of us, Cole and I enter the lobby of the building and head for the elevator. There's no rush this time, though, but our measured movement perhaps more symbolic of how we're actually feeling. There are nerves, definitely, but there's also this underlying expectation and perhaps acceptance that things need to or are about to change in the best way possible.

We are alone in the elevator leading up to our floor, and it's understandable, seeing how it's so late and the tenants are mostly wealthy early risers from the corporate sector. Cole and I stand on opposite sides and watch the numbers go up. The silence is thick with expectancy, and I have chills running up and down the length of my body.

"I was with Lan and the guys," he says quietly, taking me by surprise. I wasn't expecting an immediate explanation and had prepared myself to shove the questions onto the back burner for now. But it seems like Cole has other ideas. He leans his head against the side of the elevator, looking up at the ceiling and expelling a frustrated sigh.

"They want to help, come up with some master plan that'll help me figure out what the hell happened that night. I know…I know that I was drunk enough to not realize what the hell I was doing or with whom, but that doesn't make it okay. The look on your face when I told you about what I had done, God, it'll haunt me for the rest of my life."

I open my mouth to interrupt but he shakes his head, begging me to let him finish.

"I need to know everything about that night, Tessie. If I don't, then I'll spend the rest of my life wondering whether or not I was weak enough to do that to you. Because some part of me believes that I would never do that to you, that I would rather die than cause you so much pain."

Blinking back tears, I ask him gently, "And did you? Did you get the answers you wanted?"

Because how could he get answers without talking to the only person that had them? The thought of him with Erica in any capacity made my stomach churn. If he'd gone to see her and not told me, then I did not know what I would do, and the prospect made me tremble.

He exhales heavily. "She's been trying to talk to me for a while, I guess. The day I went to see her before the graduation party, she tried so hard to avoid talking about that night, and that's what made me suspicious. But she left town the next day, and there's been no words from her since. I guess we could put it behind us since I didn't sleep with her," he grimaces and his face scrunches up like he's swallowed something bitter, "But I need…"

"Closure—we both need that," I affirm.

A bell chimes, alerting us to the fact that we've arrived at our floor, and Cole walks us out with a hand at the small of my back. Unlocking the door, I lead us inside and head straight for the fridge, the clicking of my heels magnified by the silence. Grabbing a water bottle, I gulp down the entire thing, attempting both to draw out the conversation and soothe my parched throat. I need to be less buzzed in order to deal with what Cole is going to say.

He leans against the kitchen counter, his eyes never wavering from my face. "Lan's been digging around for me." He stops and lets out a laugh. "He was always convinced that Erica belonged in the nut house. He's having one hell of a time making me feel like shit now."

"You couldn't have known that she was a psychotic bitch any more than the next person," I say, and Cole grins. Only a few people manage to bring out my vindictive side, and his personal crazy lady is right on top of my shit list now, with Nicole definitely knocked down from that spot.

"Well, now I know, and we've been trying to find her. I should let it go; God knows I never want to see her again, but there are so many questions in my head, and I can't look at you without feeling like a complete asshole that doesn't deserve an ounce of your loyalty."

"I get it, Cole; you don't have to sneak around behind my back while you're looking for whatever answers you need. It's important to both of us, and I'll try not to have a complete meltdown if you ever have to confront her again. You might have to persuade her to wear bulletproof clothing, though."

His face breaks into a huge smile and so does mine. He seems relieved that I'm not ending us again just on the basis of the fact that he needs to know why we put ourselves through months of misery. Maybe I've been prone to overreaction; maybe it's totally justified that I have. Whatever the deal is, we both need time to fully convince ourselves that the other isn't going anywhere. The fear is still there, haunting us and making us fearful of the loss we've already had to face once, but then I guess that's what love is. Love means to be brave despite knowing the kind of agony that comes with a broken heart.

And I think it's about time to put on my big-girl panties.

"So, was this the conversation you were so worried about?" I tease, and watch as his eyes turn a shade darker than their usual mesmerizing ocean-blue. I gulp as he strides toward me, like a confident predator. He gently removes the water bottle from my hand and throws the empty bottle in the trash, making a perfect shot in the can without even looking.

I raise my eyebrows at him. "Impressive."

He grins, wrapping his arms around me and pulling me to his chest. "You haven't seen anything yet."

And then he kisses me.

Like really kisses me, smack-dab on the lips.

I moan as he presses his lips to mine in a kiss that starts out slow, sweet, and poignant but quickly turns into frantic and wild, passionate and searing. The time apart makes this a bittersweet moment. Of course, there's happiness in coming back to each other, but the desperation behind our kiss hints at the pain we've gone through. I tug at Cole's hair as he bites and nips at my lips, running his tongue over them, soothing and salving the sting. I push my hands under his shirt, tugging at the hem. Cole gets the point, breaking away only to pull the shirt off and then going right back into kissing me.

My hands greedily explore his chest, fingers trailing over his shoulders, his incredible abs, and the taut skin of his waist. His muscles strain beneath my touch, and he groans into my mouth. In one fell swoop he picks me up in his arms and carries me to the room he's staying in, kissing me wildly all the while. Abruptly, he drops me on the bed. We're both out of breath and panting like crazy. But I don't care; I need him to kiss me some more. And perhaps touch me, all over and right now.

He looks at me longingly, like he's in pain, his chest rising and falling rapidly.

"Why did you stop?" I say breathlessly, and he groans a little.

"We've both been drinking, Tessie. What if you regret this in the morning? We should wait…maybe when you're sober." He gulps and looks away, shoving his hands in his hair.

I fall onto the pillows with a loud thud. "You've got to be kidding me. I thought you wanted to…at the club and in the taxi, you were all…this is so embarrassing," I whine, covering my face with my arm. My heart rate is slowly going down, but now my face is as red as can be. What did I think? That we'd do the deed tonight? I'd so brazenly attacked him that I didn't even consider that Cole would hesitate, that he would never take such an important step when we'd both obviously been drinking.

I didn't mind, though, and that in itself should make me feel ashamed. Didn't girls usually want to be completely sober during their first times? Though I have no idea why, alcohol would totally help with the pain.

Oh well.

I feel the bed shift as Cole lies down next to me, removing my arm from across my face. He's still shirtless and not helping the situation in any way.

"Are you disappointed?" he asks as he kisses me softly.

"I don't know. Maybe it's for the best; we did talk about baby steps, right?"

"You blew that when you wore this dress, babe." He grins and I blush, ridiculous, considering how I'd just been mauling him a few minutes ago.

"So, we definitely suck at taking things slowly. It's either nothing or full throttle, huh?"

"It's never nothing with us and it never will be."

"Stop being so sweet and shirtless; you're making me horny."

Shit, did I just say that? I clasp my hand over my mouth as Cole bursts out laughing and continue to do so for at least five minutes as I lie there in utter humiliation. Why, oh why, did I drink? It is totally ruining my game here. This time I push myself up from the bed and pretend to need to use the bathroom. I hide in there for a good ten minutes, running the faucet for longer than I need to take my makeup off. Cole knocks much later than I expected him to and comes right in without waiting for permission. He looks a bit apologetic and still shirtless.

"I shouldn't have laughed; I'm sorry."

Biting my lip, I hop onto the counter and study the tiled floor. I'm beyond embarrassed. It seems like the only thing on my mind is sleeping with him, while he couldn't be less interested. In reality, I know that that's not necessarily true. For a girl who has spent her entire life seemingly loving people more than they love her, his reaction brings out my insecurities, which are always itching to resurface. Those little, blood-sucking leeches.

"It's okay," I mumble, twiddling my thumbs.

It's stupid and immature to be hurt by this, he'd only been joking, but like I said, my insecurities seem to like sucking the joy out of everything.

"How do I keep managing to screw things up with you?" he says hoarsely, coming to stand in front of me and tilting my chin up to look at him.

"This isn't about you; I just need a minute, okay? I'll be right out." I smile at him, but he sees right through it. Pain darkens his features as he closes in on me. "I hurt your feelings, and that's not okay."

"Cole, please, it's not a big deal. You were just trying to do the right thing, and here I am acting like some sex addict with a one-track mind. I made a fool out of myself out there; anyone would have laughed."

I'm blushing furiously as I say this, humiliation washing all over me. But when I look at Cole, I don't find pity or disgust at my behavior; he looks almost angry as he takes my mouth in a punishing kiss. Spreading my thighs, he moves into the space between them and moves me so that I sit at the very edge of the counter. The kiss is meant to affirm, to tell me how he feels, and it's doing a pretty good job of that. We break apart after a while, lost in a lust-filled haze as Cole nuzzles his face into my neck.

"I love you so much, Tessie, and I want you like crazy. You drive me insane; whenever you're around, I can't think straight. Whatever control I have is hanging by a very thin thread right now. If I wasn't so fucking terrified of somehow losing you again, I'd make love to you right now. But I won't, not because I don't want to but because I know the wait will be worth it. When I'll be with you, it'll both rip me apart and make me whole at the same time."

If he feels how fast my heart is racing, he makes no mention of it. But damn, it's a miracle that I'm still upright. Goose bumps form over my skin, and I shiver due to the power of his words. I've never been spoken to like that, not even by him. His words are so raw, so passionate, and so unbelievably romantic that I want to cry. In fact, I do tear up, but that's just routine now.

"Cole?" I say after we just hold each other for a while.

"Yeah?" he asks, kissing my neck.

"You should take me to bed now and cuddle. I would really like to cuddle right now."

"Anything you want, Tessie, anything."

And so, he carries me out, settling me on the bed as if I were made of glass. He then proceeds to get pajamas for me, the Scooby ones I never threw out, and undresses me without ever looking away from my eyes. It's the most erotic experience of my life. We fall asleep with my back pressed to his chest and his arm slung over me, our legs tangled together and his head buried in the crook of my neck. We vaguely hear our friends stumble in, midmorning, but I don't even pretend to worry about what they might think.

I'm in heaven.

CHAPTER SEVEN
We're Not Bunnies

The sound of a running shower is what wakes me up the next morning. Well, that and the fact that there's the unmistakable hangover headache that's desperate to make its presence known. Groaning, I lift my head up, only to find its weight unbearable. With a thump, I fall back into bed, cursing myself for last night. Simultaneously I thank Cole for having the foresight to make me drink a whole bottle of water and take two aspirin in the middle of the night. Had it not been for him, Damien, the devil child from *The Omen*, would have nothing on me. Obviously, I don't do well with hangovers, just like every other person out there, and that still didn't stop me from imbibing my body weight in tequila last night. Fine, that might be a bit of an exaggeration, and I'm grateful for not drinking as much as I'd been planning to, but someone needs to make the pain go away! Mentally, I stomp my foot, since physically moving would be a one-way ticket to the bathroom and would end with me hugging the toilet bowl.

"How're you feeling?"

I mumble an incoherent answer, hugging a pillow closely to me. It smells like Cole. I like it when things smell like Cole. I'll have to do with them since I can't really bear the sound of his amused laughter. He's a cruel, cruel man.

"Tessie, come on, you need to get up and eat something. You'll feel better," he says more softly and I open my eyes. Well, I'm not exactly capable of opening them; it's more like squinting when someone's got a flashlight all up in your face.

"I don't want to," I whine and shove my face back into the nice-smelling pillow. The thought of food is nauseating.

"You're going to have to. We've got plans today, and you need to get out of bed."

I grumble, but at this point I'm dozing off, and sleep is welcoming me with open arms. Ah, sleep, my oldest and closest friend. No wonder we get along so well; it's always there to take away my pain and the consequences of my various mistakes.

"I don't have to do anything. I'm on vacation, remember?" I huff, making the effort of glaring at Cole before turning my back on him and preparing myself to go back to sleep. In my haste to slip back into oblivion, I don't think too much about the fact that Cole's not wearing a shirt. That said, a sleepy smile makes its way across my face when I think about instituting a law that requires Cole to walk around shirtless all the time. Now, that would be a wonderful amendment to the Constitution, wouldn't it?

"Fine, but you asked for it." Maybe I should be more fearful of what he's about to do, but it's not an immediate concern, so I dismiss the warning I'm receiving from the part of my brain that hasn't been destroyed by alcohol.

"Since you want to sleep, we obviously need to cancel our plans. There's no need for me to get dressed; actually, why wear any clothes at all? All I have to do is take off this towel wrapped around my waist. Maybe we'll make a day of it; how about it, Tessie? Let me just take this thing off…"

Wait—what?

He's getting naked?

Now?

"WAIT!" I shout and cover my eyes with one hand, flailing the other about in space. "Keep your clothes on, Stone; I'll get out of the damn bed, just don't get naked."

"Oh, so you want to undress me yourself? Can't complain there, but why don't you get some food in yourself first?"

I want to die. He's totally feeding off of my embarrassment, and I'm letting him. How sad is this? Why can't I flirt like the pro I'll never quite be at exchanging sexual innuendos? Maybe I need lessons; do they have a hotline for that?

He laughs then, and it's the most wonderful sound, even in the given situation. I haven't really heard enough of it and find myself cracking up, too. "You're actually wearing jeans, aren't you?"

"Yeah, shortcake." He pulls my hand away from my eyes and kisses the top of my head. "I just wanted to know how you'd react. Good to know the idea of making me naked traumatizes you." He shoots me a wounded look and I shove at his chest, not even moving him an inch. I'm sitting upright and he's standing at the side of the bed and, upon inspection, I do see the jeans and the exposed, coveted "V" of his hips but quickly avert my gaze. I need to stop eye-molesting the guy.

"I don't feel so good," I mumble, looking longingly at the pillow that I've now placed in my lap.

He ruffles my hair gently. "Why don't you go take a hot shower, and later I'll make you my hangover-cure breakfast."

I must start looking a little green since he chuckles and tips my face back to meet his gorgeous blue eyes. "You'll like it; I promise."

Smiling at him, I rest my forehead against the still unclothed chest. "I know I will."

***

Hot showers are a godsend, let it be known. I feel relatively human again as I stumble into the kitchen forty minutes later and comfily clothed in a trance-like state, following the smell of coffee. I pour myself a huge mug and add in copious amounts of sugar and creamer, taking big gulps of the scalding liquid.

"Easy there, tiger, you'll burn your tongue or something."

I look up at Cole, who is both frying up some eggs and watching me with amusement. "I already did." I grin and keep drinking. It definitely deserves to be called the elixir of life; caffeine is like no other substance out there, and there's only one thing in the world more addictive than it.

And he's staring at me like he wants to commit everything about me to memory.

As I shamelessly gawk at his gray-T-shirt-clad body and his jeans, which cling to all the right places, I find myself doing the same. But no amount of time being away from each could have possibly made me forget how his blue eyes become darker when he's angry or elated. I can't forget that he gets annoyed by how stubborn his hair is in the morning and that he's given up on it, making him look impossibly sexy with the Andrew Garfield hair. And what I definitely couldn't ever forget is how he looks at me, like he's been waiting for me forever. That look tends to stay with a girl for a lifetime.

"What?" I ask him, sounding rather breathless.

He gives me a heart-stopping grin. "It feels good to be with you like this again."

Warmth fills me, along with a kind of happiness that I haven't experienced in so long. He's right; it does feel good. It feels like we're back to who we were, but stronger. So what if we don't have all the answers right now, and he needs some twisted sort of closure from the redheaded witch; that doesn't really matter, not when being with him feels so right.

"Is there some kinky kitchen action going on?" Beth's head pops out from the room that was supposed to be Cole's. I can only imagine the thoughts running through her head when she found out that our shared room was otherwise occupied. Mentally groaning at the amount of teasing I'm going to have to endure, I twist my body to give her a pointed glare.

"We're not bunnies," I huff, but any annoyance at her evaporates when I notice that her pajamas are my brother's former baseball jersey and sleeping shorts with his number on them. I'll tease her about them later, but right now, it melts my sappy heart. Jenny, Travis's conniving, backstabbing ex-girlfriend wasn't really the supportive kind. She enjoyed the privileges that came with being Travis O'Connell's girlfriend, but that was about it; when the ride ended, she left. Knowing that now my brother has someone like Beth, and that she has him, makes everything right in the world.

"Don't look at me like I'm a heroine from one of your novels," she says while rubbing her tired-looking eyes. She's definitely hungover, much more than I am, and it's showing. It wouldn't be really nice of me to pick on her right now, but she looks just so darn adorable!

"But you look so cute in that outfit! Does Travis know you wear this to sleep?"

She arches an eyebrow, as if asking me why wouldn't Travis know about what she wears to bed, and the tips of my ears feel hot.

Oh God.

Is she insinuating what I think she's insinuating? Gross!

Cole coughs awkwardly. "Okay then, ladies, now that we've got that out of the way, how about some breakfast?" He gives us a pageant-worthy smile and offers us two plates. Beth and I reconcile in our attempts to rush to the nearest available toilet.

***

Afterward, when I'm finally able to keep food down, and Alex and Megan stumble into the kitchen, we all make our plans for the day.

Everyone's pretty okay with a plan to lie low for the morning and evening recovering from last night. Honestly, it's a bit disappointing since I'm feeling okay and want to go out and enjoy the fact that I'm not home anymore. It's not like I haven't been to New York before, all of us have and done the touristy things, but there's definitely more fun doing all those things again with your best friends and not your uppity grandparents.

I lean against the dining table watching everyone finish their breakfast and retreat back into their rooms as if the sunlight from the open windows literally burns them. Beth is already on the phone with Travis, and I shudder thinking about the things they talk about. Megan looks at me apologetically, but, given the fact that she's been sick the entire night and that Alex has been up taking care of her, I let her go. The three of us will still get to enjoy our best-friend road trip; today's just a small bump in the road.

Cole snakes an arm around my waist and pulls me back into his chest. Any hesitation he had about touching me is gone. He's been finding subtle ways to touch me all morning. Brushing past me, leaning against me and whispering in my ear, it's been driving me crazy. And now we're alone, completely alone all over again. Someone needs to bring out the heavy-duty rope here so that I can keep my hands to myself. There are some things I can conclude certainly about myself, and being a nymphomaniac was never in the plans. That's what Cole Stone can do to you, though.

"How about you and I get out of here?"

I perk up immediately and twist my neck to look at him, smiling as widely as possible. "What did you have in mind?"

"Well, so far all I have planned is ice cream and then maybe a walk; I just want to be alone with you."

"I'd love that, especially the ice cream."

He laughs, turning me around and enveloping me in his arms. "Is it stupid that I'm jealous of two really old guys called Ben and Jerry?"

I shrug playfully. "If you make me my favorite ice cream, I'd place you right up there with them on my list of people I worship."

He grins. "Oh, I think you'll worship me for a whole other set of reasons when I'm done with you."

There goes my mind into the gutter. Does he do that on purpose, or does he seriously not know what he's insinuating right now? I know I'm giving away my dirty thoughts by the look of amusement on his face and, well, by the fact that my cheeks must now be like cherry tomatoes.

He leans in closer and whispers huskily, "Yeah. Wait till you get to experience the most decadent and sinful pleasure known to man. You'll be addicted once you get a taste, Tessie."

My heart is racing wildly; my insides are on fire. I'm almost ready to jump out of my skin; that's how tingly and nervous I am. His voice is like pure honey, smooth and silky, but there's an edge of roughness that does the trick. Man, he's good.

"I've been told before, but you'll be the best judge there is, so do you want to, Tessie? Do you…do you want me to make you…" He pauses.

"Make me what?" I squeak, on edge with my mind buzzing and thoughts flying in every direction, or, well, one particular direction.

He straightens up and with a straight face that has me unnerved says, "Would you like me to make you my famous triple-Nutella-layered fudge brownies?"

Suffice it to say I don't talk to him for an hour after that.

***

Even though I'm still super irritated with Cole for the stunt he pulled, that's not enough to stop me from getting ready for our pseudo date. Since Beth decided to go back to the room she slept in, I'm left with Cole as my roommate, and he watches me as I bang closet doors and throw stuff around looking for an outfit.

"Are you still mad at me?" he asks from where he's sprawled on the bed, leaning against the headboard, his arms crossed behind his head.

"Asking that question the fifth time won't change my answer, you know." How come I have no cute shoes? How is it that I only packed my most mangy-looking flip-flops that are almost in tatters? Wonderful, now I'll be the girl with the ugly, homeless-person shoes. And what's with all the shirts I have? Why didn't I raid the closet filled with the clothes my mother had bought me? Oh, right, it's because my mother bought me the clothes. So, as I dig through one unflattering top after another, I don't feel him approaching until he's crouching down next to my open suitcase, which, by the way, looks like a crime scene.

"I'm sorry if I hurt your feelings. You know that I wasn't making fun of you, right?"

I throw away the tank top that I'm currently mangling and avoid looking at him. Of course I'm being a bitch, and he doesn't deserve that kind of behavior, but sometimes a lot of feelings get bottled up and then burst open at the worst of times.

"I know, I'm sorry, you were kidding, and I overreacted, as usual. It's all I seem to be doing with you, and I know it must get annoying, but it's just self-preservation, Cole."

I sit down cross-legged on the floor and play with the hem of my shirt. Cole sits back too, pulling his knees up and watching me with concern and a bit of confusion.

Exhaling, I prepare myself to say something that might hurt him, but it's something that needs to be said. If I keep these feelings to myself, it'll spread like poison and possibly ruin our relationship—again. So now I need to be honest.

"Sometimes I get scared that maybe what I feel for you is more than what you feel for me." He opens his mouth to argue but I cut him off. "I know that's stupid, okay, and that I'm wrong. You've never made me feel like we're on an uneven playing field. You've…you've liked me for longer, so what I feel doesn't even make sense, right? But after everything, I'm still a bit scared to come off as being more in love with you, because that makes me feel weak, and it takes me back to how badly I broke. That's why when you joke around and I fall for them, it scares me. That's not your fault, it's mine, and it's something I have to work on. I can't let what happened keep messing us up, you know?"

Cole watches me with an intense gaze when I finally look at him. There's pain in those eyes and guilt, emotions I never wanted to see again but, way to go, Tessa, they're back. He doesn't deserve what I put him through, but he's still there every single day, looking for more ways I can hurt him.

"Do you remember what I said to you last night? I told you that my worst fear was losing you. That's what's on my mind all the fucking time. Whenever I look at you, I realize how easily I can lose you, especially now. So, when I'm joking around, it's partly because I'm trying to chase away that voice that tells me that sooner or later I'll do something that'll make you leave me for good. But mostly because teasing you is what reminds me the most of how we started, literally when we were kids. It was always my MO to get your attention, to see that spark in your eyes. I figured that if it worked when we were five, it would work now, too."

His mention of our childhood instantly makes me smile. God, he tormented me so much, and I hated him from the core of my being. Whenever I saw him, I'd immediately fear the worst for the rest of the day; he was like the kid from *The Omen*. Now he's like that really cute guy from *Clueless* whom I dreamed about for ages.

Except he's not my former stepbrother; that would be weird.

Moving on…

I cross on over to him and cup his face in my hands, kissing him soundly then leaning back. "Have I told you before that I'm madly in love with you. Cole Stone?"

He looks relieved and a bit surprised but, given the way he

pounces on me, tackling me to the ground, I can tell that mostly he's happy.

"I'm madly in love with you, too, Tessa O'Connell."

And then he kisses me forever, or so I wish.

***

When I finally find an outfit—a difficult feat, given how Cole's hell-bent on distracting me—Cole and I leave our friends from *The Walking Dead* at home and head on over to a nearby park that's chock-full of people enjoying their summer. After getting and eating my promised ice cream, we find a secluded spot beneath a massive old tree and settle down. Well, I sit and Cole lies down with his head in my lap. Sighing contentedly, I lean against the tree and run my fingers through his hair. His moan of appreciation tells me that he approves.

This is perfect.

We're silent for a while, enjoying some quiet after the heavy-handed conversation we had at the apartment. We're finally in a place where there are no questions lingering in the space between us. So, if any more problems were to come our way, we could face them together. Just as I'm getting lost in my thoughts, I hear Cole say something that I don't catch.

"Did you say something?"

He sighs. "I wish I hadn't."

This sounds ominous and I'm panicking already. What now? Oh, please, don't let it be the E-word; I can't take the E-word without flying off the handle.

"Your mom called me today."

Okay, that's okay. It takes a minute for me to process what he just said, but when it does sink in, I'm surprisingly okay with it. She's been calling me, too, but I don't answer or listen to the voice mails she insists on leaving every time. It's only natural that she calls Cole; cheap shot, Mom.

"Oh." I manage to say after a few tense moments, "What did she want?"

"Apparently, you don't answer her calls."

I mutter a noncommittal *whatever* as he watches my face. "She really wants to talk to you, Tessa."

"I'll talk to her when I'm ready. If I do it now, it'll only end up making things worse; I'm not exactly her biggest fan at the moment."

"That's what I told her, but she was sort of desperate. Tessa, she's in the city and she wants to have dinner with us tonight."

"No." I don't need to think about it; there's not even another option. I did have my suspicious about my mom being here, and I'd prepared myself for this. There is no way I'm going back to pretending everything's normal, not when she walked out on her family without a second thought. She's always been selfish, but her actions of late have taken it to a new level. Me being civil and fake is not on the cards, Mother.

"Look, it's just dinner. If we show up and you let her have her say, that'll be the end of it. At least it'll be better than constantly avoiding her. I know what it feels like when you cut someone off, Tessie."

Ouch, he's making a valid point and bringing up bad memories, all in one go.

"It's not the same…she…she…"

Cole lifts his head from my lap and scoots over next to me, taking my hands in his. "You feel like you hate her, like you can't ever forgive her, right?"

I know what he's thinking about right now. "It's not the same. We were different; that was you, and this is about my mom."

"We're both people who hurt you and failed you. Do this for me, Tessie; just try talking to her, that's all I ask."

"What exactly did she say to you to get you on her side?" I ask since I'm genuinely curious. Usually he lets me and my mommy issues be. He's never been this involved because I know I've made it a moot point and he doesn't want to fight, but this is the first time he's being so relentless about it.

He grins and brings his face closer to mine. "She may or may not have said that I was the only person her daughter trusts with her life and would always listen to."

"And you believed her?" I scoff, but inwardly, I hate the fact that Mom still knows me.

He looks nervous for a moment. "Maybe things have changed a bit and you don't trust me like you used to—"

I slap my hand over his mouth. "I do trust you, Cole."

His lips curve into a smile beneath my fingers and he kisses my palm. Removing my hand, I lean against his chest and ask, "Where do we have to be and at what time?"

I'm such a sucker for him.

But this is not about my mother; this is about me showing Cole that what my mom said is right and that he doesn't need to doubt us ever again.

"Love you, Tessie." He kisses the top of my head, and it makes everything worthwhile.

CHAPTER EIGHT
The Boy Band Asshat Needs to Know You're Mine

I realize my mistake the moment I step into the fancy restaurant my mother's selected. The impersonal, stuffy setting clearly shows that she's not up for a heart-to-heart. Well, good, I'm not ready for that, either. Clutching Cole's hand, I look around for a familiar face, but it's my boyfriend who points me in the right direction.

"That's her, right?"

I swivel in the direction Cole points, and the first thing I notice about the woman sitting at the table is that she looks happy. Maybe that's not something to begrudge, but I do. She's smiling warmly at the man seated next to her and is constantly touching him in some way, stroking his arm, holding on to his hand, the works. There's an easy affection that's long been missing from my parents' marriage. Maybe if she'd kept off the antidepressants and hadn't been lost in a constant haze of prescription drugs, we'd have a better relationship.

Her appearance has drastically changed; she's no longer going for the whole *The Stepford Wives* look. For one, her hair's blonder, with warm highlights that bring out her eyes. I can see she's lost weight, but that's only given her face more definition; her body from the waist up looks more toned, and, as much as it hurts, she's glowing. Her eyes gleam with adoration as the good-looking man in a crisp navy suit with the salt-and-pepper hair caresses her cheek. He's the one who notice me watching them and says something to my mother, who turns to look at me.

Our eyes meet from across the busy dinner service; she smiles at me, and I try to return it, I really do, but it's not that easy.

"Come on; you can do this," Cole assures me, leading me to the table that's set for five people. The fact that she's brought her latest fling to our so-called reunion is evidence enough that this is not going to be the scene for a mother-daughter bonding session. Still since I'm here, I might as well put a smile on my face, and get done with this so that Cole and I can go ahead with our plans. Cole places a hand at the small of my back and leads me to the table. Both my mother and her date stand, and I get a good look at her. Susan O'Connell née Ryan always dresses impeccably, come rain or shine, but it's obvious that she's changed her style, wearing a fitted navy sheath dress that hugs her curves. If the dress were even an inch tighter, it would look obscene, yet it doesn't. She looks classy and elegant, but most of all hot.

I'm glad for the impromptu shopping trip I took in the afternoon, spending way too much money on my own red wrap dress made of a fitted jersey material. I got the Megan-and-Beth stamp of approval and Cole had been rendered speechless for a minute or ten, so I must look good. Appearance has always mattered a lot to my mother. In the olden days when I was heavier, she would breathe down my neck about losing weight. I'd get daily suggestions on diets, and some days she would purposely buy me clothes about four sizes smaller just so she could point out that I needed to stop shopping in the men's section for some decent jeans. It's not surprising that we didn't get along.

Now she watches me carefully, assessing every fine detail, and there's still the little girl inside of me that wants her approval. The gleam in her eyes tells me that I've finally done something right in my life. Approaching them, we exchange pleasantries, and I stiffen a little when Mom hugs me. She holds on to me for a while and I breathe in her familiar scent. "You look wonderful, honey. That color looks incredible on you."

No hey, Tessa, how've you been, no hey, congratulations for getting into college. I guess that's what was expected.

"You look great too, Mom."

She touches her hair consciously. "It's not too much?" She grasps my hands in hers as we sit down. "I just wanted a change, you know?"

"It looks good."

"It's nice to finally meet you, Tessa; your mother talks about you all the time."

My mom's date is a Wall Street heavyweight called Patrick McQueen; the man oozes wealth and charm. Now, as he sets his eyes on me, I notice that he looks nothing like my father. For someone in his late forties, he looks impossibly fit and well groomed. He peers at me and I squirm in my own seat, unconsciously smoothing the nonexistent wrinkles in my dress.

"It's nice to meet you, too, though I wish I'd heard more about you. This is kind of a surprise." I try to sound as polite as possible, but there's not really a better way to phrase that your mother ambushed you into meeting her man of the moment. But Mr. McQueen doesn't skip a beat; he laughs and turns to Cole, who has not let go of my hand till now. I think he's well aware that I might have one of my outbursts if he lets go of me. I love him even more for understanding that I have a psychotic side. He and Mr. McQueen talk about sports for a bit while my mother and I sit in strained silence after we all place our orders. That is until her date addresses the elephant in the room and all hell breaks loose.

"So, son, are you—"

"He's her friend, dear; the Stones have always been close to our family."

"Actually, I'm her boyfriend, and we've been together for around nine months now." He grins at me lovingly and I squeeze his hand. God, I'm so glad he's here.

"Really? That's impressive, being together for that amount of time when you two are so young. What about college, though? I heard you got into Brown, Tessa; that's impressive. Congratulations."

"Patrick's right, Tessa, you need to focus on college now, and a long-distance relationship takes too much effort. I'm sure Cole will agree. You don't want to take that kind of baggage with you. A fresh start is always a better idea, and I mean that for both of you."

I want to take my salad fork and stab it into someone's eyes, preferably not the woman who gave birth to me, but perhaps someone who looks like her. Given the fact that she looks like a stereotypical Upper East Side groupie, I have my pick of the lot in the restaurant. What is she doing? Why is she doing this?

"Well, then it's lucky that we won't need to have a long-distance relationship, isn't it, Tessie?"

The smile on my face feels more like a grimace as I direct it toward Mom.

"Yes, it's really lucky that Cole's going to Brown, too."

She looks dumbstruck and…disappointed. The warning bells have officially started ringing.

"Is he? Don't tell me he changed his plans just to follow you to college?" She's looking at me and directing the question to him. If she sees the angry expression on my face, she ignores it. Clenching my jaw, I pretty much dig my nails into Cole's palm, wishing he sees that he needs to not pay attention to a single word coming out of my mother's mouth.

"That does sound pretty reckless, Cole, following your high school girlfriend to college. What if it doesn't work out? Won't you regret not going to your first choice? After all, there are so many other, better choices if you want to play ball."

It's none of your damn business, I want to tell them! But it's too late; the path to destruction has already been set upon. Maybe I'm being dramatic, but if this isn't an ambush, then I don't know what is. It's like my mother and her date are setting us up, and we just walked right into their trap.

"I wasn't thinking that negatively when I made the decision, with all due respect, Mr. McQueen. Brown's a great college, and I'm lucky to be going there. But I'd still choose that school even if they didn't give me a great scholarship offer, because I have no doubts that we will work out."

Mom ruins the effect of the sweetest words ever said by clearing her throat, dismissing the idea with a wave of her hand. "You're both teenagers; there's no need to make such long-term plans. When you're my age, you'll realize the benefits of giving yourself that freedom to explore in your younger years."

"Like your failed marriage?"

Her fork clatters to the floor as she stares at me angrily with a tight mouth. "That was extremely out of line."

"Calm down, Susan; she was stating a fact. Tessa has all the right in the world to be angry with you, as children of divorced parents are prone to be."

The man has the nerve to give me a patronizing look, and then he winks at me like we're good old pals and that we both know that Mom belongs in the loony bin.

"Actually, you're wrong. I'm angry because she knows nothing about my relationship—"

"I know that he cheated on you. Is that what you want? You want to end up with a man just like your father?"

I gasp, and Cole senses that I'm about to explode. He tries holding me down, but this dinner is destined to be doomed, as it had been from the beginning. I stand up and so does Cole, but I'm the only one glowering at my mother. It's not even anger at the fact that she tricked me into coming here or that she seems to have no sense of remorse for the past couple of months. I'm angry because she hurt Cole's feelings. I saw him flinch from the corner of my eye when she brought up the cheating; I noticed the tight clenching of my hand. He's been punished enough and that, too, mostly by me. He does not deserve to be criticized by a person who has no idea what our relationship is like. She knows nothing about him, and she certainly doesn't know me anymore.

"You know what? The only reason I came here was because this guy told me that I needed to fix my relationship with you. You used him to get me here, and now you're insulting him? That's really low, Mom. You weren't there for me for so long; he was, and no matter what happened between us, you don't get to talk to him like that. When you've accepted the fact that you don't know anything about me or us anymore, maybe then we can talk."

I'm breathing hard by the end of my tirade, and my mother looks almost glacial as she shoots vicious glares in my direction. Maybe I took things too far, but she asked for it. There's a lot of pent-up hurt in me that needed to come out, and I know this isn't the time or place for it, but no one gets to hurt Cole like that.

Especially after we've been through hell and back and are just starting to recover.

I storm away and hear Cole say something behind me, but there's so much adrenaline and frustration coursing through me that I exit the restaurant and start pacing the sidewalk. I'm sure I look like a lunatic, stumbling around in heels, but I couldn't care less.

How could she?

Why would she do that?

She knows how important Cole is to me. Why on earth would she try to fill our minds with doubts when it comes to our relationship? We haven't thought that far ahead. We don't know what the future is going to mean for us, but what I do know is that we have enough answers for at least the next four years. I don't have any need for the freedom to explore, or whatever nonsense she was going on about.

But what about Cole?

Am I going to be enough once he's surrounded by all those college girls? There will be older, prettier, smarter, thinner, more experienced women all around him. What if he realizes that compared to them I'm just this ordinary, naïve blonde with enough issues to fill a world map?

Damn it.

I chew at the inside of my cheek until I taste blood. Why haven't we discussed this? When Cole told me that he was going to Brown, all I thought about was what it would mean for us. I never stopped and considered what he would be giving up. Maybe he had better offers; maybe he'd like playing for another team. How could I have been so selfish? Angry tears rush to my eyes; everything had seemed so amazing yesterday.

Now all I have are doubts and questions.

"Hey, hey, stop."

Cole grips the tops of my shoulders and looks at me intensely. His eyes are boring into mine as he wipes away my tears. We're still on a bustling street and there are people all around us, but the world seems to stop when he's with me. I can only see him, and it's already getting easier to breathe. It's scary, this connection between us.

But it's also the most beautiful thing in the world.

"That didn't go well."

I manage to laugh through the pain; yeah, that's the understatement of the century.

He smiles, too, pulling me to his chest. "It'll be okay, Tessie. She's your mom; you two will work things out in time."

I push away and stare at him in wonder. "That's not why I'm upset. She said those things about you…she shouldn't have done that."

He chuckles, but there's a certain sadness to it. It irks me because that seems like a sign that he agrees with my mother and how she belittled our relationship. Just because we're young doesn't mean that the love that we have for each other is futile or meaningless. Love shouldn't have to be dependent on age, and the two of us need to believe in that. It terrifies me that maybe he doesn't.

"Parents aren't usually big fans of me; it doesn't hurt me, I promise. She was right in a way; I did…I did hurt you, no matter what the truth is. I can't really deny that."

"No!" I say vehemently, feeling myself getting angry again. "I've forgiven you; we're past that. She shouldn't have brought it up. I don't want you to feel like you have to constantly feel guilty about that. We shouldn't have come here; it was all a setup."

He doesn't say anything but folds me into his arms. Though I wish more than anything that we could've talked about it more, somehow, silence and denial seem better right now.

***

It turns out that Mom's plans to destroy my relationship were pretty long-term. Cole and I go home to an empty apartment, as we had told everyone that we would be late. We'd made plans after dinner but the mood had been ruined, obviously. Now the silence seems suffocating as we go about getting unready for the night. I immediately get rid of the dress I'd bought especially for the dinner, nearly tearing it off my body. Changing into comfortable sweats, I scrub my face clean of any makeup and run a brush through my hair, getting rid of the already-loose curls.

I don't want any reminders, so my OCD-like behavior is completely justified.

I find that Cole has done the same. His dress shirt and slacks are gone, replaced by boxer shorts and an old T-shirt that I love. What a waste of a perfectly delectable outfit. He's lounging around on the living room sofa, his arm stretched out over the back, creating space for me. It warms me how he always does that, and I go to him, fitting perfectly in the crook of his arm.

We watch mindless television for a while, still staying perfectly silent. But the silence is ominous; we need to have an unpleasant conversation, but we're both too scared to ruin an already-fragile thing. Suddenly we get a call from the lobby, letting us know that we have a visitor. Our friends would automatically come up, and the two of us aren't expecting anyone, so I press for details. Turns out Patrick has sent his son to talk to me; always the businessman, he wants to find a way to negotiate. Apparently, my mother is an absolute wreck after our catastrophic meeting, and he wants to help.

Well, the joke's on him because I know he's lying, or my mother is a better actress than I realize. She never becomes a wreck, never loses her composure. The drugs don't let her, and, given the hazy look in her eyes today, I know she's still popping those pills like candy. Still, out of politeness I call Patrick's son up.

Then I realize what I'm wearing.

Though, quickly, I realize it doesn't matter. I dressed up once today to meet someone's expectations and it didn't work out, so not going down that road again. McQueen, Jr. can feast his eyes on the spectacle that is nighttime Tessa and be happy with it.

"Who was that?" Cole asks as I sit down beside him again.

"Patrick's son is here. His father's sent him in hopes of, and I quote, 'negotiating with my mother.' The guy's crazy."

He tenses up. "It's okay if you mend fences with your mom. She's family, and you can't just leave things the way they are."

In genuine curiosity and a bit of annoyance, I ask him, "Why is it so important to you that my mom and I get along? She basically told us to break up, and you're still on her side. Why?"

He sighs, runs a hand over his face. I realize that whatever's coming next is painful for him to talk about.

"I'm not on her side, baby. It's just that…I think you should try to get along because not everyone gets to have that. A lot of people would just kill to have a shot at knowing their mom, you know?"

Oh God. My heart breaks instantaneously. That's what this is about; that's what he's been thinking about. How could I be so blind; how could I not see where this was going? I want to shoot myself for being so callous about everything, given the fact that he lost his mother at such a young age. He never talks about her; he's never mentioned missing her. I know he loves Cassandra like a mom but…

"I'm sorry, Cole. I…I wasn't thinking." I choke on my own words, a huge knot forming in my throat.

"I don't want you to pity me. Cassandra's the best thing that happened to my family, but just…don't waste what you have with your mom."

"I—"

There are two sharp knocks at the door, and I watch as Cole quickly shuts down that part of him. I want to scream and cry at the injustice of it. He'd just started to let me in; he never talks about his family a lot, especially his mom. He always makes it about me, and I feel like the worst person on the planet for not knowing the deep pain he carries behind those mesmerizing eyes.

"That'll be the son. Want me to scare him off?" He grins but it's forced. We both know what he's doing. Now that I know more about his deepest thought, I won't let it go. He's going to have to talk about it.

"No, you're right. I should at least try, right? Who knows; maybe she's actually feeling remorseful." He kisses me quickly, letting me know that he's happy and goes back to the TV.

Drew McQueen screams preppy Upper East Sider in a single glance. As I open the door, I find the tall, good-looking guy looking politely disinterested as he waits. When he catches sight of me, he gives me a charming smile that would've worked wonders on a girl not in love with Cole Stone.

I, for one, seem to have become immune to the hot guys of the world. They don't do anything for me, and it's scary. But I can appreciate the fact that he's good-looking in a pretty, Hollywood kind of way. Tall, lean, with dark brown hair, he looks every bit as privileged as he probably is with his pale skin, showing no hint of a tan. His gray eyes light up with amusement as he takes me in, in all my sweatshirt-and-sweatpants glory. He himself is dressed stylishly, with dark-washed jeans, a plain white shirt, and a navy blazer.

"You must be Tessa."

I stare dumbly at him for a few seconds before common sense kicks in and I nod. "Hey, and you must be, umm, Patrick's son…" Do I acknowledge the fact that I asked the receptionist for his name, or do I let him make the introductions?

"I prefer to be called Drew, but that works, too." He shoots me a flirty smile, uh-oh.

I back away from the door, offering him a silent invitation to come in. Inside is safer; Cole's there.

He comes in and looks around appreciatively, until his eyes come to rest on Cole. That's when he starts to look a bit uneasy. Cole straightens up and nods in our direction. "Drew, I presume?"

"And you're the boyfriend?"

"Cole."

There's a strained silence between the two, and I don't know if it's only me or if the two are having a stare-off. There's a silent exchange going on, and I can't understand a word of it.

"I didn't realize that you two were living together. I guess my dad left that detail out."

"Does that make a difference? You want to talk to her about her mom, right? You can do it with me here."

Cole sounds polite enough, but I don't miss the note of hostility in his voice. His walls are up; I can see his jaw flex, and I realize that he feels a bit vulnerable in light of our recent conversation.

"He's right; anything you had to say to me before, you can say it in front of me."

Drew holds up his hands defensively in front of him, still smiling. "Relax; I was just surprised, that's all. Your mom talks a lot about you, but she never mentioned that you were in a serious relationship. I'm surprised; that's it."

"We're on a trip with friends; that's why we're living in the same place."

Why did I say that? That seemed a lot like a declaration about how we weren't in a serious relationship. I'm on a roll today, screwing up everything that comes my way.

"Okay," he says simply and gestures toward the couch. "Should we sit?"

I nod dumbly and sit closer to Cole than necessary, but he doesn't wrap his arm around me like he usually does. He just sits there looking pensive as Drew sits on an armchair near us. I turn the TV off and hope that I do no further damage.

"My dad's really serious about Susan," Drew tells me as he watches me carefully. "I know that our parents are recently divorced, and it must be hard to see her with someone else…"

I snort, "You're way off, buddy. I've been watching my parents cheat on each other for a long time. That's what I've grown up with, so it's not some kind of traumatizing issue for me to see her with your dad."

He looks taken aback, like he's been put off track and doesn't know what to do next. My guess is that he had this whole speech planned, probably even wrote down the points. Now he's lost.

"You can tell Patrick that I'm willing to work on my relationship with my mother, but only if she's ready to respect my choices."

He looks immediately at Cole, whose entire body is tense, his muscles straining against his T-shirt.

"I'll pass along your message, but in the meantime, how about we get to know each other? Stay in the city for a few weeks; I'm here on break, too. Our parents are obviously close for now; why not become friends?"

"She told you she's on a road trip; that usually entails going to more than one place. We have to leave in a couple of days." Cole looks at him pointedly.

"That's not nearly enough time for her and Susan to get talking. It'll take time; she should stay for at least a couple of weeks. Isn't that so, Tessa?"

I can't look at Cole, and I don't want to look at Drew. There's no way I'm hurting Cole anymore, and the way Drew is staring at my profile doesn't sit well. He seems like an okay enough guy, but it's pretty clear that my boyfriend has problems with him. Plus, I didn't miss how he said that his father and my mother are close "for now." He doesn't expect them to last long; maybe that explains his looks.

"I need some time. My friends and I already have plans…I can't just change them."

Cole exhales, but I don't know if I've said the right thing.

"Well, think about it. We'll do lunch the day after tomorrow, and you can tell me your decision. But, if you ask me, you should stay. I'll make it worth your while." He winks at me and leaves before I can get over the shock of his parting words.

"Fucker," Cole mutters under his breath.

"He's crazy," I say out loud, and Cole pounces off the sofa, heading right for the fridge and grabbing a beer. He downs it quickly, slamming the bottle on the counter.

"Do you think that lunch is a good idea?"

I'm not asking his permission; that's not what this is about. I want his input; I want to include him in my decisions. This is as much about him as it is about me.

"Of course," Cole says, grinning mischievously, all the angst evaporating. "I'll be right there with you; the boy band asshat needs to know you're mine."

I laugh, feeling all the tension leave my body, and giddiness overcomes me at his words.

That's the Cole I know. However, I suddenly fear for the well-being of the McQueen family. If the older one's got to deal with my drug-addled mother, then Drew is certainly in for the fight of his life, because he just pissed off Cole Stone.

And you just don't do that.

CHAPTER NINE

What Do I Need to Know about Baby Dolls and Teddies?

My fingers flex around the doorknob, a guttural instinct telling me to just go ahead and open the door, but there's another part of me, the vindictive part that wants him to suffer just a little bit more. After all, these will be memories I'll cherish in the future and use to blackmail him into buying me all the ice cream I could ever want.

"Come on, Tessie," he whines on the other side. I can picture him, his powerful body hunched against the doorframe, his forehead leaning against it. His fists will probably be clenched, and there might be a risk of him punching a hole through the wall.

My dad can pay for that—I'll risk it.

"I didn't mean to hit him, I swear."

Snorting, I sit down, leaning against the door and pulling my knees up to my chest. Whenever I think about that moment, all I feel is horrible, terrible embarrassment. Of course, I'd known that lunch with Drew McQueen wouldn't exactly be a joyride, and adding Cole to the mix was an even worse idea.

But, stupidly, I'd believed him when he said that he'd be on his best behavior, that he'd try to keep his caveman tendencies at bay. Needless to say, things did not go according to plan.

"Were those your exact intentions when you punched him so hard, he flew over the railing?" I cringe as I say those words, the image of Drew being carried on a stretcher into the back of an ambulance making me want to crawl out of my skin. Not that the guy needed an ambulance; Cole hadn't done any real damage, just some minor external wounds, nothing life-threatening. But if there ever was a male drama queen, it would be Drew. He'd dialed 911 faster than I could talk him out of pressing charges. So, the theatrics ensured that everything got blown way out of proportion. I wouldn't be this annoyed with Cole if the aftermath of the entire thing wasn't so embarrassing.

"You know he deserved it. The guy kept talking about shit he knows nothing about." I can practically hear the fury in Cole's voice. He still hasn't managed to cool down, and I'm glad that Drew's currently in the emergency room, even if he has no reason to be there. Damn, pretty boy.

"So? There were other ways to get him to stop. We were leaving; I told you that we'd leave and to wait till I got back from the bathroom. Imagine my surprise when I got back and found Drew clutching his jaw in agony. How'd you even hit him that fast and hard?"

He laughs, that idiot! This is not funny; he could've been arrested for assault had I not groveled to Drew on the ride to the hospital. Yes,

I'd been the one holding the guy's hand as he moaned and complained about his knocked-out teeth on his way to the hospital. I definitely count it as one of the most traumatizing experiences of my life.

"He got worse after you left, Tessie; if I hadn't shut him up at the right time, you'd be coming back to a corpse," he growls.

I'm terrified to even imagine that scenario. But mostly I'm scared for Cole and hope that his parents don't find out about this. He doesn't need assault charges right now; Sheriff Stone would drag him to hell and back and then some. I shudder at the thought.

Getting up, I swipe my hands on my poor, blood-stained white dress and unlock the door. Before I even get the opportunity to open the door, Cole is barging in and hauling me to his chest. His chin rests on my head as he crushes the life out of me.

"I'm sorry, babe; I didn't want to mess up this day for you."

"Don't be cute; this is exactly what you wanted," I mumble into his chest, and I can actually feel the smug bastard smile. He wouldn't be smiling if he were in jail now, would he? Maybe I can hold that over his head for life. He'd be my slave for all eternity. The thought of Cole as any kind of slave turns my thoughts in the wrong direction, thoughts that are highly uncomfortable with him pressed against me like this.

"You're right; I couldn't wait to get my hands on Dickhead Drew."

"Well, you should've told me you wanted him for yourself. I'd let you two be happy, no need for violence, buddy."

"Does the fact that you're being sarcastic mean that we're good?" He pulls back and tips my chin up to meet his eyes. I'm very tempted by those hypnotizing devices he calls eyes, but I stand my ground. He went too far today, and it's not even Drew I care about. It's him and how prone he is to self-destructing. If he'd gotten arrested…

I pull out of his arms. "What exactly did he say to you? I mean, yeah, he was being a jerk, but what was so bad that you went all Incredible Hulk on him?"

"Please, I'd be Batman."

"Don't change the topic. What. Did. He. Say?"

His expression darkens, and that's when I know that Drew must have really crossed a line. I brace myself for the worst. I could call Mom or Patrick and tell them to relocate him to parts of the world unknown. But, just for a second, I do consider locking him up with Cole and letting my boyfriend do whatever the hell he pleases. The possessive part of me wants to hunt down and kill any person that's hurt this wonderful, amazing creature.

But this wonderful, amazing creature does have a penchant for making me a prime candidate to die young, probably due to cardiac arrest. I do have some sense of self-preservation. I can attempt to tame him, to make him see that he can't go about beating someone nearly to death. Even if the guy is a pretentious douche bag, you just don't do these things.

I grab his hand and drag him to the bed. Alex, Megan, and Beth agreed to give us space, but they have probably all been camped out outside since the moment the two of us stepped inside and saw Cole's bruised knuckles. After assuring them that nobody was dying or getting arrested, I locked myself in. It's been around three hours since the actual incident occurred, and my phone is going crazy with all the calls from my mom. If she dares say anything about Cole or something along the lines of "I told you so," I would lose my mind. Things might get said that neither of us could take back, so the better thing to do would be for me to ignore her calls. If only she'd get a clue.

"Tell me, please." We sit at the foot of the bed and I cup Cole's cheek. His knuckles have been bandaged, courtesy of Alex. The two know how to handle situations like these, letting me know that they've been in more than enough fights.

"It doesn't matter anymore, okay? I don't even want to think about it because if I do, I'll end up doing some serious damage."

"Oh no you don't. You are not going anywhere near the guy ever again, not on my watch."

He rolls his eyes. "It wasn't that bad."

"He's probably going to be spending thousands of dollars on dental work. It wasn't pretty." I shudder.

"Well, now we both know he should've just shut up when I warned him the first time."

"How nice of you to pre-warn him, is that a regular practice for you?"

He smirks. "You really want me to answer that?"

I can almost feel a panic attack coming on at the thought of all the times Cole might have done something similar. Only in my head, the endings don't go as well as planned. All I see is him lying in a ditch somewhere, a bloody, bruised mess. I'm forever the pessimist.

"How about later? Can you promise me that when you cool down, you'll tell me everything?"

He sighs, flopping back down on the bed and closing his eyes. "Yeah, I promise."

Great, that buys me enough time to get Drew out of the country.

***

"So, let me get this straight, Dickhead Drew basically attempted to get into your pants while your boyfriend was sitting at the table," Beth asks, stopping amid painting her nails.

The three of us are sitting at the kitchen table, all painting our nails and unwinding from a hectic day. It's not the norm for me to watch a fistfight take place live and then take a rather adventurous trip in the back of an ambulance.

Well, maybe it is, mostly since Cole's come back. At least I can't complain about having a boring relationship.

"And he pretended that Cole wasn't even there? Did he want to get hit?" Megan asks.

I blow on my nails, pretending to ignore the anger rising inside me as I remember the meeting. Dickhead Drew is such an appropriate name for the guy. I'd gone to meet him in the hopes that he would persuade my mom not to interfere with my relationship. Instead he had shown as much respect for it as she had, which was basically none. He'd barely acknowledged Cole and had flirted blatantly with me. I don't know what kind of Kool-Aid the people in New York drink, but, apparently, they don't know what to do with boundaries when they see them. Or maybe they just tend to want to demolish them in general.

I fume silently as I remember him kissing my cheek when Cole and I arrived. His lips had been stuck to my skin as if with semi-permanent glue, and I'd counted seconds till he'd back off. A kiss on the cheek is an acceptable form of greeting, and I'm not a complete prude, but as the afternoon progressed, he made sure to touch me in some way, making me highly uncomfortable. He'd drag his chair closer to mine, place his hand over mine when talking, and, more importantly, he ignored the fact that my boyfriend was barely restraining himself from bludgeoning him to death. We didn't even talk about my mom; kind of funny that that was the point of the dinner. Instead Dickhead talked about himself, and then some.

I'd excused myself to go to the bathroom, hoping that an escape route would magically appear as I pretended to retouch my makeup, but before I could tell Drew that my dog had diarrhea, I'd heard him yell in obvious pain. Chaos ensued, and I couldn't quite get to Cole and ask him what the hell had happened in a space of ten minutes.

"I should never have agreed to see him. My mom's vapid enough to know that the people she hangs out with would be the same. She's probably feeling really smug right now and can't wait to point out that she was right about Cole."

"But she wasn't; he didn't do anything wrong. Granted, he could have gone about it in a completely different way but he was defending your honor and he shouldn't be punished for that." Beth glowers at me. Recently, she's become a staunch supporter of my boyfriend, and it amuses me to no end. Sometimes I think she's trying to make up for how badly Travis still treats Cole. My brother hasn't completely warmed up to Cole again and there's certainly no love lost between the two. Beth tries to balance things out a little, especially when the four of us hang out. The fact that she's so in sync with my brother's life makes me feel all sorts of warm and fuzzy.

"I know that, okay? I'm not blaming Cole for anything. It's just that this tendency of his to get violent scares the shit out of me. I don't want him to get into trouble and ruin his life. He's been to prison at least once since I've known him and…"

"Oh, but I really wanted to see Jay get beaten up at some point. Isn't that the bright side in all of this?"

Megan looks at us expectantly and we burst out laughing, the tension dissolving easily. Maybe I need to stop stressing and just be grateful that I intervened before things got out of hand and that Cole isn't going to jail. My mother's opinion stopped mattering to me around the time she decided that being overweight made you the equivalent of a second-class citizen. There's no reason why what she thinks of Cole should be of any importance and that's that.

***

Alex has taken Cole out to blow off some steam, and by now, it's pretty dark outside. We haven't really gotten an opportunity to talk since our last conversation, and I don't know if he's ready to tell me what happened. A part of me is scared to think that someone Mom purposefully placed in my life could be so vile, but the other part wants to know so if I ever run into the woman again, I can tell her to keep her flings and their spawn far away from me.

We've decided to leave New York in a day or two; no one's really in the mood to do the tourist thing, and we've done the bar crawling. We haven't planned the next destination; it's all supposed to be spontaneous, but I'm majorly stressed that this isn't what Cole and I need right now. It's been a tumultuous couple of days; we've gone from not having a relationship to going full throttle. This fight today, and the meeting with my mom have put unneeded doubts into our heads and now Cole feels like he's got something to hide…

"He said I was dragging you down."

Startled at the sudden sound of his voice, I sit up. I'd been lying on my back on the bed waiting for him to come back. Cole looks deliciously rumpled, hot, even, in his tiredness. His T-shirt is creased, his hair a mess, circles under his eyes, but he's still the kind of beautiful that breaks your heart.

And now he's going to tell me what's been eating at him.

"What?"

He sighs and flops down next to me on the bed, taking my hand in his. His thumb traces circles over the back of my hand.

"Dickhead kept flirting with you, which was enough to make me want to tear his head off, but I didn't want to ruin this thing with your mom before it really got a chance, right? But he was pushing my buttons; he wanted me to fight him. Even when I punched him he had this smug look on his face, like I was doing exactly what he wanted me to do."

"That asshole," I mutter.

"He made sure to let me know that I was the scum of the earth, and that my being with you would only end up with you spiraling into this pit of doom. I tried to not let it get out of control but the guy's fucked up and the things he kept saying about you? He needed to shut up and I just happened to be there."

"You're editing and omitting a lot right now, aren't you?"

"I can basically see the steam coming out of your ears, babe; I'll spare the man whatever it is you're planning to do to him."

He's right; I'm furious. I'm sick and tired of judgement and of people interfering in my relationship. We're still being careful with each other, still figuring out how to go back to being us and the last thing that I need is for a self-righteous prick like Drew to make things more complicated.

"He's not worth it. The sooner we put this nightmare behind the better, I'm not letting my mom think she's won in some twisted way."

He chuckles. "I had no idea she disapproved of me that much. Do I need to dress up like a preppy asshole to get her to like me? Because you know I'd do that."

I hit his arm playfully. "Shut up. It doesn't matter to me. I know who you are; I know you, Cole. What my mom thinks, what anyone thinks, it doesn't matter."

He cups my cheek and leans in, his lips ghosting over mine. "I love how you're so defensive when it comes to me. It's a huge turn-on." He grins and presses his lips softly to mine. My breath hitches and I kiss him back, softly at first, almost revering, but then frantically as it progresses, until my hands are grasping fistfuls of his shirt, pulling him to me. He cups the nape of my neck with one hand, the other still at my cheek, tilting my face to give the right angle. The stress of the day fades away as we attempt to lose ourselves in each other. We kiss until my lips start to ache, until it becomes difficult to breathe, and even then, we pull away, only to find each other's lips again. It's magical; that's what it is.

"It's so good with you," he says gruffly, now kissing my jaw. "Everything feels so much…"

"More, it feels more," I say breathlessly, and as I say those words, I'm filled with a certain kind of conviction. Something seems to have clicked, like a hazy picture suddenly becoming visible in high definition. Right now, at this moment, I know that I'm ready.

I'm ready to take that next step with him, not just physically but with everything I've got. A part of me will always be scared of getting hurt like I had been before, but a bigger part knows that this is the guy. The guy who is it for me and that if ever he's not with me anymore, then every man who comes after him will need to match the standards he's set.

My heartbeat skyrockets as the epiphany settles in. I want to tell him, tell him that I trust him completely and that I can now give myself to him without any fears or insecurities. But today's been eventful enough without me dropping this bomb. Besides, it deserves a special occasion, preferably an occasion where we're alone.

"Hey," he asks, kissing my cheek. "Where'd you go?"

I smile, blushing at the directions my thoughts had taken. Hopefully, he won't be able to pick up on it. "I'm just really ridiculously happy right now; that's all."

He pulls me into his lap, cradling me in his arms. "I know the feeling."

***

"This has got to be the single most embarrassing moment of my life." I moan and squeeze my eyes shut. Maybe if I can imagine that I'm not in a lingerie store with my best friends pressing all kinds of skimpy underwear to my body, I'll be able to get out of this alive.

"Shush, this is going to be like the most important moment in your life. You need the right attire," Beth reprimands. She's got a scrap of black lace in her hand that she seems to think will cover my chest and torso.

She's mistaken.

"Oooh, this is cute!" Now Megan throws voluminous ivory satin at me, which seems like it's respectable enough, until I notice the slit in the skirt that goes up to parts unknown.

Holy Crap.

Do you really need to wear these things? I didn't realize that actual women wear these things when they're about to, you know…

What's the point of wearing them if they're just going to get taken off? Why not opt for comfort and simplicity, then? Guys aren't really adept at dealing with the knots and clasps that are on these things. Or maybe they are.

Maybe Cole is.

Oh God, I cover my face with my hands and groan into them. I did not sign up for this when I told my best friends about my plans. Whereas I thought they'd give me an emotional, meaningful speech and practical advice, they instead dragged me to Victoria's Secret, subjecting me to this mortification. I don't shop for nice lingerie; I buy the basic, white-cotton stuff. These things are on a whole other level, like the miracles of modern science.

"Can't I just…how important exactly is it to wear stuff like this?"

"Guys appreciate the effort—trust me." Beth winks and I cringe.

"Don't say things like that. You're dating my brother, remember."

"But if I'm going to be lending my expertise, then you'll need to hear them. Toughen up."

I turn to Megan with pleading eyes. "You…you lend me the expertise. I can't listen to her anymore."

A flush creeps up her neck, shockingly similar to her hair. "I'm not; she's more…it's awkward to talk about it for me. But, seriously, you don't need to worry. If you want to skip this stuff, then do it, but it actually makes you feel more confident, you know? When you're standing sans clothes in front of a guy, you'll want to have the cutest underwear on."

"See, now this I understand. You can stop traumatizing me now, please."

She shrugs, holding her hands up.

The girls help me find what they think is occasion appropriate. We then stop over by the food court to refuel, and my phone chirps with a text.

Cole: Lan and the guys are going to come into the city today. You won't mind if we do a guys' night out?

My heart sinks a little. It's not like tonight is supposed to be the one, but I did want to get a head start. Maybe practice a little, set the mood. But as soon as the thought crosses my mind, I realize that I'm being extremely selfish. He doesn't really get to see a lot of his friends, and I shouldn't have any problem with it. I don't have a problem with it, so this is a nonissue.

Me: Of course not. I'll make plans with the girls; spa and shopping sounds good.

Cole: Okay, babe, love you. Miss me.

Warmth spreads through me, as is prone to happen around him. It reassures me that I'm doing the right thing. Suddenly the bags of excessively expensive lingerie aren't weighing me down. In fact, I'm excited, nervous but thrilled at the same time.

Me: Love you. And I always do.

"So…what do I need to know about baby dolls and teddies?"

CHAPTER TEN

BAM, You're Naked and It's Go Time

In light of my latest epiphany, I begin to take precautions for the day to not be a total disaster. Not that I know when the exact day is; it's not really sexy if you've marked "the moment" in your calendar, and nor is it romantic. It'll happen when it'll happen, spontaneously, like it happens in the movies. One minute you're calmly sitting next to each other and the next, BAM, you're naked and it's go time.

Again, that doesn't sound really romantic, does it?

Maybe what's missing is the angst, the tension and anticipation. Maybe what I need for that moment to be special is for something big to lead up to it. It's not like I'll seduce him with my verbal prowess, or lack of, and it'll be on. No, from what I've been advised by my friends, there needs to be a perfect blend of spontaneity and planning. You cannot afford to be unprepared in a "My legs need to be shaved by a WeedWacker way," nor can you be overly eager and exuding the same sentiments of a stripper who gets paid a hundred dollars per hour. Apparently, there's a science to it that I'm trying to wrap my head around. I'm sure Cole notices that I'm different, more jittery and nervous when he's around. He hasn't said anything, though, so maybe he's willing to put up with my temporary neurosis. However, what he shouldn't have to put up with is the hell that is the dysfunctional O'Connell family.

***

One minute I'm in absolute heaven, eating my triple-Nutella-layered fudge brownies that I'd been so cruelly promised before, and the next minute, my phone's ringing like crazy and I'm fielding texts from not only my mother but my dad and Travis as well. My first instinct is fear, the fear that maybe something's happened to someone I care about. But when I do get the opportunity to go through the texts, I see that most of them are about the same thing.

Travis is warning me.

My dad wants to know if I'm still at the apartment.

My mom's telling me that she only has my best interest at heart.

Holy crap.

I have a few minutes to prepare myself before the buzzer goes off, letting me know there's a visitor. My dad is one of the people who can come up without the reception having to confirm his visit. Reading his texts has told me that he's here. Reading my mom's texts has told me that nothing good is going to come out of this.

Shooting out of the sofa that I'd curled myself in, I throw a panicked look toward the bedroom where Cole is showering. Megan and Alex still aren't awake, and Beth's gone out for a morning run.

I'm both scared and thankful about the lack of company, because even though the coming confrontation scares me, I'm glad other people aren't around to witness it.

I throw the door open, in my haste forgetting that I'm still in my pajamas, those pajamas consisting of an old T-shirt of Cole's and some halfway-decent sleeping shorts. Halfway, though, but not completely. My dad stands in front of me, a carry-on clutched in his hands. He becomes instantaneously stiff as he observes what I'm wearing, his reaction making me automatically blush. He clears his throat. "I called you," he says blankly, his face not giving away anything.

"Uh, I just checked; my phone was switched off," I tell him, trying to figure out if the situation is nearly as bad as I think it is.

"Can I come in?" He looks pointedly toward the path that I'm blocking by standing right in front of him.

Hesitating just for a split second, I immediately move to give him space to enter. His rigid posture thickens the tension that's already brewing in the room, a tension that has been lodged in my gut ever since I picked up my goddamn phone. Now, I wait for the bomb to drop, knowing that it's got something or other to do with my mother and what she thinks is best for me.

"Relax, Tess, it's not nearly as bad as it is in your head," my dad tells me as he sits on the couch, putting his feet up on the coffee table. I saw him a couple of days ago, but now he seems older, scarier, and maybe a bit more authoritative. I haven't done anything wrong, but still this feels like those times as a kid when you know you're going to get scolded for something.

"Why do I get the impression that it is? You wouldn't have flown over in a night if it weren't."

"I had business in the city anyway; when your mom called, I decided to come early."

Shaking my head, I begin pacing the room. "What did she say to you? Whatever it is, you have to know that she tried to manipulate me."

He huffs out a breath. "Of course I do, honey. I know all about the latest man in her life, and I know it's just a fleeting affair. But she recognizes a golden opportunity when she sees one and probably thought she could set you up with the son and keep it in the family."

"That's disgusting; she had no respect for my relationship, and Drew, oh my god, Dad, you can't even begin to imagine how big of a self-righteous, ignorant prick he was."

He laughs at me and shakes his head. "I'm pretty sure Cole put him in his place, if what I heard from your mom is correct."

That immediately makes me shut up. "He deserved it," I mumble, once again defending Cole against the world.

"I'm sure he did, and I'm not here to berate you about your personal life or your relationship. But your mother while being as misguided as she is, made one valid point."

Fear lodges itself in my throat; any valid point my mom makes can never be good news.

Feeling as though what he's going to say to me will be nothing but bad, I take a seat on the plush love seat opposite my dad so as to give my shaky legs some support. Maybe I'm overreacting, maybe what he has to say to me won't be necessarily negative, or, even if it is, then it shouldn't matter to me. But that theory goes to hell the moment Cole enters the room looking all freshly showered and outrageously sexy. There's a grim expression on his face, as though he's heard part of our conservation and knows that there's a problem.

"Mr. O'Connell." He nods his head toward my dad and sits down close to me. He grabs my hand in his and squeezes it in reassurance. "This is a surprise."

"Well, it was either I show up here or let my ex-wife sort it out with your family. I think the sheriff would prefer not going through that kind of torture. We compromised; I decided to come here and talk to you two, and she promised to stop being a giant pain in the ass."

I wince, a part of me still not used to having my parents talk so harshly about each other out in the open. But mostly I'm frustrated with the fact that my mom chose the absolutely wrong time to start giving a damn about my life. I have no idea what's going on in that head of hers or why she feels so compelled to interfere in my boyfriend's life. But if she doesn't stop soon, she'll have a very angry, Irish-blooded daughter to deal with.

"I guess I appreciate that," Cole tells him, and it's my turn to squeeze his hand.

"But you don't completely disagree with her, do you? There's something you find reasonable in all her madness?"

"Yes, there is one where I think she's coming from the right place."

"And?"

He sighs and rubs his hand across his jaw, studying the two of us carefully and then studying our joined hands. Then, as if thinking very carefully about his words, he tells me, "What I feel is that the two of you are young, and that it's not exactly healthy to have such a dependent relationship at this age."

My throat dries; I have no idea why I'm taking this as seriously as I am. There's no need to listen to him but, unlike my mom, Dad seems to be coming from a genuine place, and I can't find it in myself to ignore him.

"Before you start arguing with me, know that I'm on your side. Tessa, even though I haven't been the best father to you, you're still my little girl, and no man will ever be good enough for you. Knowing that, I still think this kid here is pretty good. Don't think I've missed how much happier you've been since he came back into your life."

My gaze, as if reflexively, lands on Cole, and he gives me a heart-stopping smile, melting some of the tension between us.

"But," my dad begins, and the tension comes back immediately. Ah, that dreadful *but*, "It's scary how serious you are about each other. I saw what the breakup did to you, even if I don't know the details. You guys are in it so deep, it's like you're an extension of each other. There's no middle ground here; it's either complete heartbreak or you go full throttle."

"So, you're saying that it's a bad thing if we're in a committed relationship?" I don't mean to sound as defensive as I do, but with the way Cole's tensing up next to me, this situation is deteriorating pretty quickly.

"There's committed and there's codependent. I'm on your side, Tess, but what I'm trying to tell you both is that it's not healthy to build your lives around one person when you should be discovering yourselves. You're starting college in a few months, Tess, and if I know you, then you wouldn't even have made the effort to find out more about the people you're going to meet. Tell me if I'm wrong, but is the fact that your boyfriend is going to the same college as you the most exciting prospect right now?"

I don't answer because that would be admitting he's right.

"No offense, Mr. O'Connell, but she didn't even know I was going until a few weeks ago. I wasn't a part of her plans then."

"And maybe that would've been better for you and for her." My dad's voice goes up a few notches, and this is the first time he looks slightly angry.

"The fact that you got back together and then a minute later were on a road trip together, living in the same room, sleeping in the same bed…"

My face turns red and I open my mouth to object, but he cuts me off. "I'm not an idiot, so don't even try to deny that. You're an adult, Tess, and as long as you're being safe, I have no problem with what you do with your boyfriend. What I do have a problem with is the fact that you depend too heavily on him. None of you know what distance can do to a relationship, whether it can survive being given space and time. You know what it says to me? That the two of you jumped at the chance to travel together? It tells me that you're insecure. It tells me, Cole, that you were scared Tessa wouldn't want you back if she had the time to think about it, and same goes for you, Tessa. You may have been scared that he'd hurt you again, or that you might not want to get back together after the hell you went through in that month and a half. Maybe if you spent the summer apart, spent a little time figuring out what you want from each other, it would help you when you start college."

Once his speech finishes, no one speaks for a couple of minutes. He's said so much that Cole and I both pretty much need time to soak it all in. I don't even know where to start analyzing his tirade. So much has been said, a lot of which is right, but there's a lot that's wrong, too. Why do we need an explanation for how in love we are? Aren't adults usually berating people my age for being involved in too many casual and meaningless flings? So, if I'm in a stable and secure relationship with a guy I'm in love with and who loves me, why is that suddenly starting to become such a big problem?

Looking at Cole to gauge his reaction, I'm shocked by the stony expression on his face. His jaw is ticking, a sure sign that he's angry. Maybe he's had one too many O'Connells breathing down his neck lately. He doesn't deserve the hell my family is putting him through, and I won't blame him if he storms out right this second.

"With all due respect, sir, I waited a long time to tell your daughter how I felt. She's wise, she didn't trust me at first, and she took her time to make sure that I was serious about her, about us. This isn't some whirlwind romance, and nor is it unhealthy in any way. She's my best friend; we know each other inside out. You think we're dependent on each other? Why? Since when does being in love mean we're addicted? We know what we want, and I'm hoping that she agrees with me on this, that distance or time wouldn't have mattered."

I nod immediately, knowing without a doubt that he's right.

"Then do it; take some time apart. If you're hell-bent on spending the rest of your lives together, and if that's something you're so sure of at eighteen, then give it a month, if not the whole summer. Tessa, this trip was supposed to be something you did with your best friends before you all went your separate ways. Do that, have fun with the girls. Your relationship will always be there, if you have so much faith in its longevity."

That's apparently the last bomb he had to drop since he gets up and kisses me on top of the head. "I love you, kiddo, and I'm only doing what's in your best interest. Get to know who you are before you become part of someone else's identity."

I may have nodded; I don't really know.

"Same goes for you, Cole. You're good for her, but give her the space to be something other than the town bad boy's girlfriend."

***

It's been a couple of days since my dad landed from Connecticut and wreaked havoc on my New York happy bubble. Though he only acted out of the goodness of his heart, the results have not been quite the success. Cole's become really distant and quiet; no matter what I do, no matter how hard I try, I can't get through to him. He lost somewhere inside his own head, and it scares me to imagine the kind of things he's thinking about.

But as I pack my bag, I breathe a sigh of relief knowing that we'll be leaving New York tomorrow. It would be the understatement of the century to say that things did not go as were planned and that I'll be glad to get out of here. The sooner we leave, the sooner we can put everything behind us.

The girls and I are out, spending some much-needed time on our mental health; okay, so we're shopping again, but retail therapy is the best kind of therapy. More often than not, though, I do find myself checking my phone to see if Cole's replied to any of the texts I've sent him since the morning. It's extremely unlike him to not do so, and the fact that I have no messages from him is what makes the gnawing fear inside of me grow worse. Whatever this is, whatever's changing between us, I need to confront him about it before it becomes destructive.

I'm done giving him space, and I'm definitely done avoiding what has obviously become a bigger issue than expected. After idling around the shops for a bit, I leave Megan and Beth, telling them that I'll see them later. They've decided to give us the apartment for a bit, and Alex is going to meet them. Sending them a thankful look, I trudge toward whatever it is that awaits me.

When I get back, it immediately hits me that something's wrong when I see all of Cole's bags gathered in the living room. Panic starts to claw at me as I walk toward the room we're sharing. He's there, sitting on the bed messing around with his phone. He looks uncharacteristically serious, his expression grim, and it only gets grimmer when he sees me standing in the doorway.

"Hey," he says, and I just look at him blankly.

"Alex told me that you were on your way back; I would've texted you earlier but..."

"Why didn't you, then? What's going on? Why are your bags out there?" I ask, sounding as confused and frustrated as I feel.

He sighs. I hate that sigh; the sigh is my enemy. "I've been thinking and Tessie, maybe, maybe your dad's right. Maybe I manipulated you into taking me back because I thought that if I gave you time, if I gave you the summer, you would change your mind. If I leave right now, you can make your decision without having me pressuring you all the time."

I gape at him for a few seconds before complete fury overtakes me. I'm sick and tired of people thinking that they know what's best for me. My parents and now him, they all feel like they're freaking mind readers and that, somehow, they have the godforsaken power to tell me how I feel or, rather, how I should feel. Well, guess what? I've had enough.

Trying to restrain myself and not throw something at him, I try to focus on getting my temper under control so things don't spiral completely out of control.

"Why are you so convinced that I'm an idiot?" He opens his mouth to object but I stop him. "No, listen to me. Do you think that it was that easy for you to 'manipulate' me, especially after the hell I went through after our breakup? I was heartbroken, completely crushed, and every instinct I had yelled at me to never let you in again. Don't you think I thought long and hard about what I wanted? Don't you know that I was terrified to let you back again in my life, and that if I did decide that I wanted to be with you, it was because I fought to overcome all those fears! So, don't tell me that you somehow made that decision for me. You didn't; no one did. My answer would have been the same if you had asked me next month or the next year, because I love you, damn it!"

His eyes are stormy as he rushes toward me and pulls me to him by the waist. "But you deserve better; you could do so much better. If I'm holding you back…"

"Who are you?" I ask him, completely astounded. "Where's that cocky, over-smart jerk who fought like hell to convince me that he was the one for me? Where is the guy that I fell for, because it sure as hell isn't you?"

He staggers away looking conflicted, and I know what I have to do. Too many people recently have filled his mind with doubts, playing on his insecurities, and it kills me to see this amazing guy being subjected to that. Being a person who for her entire life has never felt good enough for anyone, I know what it can do to you, how it takes away that part of you that wants someone to love them. He has to know that if anyone could do better, it's him. He's the better person in our relationship because he's stronger; he turned my life around when I was completely lost.

"Cole, please look at me." I move closer to him and cup his face between my palms, forcing him to look straight into my eyes.

"You have to know why I love you and why I choose to be with you. You make my days brighter just by being near me; I always have a reason to smile when you're around. Everything feels like it's easier; I laugh easier, breathe deeper, and feel so much more because of you. You came into my life like this whirlwind, tossed everything around, and when it settled back down to normal, my entire world was different, and it was amazing. So, if that kind of a relationship sounds unhealthy to people, then I don't care, because I'm really selfish when it comes to you. I need you to be in my life, Cole."

I choke on the last few words, trying my best not to cry, but Cole must have sensed the emotion anyway because he shakes his head, as if he were in a trance, and hugs me close to him, molding my body to his, and he kisses me deeply but without urgency, savoring the moment.

"Goddamn it, woman, how is it even possible for you to love me so much? I can't walk away from you, not after this."

"Then don't." I gulp and will myself to be brave enough to do what I want to do at this moment.

Pulling back, I start working on the buttons of his shirt when his hand shoots out to stop me.

"What are you doing?" His voice is hoarse, his eyes wide, mouth slightly ajar.

Swallowing, I push his hand aside and continue unbuttoning his shirt.

"I'm ready," I tell him simply, knowing that he'll understand.

He doesn't stop me again but does question, "Are you sure? I don't want you to think you have to do this to prove a point."

Never taking my eyes off his chest I tell him, "I've been thinking about it for a while, and I know that I want this with you."

He nods, and then the most wonderful thing happens. I get my arrogant, smirking, bad boy back, who's in control and who knows that the only thing I need right now is him.

We move gently, hesitantly toward each other knowing that we're about to do something that'll change us and our relationship, stopping it from existing as it does now and morphing into something so much more.

***

After, as we lay tangled in the sheets, not knowing where one begins or the other ends, I can't help but think that now I understand why everyone's so crazy about the sex thing. It's not just about the physical gratification but more so about the emotional connection, especially when you're with the person you love.

I definitely feel closer to Cole now, like our feelings have been magnified and externalized. I'm lying half on top of him, his arms wrapped tightly around me. Both of us are still breathing hard, covered in a sheen of sweat, and I snuggle deeper into him.

"I'm sorry I hurt you, Tessie."

I shrug, though it was quite painful, it wasn't his fault. "It was worth it, definitely."

He kisses the top of my head. "How do you feel? Was that as good as what you expected?" The insecurity is back in his voice, and I squash it immediately. "It was so much better. It felt…" I feel my cheeks turning red, but I continue anyway because he needs to hear it. "It felt amazing, even though the first time isn't supposed to feel so great. You made it amazing for me." I kiss his chest and he rolls me onto my back, using his arms to support himself as he rolls on top of me. I stare at him, our lower bodies covered by the sheets, but his gorgeous chest is exposed, and my eyes glaze over.

He kisses me softly, his hands all over me. Resting his forehead against mine, he rasps, "I never considered sex to be anything but a physical release, but with you, fuck, Tessie, nothing's ever felt as amazing as that."

Lovingly I run my knuckles down his cheek and he kisses every one of them.

"Don't ever doubt how I feel about you ever again, okay?"

He grins mischievously. "If the consequences are as mind-blowing as this, then I don't really have a better reason to not do it."

We both laugh but immediately stop when he begins to tug down the sheet that's covering my body.

"Again?" I gasp, knowing that I'm way too sore to try anything right now.

He shakes his head. "I just want to take care of you."

I watch him suspiciously as he rids me of the sheets, scooping me up in his arms and carrying me to the attached bathroom.

He puts me on my feet before starting the shower. In the bright light of the room, I begin to feel self-conscious about my body and consider wrapping a robe around me when Cole returns and wraps his arms around me.

"Shower?" I squeak as he runs his hands up and down my back reassuringly.

"I hope you don't mind, but the hot water will make you feel better, and I didn't…couldn't let go of you just yet."

Face blazing, I nod. I understand how he feels even though I'm too embarrassed to admit it.

When he feels that the water is warm enough, Cole leads me behind the glass doors, and I rely on him to pull me through since my own legs feel like jelly.

As I stand under the soothing spray, Cole presses his chest into my back and wraps his arms around me.

"Did you ever think when I first came back that we'd end up here?"

I smile. "Well, you did soak me with cold water the first time I saw you then, so I had my suspicions."

He tickles me and I writhe in his arms. "But this beats being attacked by a water pitcher."

I hum in my throat. "Definitely."

"That's all I ask, Shortcake, that's all I ask."

CHAPTER ELEVEN
I Didn't Cross the Line, I Usain Bolted Past It

I've never been a big believer in fate; it's always more practical to believe that you carve your own way in life than to think that some cosmic mojo is responsible for you failing that calculus test. That said, sometimes it's pretty apparent that some things are out of your control and that that do-or-die attitude fails to combat said cosmic mojo.

Take, for example, the fact that only a couple of days after my dad gave Cole and me his "distance is good for the soul" speech, we got the call. The call came while we were on the road, going to Charleston, and also at a time when I'd become more addicted to Cole than ever before. I know, right? That sounds impossible, but if you factor in the life-altering occurrence of making love to Cole Stone, you'll understand. That day changed everything about our relationship, if possible; it's definitely become more intense. All that unresolved tension that used to surround us is gone, and in its place is this spectacular pull that ensures that we can't keep our hands off each other.

On the flip side, Cole's caveman tendencies have increased, and if it were up to him, I'd dress like Maria from *The Sound of Music* before the Von Trapps. But I find the possessiveness incredibly sexy and give it back in spades. I'm definitely even more aware of all the female attention he gets, and lord save the bimbo who tries to make a move; things tend to get a little ugly.

But then there's The Call. We were just checking into the motel when Cole received it, and, given how his face drained of all color when he answered, I knew that something was very wrong. It took me some time to get it out of him as he made hasty arrangements to go back home. With a trembling voice, he told me that Nana Stone was sick and in the hospital. Sheriff Stone had called and asked Cole to come home right away. My heart sank and I had immediately offered to go with him, but he refused. Alex left with him, and Cole made me promise him that I wouldn't come back immediately and that I would enjoy the trip as planned with my girlfriends. It was a difficult decision but the look in his eyes, the blazing determination, made me agree. So, fate intervened and we went our separate ways, at least for a couple of weeks.

Which brings us back to now. Megan, Beth, and I did everything on our list and more. We drank, we danced, we shopped, but most of all, we grew closer as friends. Of course, I was constantly in touch with Cole and was immensely relieved to know that Nana Stone was doing well after a heart attack scare and recuperating. We missed each other, but my dad was on to something with the distance thing; it does make me feel like we're stronger now than ever before because we've done what my parents didn't think we could do. We stood the test of time and showed them that the connection we had wasn't purely physical. I guess that's something that's a bit difficult for them to absorb. The extent of their relationships post the divorce has been meaningless flings, especially in my mom's case. My dad, on the other hand, seems to genuinely be developing feelings for his secretary, now his girlfriend, as cliché as that is.

Speaking of my parents, ever since the events that transpired in New York, things have been a bit chilly between us. I haven't talked to my mom at all. I would have tried had her efforts to make amends not involve blaming Cole for "brainwashing me." She needs to learn to accept him before she can even think about being a part of my life again.

Harsh, I know, but she deserves it.

My dad, on the other hand, tries his best not to act smug, like it's his brilliant speech that made Cole and me take the decision to spend some time apart. The events leading to our separation were unforeseen, but he sees it as some kind of a divine intervention, fate, you sneaky bitch, as I like to refer to it. Anyway, when I would talk to him on the phone after Cole left, he'd sound ridiculously happy about it and would even offer to upgrade us to the best hotels in town. My patience has been wearing thin with him as well. I just don't know how to deal with the fact that my parents seem to question my relationship so much, a relationship that makes me happier than I've ever been.

***

Today the girls and I arrive back home, and even though we're dead tired from all the driving and the late nights just staying up and talking, there's a thrill in the atmosphere. It's the end of a fantastic trip, and our friendship is stronger than ever. I know we'll miss each other when we head off our separate ways, but we'll always be best friends; now I know that.

With a hug, I drop off Megan at her house, and I swear I can see her parents watching through the windows. It'll be extremely creepy if they know she's coming because it's supposed to be a surprise for our families and boyfriends. Next, Beth and I head to my house because, even though the knowledge of it makes me gag, she wants to, and I quote "pounce on Travis" the moment she can. I try to remove the visual from my head, very unsuccessfully, if I do say so myself.

The house is quiet, as expected, and, to both our disappointments, Travis's car isn't in the driveway, and neither is my dad's, for that matter. Apparently, we suck at surprises, and now it does not seem like the best idea.

But there's still one person I can get to. My stomach is filled with butterflies at the thought of seeing him, of watching the expression on his face when he sees me. A giddy smile automatically makes its way onto my face when I think of him and of finally being together. The anticipation is killing me, and I don't even bother getting out of the car.

"I know it's time to leave when you get that 'oh Cole, do me, do me!' expression." Beth wrinkles her nose and I smack her shoulder.

"I was not thinking about him doing me!" I say indignantly. She's wrong, definitely wrong. Okay maybe partly wrong.

But, seriously, it's more than the do-me part with us.

"Yeah, right," she chortles, "Who knew you'd go right from a blushing virgin to a hussy? Honestly, I'm impressed; Cole must be skilled." She winks and, ironically enough, I blush profusely.

"Don't you have a boyfriend to wait for? I thought you had a whole dramatic scenario planned," I huff out and wish for my cheeks to cool down. Beth having mentioned Cole's bedroom skills makes that rather difficult.

"Oh crap!" Beth suddenly exclaims, smacking her forehead. "I need to get started. Getting into that corset is at least going to take half an hour."

Again, a mental image I did not need but that doesn't seem to faze her, and she goes on…

"…but what's the point? He's just going to rip it off in like five seconds."

"Okay, okay, stop! You need to set up your twisted dominatrix role play or whatever it is, and I need to see my boyfriend."

She grins and hauls herself out of the car, finally, and blows me a kiss before skipping all the way to the house, her carry-ons and the unmissable Victoria's Secret bag bouncing right after her.

Ah, the things love does to us.

***

Grinning to myself, I park the car and decide to get my bags later; I cannot wait to see Cole. It's crazy how much I've missed him; it has hurt physically, and I thank my lucky stars that we'll be at the very least spending the next four years together.

The five-minute walk to his house feels like it takes forever. My pulse is racing, the fluttering back in my stomach with vengeance, and there's a rush of adrenaline coursing through me. It's crazy to miss and love someone this much; it must be. All I can hope is that he feels the same way.

I practically run the entire way, only to come to a halting stop when I reach his front porch. For a second I have that feeling, the one where you can't register the fact that you're actually seeing what's right in front of your eyes. It takes a while for your brain to catch up, and the dazed and confused feeling eventually leaves you.

But you're no less stunned, and your vision is still a little hazy.

I do see Cole hunched over the front steps of his house, and the sight of him does make my heart pound, my palms sweat, and my body thrum with desire due to his proximity, but there's something very wrong with this picture.

I'm not jumping to any conclusions, at least not yet. We've come leaps and bounds in our relationship, and the fact that he loves me is deeply ingrained in me, but this…this does not make sense.

Because sitting—thank god—a few feet away from him is Nicole, yes, the Nicole, and right now she's stroking his bicep like she's comforting him, and he's not stopping her. She's got his hands on him, this girl, my former nemesis who has openly admitted to being in love with my boyfriend, is touching him, and he's not stopping her. Nicole and I may have made peace, but that doesn't mean I have to be okay with this.

There's nothing wrong with what they're doing. They're sitting at a respectable distance and everything looks platonic, so I don't let my inner insanely jealous and irrational girlfriend out for some hair-pulling and earring-holding action. I allow myself to be the calm and collected, mature adult that I in no way am and step forward a couple of feet, enough so that when I clear my throat, they can both see me.

They don't jump apart, guilty, but Nicole immediately drops her hand and Cole jumps up. His expression, that look on his face, is everything I'd hoped for and more. He looks absolutely stunned and gloriously happy as he takes me from top to toe, with an intense heated gaze that makes my insides do somersaults.

For a moment, Nicole and her grabby hands are forgotten as Cole rushes toward me and, just a millisecond before he wraps me up in his arms, he whispers my name in his husky voice like it's a prayer, and I melt into him.

"Cole," I breathe as he pulls me into his firm chest and cups my face in his hands.

"I can't believe you're here," he says before he crushes his mouth against mine and kisses me like his life depends on it.

Like our life depends on it, and I kiss him back, wrapping my arms around his neck and standing on my tiptoes. Our kiss turns deep and longing; his hands dig into my waist as he tries to pull me impossibly close. I want more, and the sexual awareness that exists unquestionably between us now makes me want to drag him to his room.

But then another throat clears and we pull apart, panting heavily and still holding on to each other. Nicole's standing looking rather awkward at the stairs, and that's when I remember my manners. Having Cole near me wrecks my strict upbringing at times.

"Hey," I say breathlessly while trying to untangle myself from Cole, but he doesn't allow it. Instead he settles for wrapping his arm around my shoulder and pressing me to his side. He plants a sweet kiss at the top of my head before letting me turn back to Nicole. There's no tension in his body, so I take it as a good sign; I trust him.

"Hi, glad to see you're back." She gives me small smile that's so unlike her that I almost laugh and tell her to drop the act. We're amicable at best, so this politeness feels weird.

"I wanted to surprise him."

I shrug in Cole's direction, and in return he nuzzles his face against my neck while he murmurs in my ear, "Best surprise ever."

He's making Nicole uncomfortable, I can tell.

"So, what're you doing here?" I ask her as nicely as I can. In my defense, she moved to New York and vowed never to return to this town. It's a pretty big deal if she's here and feels the need to caress Cole lovingly.

Her eyes dart between Cole and me and she finally says to me, "Do you mind if I speak to you alone?"

That takes me by surprise, and Cole starts to protest, but I turn toward him and tell him that it's okay. He doesn't look nervous, not like he doesn't want me to know something. He's more annoyed, seemingly at the thought of leaving me.

"I'll be inside, like literally glued to the door," he tells me before pulling me in for another long kiss. He nods toward Nicole and heads inside, his hand lingering in mine as he leaves. We're nothing if not lovesick.

"So…" I turn to Nicole, who has sat back down on the steps. She pats the space next to her, and nervously I walk up and sit down next to her. She's quiet for a while before she addresses my first question to her.

"I know I told you that if it was up to me, I'd drive out of this town and never look back. So, it makes sense that you're surprised to see me back. But you didn't look jealous; I was expecting more of a reaction." She seems genuinely curious.

"I trust him. It's as simple as that," I tell her.

She seems surprised by my answer, and I know it's because she's well aware of my tendency to overreact. "You've grown up," she observes, and I shrug.

"Well, anyway, the reason I tortured myself into coming back into this soul-sucking vortex and why I was with your boyfriend in your absence is because I found out some information in New York. It's information that I know you could do a lot with."

"I don't understand," I tell her; this seems like the beginning of a bad episode of *Days of Our Lives*.

"Look, I won't beat around the bush here. I know why you and Cole broke up all those months ago. Your friend Lan filled me in because he apparently found out how much I hate the psycho bitch Erica."

I stare at her with a gaping mouth. "Wait, you know Erica?"

I haven't said the psycho bitch's name in a long time, and it feels as unpleasant as ever on my tongue.

She rolls her eyes. "Of course I do. I've spent summers with the Stones. I've seen that redheaded leech paw away at Cole, and I've always suspected that there's something seriously messed up about her."

I snort. "Well, you were right about the last part."

She continues, "When I found out what had happened between you guys, I knew that what Lan suspected could seriously be true. I mean she's more than capable of drugging a guy and playing her twisted mind games with him. If I could just find her, get her to talk, I knew I'd find out what really happened."

"Why do you seem so sure? I've heard she's some sort of compulsive liar."

"Oh, that she is, but she thinks that she and I have something in common; well, we used to, in any case. The thing is, she knew I had feelings for Cole, and she felt like we were some sort of kindred spirits because both of us resented the fact that you existed."

"Ouch?"

Nicole waves her hand dismissively. "Well, I don't hate you anymore, so get over it. It must have killed her, though, to obsess over Cole for so long, only to have him so completely in love with you. When she found out that you guys were finally together, there was bound to be a reaction."

"So, you believe, based on your mutual hatred of me, that Erica drugged Cole and lied to him?" I feel my breath hitch.

"Oh, I don't just believe; I know," she says confidently, and I feel a heavy weight settle in the pit of my stomach. The same adrenaline that got me to Cole's house now starts rushing back. Could I finally be finding out the truth?

"W-what do you mean?"

"Did you know that Erica's planning on going to NYU?" she asks with a smirk playing on her face.

"No, I…I didn't."

She shakes her head. "She's going to the same school as me. I found out through the class Facebook group the other day and you can imagine my surprise when I discovered her smug face staring down at me from her profile picture."

"No way!"

"Yeah, and not only that, the bitch thought we were fast friends. She messaged me and said she'd love to meet up when we both move to the city. I texted Lan and told him, and he's the one who gave me the idea."

"What idea?" My patience is wearing thin and I need to know; I need to know everything right now.

"To get close to her, to let her think we're friends, and persuade her to tell me all her dirty secrets. So, I did that. Erica's visited me a couple of times while I was in the city and I've spent the last month making her think that I hate your guts, no offense, but it worked. One night after too many beers, she told me everything."

Oh God.

"And?"

"And your boy's good. He didn't even touch her, not even when he was wasted. That's the part that pissed her off the most, that even a smashed Cole Stone wouldn't cheat on you. So, she did the second-best thing and made him think that he had. Between his issues and hers, she managed to convince him, but you need to know that he didn't do anything.

In the grand scheme of things, maybe I would have been okay even if I never knew the truth. I'd already forgiven Cole and we had moved on, but does it make me a bad person if a part of me needed desperately to know the truth about that night? I know he's sorry; I know he's done more than enough to deserve my forgiveness, but I would always have wondered, and maybe it'd always be something that could possibly come between Cole and me.

Relief like I've never felt before rushes through me, and a gigantic weight feels like it's been lifted. It's unexplainable, and the urge to get up and laugh and scream like a lunatic does get squashed. But instead, I settle for doing something equally bizarre; I hug a very shell-shocked Nicole. Standing up, ready to sprint toward Cole, I tell her, "Thank you!"

She still looks a bit dazed. "Wait, you believe me?"

"Why wouldn't I? You just gave me the best news since Beth's decision not to read *Fifty Shades of Grey* out loud to me."

Her brows scrunch up in confusion. "I appreciate that, I guess?"

"Besides, what good would it do you to lie to me? Especially when it comes to Cole."

She nods, standing up. "You're right. If anything, it'd be more believable if I told you that Cole had actually done what Erica made him think he did. But I like to think that I did this for you to make up for all those years of being a bitch to you. Take it as my biggest apology."

"Duly noted."

"And," she adds, "If it helps, I intend to make Erica my next victim. Old habits die hard and all that." She grins and I laugh.

"That's something I look forward to hearing more about."

"Oh, don't worry, you'll hear her cries of pain all the way to Providence."

"I wouldn't expect anything less."

Nicole turns to leave and I watch her retreating back. She turns back for the last time. "You were always a good friend to me, Tessa, even when I didn't deserve it, but I hope that…maybe in the future we could try again."

I smile at her. "Maybe."

She nods and heads off.

The moment I'm inside his house, Cole hauls me up in his arms so that my feet leave the ground, and I'm forced to wrap my legs around his waist. Not that it's a hardship of any kind. Laughing, I wrap my arms around his neck as he carries us to the living room and sits on the leather couch with me straddling his lap.

"Did she tell you?" he asks and then kisses me.

I nod, feeling slightly breathless.

"Do you believe her?" He looks incredibly vulnerable, and it breaks my heart to think of all our suffering, especially his. I thought I had all the facts, enough to leave him, but he lived in confusion. It must have been so hard for him to not know, to be so out of control.

"Of course," I tell him, running my hands through his hair.

I feel the tension release from his body as we once again start making out like the teenagers we are. I can't get enough of him, and I'm pretty sure he feels the same way about me. I lose track of how long we stay on the couch, content in kissing and reveling in the fact that we're both with each other again.

"Guess what?" he asks as we finally come up for air.

"What?" I pant as he slips his hand beneath my shirt, his fingers skimming the skin right over the waistband of my jeans.

"Dad and Cassandra are staying at a hotel near Nana's retirement home for the week."

My pulse starts to quicken. "Jay?"

"He's started college early, baseball camp," Cole says throatily as his hands travel up my back.

"We're alone?" I hum in pleasure as he caresses the small of my back.

"Completely."

Here's the thing about Cole Stone making love to you—nothing else quite compares. It's addictive, maddening, and so passionate that you could cry. After the first time we did it, we made love about three more times, but it still doesn't seem enough. Then to be away from him for so long, it's no wonder my body feels like a live wire.

I let him carry me upstairs to his room, where we rediscover each other all over again and, might I say, Beth was utterly correct about his bedroom skills.

***

Over the next couple of days, I find myself developing a routine. The mornings I spend with my brother and at times my dad as we discuss college and Dad's upcoming election. He's running unopposed, so things look good on that front. Travis is still catching up on his courses, and it'll take at least four to five months before he can start looking at colleges. A heavy donation from my grandfather from my mom's side to Travis's old college, the one that expelled him for plagiarism, means that he'll have that off his permanent record.

Beth is working odd jobs, but she's been quiet and contemplative recently, and I know that Travis knows what's up with her but I don't push it. She'll tell me when she wants to. She's staying with us, which means at night I force myself to sleep with music blasting into my ears as I don't want to stumble upon any…noises.

I still hang out with her and Megan, the latter being thrilled that Alex is following her to New Jersey for college as she starts at Princeton. They're also going to only be three hours away from home and four hours away from Brown, so visiting won't be an issue. At this point, I'm not panicked that the girls and I will lose touch. But I do intentionally try to spend more time with them and not with Cole because I know we'll be together in college. However, we still do spend a lot of time together, hanging out and taking advantage of his empty house. At night, we switch over between spending the night at his place and my house, never being apart. We took a trip to visit Nana Stone once, and she made me laugh until my sides ached like all hell. A near-death experience or not, the woman is definitely where Cole gets his easy charm from.

As the days to leave for college approach, I don't feel a sense of panic or fear. Largely, it's because I know Cole will be there, but also because it's time I get out of this town. No, unlike Nicole, I don't hate it anymore. A lot of things changed for me this year, and one of those changes is that instead of just representing my misery, this town has become home to all those moments that have led me to this point. I fell in love and I became brave; my family, though still far from perfect, is slowly but surely heading in the right direction, with the exception of my mother. I'm a different person, and this place is now witness to most of the greatest moments of my life so far.

I'll visit a lot; I know that since college is just two hours away. My past isn't some tragedy that I'll run away from. As I sit in my childhood bedroom amid dozens of moving boxes, I know that this place will always be home.

Downstairs, the music is loud enough to reverberate through the floor. I'd just escaped for a second to take a breather but found myself getting lost in thoughts. I'm sure Cole's going to be up any second to see if the ground hasn't swallowed me whole. Right on cue, there's just one knock on my door before he barges in looking sexy as hell in his black V-neck sweater and black slacks. He appraises me as I sit knee-deep in a sea of boxes and cocks his head to the side.

"The party got too much?" He looks at me knowingly.

My dad, in one of his brilliant ideas, decided to throw a going-away party for me and my friends and insisted on inviting the entire graduating class. Unluckily for me, most of them are still in town and are attending the party downstairs. It's not that I have anything against people in general but crowds, confined spaces, and Solo Cups heighten my anxiety levels.

I drop my head in shame. Cole's the life of the party, and then there's me. "It just got difficult to breathe, you know?"

His intense eyes soften as he kicks some boxes to the side and sits down next to me, picking me up with ease and placing me on his lap.

"Why didn't you come to me?"

I rest my head on his chest and let out a breath. "You were surrounded by your people. I didn't want to drag you away from them," I mumble.

"You're my people, Shortcake. You feel upset, anxious, nervous, happy, you come to me."

"I will," I tell him, flattening my palms against his chest.

"What's going on in your head, babe, tell me."

"I'm just thinking about how much I love you. Sometimes it scares me."

He laughs, but he's not laughing at me; it's more like he can relate to how I'm feeling. I continue, "I can't imagine how you lived with that feeling for so long. You loved me and I…I hated you. That makes me feel like such an idiot," I groan.

He chuckles and kisses my forehead. "Trust me, I don't hold it against you. I gave you plenty of reasons to hate me. It'll always be a fucking miracle that you somehow ended up loving me."

"You made it easy." I kiss his chest.

"But getting here was tough, wasn't it? I made mistakes and crossed so many line. Hell, I didn't cross the line, I Usain Bolted past it."

That makes me laugh, a lot.

We sit there silently for a while, and I'm content with forgoing my peers to listen to his heartbeat. It's tranquility at its best.

"Mind if we interrupt?"

Cole curses under his breath as the door opens and in come Lan, Seth, Jameson, Beth, Megan, Alex, and, surprisingly, Jay. I met him when he came to the party and we exchanged pleasantries, but things tend to get pretty awkward with us. Now he stands there with a faint, amused smile on his face. He does look a bit out of place, but I give him points for making the effort. He's going to Duke in the fall, and that's far enough by road to not let our paths cross too much. It's a bittersweet moment. I did genuinely believe that I loved him at one point, and knowing that there's nothing between us now does feel strange.

I laugh as I try to get off Cole's lap, but he holds me there.

"Ever heard of knocking?" he growls at our friends, and it's Seth who's brave enough to answer. I'm so glad that these guys are here; I've missed them, and I know that once college starts, we're going to get pretty close because they're going to the University of Rhode Island.

Yes, all of them.

"Well, we knew you're quite the exhibitionist, but you wouldn't let Tessa get caught in a compromising situation, so we took our chances."

He scowls at Seth. "Are you picturing my girl naked?"

Seth shakes his head and holds his hands up in surrender. "I like belonging to the living and breathing variety."

One by one, everyone makes a space to sit down and forgets about the party going on downstairs. I'm sure they won't do a lot of damage.

Maybe, I think.

But if they do break something, let it be one of my mom's vases.

We lose ourselves as the conversation flows freely. Namely, Beth drops the bomb that she's deferring going to college for the year. She'll stay here as she and Travis look for a place of their own. I'm stunned but realize quickly that this is exactly what the two need. This way I won't be constantly worrying about Travis being alone, and Beth will have more time to get her life back together.

We talk until the last of the partygoers leave. Our friends are all staying the night, and it's nearly dawn when everyone starts to get up. Cole drags me to bed once I've closed and locked the door.

"Tired?" he asks as he walks backward toward the bed.

“Not at all,” I tell him.

“What about Travis?”

“He’s going to surprise Beth with a weekend getaway in just about two hours. We should be good.” I grin at him.

“Two hours? Two whole agonizing hours!” He groans and falls onto the bed with a thump.

“Stop being a baby; if you’re not ready to sleep, I know something we can do to pass the time.”

"But I’m your baby and I love you," He says adorably.

I smack a kiss on his lips and grin. "I love you, too. But what were you planning to do?"

“You can’t be quiet enough for what I have in mind,” he retorts, and I roll my eyes. Guys and their one-track minds. He still lifts himself on his elbows and gives me his whole attention.

I bite my lip seductively and he perks up, immediately looking intrigued.

“How adept are you at Facebook stalking?”

PART 2

CHAPTER TWELVE
That's My Motto—Make Love, Not War

My Converse-clad feet skid to a stop as I try to catch my breath. Resting my hands on my knees, I manage to get my panting under control and then straighten up. Peering around the quad, I'm relieved to see that no one's seen my mad dash to get here. Running a hand through my windswept hair, my eyes dart around and try to find him. As always, I know he's here, but given the fact that class has just let out for a lot of people, Cole won't be the easiest to find.

Then I hear it.

A high-pitched giggling sound that's usually associated with someone pawing at my boyfriend. Squaring my shoulders, I head toward the direction of the squealing chipmunk and, sure enough, there's an exotic-looking girl trying to climb all over Cole like she's a next-generation spider monkey. But then again, there are always exotic-looking college girls trying to worm their way into his pants, and, two months into my freshman year here at Brown, it's something that I've had to bitterly accept. The fact that Cole constantly plays dodgeball with their grabby hands puts me at peace. I genuinely feel sorry for him, the way he has to force these girls not to come on to him too strongly. What some men might consider nirvana, is hell.

Deciding to put him out of his misery, I push past the throngs of students and get to him just as his latest fangirl reaches up and caresses his arm. She definitely looks like the stereotypical man-stealer that I've had the misfortune of running into these past couple of months. She's tall, Amazonian, even, and has tanned skin. Her mane of dark hair is pulled into that stylish-but-cute side braid that I can never master without looking like I should be in kindergarten, and to top it all off, she is impeccably dressed, even in the cold weather, with skin-tight jeans, a figure-hugging white sweater, and a belt wrapped around her waist, emphasizing just how tiny it is.

I take a moment to study my own outfit that I'd hurriedly thrown on this morning before I left home. Comfy fuzzy sweater, jeans with a pesky coffee stain, black worn boots, and a scarf that nearly swallowed me whole—I'm surely not in the same league as Miss Glamazon over there, but that's not the point. A huge smile makes its way onto my face as I happily cross over to Cole and loop my arms around his back. He doesn't jump, nor is he startled, in fact, I can feel his body relax under my touch, and it's all kinds of wonderful.

I poke my head around his side to smile at his latest admirer, whose perfectly shaped eyebrows are nearly retreating into her hairline.

"Hi, I'm Tessa, Cole's girlfriend, and I haven't seen him in nearly three days. Do you mind if I borrow him?"

Cole's body shakes with silent laughter as the girl simply stares at me. My cheeks are starting to hurt from smiling so much, but it's part of the game. You simply cannot let them intimidate you. Once that happens, they think it's okay if they casually slip their bra into your boyfriend's car.

It happened.

It's never happening again; those double Ds were traumatizing.

It takes her some time to come to terms with the fact that her newest prey is taken. But she doesn't let it show for long; shaking her head, she offers me a fake smile of her own.

"Of course. I'm Allison, Cole's partner in his psychology class. We were just discussing a time to meet up later for our project."

The way she says "meet up later" makes my skin crawl. She's added some sort of a sexual connotation to the words, and I know that she's done it on purpose because that's what they do.

"Great—so are you guys about done?"

She laughs, and it's the hollow, superior-sounding laugh that sounds pretty, yikes.

"Oh no, we were just getting started. But we can hook up, oops, I mean meet up, another time. It was nice meeting you, Teresa." Her lips attempt to pull into another condescending smile, but it's like she doesn't even want to make the effort. She gives me a once-over and then touches Cole's arm again.

"Catch you later, handsome."

She walks away then, sashaying those hips like God commanded her to do so.

Naturally, I'm fuming by the time Cole turns around and holds up his hands defensively.

"You have to know that I can't stand her, and I feel highly violated whenever she's around."

Narrowing my eyes at him, I try to find a lie in his hypnotizing blue eyes but come up empty. There's not even a hint of a doubt in my mind that he's being honest and that that's all he's ever been.

Besides, I can't really be angry at him when I've missed him so much these last few days. I left to go back home on Friday and couldn't see him because he had practice. Of course, he offered to drive down to me to our hometown of Farrow Hills since it's only two hours away, but I knew that he had a big test today and needed to study. That doesn't mean that I haven't wished all weekend that he'd show up out of the blue. Now, as I take in his chiseled face, perfectly messed-up hair, pouty lips, and those damn eyes that get me every time, I can't find it in me to be angry for always having a succubus around.

It's not his fault, really; he's just that amazing.

I break into a grin and launch myself at him, wrapping my arms around his neck as he hauls me to his chest. Cole buries his face in my neck and inhales; he tells me that he loves my smell, so I never find it weird that he casually sniffs me whenever he wants—I tend to do the same with him. His arms tighten around my waist and I lay my head on his chest, against his heart, listening to it beat furiously. Neither of us cares that we're surrounded by people because when we're together like this, the world seems to disappear.

Pulling back, he kisses me nice and slow, as he does when he's trying to savor the moment. I rise on my toes and press my lips to his harder, telling him that I missed him. We only stop once the whistles and the catcalls begin. Embarrassed as usual, I hide my face in Cole's chest, which rumbles in laughter beneath my cheek.

"I'm assuming you're going to switch partners soon?" I ask, toying with the hem of his cardigan.

"Already asked the TA. That girl's a sexual harassment case waiting to happen."

"Aw, poor boy, does it get hard to have all these gorgeous college girls falling all over you?"

I know my words make him mad because his entire body stiffens. Holding me at arm's length, he tips my chin up to meet his eyes.

"You know I only have eyes for one girl, right? None of them matter, not one."

I sigh contently, feeling stupid for projecting my own feelings on him. He's never done anything that contradicts his words, and one of these days, he's going to get tired of my insecurities.

At least it's not today.

"I do know, and I'm sorry. Can we have a do-over?"

He hugs me to his side and begins walking. Cole's done with his classes for the day, and I don't have any till later in the day, so we head over to his apartment because, seriously, we have a lot of catching up to do.

No, not that kind of catching up!

***

When Cole told me all those months ago that he'd be coming to Brown with me, I felt a lot of things. Mostly I felt terrified because at the time, our relationship wasn't in a good place, and I didn't know what it would mean if he were to be around me all the time. Later, when we got back together I was still scared, but for a different reason. I didn't want us to be one of those high school couples who drifted apart in college, became different people and wanted different things from life. But with that worry came a sense of peace from knowing that distance wouldn't be yet another thing standing in our way. We could be together, learn to grow up and find ourselves without growing apart. That sense of peace prevailed and took down the fear a couple of notches.

Now, I take one day at a time, and it's going great. He lives in an apartment and I live in the dorms; both of us have roommates, so we know that it's not the best idea to spend all of our time together. The fact that my parents were worried about us being too "attached" makes me laugh now. Clearly, they overestimated how much college dorm room or apartment space one could get out of an eighteen-year-old's savings. We have to be creative about where to spend time and when, given our busy schedules.

It's nice to have time apart, meet new people, but at the same time, it's horrible.

Something I've realized about myself is that I suck at being around new people, but that's always been the case. In college, everything's so unfamiliar and new that my social awkwardness has risen to an entirely new level. With the exception of my roommate, Sarah, it's been hard to make friends or meet people in general. That means that Cole's my only tether to the world and to myself. I always find myself needing him, wanting to be around him, and it's not good; I know that.

But it truly feels like when I have him, I don't need anyone else.

***

"So, how did the moving go?" Cole opens the door to his two-bedroom apartment, one which he shares with a nice guy named Eric who's a junior at Brown. He mostly spends his time at his girlfriend's place on weekdays, and then she comes over on the weekends. After the initial awkwardness of running into him during our first few weeks here, he's started to grow on me, and I'm no longer embarrassed to death when Cole and I emerge from his room after our make-out sessions.

"There really wasn't a lot of stuff to move; their new place is the size of a shoe box." I toss my purse on the couch and settle into it, pulling my knees up to my chest. Cole sneaks up behind me and pulls my back to his chest.

He laughs. "But Beth's still going to sell the house?"

"Yup, and Travis is going to support her no matter what she decides to do. He could've found a better place for them, but she wanted to split the rent fifty-fifty, so they settled for something small." I tell him all about my brother and best friend's new place and how the bathroom, dining room, and bedroom are all one big open space simply separated by curtains. They'd decided to move in together shortly after we left for college and finally found a place that both agreed to. Yes, it's a lot smaller than what either is used to, but seeing them together this past weekend nearly made me cry with happiness. Travis has struggled with his addiction to alcohol in the past, and it nearly stripped him of the great person that he is; it took some effort from his family and a girl knocking him off his butt to make him see that he could be so much more than his weakness. Beth, too, had suffered an unimaginable tragedy by losing her mother, a mother with whom she already had a strained relationship. Travis and Beth were two broken people who'd somehow found themselves in each other.

Much like the two of us.

And we're making it work, too, despite every curveball thrown our way. Yes, our schedules don't quite match, yes, he's already got a whole new group of friends, and yes, I still prefer solitude to frat parties but hey, we're hanging in there.

We relax on the couch for a bit and I update him on my Skype call with Megan. We're all planning something big for winter break, a ski trip of some sort, and I'm struggling to work around everyone's schedules. He listens to me vent and be frustrated, then offers to drive me to work because, apparently, it's getting dark outside.

I work at the local children's bookstore, mostly on weekends and twice on the weekdays before class. It's because of this job that Cole and I veer toward a familiar argument. He's walking down the street, with my hand in his as he casually asks the question I know he already knows the answer to.

"So, some guys from the team are throwing a party this weekend."

"Cole…"

"I know, you don't want to go, but I hate going to these things without you."

A part of me wants to ask why, if he hates these parties so much, does he need to attend each one. But then the rational part reminds me that he's part of a team, a close-knit football team where you need to show up at your teammate's party; there's no questioning it. I went to the first few at the beginning of the semester and quickly realized that I could never fit in with these people. For the most part, I tended to fade into the background, away from judgmental stares and the incredulous expressions on people's faces when they find out that I'm dating Cole Stone. So, by the fifth party, I put my foot down and haven't been to one since. I like to think that he understands, but then times like this make me feel like he wishes I could be someone different.

"I work on the weekends and then I need to study; you know that, Cole." My voice is laced with frustration.

He sighs. "Yeah I do. I know that."

He kisses me on the forehead, his lips pressing hard before he cups my face in his hands and just stares at me intensely for a while. I'm clueless as to what he's thinking, and before I can ask him, he's already halfway to his car and then driving away.

For some reason, I want to cry real bad right now.

***

When I get back to the dorm, thankfully my roommate, Sarah, isn't there. I love her and her quirky personality, but right now I just need to be miserable alone.

Or I could use some company.

My fingers dial Beth's number before I can back out, and she answers the phone on the second ring.

"Remind me why I didn't take up your brother on his offer of a palatial, three-bedroom apartment in the good part of the city?"

I laugh despite my mood. "Because you wanted to prove to yourself that you're a big, strong independent woman."

She sighs. "Why can't I be a big, strong, independent woman with a bigger apartment? This place is giving me claustrophobia."

I laugh again because I know she's not even remotely being serious; Beth loves her new place, loves that she's paying for it on her own, and loves that she's sharing it with Travis.

"Anyway, what's up? Trouble in paradise again?"

"Something like that."

I then proceed to tell her about feeling like I'm constantly letting Cole down. I tell her about our conversation today and how things got a little weird afterward. She listens to me patiently, even when I talk about Allison the Exotic; at the end of my tirade, she just snorts and plummets through my doubts.

"Remember how yesterday I was making fun of your brother's polo shirts?"

I scrunch my eyebrows in confusion. "I do, but what does that have to do with anything?"

"Well, you're talking about being too different for Cole and not being enough for him, and it's the same as me hating Travis's polo shirts with a passion. I never thought I'd be with a guy who wore them to the country club, but I am. But that doesn't mean that I'll put on a freaking yellow sundress and pretend to sip martinis at happy hour with the zombie suburban wives, you know?"

"I think I understand."

"It doesn't matter if you don't have the same interests or social circle, as long as that feeling's still there, that feeling that tells you that when you're together, it's the most perfect thing ever."

I hum in satisfaction; that feeling's there in dozens.

"So, if I can't be the partying, bar-hopping kind of girlfriend, then that's okay?"

"Of course it is; he won't expect that from you, just as you don't expect him to spend all his time listening to Adele and stuffing his face with Nutella."

"Hey! That's not all I do."

"My point is that you guys are different, and those differences will become more apparent in college. Don't let it get to you; he fell in love with who you are and not who you think he wants you to be."

Her words are oddly profound and have a calming effect on me. She's right, of course she is, and I need to stop freaking out because Cole has always, always understood me better than anyone else.

"What would I do without you, Bethany Audrey Romano?"

"Die, probably, it's like I single-handedly provide you O'Connell siblings the will to live."

I think she's probably right.

***

When I sneak into Cole's bed later that night, I'm glad that he's deep asleep. He would spit fire if he saw that I'd walked to his apartment building alone at nearly one in the morning. Oh well, he can do it tomorrow. Lying in bed, I knew that trying to do homework would be pointless when all I wanted was to take away that hurt on Cole's face when he left me earlier that day.

He's lying on his back, the blanket barely covering his hips and revealing all of his delicious chest. I take off my sweatshirt, one which I'd thrown over my pajamas, and climb onto the bed, draping myself all over Cole and snuggling deep into him.

Even in his sleep, he so completely adorably pulls me closer, and I kiss him softly on the lips. It's moments like these that reassure me that we'll be fine, absolutely, completely fine.

"You know you're in trouble for not calling me to walk you over."

Because really, how could you not want to spend every moment with this guy?

Huddling closer to seek his warmth, I kiss his cheek and murmur sleepily into his ear, "How about we snuggle now and argue later."

He hoists me higher onto his chest and tangles his leg with mine. "Good idea, Shortcake; that's my motto, make love, not war."

To emphasize his point, he rolls me onto my back and rises above me on his elbows, waggling his eyebrows at me.

I burst out laughing. "I'm sure that's not how it was meant to be used."

"I like to think it's open to interpretation."

"Well, I like to get sleep before my eight a.m. class, so I'll pass tonight."

He fakes being devastated but immediately falls back onto the bed and pulls me close, repositioning me on his chest and pulling the blankets around us.

Ah, heaven.

CHAPTER THIRTEEN
The Man Can Get Dirtier Than the Inside of an Erotica

Friday night, I stand in the middle of my dorm room busy contemplating my two wild, wild options for the night.

I could a) do my laundry or b) do some assigned reading; exciting times are bound to be in my future, regardless.

Trying not to let my snark overrule what could be a productive evening, I groan and decide to tackle the mountain of dirty clothes in my closet. The thing about having a lot of clothes is that you don't feel the need to wash them regularly because hey, you could always pull something clean off the shelves. The end result, though, is as scary as probably the inside of Nicki Minaj's closet.

But I digress; there's no way I can prolong this painful experience any longer. I grab my basket, dwarfed by the stack of clothes, and waddle my way to the laundry room.

In a not-so-surprising turn of events, the dorm is more or less empty as the occupants have abandoned it for a night out. But once the initial mixers and frat parties had worn off, so had my curiosity for them. Parties were parties, even in college, and I don't have any plans of using the fake ID Beth sneaked into my bag. She'd be so disappointed in me; oh well, at least I'll have clean clothes.

As the first load of clothes goes in the washer, I dig my phone out of my back pocket and check for any messages. There's none, and I sigh, leaning against the machine. Nights like these are becoming a norm for me, and a part of me is seriously starting to resent myself. This is college; I'm supposed to be out having new experiences and meeting new people, making new friends, but instead I'm doing laundry, laundry!

Not to mention that I'm constantly disappointing my boyfriend, Cole doesn't say a lot on the topic. When he told me today that he and the rest of the guys on the football team were having some sort of a team bonding session at a bar, he never asked if I wanted to come along. Yes, I'd been hurt, but I'd also accepted that it was my own fault, for always saying no when he'd invite me to some party, especially after the first few weeks of college.

I think about texting him, about asking him how the team building is going and if I could stop by for some time, but the thought of putting myself in that situation, with a bunch of jocks who can be really, really crude, terrifies me and, quicker than is possible, I slip the phone back into my pocket.

It's official; I'm a coward, and in the very near future, some outgoing, cheery, spontaneous girl is going to steal my boyfriend because I'm lame.

"Oh My God! I can't believe you're here!"

The sound of a squeal in my immediate vicinity nearly gives me a stroke, and I realize that I'd zoned out so much that I'd missed the girl clad in pink pajamas standing at the machine next to me looking slightly starstruck.

Startled, I jump back and place a hand over my heart, trying to calm myself down, because, for a moment there, I thought I'd definitely end up like those blondes in the college slasher movies.

Yes, that's why I didn't join a sorority, the stereotype would just be too close to coming true.

"I'm so sorry! Shit, I didn't mean to scare you."

The girl's blond, around my height and build with big doe eyes that are staring at me apologetically and waiting for me to respond. Suddenly I realize that aside from my roommate, people in class wanting help, and some of Cole's friends, this is the first time that someone's interacted with me, and I'm coming across as a complete nut, so talk, Tessa, talk!

I plaster a smile on my face and try to get my panic under wraps. "No, it's totally my fault. My head was someplace else, and I didn't see you."

Her face breaks into a huge, beaming smile. "Still, that was such a dumb move on my part. Creeping up on you in the basement at night? Yeah, you probably thought I was Freddy Krueger or something."

I laugh at how close she is to what'd been going through my

mind, then she stretches her hand toward me. "I'm Cami, by the way. It's fair enough that you know my name since I know yours."

I shake her hand and let go, feeling slightly confused. "You do?"

She rolls her eyes and leans against one of the machines. "Yeah, I do; everyone in the hall does. You're only dating one of the hottest guys on campus."

That stings a little to find out that people are only interested in me because of who I'm dating, but given the fact that I'm a bit desperate to make friends and show Cole that I'm not completely miserable, I morph my face into what I assume is a neutral expression and feign genuine curiosity. "Wow, really? I didn't know our relationship was that high profile."

She smacks the top of the washing machine. "Are you kidding me? There's a line by the elevator whenever he comes to see you or drop you off because everyone on this floor and, well, all the ones above and below, wants to catch a glimpse of him." She sighs dreamily.

"That's…good to know?"

Immediately, she looks a bit guilty and sorry. "Not that any of us are trying to steal your boyfriend. Oh no, I personally think you guys look so adorable together. How'd you meet?"

Thus begins the thirty-minute conversation with this quirky, enthusiastic, and rather endearing stranger who wants to know every single thing about my relationship with Cole. I like her, I really do because for the first time it seems like she's not using me to get to Cole and is just genuinely curious, interested in my life and actually cares about our story.

It helps that talking to her makes it feel like the laundry got done quicker; I think she's my new best friend already.

We're both folding our clothes to take back to our rooms and she invites me back to hers once I'm finally rid of the dastardly basket. In her room, she disappears into her closet, only to reappear seconds later sans basket. I love how she's wearing Hello Kitty pajamas and not caring at all about it. I'd been careful to pack sensible nightwear for college, not childlike, not slutty, but sensible—as in the kind that would not get me noticed. My entire wardrobe has a signature theme, which is basically to make me wallpaper. Cute yet easily dismissible wallpaper, which isn't entirely unpleasant to the eye but doesn't catch attention. It's sad, I know it is, and seeing Cami rock her fluorescent pink choice makes me wish I wasn't so afraid all the time.

"Sit anywhere you want, my roommate isn't around much, she probably won't even come home tonight."

She bites her lip as she says this and sits down on her bed, legs crossed and hands clasped. I sense her unease around the topic of her roommate and purposefully avoid sitting on her bed. Instead I sit at Cami's desk, my eyes taking in the colorful items strewn all over it. She seems like a very vibrant, buzzing ball of energy of a person, and I feel good about this, about being here.

Maybe I could make a friend; who knows?

"So," I whirl around in the chair and point to her wall, which is the first thing anyone might notice when they walk into the box-sized room, "You like quotes?"

Her side of the room is completely covered with them, paper clippings, banners, posters, printouts, it's all there, and I get dizzy trying to read them all.

She nods enthusiastically. "I love quotes! Don't you think it's important to always have a reminder to be the most positive you can be in life? All these people who've seen so much of the world share their wisdom, and it's good to know that no matter how bad life seems right now, it's never as bad as you think it is."

I'm taken aback by her sudden seriousness, not expecting these deep words to come from someone who seems so exuberant.

"Which one's your favorite?"

She plops down on her bed and stares at her wall, squinting her eyes and thinking hard. "I don't know; it's really hard. All these quotes mean something to me, have meant something at some point in my life, and there's a reason why they're on the wall. You have to be really special to be on the wall. I just put this one up yesterday, so I guess this one's my favorite right now."

She points to a printout stuck right in the center, big, bold, black letters saying:

"Aut inveniam viam aut faciam."

"Hey, I know that. It means I'll either find a way or make one, doesn't it?"

"Yup, I'm kind of struggling with the whole college thing right now, but going back isn't an option, so I look at the quote for inspiration."

When our eyes meet, a silent understanding passes between us.

She knows I'm struggling with the college thing, too, struggling with being so out of my depth in a place so different from what I've always known.

"Do you mind if I ask why you're in the dorms on Friday night when you're dating Cole Stone? I bet you guys get invited to tons of parties."

I sigh and spin in her chair a couple of times, blowing out a breath. This is the point where I tell her about my antisocial tendencies, about how I may be screwing up a perfectly good relationship. Maybe she'll run screaming for the hills, traumatized by how I'm butchering my role as the quarterback's girlfriend.

"We do; well, Cole does. I went to a bunch of them in the beginning but realized pretty quickly that I didn't fit in with them. Everyone looked at me like there was something wrong with my being there, like I wasn't the kind of girl someone like Cole should be dating."

It feels strange to share my life story and deepest, darkest emotions with someone I just met, but sometimes you just meet people who you feel like you've known your entire life. So, I can either use this opportunity to get rid of the pent-up frustration inside, talk to the first person in months that's not giving me social anxiety, or I could make up an excuse about flossing and make a run for it.

She studies me quietly for a few seconds before she jumps from the bed and starts pacing her room like a maniac. All I can do is stare as she huffs and begins her rant.

"Why would you do that? Why would you distance yourself

from someone who's pretty much looking like the boyfriend god because of some dumb potheads who get hives from just thinking about commitment? Cole doesn't feel the way they do, so why does it seem like you're punishing him for being popular? Of course he's going to be popular, he's the fucking QB."

Theatrically, she falls back onto the bed, and all I can do is stare at her, mouth hanging open and jaw unhinged.

"Sorry if that got too real. I'm taking all these psych courses, and I'm pretty much addicted to the idea of being a relationship therapist, save the world one marriage at a time. Sometimes I forget I can't do that yet."

"No, no, you'll be a great therapist; that was some good advice. I just…"

She gets up and faces me chewing her fingernails. "I've freaked you out, haven't I? Perfect, just perfect. I mean, I've been only working up the nerve to talk to you for like the past month, and the moment we might potentially start becoming friends, I have to word vomit all over you! My friends were right; I don't deserve to interact with normal people until I get my head screwed on straight."

"Wait, they actually said that to you?"

And I suddenly feel terrible for this strange, yet oddly appealing, person who seems to feel like as much of an outcast as I do.

She bites her bottom lips and wraps her arms around herself. "I came her with two of my best friends; we were so happy to have gotten into our dream school together, you know? It was our little miracle, but then they rushed sororities and I didn't. They moved into the house together, and I had to leave my luck to the lottery system. But yeah, I mean they stopped inviting me to their parties and nights out a while ago; we barely hang out, so I'm pretty sure they're embarrassed to be seen with me."

There's our connection; see, there was something there.

"You know, you're not the only one who's had a friend bail on them because they're embarrassed to be seen with you."

***

It's been nearly two hours since Cami and I started talking, and it feels like no time's passed at all. She's so much like me, well, a version of me on serious steroids, but there are a lot of similarities, and I'm so glad I decided to put myself out there or, well, let her drag me out there.

When my phone buzzes, I realize how I've lost track of time, and when I see the text I've received, my chest warms.

Cole: Wish you were here to take me out of my misery.

Talking with Cami has helped so much, especially with the absurd resentment I'd started building toward Cole in my head. The girl in question scoots forward in her bed and eyes my phone like it's more precious than a Nutella-filled donut.

We love Nutella; she loves donuts—it's a match made in heaven.

"Is that him?" she asks in a hushed whisper, like Cole could actually hear her, and I grin, another day, another fangirl.

"Yep, would you like me to pass along a message?"

"No! I mean, I would love to meet him, so you know, if you ever want to introduce your new best friend to your boyfriend, I'd be so up for that, but not now. Do your adorable couple thing now, please, and let me watch."

I laugh out loud and proceed to do my adorable couple thing.

Me: Wish I was there and scaring away your groupies.

Cole: You do genuinely terrify them; they've started scanning the perimeter before trying to come near me.

Me: ARE they near you?

Cole: Put your claws back in, Shortcake, I'm not great company tonight. They've moved on to someone who isn't checking their phone every two seconds for their girlfriend's text."

"Aw, he's so adorable!"

Of course Cami's standing over my shoulder and reading my texts; of course she is.

"You know what you should do? Surprise him, get dressed up and go to wherever he is and stake your claim." She's shaking with exciting and it's infectious. Suddenly I don't want to be trapped in my room on Friday night and let other girls eye up my boyfriend. I'm going out, I'm having fun, and I'm staking my claim!

Going to my room, I leave behind a beaming Cami, who calls out outfit ideas over my shoulder, and get rid of my ratty clothes. In my closet, I reach for the first time for the dressier, tighter clothes. I choose a pair of skinny jeans that fit really well and pull a black cropped sweater over my head; it's a sweater that hugs my curves nicely and has Cole's hands all over me when I wear it. I finish them with my favorite black suede boots with a chunky heel. My hair's manageable as I'd straightened it earlier in the day, and I spray in some texturing spray and fluff it up, adding on some light makeup.

I grab my bag and knock on Cami's door; she's still in her Hello Kitty gear.

"Wow, you look great! He's never going to know what hit him." She sounds wistful and dreamy, which only reinforces my decision.

"Well, why don't you get dressed and see the expression on his face yourself?"

Her face lights up with excitement immediately but then falls; she's making my head spin with all these mood swings.

"I…I shouldn't, I'll just be in the way, and, well, I'm a social disaster."

"So am I; get ready and we can be social disasters together. I promise Cole won't mind; in fact, he'll love to meet you."

"Well," she grins, "In that case…"

***

Twenty minutes later I've driven Cami and myself to Ralph's, a popular sports bar downtown. It's nearing midnight and the place is jam-packed with patrons. Luckily finding space to park, I give myself a mental pep talk and head for the bar. Next to me, Cami is a ball of nervous energy, a really hot-looking ball of nervous energy. When she emerged from her room wearing a tight knitted dress and leggings and some kickass boots, all I could do was stare. The girl has some serious curves that'd been drowning in her baggy clothes, but now? Well, she's a total knockout, like apparently every girl on this campus. But she's nice and the only thing close to a friend I have, so shove it, insecurities, shove it.

The inside of the bar is as busy as the outside, and the two of us push through the incredibly overstuffed room. Fortunately, they didn't card us at the entrance, and since I'm not looking to get particularly buzzed, I won't be needing my pathetic-looking fake ID.

I look over the entire space, trying to find Cole, but it's so crowded that you can hardly tell one person from the other, though I recognize some of Cole's teammates. The replay of a game's on the big flat-screen television, and it's got everyone sucked in, which is why we get glares when we move past them.

"Wait, isn't that him?" Cami grabs my arm and spins me in the direction of the bar, which is rather deserted because it's positioned at an angle that makes it impossible to see the screen. Sure enough, when I look, Cole's there sitting at the bar, shoulders slumped and busy on his phone. Instinctively, I take out my own phone because I'd put it on silent on the way here, and I immediately see texts from Cole, texts he's still sending.

My heart can't help but sink. I know he feels guilty for having to choose between his obligations toward the team and me. He shouldn't have to do that, shouldn't feel bad for leaving his loner girlfriend behind because really, I do this to myself. Now he's sitting here instead of doing what he's supposed to do, getting along with the guys on his team.

Well, shit.

"I'll be right back," I tell Cami, already making my way to my boyfriend.

"Take your time; I'll go get some popcorn!" she half yells over my shoulder and I laugh; she's a total character.

Being as stealthy as possible, I sit one seat over from Cole and lean across the bar. He hasn't even glanced up from his phone yet, brows furrowed adorably as he literally smashes his fingers over his phone.

"Is this seat taken?"

I desperately hope I sound like one of those super-sexy older women who hit on lonely men in bars and not like the annoying preteen we all were, the ones that dressed up in slutty clothes and looked like, well…preteen hookers.

"Yes," he bites, not even bothering to glance in my direction, and I love it!

"Why? Are you waiting for someone?"

"Yes."

"Well, what if she doesn't show up? I can sit here while you wait for her."

"You know, that sounds like a great idea. How about we sneak in a quick trip to the men's room while I'm waiting for my girlfriend?"

I gasp and punch his shoulder. "You butt licker! Would it kill you to go along with me for once in your life?"

He finally, finally graces me with his gorgeous face and grins. "Don't tell me you don't like it when I get dirty."

I blush; the man can get dirtier than the inside of an erotica when he wants to, but now is not the time to remind me!

"Ugh, stop, we're in public."

He groans, "Don't remind me." But then instantly he's on his feet and hauling me to his chest. He buries his face in my head and inhales. "You smell too good to just be a dream."

"Surprise?"

He wraps his arms around me and whispers in my ear, "The best one ever."

And that makes my mini panic attack worth it.

The sound of someone's throat clearing makes us break apart. I see Cami standing near us, clearly not uncomfortable with our PDA, but feeling out of place in such a rowdy crowd.

"Oh, Cami, sorry, I just…"

"It's okay, I was having fun, it's just that some guy tried to lick my elbow, and if that's not a cause for concern, I don't know what is."

My face scrunches up in disgust while Cole just takes a second to allow all that is Cami to sink in.

"You guys know each other?"

"Right," I smack my forehead, "Cole, this is Cami, my neighbor and new friend. Cami, this is Cole, my boyfriend, as you already know."

She immediately extends her hand toward him. "Cole Grayson Stone, it is such an honor to finally meet you in person and not spy on you from my barely cracked bedroom door." She says this without missing a beat, and Cole's starting to get increasingly confused, perhaps a little alarmed.

"Uh, that's good to know. Nice meeting you, too, Cami; that's an interesting name."

“Isn’t it? My parents desperately wanted to name their firstborn Cameron. But when they got me, they didn’t think I’d appreciate having a guy’s name, so I got Camryn; isn’t that clever? But I go by Cami because they ended up naming my brother Cameron, and I should probably shut up now because I’m freaking you out.”

Her cheeks turn red as she watches us nervously, but when Cole laughs, she literally starts to gleam. The Cole Stone effect is unstoppable, and she’s certainly having the pants charmed off of her right now.

“I’m so glad Tessa found you; you guys are going to get along great.”

I grin at him. “I know, right? It’s like the heavens took pity on my loner self and custom made her.”

“Right down to the neurotic rambling, it’s like you guys could be twins.”

“HEY!” We both yell at him at the same time, and he actually clasps his hands together and looks toward the ceiling. “Thank God I don’t have to talk about cramps anymore.”

***

Cami’s sitting with one of the guys on Cole’s team, and he looks absolutely dazzled by her. I know the guy, he's Parker, and probably the only decent person besides Cole on that team, so she's in good hands.

Speaking of hands, I swat Cole's off of my backside. "Need I remind you we're inside a very crowded bar?"

"Need I remind you that I don't give a shit?" We're standing chest to chest, Cole's back pressed against a wall, the screen over my shoulder, and he's pretending to watch the game while he's groping me quite publicly.

"Well, I do." I relocate his roaming hands to a safer location. "So, you want to tell me why you weren't bonding with those meatheads when I showed up?"

He sighs, leaning back slightly. "I was wondering when you'd bring that up."

I wait for his answer, dreading it just a little.

"These guys are…well, they're not the best, but most of them are good guys, but they've come to college with different goals in mind."

I pause, and it seems like it's taking a lot for Cole to tell me this. It makes me wonder if I make him feel like he can't talk to me about these things, and suddenly I feel as good about myself as Miley Cyrus probably does when she looks at those Hannah Montana albums.

"They don't understand commitment, don't understand why I choose a single girl for probably the rest of my life over a different girl every night. When they talk about stuff like that, try to bring me to their side or whatever, it pisses me off."

I go through a myriad of reactions while he's telling me all this. Elation when he mentions a forever, fear when he talks about other guys not wanting the same, and anger when he says that they're trying to change his mind, too.

Change his mind how, exactly?

"What do you mean? What do they do?"

“I don’t want you to get mad, okay? It’s nothing, and if I see the situation getting bad, I get the hell out of there.”

“Cole, tell me, please. I know you wouldn't do anything, but I just…I need to know.”

“Fuck. Look, the team has this bunch of girls that hangs around when they’re needed. Some of them go to our school; most don’t. And whenever they come around, you know they’re going to try to flirt, try to hook up with the guys.”

I feel bile rise up my throat; he notices the look of utter horror on my face and cups my face in his hands so that our foreheads touch.

“I would never put myself in a position like that, Tessie. That’s why I was sitting alone, because they called the girls when this was strictly supposed to be a team-only thing. I’m pissed off and they know it. It’s hard for me to get along with them because they keep pulling shit like this, but that doesn’t mean I’ll ever compromise what we have for them. I’d rather die than do that.”

A moment of utter silence passes between us before I mash my lips to his and kiss the hell out of him, slipping my hands into his hair and smiling against his lips when he groans against mine. This time I don’t stop his hands from reaching down toward my butt, because why the hell should I?

When we come up for air, Cole looks slightly dazed. “Whoa, what was that for, Shortcake?”

“Did your groupies get a good look?” It takes him a few minutes to process what I’m saying but then grins a massive, stupid, goofy grin and kisses me again.

"It's so hot when you get possessive."

"Well, you better get used to being constantly turned on, because from this moment onward, I'm not letting you get molested by a bunch of pot-smoking coeds, the highlight of whose life will be being named employee of the month at Hooter's."

"Can we seriously get out of here? Everything coming out of your mouth right now is just killing me."

Smirking, I grab his hand and take him to where Cami's sitting with Parker, coincidentally right next to a bunch of the other guys and their fan club.

"Oh no, we're staying, and we're socializing, and you better be all over me, mister."

He clutches his chest theatrically. "Damn, this is definitely what heaven's going to look like."

CHAPTER FOURTEEN
Do You Really Need the Extra-Large Can of Whipped Cream?

"What do you think? Sexy nurse or French maid?"

"Neither."

"But you have to pick one; you can't be without a costume on Halloween."

"I'm not opposed to costumes, just ones with the word *slutty* in them."

Cami sighs and plops down on my desk chair. "You make my job so difficult."

I finish typing up an e-mail to my professor and face her. "I never gave you the job description of 'help Tessa get rid of the crazy hoes who are superglued to her boyfriend.' Besides, I don't think I could pull off those looks, right, Sarah?"

My roommate, Sarah, is the total opposite of Cami in the way that she's really shy around new people. It was a really awkward experience for the both of us to be sharing the same small space the first couple of weeks after moving into the dorm. But one night I heard her fighting with her boyfriend on the phone and tried to console her; we had a heart-to-heart abusing all men on the planet, and soon got along great. She's a Texan, absolutely gorgeous with her big brown eyes and curly dark hair, but looking at her it's easy to tell that she's not aware of that. With me, she's started coming out of her shell and opening up, but I'm starting to think Cami terrifies her.

She pokes her head up from the textbook in her lap and glances toward Cami, who's watching her intently, and that can be pretty intimidating, but Sarah squares her shoulders and declares, "I think you should wear the costume Cole got you; it'll definitely keep the hoes away."

I nearly double over when I hear the word *hoe* coming from her prim-and-proper mouth; the girl wears a pearl necklace to class, for god's sake! But I definitely appreciate the support and grin at her.

"I know, right? Why be a slutty anything when I have the greatest costume ever in my possession already?"

"Wait, what costume? Why have I not heard of this?"

In the three weeks that I've come to know her, it's become apparent that Cami's the kind of person who fits into your life so seamlessly that it feels like they've always been there. I have no objections to her suddenly being a big part of my life because it doesn't seem like she's imposing.

"Because I really like it, and I didn't want you to take your scissors to it."

"But…but can't I at least see?"

"You will in a couple of minutes," I tell her as my phone blinks with a text, and a huge smile comes across my face. "Just a slightly different version of it."

She's confused, and Sarah blushes because she actually knows what's going on, and the presence of a certain male always makes her flustered.

Right on cue, someone knocks on the door and I rush to open it, flinging my textbooks aside. Outside I see Cole in all his sweaty glory and kiss him quickly on the lips before dragging him inside.

"Hello ladies."

Both of them, no matter how different, turn into giggling preteens as my boyfriend directs his blinding smile toward them.

Cami sits up straighter, and Sarah tries to cover up the fact that there's a huge Tweety bird on her bed, sent to her by her boyfriend a couple of days ago. I almost laugh at how nervous they are, given the fact that they see Cole all the time.

When all he gets is star-struck smiles and a partly manic wave, Cole turns to me and gathers me in his arms. "You all set?"

We're going home this weekend because it's been a couple of weeks since we've seen our families. It's also the only week Megan and Alex can come down and visit, so it seems as good a time as any. Cole and I have also been struggling to find some time to spend together, and this feels like the perfect time. Even though being on campus has started growing on me and I've met people I get along with, there's an excitement coursing through me at the prospect of being home and with my friends.

Yes, the same town that I couldn't wait to run from is now home, strange times indeed.

Telling the girls goodbye, Cole and I walk to his car that's parked outside my dorm. Now that Cami's made me aware of it, I do see how much people stare at us when we're together. Half of the time I'm trying to figure out whether they're looking at Cole and having the obvious reaction to his enormous presence, or whether they're looking at me and wondering why he's with me. But I need to constantly remind myself to not think about other people and not allow them to affect my relationship; I'd made that mistake before, and it wasn't happening again.

Cole is oblivious to my mental tug-of-war and is unaware of the number of eyes following us. I only breathe easier once we're in the car, having loaded our things. When we finally pull away from campus, I relax and let Travis know we're on our way.

***

"So, my parents were wondering if you'd have dinner with us tomorrow. Do you have any plans with your dad?"

Cole's hand rests on my knees as he drives, and it's exhilarating to know that he finds ways to touch me whenever he's near. I lean back in my seat, put my book aside, and hum contently.

"No, well, not anything formal. I'll have dinner with him tonight, but I'm pretty sure he'll be with his girlfriend tomorrow."

I don't even cringe at the word *girlfriend* anymore. My father is honest-to-god trying to be a better man, and it's good for him to be with someone other than the vicious person my mother has become. This someone may be over ten years younger than him and possibly be after his money, but hey, at least he's back in the game.

"Great, I'll tell them to keep their hands to themselves and not embarrass me."

I smack his arm. "Your parents are cute and crazy in love! It gives me hope for the future, so don't you dare say anything."

He grins at me. "You're hoping I'll be like my dad, a romantic sap, in about twenty years' time?"

I don't let on how much happiness I get from the fact that he always talks about our future so assuredly. "You're a romantic sap now; I doubt that'll ever change."

"What can I say? You bring out the best in me."

"And you say your dad is mushy, jeez."

But he's so perfect, and I doubt he can't see the big fat smile on my face. As always, my eyes go to the charm bracelet on my wrist, a birthday present from Cole. Among other things on there that symbolize our relationship, there's also a ring charm, subtle enough not to make me freak out but still a constant reminder of where he sees us going, and I'm so on board.

"So, Jay's going to be there as well," Cole tells me quickly, and I smile thinking about his stepbrother, my friend and former crush. Jay and I don't have the best history, and our friendship is tentative at best, but he was around during a tough time in my life, when I thought Cole had cheated on me. He was there as a constant support, and I do feel like I owe him for that, regardless of our past.

"That's nice; I haven't seen him for months."

Cole grunts; things are still a bit tense between him and Jay. Not as bad as they were before, back when Cole thought I would forever be in love with his brother and that he would come second. It took a lot of time and persuading to show him that what I felt for Jay was never love and that what I feel for him is infinitely stronger. Of course, he doesn't doubt my feelings now, at least I hope so, but he still thinks Jay wants me, which of course leads to things being really awkward in the Stone household.

"He texts you enough to not let that be a problem."

Once, just once Cole caught a text from Jay, and he's taken it to mean that we're the best of buds. Yes, Jay does send the occasional text asking me how I'm doing, and I give the acceptable reply and that's the end of it. But trying to convince Cole is about as useful as playing tennis with a brick wall.

"Do you really want to go there? Need I remind you of the number of girls that text you because they need your help with their 'homework'?"

"Come on, they have my number on the class roster, how am I supposed to stop them?"

"Exactly! How can I just ask Jay to stop texting me? We're…friends."

"But he wants more."

"He's a baseball player in college, for Christ's sake, it's not like he's going to be lacking female attention and pining for me."

"You seriously underestimate yourself, don't you? If I were in his place, and I thank my lucky stars that I'm not, I'd do everything in my power to make you mine."

I blush; even after all this time, I blush. Placing my palms against my cheeks, I feel how heated they are and look over to Cole, who's looking at me with an intensity in his eyes that makes my skin feel like it's on fire.

"What?" I ask, feeling a little breathless.

"I just really love you, you know that, right?"

I place my hand over his on my knee and squeeze it.

"Yeah, I do, and I love you, too."

***

When we get home, it's around six in the evening, and Cole drops me off at my house, telling me he'll be back in around fifteen minutes. I let myself into my empty home, but with a stocked fridge courtesy of the housekeeper. Now in my room, I'm sifting through my clothes and trying to find something good to change into when I'm attacked from both sides by what feels like twin poster children for a Chanel perfume, and the next thing I know, I'm lying on the floor, the air being squeezed out my lungs by two very overenthusiastic huggers.

"Guys! Can't breathe here." I choke as my best friends continue to shriek and laugh. The lack of oxygen stops mattering, and soon I crack up, too, as Megan and Beth roll onto either side of me.

"What was that?" I ask between laughs.

"An ambush."

"Our strategy was to barge in with our eyes closed so that we wouldn't catch you and your man with his hands all over you."

"Hey! We do have some restraint, you know." We are all laughing breathlessly at this point for no reason, and it's the best feeling ever. I stretch my arms on either side so that I'm giving them both a one-armed hug, "God, I've missed you guys."

Because Cole doesn't show up immediately, I know he's giving me space with my friends, which I appreciate a lot. Skyping is never the same as being in the presence of these two, and now that we're back to those days when we'd just sit on my bed and talk for hours, it feels like we were never that far away from one another.

"I didn't think it was possible to laugh that much." Megan clutches her stomach as she falls onto her back on the bed. "Did that really happen?"

Beth snorts. "Yes, I almost beat the shit out of my boyfriend because he tried to spoon me. In my defense, I'd worked a twelve-hour shift and was completely knocked out when Mr. I-like-cuddling-unsuspecting-people tried to make a move on me."

My eyes start to water at the image; of course, Travis hadn't mentioned that Beth had given him a black eye.

"Well, at least you get to spend the night with your boyfriend. Alex and I hardly ever get to do that with our roommates around."

I hadn't quite realized how lucky I am that Cole found an apartment and didn't live in the dorms because, given the struggle we have now to spend time together, it'd be a nightmare if that were the case.

"But you guys still find time to hang out, right?"

Alex plays for the state university's football team, and if anyone knows and understands the pressures of dating a jock, it's Megan. I've confided in her a lot because Beth tends to dismiss my insecurities as being stupid. I like to think that if she'd been with Travis in high school, she'd understand my situation much better.

"It's really hard to find time between studying and work, but we make it work. Alex is…" she sighs dreamily, "he's perfect for me. I never thought a guy would put up with how neurotic I can get about school, but he's so understanding. I know how frustrated he feels when I cancel plans because I need to complete a paper, edit an essay, study for a test, whatever, but he never shows it, even if I miss a game. So, we're okay; we're going to be okay."

We're quiet for a bit, trying to process the seriousness of the moment and trying to process how far we've come. At this point last year, I was struggling to come to terms with my feelings for Cole, still held back by the opinions of other people and haunted by my abandonment issues. My friends suffered right alongside me, for something they never deserved to be punished for, but they stuck by me. We're at such different places right now, but it feels like the only thing that's changed is how we feel about ourselves.

"Wow, who would've thought we'd have relationships, much less relationship problems." Beth echoes my thoughts. "Who knew I'd not only fall in love with someone but end up moving in with him, too; it's crazy."

"But crazy good, right? I've never seen you or my brother happier." I hug me knees to my chest, wrapping my arms around them. The charms in my bracelet glitter under the lights, and I'm blinded once again by the sight of the ring.

"I am, you know, happier than I've ever been in my life.

Sometimes it feels too good to be true; yeah, I had a rough year, and it's still difficult to remember to breathe at times." She stops, blinks rapidly, trying to get rid of her tears like she always tries to do. Beth's mom passed away in a drunk driving accident over six months ago, and despite the fact that she doesn't like talking about it, we know she still battles guilt over her death every single day since it happened. My brother's been really good for her; he knows a lot about using communication as a means to fight those feelings of helplessness, and he's definitely done a great job of making Beth be at peace with what happened.

She clears her throat and chucks a pillow at me. "Now that you're done psychoanalyzing me, tell me about these Yolandas that seem to be sucking the joy right out of you."

It feels a bit petty now to whine about something that doesn't really require whining. I need to remind myself about how lucky Cole and I are to have each other and to have the opportunity to be together, so the Yolandas can keel over and die; I'm not bothered.

"Wait, who's Yolanda?"

We turn our heads to see Cole and Travis standing at the door. Ignoring Cole's question, I run over and hug my brother tightly. I'd missed him so badly, especially these last few days.

"So good to see you, Tess." He hugs me back before we release each other. Looking at him just fills me with warmth and a sense of family and home.

"I just can't get over you not living here." It feels so weird, even though it shouldn't. He's twenty-two now, more than old enough to live with his girlfriend and not under his parents' roof. And even though I'm not home most of the time, it feels so strange to come here and not have him in the room down the hall.

"I think we should both be glad that I'm not down the hall anymore."

It doesn't come as a surprise when Cole and I both hit him, and Beth throws yet another pillow.

***

The girls and I go out to the local grocery store to stock up on our favorite items for our sleepover. Five bags of junk food and a handful of DVDs later, we're setting up in my bedroom when I hear Cole call for me. He's been out with Travis and Alex, presumably doing guy stuff. I dare not suggest he include Jay in his plans.

"Hey, what's up?"

"Cute PJ's, Tessie."

Yes, they're the Scooby-Doo ones I still get horribly embarrassed by in front of Cole. There are some things your boyfriend doesn't need to see you wearing; pajamas that make you look twelve would be one of them.

"I thought you were spending the night at Travis's?" I walk down the stairs cautiously as he extends his hand toward me. When I reach him, he pulls me closer and tucks me under his chin. I have a feeling I'm not about to hear the greatest news.

"You know how we have a really important game next week?"

Uh-oh.

"Please don't say what I think you're going to say." I start to pull away but he only holds on tighter.

"You know I don't want to leave, right? But the guys want to practice, watch tapes. They have these unofficial practices all the time and…"

"You have to go." I try not sounding angry. It's okay; I mean, it's not like we won't see each other again come Monday. But that's the thing, we haven't been able to see each other a lot, not with his crazy practice schedule and me trying to keep up with my classes. I wanted to have this weekend so that we could catch up, and I would be able to get rid of this nagging feeling in the pit of my stomach, but clearly that's not going to happen.

"Do you have to go now?"

"Yeah, all day tomorrow as well." He bites his lip and looks at me worriedly, afraid that I'll freak out, but hey, talking to Megan has made me try to deal with this situation differently. Instead of being mad, I'll be cool, calm, and collected.

Because that's just who I am, right?

"Oh, okay, I'll get Travis to give me ride then."

"No! I wasn't going to just leave you here. I'll come back for you on Sunday; we can go together."

I move away from him and lean against a wall, crossing my arms over my chest protectively.

"You'll be tired, and it's pointless for you to make the same trip four times. I'll manage."

"No," he comes closer, cups my cheek in his hand, "You're mad; please, don't be mad. I can come take you, it's—"

"Not a big deal, Cole." I force a smile and place a hand against his chest, silently pushing him away. "Duty calls. You have to go, and I don't want you to have to worry about me, so go. I'm not mad; I just think this is a good thing, right? I get to spend some more time with the girls."

He backs away and has the nerve to look wounded.

"If that's what you want, then yeah, just let me know if you need the ride."

Still looking hurt, he walks away from me, toward the front door, and I feel like I should say something to try to salvage this disaster.

"Am I still having dinner with your parents tomorrow?" I call out in a moment of utter stupidity.

"Do whatever you want, Tessie."

He slams the door when he leaves.

Jesus Christ, what am I even doing right now?

***

"That did not sound good." Beth stands by my door with a hand placed on her hip, looking quite intimidating.

"Did you guys hear all of it?"

"Well, you weren't exactly being subtle. What the hell was that about?"

"Nothing, it was stupid. He wanted to come pick me up on Sunday, and I didn't because gas is expensive, you know?" I feel the hysteria building up inside me. "We're good."

"And are we just supposed to overlook the fact that you're shaking like crazy, or that Cole slammed the door so loud, your next-door neighbor heard the noise?" Megan grabs my trembling palm to show me.

"I said it's nothing. We fight at times; all couples do, right?"

"Yeah, they do, but Cole goes the extra mile to try to not let that happen, not after everything. So, what's this about?"

Deep breaths, Tessa, just don't have a panic attack and we'll be fine.

"I…I…try so hard to keep up with the person he's becoming, the person other people think he is. Most of the time, it feels like they'd do anything to get rid of me, and that's not the part that has me terrified. I know he loves me, I know he'll never do anything to hurt me on purpose, but everything's changed so much. I'm worried that I'll hurt him because I can't handle it."

They're both quiet for a while as I process my own thoughts. I may have overreacted with Cole, but I have my reasons. Recently, it's starting to happen more and more often that he has commitments that cause him to cancel our plans, and I know that he hates it, but I'm getting tired of being disappointed all the time.

It tends to take a toll on you.

The girls attempt to distract me for the remainder of the night, and I try not to let my dark mood affect what's supposed to be a great time. I also do my damned best not to check my phone, but in the early hours of the morning, when my friends are asleep, I do check it and am once again flooded with disappointment when I see absolutely nothing.

On Saturday, I try not to mope around and instead go to the mall with Megan and Beth. Let's just say my credit card sees some major action, because there's no therapy like retail therapy. Of course, I would never be able to afford the things I buy on my own meager savings, but my parents' guilt money is definitely put to good use.

Those shoes will definitely keep me company in the long, cold winter. And yes, times like these are when I unleash my inner hoarder.

"Why do you need…" Megan pauses to count the contents of my cart, "Fifteen jars of Nutella and eight pints of ice cream?"

"Isn't it obvious, Meg, Tess here is about to embark on a pilgrimage. One where she finds her true self by getting diabetes and a permanent sugar high, possibly some tooth decay."

Ignoring them, I scour the aisle for more supplies. I need sugar and I need it stat; I also need to buy a pie for Cassandra.

I will go to that dinner, and I will go proudly bearing pie. Yup, the blueberry one that is Jay's favorite, I hope he Instagrams the shit out of it so that his meathead brother notices.

I've moved on from moping to anger at this point. How dare he bail on me repeatedly and expect me to be patient and understanding all the time? I've taken off my pretty dress and makeup enough times for it to hurt quite a lot, so he'll just have to suck it up and deal with my reaction.

"Wait, do you really need the extra-large can of whipped cream?"

Yes, yes, I do.

Dinner goes reasonably well, and I try my hardest not to get myself banned from future dinner invitations. It's always nice to see Cassandra, who'd been like a mother to me when mine bailed. Sheriff Stone is an intimidating man, something his job requires, but it's quite easy to guess where Cole gets his charm from. Once you win the man's approval, the sheriff is just about as hard not to like as his son is.

Speaking of his son, Cole's rarely mentioned after an awkward slip from Jay, who, as per usual, is clueless as to my feelings. It's embarrassing to know that the Stones know about our fight, but they never bring it up, and Cassandra even gives me a casserole to take home, so I take it as a good sign.

Jay offers to walk me home.

He still looks the same, and it's extraordinary how those looks do nothing for me now. His hair's too blond, his eyes are the completely wrong shade of blue, and his smile lacks that deviousness that makes my insides do backflips.

God, I miss Cole.

"Do you want to talk about it?" He shoves his hands deep inside his pockets and walks leisurely besides me, when all I want to do is race to my bedroom and hide inside my blankets.

Cringing, I give him a weak smile. "Not really."

"Well, you know where to find me if you need to talk. Also, if you need someone to drive you to school..."

I pause, because seriously, how is it that he still says these things?

"You and I both know how well that's going to go down."

He sighs. "Yeah, I do. But why does it always have to be about what he wants? Why can't we be better friends without worrying about hurting his feelings?"

"Hey! Stop making it sound like he's the bad guy. You and I are never going to be best friends because of how I feel, not because of Cole. I appreciate that you've been there for me during some pretty tough times, but it's not going to make all those years of you taking advantage of my feelings go away."

"Tessa…I'm sorry; I didn't mean it like that."

"Just don't say things like that about him and we'll be fine."

Having completely ruined the prospect of walking me home, Jay stands there awkwardly as I leave. Jerkhole, he's always had the worst timing.

I'm supposed to be meeting up with Travis so that he can look for a birthday present for Beth, but I have an hour to fume, and I plan to use it well.

I grab my phone and dial, lesson for everyone out there, angry dialing is way worse than drunk dialing. You may actually end up saying something nice when you're drunk, but there's nothing nice about what's going to happen.

"Tessie, are you okay?"

"No, you asshole, I'm not! I just had dinner with your parents, Jay's being a jerk, and I've gone absolutely mental—this is all your fault."

Yes, I've officially lost it. On the other end, he's eerily quiet.

"What did he say to you?"

I groan; of course, it's the only part that he picks out.

"I don't care about what he said, what I care about is that I have no idea how you feel, and you're shutting me out, Cole."

"It's not me who decided to put a wall between us. You don't want to talk about what you're feeling, and I don't know what to do." He's breathing heavily, and I want to wrap my arms around him, tell him that we'll be fine.

Someone calls his name on the other end and I freeze.

Because it's a girl.

"Who was that?" I don't want to jump to conclusions; he'd never do that to me…again. But trust works in funny ways.

"Just a teammate's girlfriend, they're setting up for the game. Wait…who did you think it was? Tessie…"

It's my quick intake of breath that tells him exactly what I'd been thinking.

"I think I should hang up now."

"Yeah, maybe you should." Cole's voice is emotionless and somehow manages to drain all of mine, too. I just feel tired now.

"I guess I'll see you on Monday."

"Yeah."

He doesn't even let me hang up first.

CHAPTER FIFTEEN

I'd Meant to Sweep You off Your Feet, Not Injure You

Somehow, I surprise myself by surviving Sunday lunch with my dad. He'd bailed on me for our originally scheduled dinner on Friday, and I could not have been more thankful for it. The last thing I need is for either of my parents to say those detested words, the ones every parent is dying to say when reality slaps you in the face: "I told you so."

Instead I put on my happy, well, relatively happy, face and we went for lunch, minus Travis, to the fanciest restaurant in town. I tried not to play with my food and he tried not to push any buttons that would make me explode. Perhaps Dad convinced himself that I was going through PMS; hence, he just ordered me a large ice cream sundae and we went on with our lives.

"So, how's everything at school?"

"Good."

"Yeah? How's that economics class you were telling me about?

Still tough?"

"Pretty much."

"Well, you don't seem too worried about it."

"I'm not."

The pattern continued for a painful five minutes before he gave up and let me hack at my ice cream. I'm pretty sure that at this point, if someone drew my blood, they would actually find huge chunks of ice cream floating around in my bloodstream.

But, oh well, possible risk of disease aside, I did manage to survive the rest of the day until Travis drove me back to school. I'd learned the important lesson of never leaving my own car behind and being at someone else's mercy, because my brother took the opportunity to try to lecture me. I'd already beaten myself up enough over how disastrously I'd handled things with Cole that hearing someone else talk about it just made me feel like throwing myself in front of a semi.

Yes, I'd been feeling pretty morbid, and no, I'm not suicidal, just really hurt. Megan and Beth had let me go quite reluctantly, and it sucked knowing that I wouldn't get to see them until Thanksgiving break, but the grown-up thing to do in this situation is not to hide in my childhood bedroom. I even managed to ditch those cursed Scooby pajamas that got me in trouble in the first place.

Yes, it's all their fault; maybe they had remnants of Nicole's voodoo magic on them.

By the time Travis drops me off in front of my dorm, I'm emotionally exhausted. My head hurts from thinking so much about what I'm supposed to do now, and my body's suffering from the lack of sleep. My brother looks at me with barely concealed pity in his eyes.

"Go talk to him, Tess; I'm sure it's not as bad as you think."

"I know…I know that if I go and apologize, maybe things will be okay. But I don't want them to be as they were before. I feel like we were both hurting each other unintentionally, and it needed to come out in the open."

He sighs. "Well, it is now. Use the opportunity to talk about your problems; that's the way relationships work. I look at you two sometimes, and it seems like you've got everything figured out, that you're so sure of each other, but then…"

"We screw up just like any other high school couple?"

"Don't do that; don't undermine what you have. You guys are lucky to have found each other so soon; what you need to do now is work hard at keeping it."

I wipe a stray tear off my face and kiss my brother's cheek. "Hanging out with Beth seems to have made you really smart."

"Yeah, and I'm telling you that you guys need to talk to each other; now go and do it."

Nodding to him, I say goodbye to Travis and trudge up the stairs to my dorm, with my duffel lagging behind me. I must come across as a sorry picture; maybe a coat of lip gloss or mascara would have helped.

Thankfully, I don't run into anyone I know by the time I make it to my room. Quickly unlocking the door, I shuffle inside and collapse on my bed.

"Well…hello to you, too."

I don't even open my eyes; I feel so tired and deflated that the only thing I'm capable of at the moment is breathing. I'm probably freaking Sarah out, but she respects the roommate code, never question your roommate's crazy.

"Hey."

"I'm assuming the weekend didn't go as planned."

I sigh. "Not at all."

"Well, if it makes you feel better, I fought with my boyfriend, too. Closed the Skype chat right on his face!"

The way she says it makes me laugh because she's pretending to be tough. Sarah fights with her boyfriend all the time, quiet as she is around other people. They make up within twenty-four hours, so I'm not about to sympathize.

"Wait, how do you know Cole and I fought?"

I sit up straight and look her right in the eyes so that she can't lie to me. Sarah's sitting at her desk, book in hand, and looking at me with slight panic.

"Did I say that? How would I know…I just assumed…"

"Sarah, did you talk to Cole?"

She doesn't take long to break under my rather intimidating stare. "Okay, okay, stop looking at me like that. He stopped by to see if you were back; actually, he came up a couple of times. I didn't want to pry so I didn't ask him, but he may have mentioned that you had an argument."

The fact that he checked up on me makes me happy; the fact that he's ignoring my texts makes me mad. I'm such a mess right now that it would be right up my alley to walk right up to him and give his groupies some really entertaining material. But I realize that before any sort of confrontation with Cole, I need to be calmer, because look how well the last time turned out. Staying cooped up in the dorm room isn't going to help; all I'll do is gorge myself on more sugar; isn't that what they call the silent killer?

Speaking of…

I take out my stash of Nutella from the duffel and place the jars on Sarah's desk. "That's for being an awesome roommate and not asking for a switch."

Her big brown eyes light up as she takes in the treasure in front of her, and not even bothering to look at me, she says, "Any time, Tessa."

I leave her to have a moment with Nutella; every girl deserves to have that special bonding time.

From our shared closet, I grab my workout clothes and quickly change into them while Sarah's distracted. I throw my hair up in a bun and grab an energy drink from our minifridge. No time like the present to exercise some frustration.

"If he comes by again…"

"I'll tell him to look for you in the gym."

If he wants to kiss and make up, then he'll have to do it when I'm at my sweaty best; if that's not a relationship test, then I don't know what is.

"Thanks."

The treadmill and I became friends back in the days of Fatty Tessie; while most people prefer running, I'd coveted the treadmill at my home gym. When you have as many body issues as I had, the last thing you want is people to see you panting and heaving. The summer that I lost all my excess weight included a lot of bonding time with the treadmill, so whenever I get on it now, it gives me a sense of comfort. I run, pushing everything out of my head and only concentrating on the task ahead, which is running till I can't possibly go any further.

An hour later, I'm the promised sweaty mess and breathing hard as I towel off before hitting the showers. I'm doing some simple stretches when a pair of Nike-clad feet come into my line of sight. My heart rate's already crazy, and I didn't think it would be possible for it to accelerate any more, but it does, and I look up.

Only to be bitterly disappointed.

It's not Cole, and of course there's a possibility that he might not even know that I've come back, but still, it does suck that we've gone about two days being angry at each other.

"That was quite the intense workout." The guy is in workout clothes as well, but, unlike the rest of his fellow gym buddies, there's not an ounce of sweat on him, or extra fat. He's tall, around six feet, with muscled arms and a well-toned chest. His hair, which he sweeps off his forehead as he smiles at me, is dark, almost black, matching his eyes. They match perfectly with his naturally tanned skin, and, for a moment, I'm taken aback.

Cute guys tend not to approach me, and when they do, bad things happen.

But, given the fact that I look like someone tried to drown me in a pool of my own sweat, there would be no way that he's hitting on me.

"Thanks, I guess." I look around awkwardly, not knowing as usual what to do in situations where other human beings talk to me.

"I haven't seen you here before; is this your first time?"

"No, I usually come really early in the morning, so that might explain it."

He laughs and rubs the back of his neck. Wait, is he nervous?

"I'm not a stalker or anything, actually, I'm a trainer, that's why I was asking. I didn't creep you out or anything, did I?"

The poor guy's flushing, and his unease immediately thaws out my anxiety; he's as socially inept as I am, so, basically, there's no need to worry.

"No, of course not! But if you hadn't been a trainer, then I might have asked you how many bodies you've got stashed in your ice cream truck."

It takes a horribly awkward minute for the joke to register before he laughs and offers me his hand.

"I'm Bentley, senior and part-time gym trainer."

"Tessa, freshman, and a rare exerciser."

We fall easily into a conversation about school and our majors before I leave him to hit the showers. I thank my lucky stars that I brought decent clothes to change into, even if they are my trusty yoga pants and a gray, long-sleeved top that fits nicely.

I walk on over to where Bentley is helping another student in the weights section, and when he sees me, he holds up a finger, indicating that I should wait.

I stand there and on a whim, check my phone, noting that the screen is still blank and my texts are still unanswered. I'm brooding over these issues when Bentley taps me over my shoulder.

"So, are you heading out?" I notice the way his eyes roam over me, nothing creepy, but he definitely checks me out.

"Yeah, I usually just do the hour of cardio, not really an expert on the rest."

His face lights up when I tell him this. "I could help you with that; just log on to the gym's website and schedule an appointment with me. If you're more comfortable working out in the morning, I could switch shifts; we could start you up with some basic strength training…"

He really does tend to ramble when he's nervous, and right now he's biting his lip as if he's somehow scared me away, but I tell him that I'll definitely look into making the appointment and smile at him as I leave.

It's only then that I notice him leaning against the wall of the entrance to the gym. As per usual, Cole looks incredibly stunning with jeans and a white T-shirt with a black jacket over it. His eyes give nothing away as he watches me walking toward him. I reach for him automatically whenever he occupies the same space as me; it's impossible for me not to. Even now, when I fear the outcome of his ambush, I can't help but walk right up to him, until there's enough space between us to be pushing what's socially acceptable.

I notice immediately that he's been having as difficult a time dealing with how we hurt each other as I have. There's a nearly two-day stubble on his face, and his eyes look tired, defeated. He's the exact mirror of me.

"Hey," I say softly, but there's no telling what he's feeling, not with the blank expression on his face.

He's glaring at something over my shoulder, and I look over to see what's caught his attention. Cursed as I am, it turns out that Cole and Bentley are locked in some kind of a stare-off, neither willing to back off. This continues for a good couple of minutes before I decide to step in. I cup the side of Cole's face knowing it'll bring his attention back to me immediately.

"Hey," I repeat, "What are you doing here?"

It takes him a few moments to make sense of what I've asked, and then I receive the answer in the most glorious way possible. His hand goes to my nape as he brings me forward, and he crushes his lips against mine in a frenzied, hotter-than-hell kiss.

Of course, I forget that we're in public, of course, I forget that we need to talk about our issues, because when he kisses me, nothing else matters. That's how it's always been, and I'm not sure whether it's good or bad, and nor do I want to know.

My arms go around his neck as I stand on my tiptoes to return his kiss. His hands rest on the small of my back, just a few inches above my butt, and I know it takes him a lot of self-restraint not to move lower. We kiss, it's angry and messy, and it shows how we're feeling; it's nothing like the soft kisses he gives me right after he's told me that he loves me. I can actually feel the hurt rolling off of him, and that's what makes me back off.

I'm breathing heavily as I put my hand on his chest and create some space between us. "What was that for?"

The fact that he glances back at Bentley before giving me his answer has me furious. Of course, he'd just been marking his territory, like all men seem to think they need to do. I push away from him and turn to see a dejected-looking Bentley standing there, looking extremely uncomfortable. I want to go and apologize to him, tell him that my boyfriend's not always such a jerk, but the fact that Cole's standing there looking smug makes the situation all the more embarrassing.

I rush out of the gym and I know he's close on my heels.

"Tessie, wait!"

Ignoring him, I push past the latest crowd of gym goers and continue to storm toward my dorm. He won't be able to get in until I provide my ID, so there's a huge chance of him being out in the cold all night. Of course, given the fact that he's taller than I am and has legs that make mine look like stumps, he catches up with me in no time and pulls me back by the arm. I struggle, and he cages my back against his chest, wrapping his arms around my waist.

"Stop fighting me," he croons in my ear, like I'm a child. It does give me the urge to stomp on his foot, so maybe he might be on to something.

"Let me go, you oaf!"

He chuckles; he actually has the nerve to laugh at me right now. "I'm not letting you go, ever, now stay still."

Because we're hidden by the shadows of various campus buildings and because it's gotten relatively empty out, it gives him the perfect opportunity to press us against the back of a building. His lips find their spot on my neck, and as he begins to plant small kisses there, some of my resistance begins to fall apart.

"Why'd you do that? Why did you kiss me like that?"

"Like what?" He hums against my skin.

"Like you were mad at me."

He freezes for a second, his arms go lax, and I feel a sudden chill take over me. Cole presses his lips to my cheek and then turns me around to face him.

"I didn't mean for it to be like that but…"

"You were jealous! The stunt you just pulled there, what did the poor guy do to you?"

"Poor guy, my ass, he was basically peeling your clothes off with his eyes!"

"That's crap and you know it! He was being a nice person; you didn't have to embarrass him like that."

To his credit, Cole starts to look a little apologetic. "Okay so maybe I handled things the wrong way but you have to know that he likes you right?"

"No Cole, that's not right. Not every interaction I have with a man has to become sexual. He's going to be my personal trainer and you need to get over your Neanderthal mentality and accept it." I might be putting my foot down but 'm not really sure about the personal trainer part, I might never have the nerve to face the guy ever again after what Cole just did, but he doesn't need to know that.

Then something clicks; somehow, the reason for his overreaction becomes apparent.

"You're angry with me, aren't you? I hurt you by not trusting you; it's okay to feel that way. Be mad at me; tell me that I'm wrong. Just be honest, please, what is this even about?"

His shoulders slump in defeat. "Shit, I'd meant to sweep you off your feet, not injure you. You need to know that I want you to be able to trust me; there's nothing I'd value more than knowing that I've earned that trust. But, Tessie, you've got to learn to stop doubting us. I can't fix us if you're the one who doesn't believe that we can work."

"I never said that! I trust you, I do, but you've been so distant lately. All I ever hear are promises that you don't get to keep. That's what hurts me, Cole."

He's quiet now; we both are. I've rarely come right out and told him how much I'd hated the way his life has changed so much since we got to college; I'd refused to even admit it to myself. But the more popular he got and the more new people that came into his life, the worse I'd started to feel about myself. For a girl who'd always had insecurities, and had them for good reason, seeing constant judgement in people's eyes isn't really healthy. But I did try my hardest to go along with it, to not let it become too obvious how much I've been affected by people seeing me as nothing but Cole's plain-looking girlfriend. I know there's so much more to me that these people don't see. They don't see the long hours I put in at the library or how well I'm already doing in my classes. They don't know about all my hopes for the future and how hard I'm working to make those dreams come true. These people, the ones who just want a piece of Cole, don't define me, and I won't let them, but sometimes it hurts that they don't try harder to get to know who I really am.

"I'll quit the team. If that's what you want, I'll quit it right now."

"Of course that's not what I want," I cry out, "I just…I don't know how I'm supposed to fit into your life right now."

"I love you, Tessie; you're the most important thing in the world to me. Nothing matters more than you do; you need to believe me." He leans in and kisses me deeply, and when he pulls back, there's a sense of peace that comes with it.

"I believe you, Cole, but what you're seeing here isn't about you. I'm not in a good place right now." Then I voice the fears that I should have told him in the first place. "Being at college is not what I thought it was going to be like. Sometimes it feels like I'm still stuck in high school, and…"

"I only make that worse, don't I? That's why you never go out to parties?" He looks devastated right now because he knows how much I'd looked forward to being here, how it'd always been a dream of mine.

"No, you've always made things better. I need you to understand where I'm coming from. If I do stupid stuff, if it's hard for me to trust you, you need to know why. I need to know if things will be the same for a while, me being disappointed every time you fail to show up."

"I'll never let you hurt again, Shortcake; I'm so sorry."

Someone said that the road to hell is paved with good intentions; I just hope that the saying came to bite them in the butt.

CHAPTER SIXTEEN
I'll Never Look at Hot-Pink Fuzzy Handcuffs the Same Way Again

"Boo!"

In usual Tessa fashion, this age-old trick works on me, and I drop my toothbrush in the sink.

Goddamn it, I hate it when that happens.

But I love it when Cole wraps his arms around me and presses his naked chest to my back; that is always great.

"Why'd you do that?" I rinse my mouth and rescue my toothbrush.

"Because you're fun to play with, and I'm in the mood to play." He kisses my cheek as his hands start to wander, and I let myself enjoy it for a few minutes before pulling away. We have things to do today, plans which mean that we can't get into the other stuff.

Distractions, although it is the best kind of distraction.

"Hands off, Stone, go put some clothes on and then make me breakfast. We need to go costume shopping before all the good ones are gone."

He groans and tugs at the hem of my sleep shirt, which just coincidentally happens to be his. "Why? It's nine a.m., the party doesn't start for another eleven hours. Eric's gone to his girlfriend's, we have this whole place to ourselves. Don't you want to do something more…exciting than to shop?"

He's got a very good point there, very good indeed, and he starts proving it by sucking my earlobe in between his lips, knowing that it does crazy things to me.

I begin to breathe heavily. "What did you have in mind?"

"Well," he lets my ear go and begins placing kisses down my neck, "It definitely wouldn't involve me putting on clothes. Quite the opposite, really."

He tugs at my shirt again, and this time, instead of pulling back, I lift my arms.

***

We manage to get out of the apartment two hours later, hand in hand and ready to take on the world of costume shopping. I don't tell him that I'd planned my costume weeks earlier, the one I'd been telling Cami and Sarah about, but that in light of recent events, I'd had to completely scratch it and start afresh. Because I'd gotten a jersey, a football jersey with his name and number on the back, had it completely tailored to fit, gotten the matching shorts, had "Number One Fan" printed on the front, too.

But, things were obviously a bit different now.

We'd had the big heart-to-heart, the one where I confessed that I didn't feel like I fit in his life anymore, and, ever since that night two weeks ago, he'd been trying to chase my fears away. He'd find little ways to tell me he loved me all day, he'd show me off in front of his friends, made me come watch him practice so that I'd see that not all the guys on his team were arms up against commitment and monogamy.

I definitely appreciate his efforts.

And because he's working so hard, I've decided to work on myself, too. He deserves someone better than a person who's always going to think less of herself, who'll never have the confidence to claim him, love him, and be with him like he deserves. I needed to fix myself for him and for me. So, I'd randomly started looking up therapists in the area. Cami indirectly gave me the idea to talk to a therapist because she'd bring up a lot of the things she learned in her psych classes. I'm not sure right now if that's what I need, opening up to a total stranger, but I'm looking into it.

"What's on your mind, Tessie?" We're walking to the nearest mall instead of driving. It's cold outside and we're bundled up in our coats and scarves, but it's still nice, perfect to have him keeping me warm. Cole's arm is slung over my shoulder, and, as he asks me this, he tighten his hold around me.

I don't try to hide things from him anymore; if I'm feeling something at a particular moment, then I tell him. We've both seen how poisonous bottled-up feelings tend to be.

"I like us, just like this. Things are good now, aren't they?"

He smiles and kisses the tip of my nose. "Things are always good with us, Shortcake; that's the best part. Nothing that'll ever happen is going to make me question us. We're fighters; you need to remember that."

It's when he says things like this, things that make happiness spread to my bones, that I remember why I'd been through hell for him and why I'd actually not mind going through it again.

Only if it led us here to this point.

It's not the greatest idea to shop for your actual costume on the day of Halloween itself, but hey, we're students, and we barely get time to eat, sleep, breathe, and shower—in no particular order, so the store managers need to stop rolling their eyes at us.

"Ugh! Why does this costume industry insist that women demean themselves by wearing something that wouldn't even cover a newborn child!"

Cole stands in the corner of the latest store and coughs, trying to muffle his laughter. He's enjoying this, enjoying watching me squirm. Because yes, I did walk into a sex shop and sift through dominatrix costumes for a good fifteen minutes before I realized where I actually was.

I'll never look at hot-pink, fuzzy handcuffs the same way again.

And my so-called boyfriend just stood there, watching me stand with a whip in one hand, handcuffs in another, and think about my outfit out loud.

I feel my cheeks get hot as I remember his face when realization finally dawned on me. Let's just say he's going to have to work really hard to get a repeat of this morning.

"Well, we could always go back to the other store and get you that leather bodysuit…"

I whirl around from the mirror and shake my finger at him. "Stop right there, buddy, you are supposed to erase that memory from your head. It never happened; I'll deny it if you ever bring it up. Ha!"

His face turns red, he's trying that hard not to laugh, and then fails. The manager walking around scowls at us, before eyeing the crumpled-up dress in my hands. It's not a dress; it's a piece of floss that's supposed to make me look like I'm a cat.

Desperate times for Tessa O'Connell.

"You buying that or not, lady? It's one of our most popular options, and you're creasing it."

Humankind needs to do a lot of hard work to restore my faith in it. I shake my head and give the dress back to him, returning to the racks to peruse my choices that won't get me arrested for public indecency.

"Why aren't you looking? I thought you needed a costume, too," I ask Cole absentmindedly as I contemplate going as a fried egg; everybody likes eggs, right?

Then I remember that this party is being thrown by one of the more popular fraternities. Cami's on-again, off-again friends invited us; well, they invited Cami, who was asked to invite Cole. I assumed that as an extension, I was also invited. Even if I wasn't, I'm working on allowing these kinds of things to slide.

That doesn't mean that I'll go looking like a freaking friend egg.

"I'm a guy; I'll slap on a suit and say I'm James Bond."

The man does look good in a suit and tie.

"Well, work harder; be more creative." If I have to traumatize myself in the process, then he should, too.

"If you figure out what you want to go as, let me know; we'll coordinate." He shrugs his shoulders like it's that easy. Of course it's not, the pressure of being a couple on Halloween is more than dressing yourself as in individual. You can't be cheesy, have to avoid being "that" couple at all costs. The one that freakishly color-coordinates every part of what they're going to wear or, even worse, match! If that doesn't scream codependence, then I don't know what does.

"What if I decide to go as Jay-Z, would you go as Beyoncé?"

My goofball sticks his chest out and flips his imaginary long hair. "Everybody wants to go as Beyoncé; few can pull it off."

This is going to be a long, long trip.

***

In the end, we do figure out what we're going to wear that night, and I say goodbye to Cole for a few hours to get things in order. He doesn't know what I'm wearing. I found the perfect thing while he'd excused himself to get some sustenance, which basically meant he'd left me alone to hang out in the food court for no other reason than that my indecisiveness was giving him a headache.

Well, I showed up, I found the greatest costume of all costumes, and he wouldn't get to see it until I wore it for the party. Which also meant that he bought one for himself and wouldn't let me see it, either; we're compatible, if nothing else.

I stow my finds for the day in my dorm and am about to leave again when I run into Sarah coming back. Her eyes look puffy and she looks physically drained. I immediately go into the "good friend and roommate" mode; she's been there for me more than enough recently, and it'd be nice if I return the favor.

"Hey." I open the door for her and watch her sink down on her bed, curl up on her side, shoes and all, and pull her duvet on top.

"Hey," she sniffles.

We have the supplies for making hot chocolate in our room for such occasions, and I immediately get to task. In the short six weeks I've known her, Sarah and I have developed our very own rituals, and this is one of them. I make her one big steaming mug of the good stuff and set it by the table.

Sitting on my own bed, I try to get her to talk.

"Another fight?"

At first, I didn't take her constant arguments with her boyfriend seriously. They'd always make up the next day and go back to their late-night Skype calls that made me put my headphones in. But recently, it looks like things are going from bad to worse with her and Grant, the boyfriend.

She nods her head and sniffs.

"Do you want to tell me what happened?"

This time she shakes her head.

"It'll make you feel better, and we can call him horrible names together; that always helps."

She takes some time before responding but then gets up and

leans back against the headboard of the bed. Grabbing her mug of hot chocolate, she stares at it intently before looking at me with her watery eyes.

"I think we just broke up."

Whoa, was not expecting that.

I try to make sure my mouth isn't hanging open.

"Why would you say that? I'm sure it's just a fight…you guys will pull through. I'm sure."

She doesn't look convinced.

"I told him that I was tired of him calling me at odd hours and that he needs to value my time. I plan my day according to his schedule, whenever's convenient for him and the crazy hours he keeps with that band of his." She takes a long, draining sip of her hot chocolate. "That's not right, is it? It's one thing for me to want our relationship to last, but it's like he forgets that he needs to make an effort as well."

I stay quiet for a while and let her dwell upon her thoughts; it's all hitting a bit too close to home for me to give her any advice. It's not like I hadn't felt something similar a few weeks ago.

"And what did he say?" I ask her softly.

"He doesn't get it! He never does; he thinks I shouldn't have gone to school so far away, should have stayed with him in that suffocating small town. And even now, he makes it seem like it's all my fault that we hardly have any time for one another. He knew it was going to be like this; he told me he didn't want to break up. I…I believed him. God, how could I be so stupid?"

She starts crying in earnest right now, and I immediately cross over to her and wrap my arms around her frail shoulders. She's shaking so much, and I'm hurting for her because I know what this kind of pain feels like. But I also know that nothing I can do or say is going to make her feel better; she just needs to feel everything until she's okay with feeling it.

***

A couple of hours later, Cami has joined us and is attempting to cheer Sarah up by teaching her about the three S's of Halloween costumes.

"You can either be sexy, scary, or shut the fuck up, I don't want to play dress up."

She's not really being successful at the cheering-up part.

"But the choice between the three is pretty easy. I could rock the scary look because hey, it's not like I have guys looking at me. Nope, so if I want to put in fake fangs or fake blood and guts coming out of me, then I'll do it," she declares emphatically.

Sarah is curled up on her bed; her eyes still look bloodshot and puffy, and they would, given the amount of crying she's done. But we've surrounded her with lots of ice cream, loaded the latest feel-good rom-com on her laptop, and have our in-house comedienne dishing out her best.

But she still looks so sad.

It even manages to make Cami's confidence falter. She shoots me a panicked look and then reaches for the shopping bag that holds my outfit for the ill-fated party.

Obviously, I'm not going anymore, not when Sarah's this

devastated.

"Let's see what Tessa got since she needs to be on top of her game. We've got all these vultures just looking for the right opportunity to swoop in and sink their claws into some Sexy Stone. So, this costume needs to be one hell of a sexy one."

She peeks into the bag, and I know she's put the pieces together without even seeing all of it. The wig is sort of a huge giveaway, and all the sequins are just plain obvious.

"No way!" she squeals, and even Sarah looks up; yup, that's our in.

I shrug. "I saw it and remembered something Cole once said to me, maybe we were watching it on TV. I don't really remember, but it just sort of stayed with me, and then I found this and knew it was meant to be."

Maybe I'd get another opportunity to wear it, Cole and I could try something new, god knows he must get bored of how scared I am of trying new things.

Getting back on track…

"It's absolutely perfect! You are going to look so good, Tessa, and with the right makeup…"

"I'm not going." I try not looking directly at Sarah as I say this, and hopefully she doesn't catch my eye. "Cole and I are going to do something next week instead; it's not a big deal."

She opens her mouth to argue, but I shake my head and nod toward Sarah, who has started staring into the distance with a really eerie, blank look on her face. You don't leave a person alone when they're like this.

"Oh." Cami bites her bottom lip. "I guess that makes sense."

Looking at the clock, I see that it's well past six and that Sarah hasn't moved from her spot in over five hours. She abandoned the hot chocolate halfway and obviously hasn't eaten anything since morning. I'm about to tell her to get up and go with me to the cafeteria when there's an insistent tapping on our door. It must be Cole; it's going to kill me to tell him that we're going to have to cancel our plans because we were both so desperate to have this one night of fun. One night where I'd prove to both him and myself that I was over my silly fears.

Putting on my brave face, I open it and prepare myself to tell him the bad news, but he surprises me by grabbing my wrist and pulling me outside. He gently closes the door behind me and holds me by the waist.

"I found this guy outside." He nods to his side, and that's when I notice the tall, dark-haired guy standing a couple of feet away from us. If it weren't for the fact that he was completely rumpled, with his well-worn clothes, messy hair, and tired-looking face, I'd say he was…

"No way! You're Grant, aren't you?" I slap my hands over my mouth.

His exhausted blue eyes seem to get some light in them. The more I look at him, the more he looks like the guy in Sarah's pictures, just as good-looking as she said, but right now he looks like he's been through hell and back.

"You're Sarah's roommate, I…I saw a couple of photos on her Facebook. Is she inside? Can I go in?"

"How'd you even get here so fast? You guys broke up less than ten hours ago…she's still crying her eyes out for you!"

He flinches. "I got on the first plane I could find…just can I see her, please?" His southern accent coupled with how polite he's being pretty much makes my decision for me. I look at Cole, and he gives me a lopsided smile, like he's with the guy.

"Just one sec."

I go inside and grab Cami, who's still trying to salvage her one-woman act, and drag her outside. Sarah is barely registering us, so I manage to do so without giving away the big surprise that awaits her.

"Why'd you do that? I was just about to get a smile out of her!"

Shutting the door gently behind me, I say, "Cami, meet Grant, Grant, meet Cami, and then go inside and make your girl happy, please."

I've never seen a man say hello and run so fast; the next thing we know, he's left us and inside, and Cole, Cami, and I are just standing there, feeling a bit shell-shocked.

"Can you believe he came all the way here from Texas? Talk about a grand gesture." We're both pretty much swooning at this point.

"I know! It's so romantic."

I sigh and Cole nips at my lips with his, "Hey, if all it takes is getting on a plane to win you over, you should've told me earlier, before I robbed the state's Kit Kat supply."

I snuggle into his side and kiss just beneath his ear; Cami's got her ear plastered to the door of my room now, so PDA isn't a concern.

"I'm glad you don't have a reason to hop on a plane and travel two thousand miles to see me. I'm glad you're right where you are."

"But it would be like she said, a grand gesture. Wouldn't you like that?"

I fold myself into his chest. "Nope, nothing's worth that kind of a distance."

"Ten bucks says they're having makeup sex in there," Cami whispers conspiratorially.

And yes, that does ruin the mood a little bit.

***

In the end, we do decide to go to the party since things were obviously going better for Sarah. It was a bit awkward when I went in a little while later to pack an overnight bag and give her some time alone with Grant. They'd obviously been kissing and doing a bit more and looked absolutely disheveled when they sprang apart. I quickly grabbed the essentials and my costume before saying goodbye.

I'm so ridiculously happy for her!

Now we're back at Cole's and getting ready for the night. It's been quite the emotional day, and I'm in the mood for some fun. So, I've kicked Cole out and taken over his room, getting ready to give him the surprise of his life.

When I saw the dress, I'd been a bit concerned about being able to pull it off because it's definitely a lot more daring than anything I've ever worn. But I imagined his reaction, and that's what's driving me to go through with this.

After a nice long shower, I put on a robe over the matching underwear I'd scrounged for in my collection and dry my hair. Because it's going to be trapped under a wig tonight, I don't pay much attention to it and, after air-drying it, pull it up into a bun. I concentrate on making sure my makeup is right for the getup I'm planning. Pulling up some pictures on my phone, I try to match it to the real thing as much as possible. After getting as close as I can, I take a deep breath and go for the dress. Praying that it's the right size, I slide myself into the sparkly red fabric. It clings to every curve I've got, and I'm glad that I've kept working out after getting here. After I've pulled it up to right over my boobs, I examine myself in the mirror.

Well…it could've looked worse.

It doesn't look as obscene as I thought it would. The dress is tight, but instead of making it look like I'm purposely cutting off my air supply, it looks…good and emphasizes all the good parts of my body.

My boobs aren't on show, but the strapless, sweetheart neckline creates a nice cleavage, but the kicker, well, the kicker is the slit that runs the length of my right leg, going a good few inches over my knee but stopping before I pull a Kendall Jenner, nope, no hipbones here.

I've never worn something like this, but Halloween seems like the best opportunity to be brave, to try something new and terrifying, right?

I reach for the wig, the iconic redheaded waves that were part of the fantasies of many, many guys and still are. When I secure it over my head, it doesn't look like a cheap knockoff, and maybe that because I did spend a good fortune on this whole look. The hair looks real, waves tumbling down one side, obscuring part of my face while the rest forms a thick sheath down my back. It’s a deep, rich red that complements my skin tone and my red lips.

Oh-kay, this is working.

The last thing I go for are the purple, elbow-length gloves, and as I slide them on, I do feel sexy, like Cami said.

Sexy and ready to keep the vultures away from my man. If it takes channeling Jessica Rabbit to get them to back off, then bring it.

***

I open the door to see Cole’s back and catch sight of a black jacket. I still don’t know who he’s going as, he’s been getting ready in their spare bathroom and being stubborn and mysterious.

But he hears the click of my heels and turns.

And that look on his face?

Yup, definitely worth it.

“Holy Shit,” he swears under his breath as his eyes look hungrily over me, and I find myself doing the same to him.

James Dean.

He’s going as James Dean.

My bad boy is going as the ultimate one, and I’ve just died and gone to heaven. I watch him hurriedly cross the room and get closer to me. He's put product in his hair in an attempt to get it to behave and pushed it up, wearing a black leather jacket, white T-shirt, and dark washed jeans—he looks like a dream.

Well, he always does, but whoa, when Cole Stone makes an effort to look good? Lord have mercy.

But right now, he's devouring me with his eyes; his hands are skating over my arms, my sides, my face. It's like he doesn't know where to touch me first. I notice his eyes zooming in on the expanse of the exposed skin of my leg, and his jaw begins to tick, his eyes dark.

"Fuck, you look…"

"Surprised?"

It seems like it takes him some effort to take his eyes off my leg and to my face, but when he does, I notice those piercing blue orbs are smoldering.

God, he's so hot.

"Let's just say you'll be lucky if you're able to walk tomorrow, Tessie."

Oh My.

He grabs my hand and begins to pull me toward the door. "The sooner we get to this thing, the sooner we get back. Now come on."

I scramble and grab my clutch and phone, a coat to throw over the dress, and Cole's keys, because he sure as hell isn't going to remember to take them. The man's on a mission, and I am so looking forward to how well he manages to accomplish it.

CHAPTER SEVENTEEN

I'd Be the Guy from *Twilight,* but the Store Ran out of Body Glitter

I swat Cole's hands off of me for the fifteenth time in five minutes. It's not the easiest task because he's so determined, but I've been getting way too many longing stares projected in our direction for me to be comfortable with it.

An exhibitionist I am certainly not. Just the thought of some girl looking at us, imagining herself in my place and picturing my boyfriend naked, makes my skin crawl, so I try my best not to give them visual representations to shape their fantasies after.

But the stubborn hunk of a man attached to my side isn't making it easy for me; his hands keep wandering, his lips often finding their way to mine and his arms wrapped around me. It's also convenient because he glares at anyone within a five-foot radius, so that we're left relatively alone. That doesn't, however, mean that I don't feel the laser-beam-like wistfulness of all the women and some of the men here burning into the side of my head.

"You put that dress on knowing what it would entail, Tessie; don't play with me."

Good point.

I'd known dressing up as the fantasy of most prepubescent boys, aka Jessica Rabbit, would get me in a bit of trouble with Cole. I'm testing him, and I did it on purpose, so if it means dealing with his grabby hands, then so be it.

It's not like it's much of a sacrifice, right?

The sorority house is decked out to the extremes for Halloween, and, in typical college party fashion, it's not really about who dressed up the scariest. It's just a bunch of stressed students blowing off some steam before going back to the books. Drinks are flowing freely, the music is loud and buzzing, everyone's dancing, and the ones who aren't are catching up with their significant or not-so-significant others.

Cole said hi to the bare minimum of people I knew, and I had to drag him to the girls, Cami's friends who invited us, since they looked like they were ready to start slobbering once they saw him. Even though they haven't exactly been the nicest to my new friend, the manners my mother forced into me at a very young age made me subject Cole to the mind-numbing torture of the two girls fawning all over him.

Now they've finally let him go, and we're getting a feel for the place. Of course, Cole insists on going back to his apartment but hey, as delicious as he looks, I've put some serious time and effort into this look, and if he has to put a lid on what he needs, then so be it.

"I thought you didn't like parties," he grumbles beside me; he's been nursing the same bottle of beer for the past half hour, and it seems like he isn't in the mood to get more than a little buzzed. I, on the other hand, could use some liquid courage tonight. We're getting stared at, and we're definitely getting stared at a lot. But what's surprising is that I'm not getting vicious glares sent my way, well, not mostly. What's got Cole in a cranky mood is the fact that it's the guys who can't seem to stop looking in our direction.

It's flattering, of course, but it's also making me feel highly uncomfortable, like they're all picturing me naked, and this dress definitely doesn't leave much to the imagination. That explained why Cole had been so insistent on dragging me to a corner and covering my body with his, shielding me from those hungry eyes. But then we were back to square one; I was being insecure and scared, and he had to spend his time playing hero, always rescuing me.

"I don't like them," I confirm, "but this is a Halloween party, we're all in costume. If someone doesn't like me, then at least I can blame Jessica for it." I gesture toward my dress and the wig.

He groans, following the movement of my hands. "Baby, half of the room is salivating looking at you. The only reason someone won't like you is because you've got their boyfriends' eyes glued to you."

"But I only care about one boyfriend's eyes—mine." I flash him a grin to put him at ease. He needs to think I'm having fun and that my social anxiety isn't creeping all up inside me. Because this guy has put himself out there for me enough times, and he deserves to have a girlfriend who isn't so neurotic.

"Hey, isn't that Justin? He's coming this way; we should say hi."

Even though I'd love nothing more than to stay wrapped up in our little bubble all night, it would make this entire exercise pointless. Which is why even though Justin is one of the most sleazy and moronic guys from Cole's team, I pretend to be as happy to see him as I'd be to see a leprechaun atop a unicorn.

Suffice it to say, I'm a damn good actress.

But Cole's not in the mood to be playful; as the jock approaches us, his body becomes stiffer and he stands half in front of me, his arm going around my back.

"Nice to see you got away from the ball-and-chain, Stone."

Sighing inwardly, I clasp my hand around Cole's shoulder to spare Justin his life.

The team would really miss its running back, were he six feet under.

"Always a pleasure seeing you, Justin," I interrupt before this guy continues putting his foot in his mouth.

His eyes widen and he rakes his gaze over me, once again making me feel slimy.

"Whoa, Tessa, I…I didn't recognize you there. Jesus, you look…"

His eyes must remain on my chest a bit too long, so Cole fully stands in front of me and slaps Justin's back, a bit too forcefully, given the wince on the guy's face.

"Nice costume, so who are you supposed to be?"

It looks like he'd been going for the common white guy approach with his pinstriped shirt, a clip-on tie, black slacks, and dress shoes. How on earth this became a Halloween costume, I have no idea.

"I'm a real estate agent!" He bursts out laughing as if he's said the funniest thing on the planet. "Made my old man really happy to see me going for the family business. Told me middle-aged divorcees always make for the best…"

"Okay, then." Cole slaps his back again, promptly shutting him up before Justin launched into a very vivid description of what he'd like to learn from a single woman in her forties. "Why don't you get us some drinks and wait by the bar? That girl dressed like Little Red Riding Hood has been eyeing you for some time."

Like a dog with a bone, Justin's eyes zero in on the girl dressed like the fairytale character…only sluttier, because Little Red Riding Hood's grandma wouldn't really approve of leather skirts and fishnet tights.

He chases her down immediately and leaves us in peace. But once at the bar, he keeps shooting Cole smug looks and hollers at him to join him and some other teammates that are there. I know he doesn't want to, but I push him toward them.

"Go! I'm not going anywhere." My hands tug at the lapel of his leather jacket, one that I can't seem to stop touching. "Bond with the guys; I want to do some people watching. Beth and Megan need evidence that I actually made it this far."

He looks uneasy but laughs anyway, kissing me possessively for a while and ignoring the wolf whistles of his teammates. Then he walks away, and I fight the urge to go to my Plan B, as in grab my phone from my clutch and play Candy Crush but look like I'm texting someone really important.

Predictability, thy name is Tessa.

"Tessa, is that you?"

The sound of a friendly, familiar voice makes relief flood through me, so much so that it staggers me, and, as I search for its source, I come across a vampire.

Literally.

But it's Bentley; I can tell from his build and his dark, strikingly black eyes. So even though there's fake blood smeared across his chin and he's got fangs and a cape on, I still know the guy. I've started working out a lot more regularly and often run into him. It's strange because even though he's told me that he trains the evening batch of exercisers, I more often than not run into him in the mornings. But still, despite how embarrassed I'd been to face him after the Cole fiasco, we've become good friends, and it feels great to see him here.

"Hey! I didn't think you'd be here."

He shrugs, and I notice him taking in my appearance but, surprisingly, it doesn't make me feel dirty, just a little embarrassed.

"One of my regular clients is in the sorority and she insisted, so here I am." He does an awkward bow with his cape and I laugh.

"So, you're Dracula?"

"Well, I'd be the guy from *Twilight*, but the store ran out of body glitter, kinda ruined my whole look."

See? This is why it's so easy to be around this guy, he makes me laugh until my cheeks hurt, and he gets my kind of humor!

"And wow, you're like every guy's childhood fantasy."

He blurts this out and then his face colors, still visible under the white paste he's got on it. Immediately I blush too, because we're just one big awkward mess.

"Thanks…I, well, thanks. I didn't realize guys were that into a cartoon character."

"She's not just a cartoon character!" He seems insulted. "Jessica Rabbit is what every guy shapes his perfect woman after. She's it, Tessa."

"Well, damn, so if I'm not wearing a red wig and tight dress, I'll never be *it* for someone?"

He stutters and I put him out of his misery. "Kidding! I just have a sensitivity to redheads, long story, don't ask. It took me a while before I could look in the mirror and be okay with this hair, not planning on looking like this for long."

He squints in concentration, trying to understand what I'm saying, but comes up short. "Well, uh, I think your hair's great the way it is. Not Jessica great, but still, uh, it's shiny."

I cough in order to hide a laugh. Shiny? What are we? In second grade?

But he's blushing, which is pretty adorable.

"Now I see why you don't like coming to team parties. The guys are assholes." Cole comes back, but his head is turned away from us, which is why when he sees Bentley with me, his face drops. But it doesn't take him long to get the composure back; keeping a frighteningly blank expression on his face, Cole acknowledges him.

"Bentley."

"Mr. Dean." He nods.

What can I say? The guy's a dork.

"So," Cole stuffs his hands in his jeans, "do you mind if I borrow my girlfriend? Thanks for keeping her company."

Bentley bows again, the damn cape slapping me in the face. "The pleasure has been all mine." Before Cole can react, Bentley leans in and kisses my cheek before flapping away.

Uh-oh.

Cole glares in the general direction Bentley disappeared. He's been doing a hell of a lot of glaring tonight; distraction required immediately!

"What were you saying about the guys? Not all of them are assholes. Parker, Parker's nice." I make a feeble attempt to grab his attention by looking toward the spot where Cole's nicest teammate is flirting quite heavily with Cami. I've seen them spend a lot of time together, and although she brushes it off whenever I ask her, they definitely look cozy. She's dressed up as one would have predicted—a sexy cop, and maybe it's a complete coincidence that Parker dressed as a burglar, ski mask and everything.

Hmm, might have to try to make her fess up.

But currently, I need to keep an eye on my boyfriend who keeps muttering *asshole* under his breath. His body is locked tight and any of the guys who'd previously been shamelessly staring at me begin to avert their gazes because of protectively Cole hovers over me.

"Do you want to dance?" My attempt at distraction is not so subtle as I try tugging Cole towards the dance floor. He follows reluctantly and is still busy glaring down any guy who think it's okay to stare at my boobs for more than two seconds.

"Hey, stop." I force him to look at me. "We're here to have a good time and I'm not okay with you paying more attention to some jerks than you are to me." He turns toward me and I think it's working. The longer we're here, the more the frat boys are veering towards the sexy French maids, the sexy cops and the sexy nurses.

"Do you have any idea what those guys were saying about you?"

"Honestly? I don't care and heck, I know it's pissing you off but after all the effort I've put into this costume it's nice to know that it's being appreciated." I try joking but I don't think he's too impressed.

We're in the middle of the room and blocking people's way, so I take Cole's hand, and he lets me lead him to the dance floor. It's dark and crowded, the music is loud, and no one's interested in anything but getting lost in it.

"Dance with me, okay? We're here to have fun; relax and dance with me."

I can feel him giving in to me, feel his body go lax as he wraps his arms around my waist and hauls me to him. I place mine around his neck and press myself closer. The thin material of my dress and his T-shirt means that little to nothing separates us, and with my heels, my lips are in direct contact with his.

"Kiss me," I tell him softly, partly to get him to cool off.

But it has entirely the opposite effect.

He kisses me both harshly and softly; he kisses me with possession and love, fiercely and tenderly. He's making a statement, not just to everyone around us but to me. It's a dirty, wet kiss, and when we come up for air, there's just one statement in his eyes, clear for me to see.

You belong to me.

Because I do, and he does to me.

The lyrics are crude and blunt, the music rocks, and the beat pulsates around us. I angle my head closer and reach for his lips again, we kiss and we sway. Our hands are eager to touch and discover, and by the time the song ends, my lips feel swollen, dress askew, and I'm completely out of breath.

The best part?

Cole hasn't fared any better.

We dance to few more songs and then join a group of acquaintances, plus Cami, for a showing of *The Rocky Horror Picture Show*. I'm having fun, even taking a few pictures to send to my best friends, and I realize that even though I came here for Cole, I'm happy because of me, of what I've achieved.

It's a great feeling.

By the time we're ready to leave, I take a quick trip to the bathroom to freshen up my makeup and make sure my wig's still secured. Yup, good to go! Because, given how hot and heavy things have gotten, my face is all flushed, my eyes shine so brightly they scare me, and there's a ridiculously big smile on my face.

Things are only going to get better…

With that thought in mind, I leave to look for Cole and there he is, standing with his groupie squad. I've stopped paying attention to them, or at least I try not to let it get to me too much. But when they're all grabby with him, it tends to get on my nerves.

Right now, he's keeping them at a respectful distance, and I see how uncomfortable he is, shrugging out of their touches. That snake Allison's there as well, the one who loves reminding me what a perfect study partner Cole is and how she's made him promise to study with her for all their common classes.

I bet she switched her major just to be with him. Went from an acting major to an engineering one because, I admit, she even makes me doubt my relationship for a millisecond.

Just a millisecond.

I watch them from a distance until it becomes painful to see Cole put on the spot like that and move in to save my man.

"Ready to go home, babe?"

He looks so happy, I could cry. "Yes, please! I mean, yeah, you're probably tired, honey."

I twine my body all around him like a vine and repel the man-stealing vultures away. "Yeah, let's call it a night." I wink at him and he grins mischievously. These ladies are obviously in for a show.

"Well, I wouldn't quite say that; it's still going to be a long night."

I hear their quick intakes of breath, the dreamy sighs, see their jaws dropping.

"Again? But I'm still sore from last night."

Cue the bulging eyes.

"I'm sure you can keep up, if not, I can always do that thing I do with my hands…"

"Oh," I groan theatrically, "Yeah, that's so good. But did you remember to buy the extra-large whipped cream?"

Someone moans; I bite my lip to stop myself from laughing, and so does Cole.

"That's not the only extra-large thing I got."

Holy Shit.

I can't believe they're all still standing there listening in. But the groupie squad looks like it's about to faint; their eyes are glassy, envious, and all of them are probably coming up with a hundred and one ways to kill me.

Oh, well.

On that note, my boyfriend and I make our dramatic exit.

***

We're still laughing as we drive back to Cole's apartment. I just can't get their dazed looks out of my head.

"Shit, I think we scarred them for life," Cole says between laughs and I double over.

"That last line was a killer! You have no shame, do you?"

"Hey, you started it; I just followed your lead."

"One of them could've had a heart attack, you know; tone down the sexiness, Stone."

"I don't know if that's even a possibility, Shortcake; sexy is who I am." He waggles his eyebrows and I swat his arm.

“Eyes on the road.”

We make it back a little after one a.m., but people are still out and about on the streets, so for us it’s an early night in. Cole locks the door behind us with a click that resonates inside the entire space, making me shiver.

I turn to look at him, and that look is back in his eyes, the predatory one he had before we left for the party.

He glides toward me, in all his bad-boy glory, and grabs the nape of my neck, pulling me in for a long, deep, drugging kiss.

“Take the wig off; I want to see only you, Tessie.”

I listen and he watches me take it off, watches me release my own messy blond fall of hair, and his eyes darken. He tugs at a lock. “Missed this.”

Stepping back, he studies me; I’m still wearing the dress, but without the shield of the hair, I feel a bit intimidated, scared, like I’m a little girl playing dress up.

“God, you’re so beautiful, Tessie.”

It gets harder to breathe, and then he takes his jacket off, and I concentrate on the flexing muscles of his biceps as he throws it on the floor. I gulp looking at the heat in his eyes, but the nervousness disappears as he cups my face and kisses me. As he does this, his hands go to the back of my dress and he unzips it. Almost at once, the material pools at my feet. He sucks in a breath when he sees what I’m wearing underneath.

Crimson lace-and-satin does wonders for a girl’s confidence.

His kiss becomes more intense, his movements hurried. I grab the hem of his T-shirt and he pulls his over his head and it joins my dress on the floor. I trace my hands all over his solid chest; that eight-pack still manages to do all kinds of things to me. But before I can trace it with my hands, my tongue, Cole has scooped me up in his arms and is carrying me to the bedroom.

"Can't wait to see you in my bed, looking just like this." His voice is thick, hoarse, choked with emotion as he leads us in and places me on the bed. For a few minutes, he just stands there and watches me. Any other time, I'd feel self-conscious, shy, but he's made me feel so beautiful tonight, every night, and I can't find it in myself to be scared anymore.

My arms reach for him, and he finally, finally climbs on the bed, on top of me. He's still wearing his jeans while I'm almost naked, and the contrast is a bit jarring. When I reach for the button on his fly, he catches on, and in no time, his jeans are off and land with a thud, somewhere in the room.

He's so perfect, everywhere.

And then he kisses me, everywhere, undresses me fully. No part of my body is left untouched by his lips; he worships me with his fingers, his lips, his tongue, until I'm crying out his name and clutching the sheets.

Desperately I reach for him, hooking my arms around his shoulders.

"Please," I beg.

"I love you, love you so much, Tessie." He groans in my ear; with his free hand he reaches inside the bedside drawer and grabs a foil packet. Once that's done, there's nothing left but for us to be together, to join in the most intimate way possible.

There's a possessiveness about him tonight. He's marking me as his, and I have no problem with that because I leave marks of my own all across his back.

He loves those.

Between rounds of rigorous kissing, he tells me he loves me, tells me how much I mean to him and that he'll never hurt me, never leave, and that I'm his world.

I tell it to him right back.

And we hold each other, all night long.

CHAPTER EIGHTEEN
Caffeine Is My Natural Habitat

I stumble across my room in a desperate attempt to get dressed in time, but I know nothing short of me walking out the door in my sleep shorts and tank top with unbrushed teeth will make that happen. So, I mentally accept that I'm going to be late, but make an effort to be as little late as possible, and if that entails shoving both my legs in my yoga pants at the same time, then so be it.

I grab the first warm item of clothing I see and pull it over my head. Immediately, I'm surrounded by Cole's warm scent, and I know I've put on one of his sweatshirts that almost drowns me, but it's comfortable and snuggly, and I don't have time to wear anything else.

I get done in the bathroom and wrestle together my textbooks for the day and my laptop. Throwing those in my tote bag, I lug myself all the way to campus half sprinting, half dragging.

I'm still over ten minutes late because I slept in way past my alarm.

And whose fault would that be?

Cole had an away game yesterday and arrive back to his apartment late last night. We talked on the phone for over two hours and I fell asleep sometime around three a.m., not the greatest move on my part, since I have an eight a.m. class. Everyone knows how nuclear I can be without sleep, so I do fear for the general well-being of the people around me.

I make it to class just as Professor Gingham is getting around to starting the lecture after setting up his mandatory slides. He gives me a curt look as I pass him by but doesn't say anything as I scurry to my seat in the middle row. This is the first and only time I've been late for class, so he's giving me a free pass; all hail being a Goody Two-shoes.

If only my luck were to continue. As I'm passing the aisle to get to my seat, a foot shoots out of nowhere, and the next thing I know, my knees are buckling and I've face-planted onto the floor, my butt sticking out for all the world to see. My laptop crashes to the floor loudly as my books land with a loud thump; my tote cushions my face from the impact of the ground. For some unexplainable reason, it takes me a while to actually register that I'm on the ground and that I should probably stand up. But when I do try to stand, the devil's foot manages to trip me again, and this time I hit pretty hard on one of the ridges that make up the stairs of the auditorium. My cheeks are fire-engine red with humiliation as I try to collect myself.

The snickering starts slowly, mostly from the side of the room that has witnessed my fall, and spreads slowly around the auditorium as the rest catch up.

"Miss O'Connell, kindly take your seat; you've already disturbed my class once, I'd appreciate it if you wouldn't for the second time."

My face feels like it's on fire as I sidle over to my seat. The girl who sits next to me and occasionally borrows my notes gives me a sympathetic look. "You realize this is going to be all over Facebook by the end of the class, right?"

My mouth hangs open. "They were taking pictures?"

She nods solemnly.

"Wait, did you see who tripped me?" I ask in a hushed whisper. Because even though I know I'm clumsier than I can afford to be, even I would've seen that high-heeled, boot-clad foot appear out of thin air.

"Well…" she hesitates and I see her gaze travel down to the aisle where I had the mighty fall. "I'm pretty sure it was one of them; Allison Vega and her friends sit there."

Ah, so she strikes back. I know that my little stunt at the Halloween party with Cole wouldn't go without consequences. These girls sure as heck know more about playing the game than I do, and they're pretty good at it. And now I'm left wondering if I've bitten off more than I can chew by poking the vultures in the eye.

***

Any suspicion I have over who tripped me vanishes when class ends and we leave. I'm walking away when the wicked witch of Providence calls out to me.

"Nice underwear, Tessa. How many grannies did you have to

beat off to get to them?"

Her comment doesn't get to me for a lot of reasons, mostly because I know my underwear wasn't visible for the world to see. But more so because my decision to wear comfortable clothing is just oh so embarrassing to people like her, not me. That ship sailed when I tried wearing thongs for a couple of days straight and waddled around like a penguin. I'm not questioning my choices ever again.

I spin around to face her, and the smug expression on her face infuriates me.

"Should I be concerned about the fact that you paid enough attention to my underwear in the thirty seconds I was on the floor to tell what type it is? Are you generally that observant, or am I special?"

To my utter delight, her face turns pink, as if the prospect of liking a girl is that heinous to her. Great, on top of being a vindictive bitch, she's also a homophobe. Such a pretty girl, such an ugly inside.

"Don't flatter yourself; you're not my type. Your boyfriend, on the other hand…"

She lets her words hang in the air, and it takes every ounce of willpower I have not to claw her face out. The most basic instinct I have is to remove that smirk from her face with my bare hands.

"Oh, that's right, you have a massive crush on him, right? It's got to hurt that he can't even stand you enough to be your partner next semester. Besides, I don't think shallow, petty, and immature are his type."

Not in the mood to hear more of the wonderful words that might come out of her mouth, I walk off feeling all kinds of mad. I'd left this world behind and have experienced more bullying than anyone would be okay with. The thing about college, I'd thought it would be that people were grown up and would have moved past all the high school mindset and antics. I'm shivering, and it's not because of the cold.

Not again, please, god, just not again.

I storm toward my dorm; my next class isn't until the afternoon, so I'll either take a nap to try to get rid of the anger, or I'll hit the gym, go chat with Bentley and hope that it's not because I'm mad at Cole.

Because it's not really his fault that the girls who crush on him seem to take out all their frustrations on me.

Right?

Sarah's about to leave for her own block of classes when I enter, and she immediately picks up on the dark expression on my face. She slides off the strap of her backpack and lets it fall to her bed.

"Uh-oh. Did your professor get mad about you being late?"

"No, I just had a major déjà vu moment in class." I walk past her and collapse onto my bed.

I know she's standing at the foot of it waiting for me to continue.

"One of the groupies thought it would be fun to make me face-plant for the world to see. That's not the problem, I can deal with girls like her, I just didn't think I would have to."

"I'm sorry, Tessa…but wait, what do you mean you're used to it?"

I sigh, not really in the mood for a retelling of my sob story. “I don’t feel like talking about it now. You should head to class; I think you’ve got about five minutes to make it.”

The poor girl has a true struggle in front of her, to try to make sure her crazy roommate doesn't slit her wrists, or be late to class. She wouldn't be Sarah, though, if she didn’t pick the latter, and even though I can feel her disappointment at my not having opened up to her, I just close my eyes and try to go to sleep as she leaves.

***

I do actually end up falling asleep and feel considerably better once I’m up. The Allison incident isn’t a big deal, and it’s not why I had the reaction I did. I’m just tired of the stupid game and have played it long enough to never want to ever again. But the groupies aren’t going away and some will get vicious; I just need to keep fighting.

I totter around the room for a bit and finally change into acceptable clothing. I put on some light makeup and decide to head to the campus coffee shop. My phone tells me that I’ve missed some texts from Cami, who wants to hang out, so I text her and let her know where I’ll be.

There’s also a text from Cole, but I ignore it for the time being. He texts me every morning, whenever he wakes up, and it’s usually something like an “I love you” or “Good morning, have a great day, Shortcake.” I’m not going to lie; his texts do make my mornings, but I don’t get around to reading it today.

I find myself an isolated table and after getting myself a croissant and a hazelnut latte, set up my laptop and begin working on my essay. And under no circumstances do I allow myself to check Facebook, nope, not at all.

"Have you checked Facebook?"

Apparently, Cami has different ideas.

She takes the seat across from mine and shoves her phone into my face. Sure enough, there's a photo of me with my butt in the air and my sweatshirt wedged up quite painfully. I scrunch my nose in disgust and push her phone away.

"I already experienced that once; do not need a reminder."

"But why didn't you tell me about this? Who did it? Did you fall, or did someone think it was funny to mess with my new bestie?"

I smile at how angry she sounds on my behalf. She reminds me of Beth sometimes, but then again, she's not like Beth at all.

Weird.

"It was just an immature prank by one of the groupies, nothing I can't handle."

"Oh, from what I heard, you handled it really well. There's a video going around of your little spat, and I have to say you completely verbal bitch-slapped her."

I groan. "How do people even record these things so fast and make them spread out?"

"Through the student group on Facebook, duh. There's a reason why I've been asking you to join it."

"I'd rather not."

"But…"

"Hey, Tessie." My eyes widen in panic as Cole sits down next to me and kisses my cheek. I try having a silent conversation with Cami, making sure she knows that Cole doesn't need an update on how wonderful my morning has been. She looks at me a little weirdly but pockets her phone.

"Uh, hey. How'd you find me here?"

He looks at me a little weirdly before giving me an uneasy smile.

"Well, I texted you a couple of times, but you didn't answer. Then I went around to your room and you weren't there, either, so I thought I'd check this place out since…"

"Caffeine is my natural habitat?"

He laughs, a relieved expression evident on his face now that I've broken that awkward tension between us. "Something like that."

"Sorry I didn't answer your texts, though, I was just caught up in finishing the essay."

He nods and kisses the top of my head before leaving us to go place his order.

Cami has watched the entire exchange and, as soon as he's out of earshot, hisses at me, "He doesn't know? His fangirls are plotting to send you to an early grave, or at least as far as Timbuktu, and you're not telling him?"

"Be quiet! It's not his fault, okay? And he's already trying really hard to make sure football doesn't ruin our relationship. He offered to quit the team for me, if I tell him about Allison or the rest of them, he'll try to do something just as drastic."

"He'll find out one way or the other, Tessa; cyberspace doesn't work as slowly as you're guessing it does."

"Well, lucky for me, Cole hates social media. He doesn't have accounts on half of the things, and it's lucky if he checks his Facebook about twice a month. I'm not worried about him seeing me with my butt in the air and wedgie to go with it." I'm hoping she misses the bitterness lacing my voice.

She settles back in her chair and stares at me. "Wait, do you blame him?"

I shake my head a bit too forcefully, and the all-seeing thing that is Cami catches it quickly. "Oh My God, you do, don't you? You think this is all happening because of him?"

"No, of course I don't! He's not responsible for what the groupies do any more than I am for Jay's stupidity," I continue without stopping to tell Cami who Jay actually is, which clearly means that the explanation is more for my benefit than hers. "It's just that…at times it feels like Cole and trouble come as a package deal."

Now that the words are out there and I can't take them back, I think over them really hard and try to figure out if I really, truly mean them.

But Cole comes back then with his own coffee and a sandwich and sits down as close to me as possible, his thigh pressing against mine as he places his hand on my knee.

"What were you guys talking about? It looked pretty serious from back there."

So, I do what I'd promised myself to never do again; I lie to him.

***

"You okay?"

Cole and I are walking back to my dorm after our last class together. He has practice right after, so he offered to walk me back, and then he'll be gone till late, and I'll probably see him sometime tomorrow evening as I have a study group taking up most of my day. After having coffee with Cami, Cole and I sat through two classes, and I'm glad that he missed a lot of the looks thrown our way or rather, my way. I'm also glad that no one had the balls to come right up to him and tell him about his girlfriend's rather embarrassing moment being advertised for the world to see.

I want to tell him, but I know how he'll react, his protective instincts will take over, and even though I know he would never hit a girl, chances are he'll get himself into trouble. Allison what's-her-face isn't worth his time or mine.

"Yeah, of course," I tell him.

"You've been really quiet today, Tessie. If something's wrong, tell me."

I stop walking and tug on his hand to do so as well. I cup his face in my hands and kiss him. "I'm fine, I swear, just a little tired."

He looks really guilty. "I shouldn't have kept you up, god, I'm such an asshole. You had a class this morning and I didn't even think about it."

I let him beat himself up for a few minutes because it's better he think that was the reason why I've been in such a weird mood all day.

"Let's just try restricting ourselves to an hour next time you decide to call in the middle of the night, okay?"

He pulls me to him and buries his face in the crook of my neck.

"I missed you in my bed, Shortcake, especially after the Halloween weekend…"

My face heats up at the memories; let's just say dressing up as Jessica Rabbit was the absolute best decision.

Shivering from his touch, I pull back. "We don't have time to talk dirty, mister, you have practice, and I have lots of assigned reading to get to."

He sighs dramatically and we continue walking to my dorm. Once inside, I'm instantly on alert when a couple of girls spot me first, before seeing Cole, and start laughing a bit too loudly. I ignore them and push the button for the elevator that'll take me to my floor. Cole frowns at the giggling pair.

"Something funny?"

I make a huge deal of rolling my eyes. "I think that's an automatic reaction to you being around. Women all over the world tend to become reduced to overenthusiastic toddlers."

He doesn't buy it and looks toward the girls again, but our elevator arrives before he can ask them why they're still laughing, and I pull him inside. I push a couple of buttons so that it buys us some time alone and I can try to distract him.

"Who keeps texting you?" His phone's been going crazy for a while, and I'm half afraid that it's someone forwarding him the photos and video from earlier.

He grimaces like he's tasted something foul and shoots me an apologetic look.

"It's Allison."

Wait, what?

I try not to throw a full-blown tantrum. He doesn't know, he doesn't know, I chant in my head.

"Why? I thought she wasn't working with you anymore?"

"Well, yeah, in the psych class, but somehow we got partnered up in our 100-level engineering class and the TA's refusing to change the pairings."

My jaw might just become unhinged from how far I've let it drop.

That manipulative, psychotic, little she-demon!

"Oh." I've curled my hands into fists and I'm ready to pound them into the walls when we arrive on my floor.

Cole walks behind me a little cautiously as I use my key to let us inside the room; thankfully, Sarah isn't back to witness yet another thing in my life going wrong.

"There's nothing to be worried about, Tessie; you know I don't like her."

But she's freaking obsessed with you! Just like Nicole was, just like Erica was, I want to scream at him.

"I know, and I trust you; I just really don't like that girl."

"Well, I'll try getting done with our project as soon as possible and submitting it before the end of the semester, okay? I don't want to work with her for that long."

He tips my chin up to meet his eyes. "If something was wrong, you'd tell me, right?"

I nod and he carefully studies my face.

"I love you, Shortcake."

"Love you, too, Cole."

He kisses me soundly before he leaves, and after he does, I collapse onto my bed and find that my eyes are stinging. I throw my arm over my eyes and scream into my sleeves. I hate overreacting; I hate being this weak. If I need to fight to keep Cole, then I will.

The problem is that I shouldn't have to. He's mine now, my boyfriend, and sometimes even the word boyfriend doesn't seem like it's enough. I'm secure enough in our relationship to know that we're in a good place, but if I'm still left battling every woman who thinks she could be better for him than I am, then what's the point of this security?

CHAPTER NINETEEN
Just Around the Time You Stole My Virtue

"Your boyfriend's dad is the sheriff; I'm thinking I'll get be able to get away with murder."

"I don't think Providence falls under his jurisdiction, Beth, but I appreciate the sentiment." Balancing my cellphone between my ear and shoulder, I shove a bunch of books and notebooks into my backpack. My watch tells me that it's six thirty in the morning, which means that I'll get a solid block of time in the library if I get there now. Finding an available desk, on the other hand, is a power struggle on its own; maybe I'll ask someone nicely or bribe them with my stash of Kit Kats.

Yes, that's how badly I need a damn desk this time.

"Listen, if they keep their shit up, you need to tell Cole. This isn't fair on you, and he needs to tell those skanks to back off."

"I don't need his help, and the skanks are the least of my worries." I slip on my faux-fur-lined boots and wind a scarf around my neck. I am in standard midterm garb, sweatshirt, warm leggings, and a warmer coat on top. All the layers make me wobble around like a penguin, but I force myself out the door.

"Oh yeah, how goes the Ivy League academic hell, god, I don't miss that shit at all."

I snort and walk quickly down the abandoned halls. It's a ghost town around here, and the thought worries me. I've never been Megan smart but I manage; I'm here, aren't I? But every person in this school is smart, and it makes you rethink whether you should be here in the first place.

I don't have time to be all mopey and depressed about this, though; I've got three finals in the space of a day and a half and not enough prep done to ensure that I pass.

"It's hell, all right. But I've got about a week to make sure I don't flunk my freshman midterms, so that's a good thing. Maybe I'll come visit you guys this weekend, get in the zone."

"Yeah, you should; we'll research voodoo dolls."

"You're taking this more seriously than I am."

"Because you're not going to do anything about it. I get that you're all big and brave now after facing Nicole, but these girls target something completely different, and you're letting them get to you."

"I'm not; I just don't want to play their stupid games. We're in college, for crying out loud."

The campus is quiet as I trudge through it, given that it's early or very late, depending on how you see it, people are still asleep. But those are the ones who didn't have to work very hard to get into the school in the first place; they can afford sleep. I know I'm right when I walk in and find more than half of the individual study desks taken. I hide from the librarian and stay on the phone with Beth as I stash my books on my first-choice table. Then I leave to go to the on-campus cafe and get myself a much-needed large coffee.

"Why are you this early in the first place?" I ask her as I stand in line for my coffee.

She yawns. "I had a late shift at the restaurant so I haven't actually been to bed yet, drank way too much coffee, and I can't go to sleep now."

Knowing my brother shares the same genes as me, I can confidently say, "And Travis is out like there's no tomorrow, right?"

"Well, in his defense, he was a very good boyfriend who stayed up for me half the night, so I'm letting him hibernate."

It makes me laugh; I'm glad he's being taken care of. "We're coming down for Thanksgiving next week, remember, can't wait to catch up with you guys." There's a note of wistfulness to my voice that Beth doesn't miss.

"You're supposed to be having the time of your life, Tess, don't let those miserable bitches get you down. You've got the guy; he's not going anywhere. Own it and throw it in their faces."

"So, you'd suggest the aggressive approach as opposed to my passive-aggressive one that I've perfected so well?"

"Do I look like I even know what passive means?"

"Good Point."

We end the call, and I get myself a large cappuccino and a bagel, which I stuff my face with before going into the library. I knock out a few good hours there, knowing that my intro-level history course would be a pain in the butt regardless of how hard I try, but this way at least the butt-kicking will be less painful. Next, I study my economics and statistics notes and wonder why I don't have Cole studying with me right now. He's good at this stuff; any math-related thing and he's great at it. The thought makes me reach for my phone. It's about ten a.m. now, so he's already been up for a couple of hours. I start to text him when I think the better of it and shoot Megan an e-mail instead. We have study session over Skype often, where basically she teaches me things that I would've known had I taken the same AP classes as she did. Because she's already taken so many college-level courses in high school, the girl's acing her way through college.

I study as much as I can and cram as much information as my brain can handle. I leave my Introductory English Lit prep till the end because that's something I know I can do well without wanting to tear my hair out.

I leave the library after six hours with a rumbling stomach. When I pull out my phone to check my e-mails, I notice that I've missed a few texts, and one's from Cole.

Cole: Breakfast?

Cole: I'll bring those chocolate hazelnut French toast things you like so much

Cole: Shortcake…

Cole: Seriously I'm getting worried now, where are you? You're not in the dorms.

I call him immediately and he picks up, a little out of breath.

"Where've you been? I've spent the entire morning trying to reach you."

I hear someone giggle in the background and ignore it; there's always someone giggling in the background.

"I was in the library; I thought I told you I'd be there this morning."

Shivering in the cold, I walk faster to my dorm. I plan to nap for an hour or so and then go back to studying. Cole won't be pleased.

"Well, you didn't; Jesus, Shortcake, you gave me a heart attack."

My insides warm at the concern in his voice. "Where are you right now? I could eat—"

"Hold on a second."

I hear him talking to someone, a someone with a high-pitched, girly voice that makes me grit my teeth. The classes where he has to partner up with someone for a project usually ends with the partner being a girl. I'm not a complete psycho, I know that not every woman is out to get him, but some just make it so obvious. When he comes back on the phone, he sighs, "I'll catch you in the after, babe, apparently the prison warden won't even allow food breaks." I hear the high-pitched voice yell something and it makes me happy; suck it, Yolanda, he doesn't want to be with you.

"Okay, well, I'm going to take a nap. Maybe we can study together later?"

He sounds affronted that I said that. "Why are you even asking?

You and I both know you'll fail your stats class without me."

"Because of course you're the only person in the world who's capable of teaching me."

"Maybe not, but I do have the best incentives. Get a question right and you'll get…"

My cheeks heat up, which is a miracle and a blessing, considering the weather. "Do not finish that sentence in front of other people!"

He chuckles. "I was going to say gummy bears, the red ones, too. What's so wrong about that?"

I roll my eyes and I know he can visualize my reaction. "Of course you were, and you know what I'll hold you onto that. Just the gummy bears, Stone."

He makes an outraged sound on the other side like I've seriously offended him. "Don't mess with my tutoring mojo, Shortcake. My methods are very effective."

I'm about to respond when his partner calls out again and Cole sighs defeatedly, "Yeah, I got to go. The sooner I go, the sooner we finish this." He says the last part louder than necessary and I laugh; the poor girl's going to have to deal with a grumpy Cole.

***

I wake up to soft lips trailing down my neck and strong arms wrapped tightly around my waist.

"Go back to sleep, Tessie, I just want to hold you for a bit."

I sigh contentedly and close my eyes, sinking into my happy place.

***

We're at Cafe Rock, the on-campus café, again, and pretending to study. Well, I do have my books out and ready to learn, but Cole's distracted. He's making funny faces and trying to kiss while I want to shove my $200 textbook down his throat. It's not helping that Cami's with us and being highly amused by my boyfriend's antics.

"You know what we should do?" She thumps her fist on the table like she's had the best idea ever.

"We should go out, go drinking and clubbing, and get a hangover so bad, we could die from it."

"Well, that sounds particularly pleasant, but no?"

Leaving campus before and during finals? That's crazy talk!

"Oh, but you'll be able to focus on studying so much better once you get the fun out of your system. You won't be sitting in some abandoned corner of the quad forcing all this gunk into your brain!" She slams her fist down again.

"I take it you want to go out?" Cole raises an eyebrow and stretches his arm over my shoulders.

"Yes! For the love of god, yes, take me out of here."

"No, absolutely no! We're not leaving; I have so much work to do and—"

"Shortcake," he cuts me off with a kiss, "I think we could both use a night out, unwind a little. Afterward, I'll teach you everything you need to know, without the distracting incentives."

"You're bribing me with tutoring me by not tutoring me?"

"If you put it like that…"

"Come on, Tessa," Cami whines, "Don't you want to just get off campus and get away from those—"

I stop her midsentence, but it's too late. Cole looks at us suspiciously. "Get away from whom?"

I discreetly elbow Cami and wave my hand dismissively. "Those massive, massive piles of books."

He doesn't seem convinced. "I'll find out eventually."

"There's nothing to find out."

"That's what you want me to think, don't you?"

"I don't know what you think I want you to think."

"Well, I think I know what you know what I think you want me to think."

"Wait, okay, hold up, guys. I can't keep up with this conversation, and I won't be able to tweet about it!"

Cole and I stop our staring contest to look at Cami, who doesn't look up from her phone.

"You tweet about us?"

"At least three times a day. Your fans want to know where your relationship's at."

"We have fans?"

"Of course you do. You guys were voted freshman couple of the semester like last week on the student group page. I made an acceptance speech on your behalf, no worries."

"You scare us." Cole moves closer to me.

"Don't be! I make a fantastic fangirl."

I turn to my boyfriend. "I'll go out, on one condition. Just make sure to get me really, really drunk, okay?"

***

I slam the martini glass on the counter and signal the bartender for one more. Next to me, Cami wolf whistles and swallows her own shot. We're giggling uncontrollably about nothing at all, and it's the best thing ever. Cole keeps us in his line of sight as he talks to one of his friends. His teammate Parker decided to join us, and he can't take his eyes off Cami.

"Why don't you give the poor guy a chance?" I ask her once we have our drinks and stop laughing.

Her cheeks turn red. "Parker? He's not…we're not…"

"Come on, give it up. You guys like each other; why don't you go out?"

"Because, Tessa," she sighs heavily and looks longingly toward Parker, "honestly, I wouldn't be able to put up with the kind of cattiness that comes from all their groupies without killing someone."

A twinge of hurt is amplified by the alcohol and rises to the surface. I glance at Cole and then at the empty glass in my hand.

"You learn to deal with it and move on with your life."

"Look, I support your relationship more than I probably should, but doesn't it drive you insane? To get that amount of negative attention?"

"He's worth it. I mean it's not like I never questioned it, especially this past week, but I like looking at the bigger picture."

"And what a damn fine picture it is."

Cole walks toward us with a predatory gleam in his eyes; he

grabs my hand and begins walking me toward the dance floor.

"Did I mention how much I love this dress?"

It's short, tight, black, and lace—there wasn't a shot in hell he'd dislike it.

I wrap my arms around his neck. "Just a couple of times."

We dance for a while, him holding me close. I try to forget about my mental to-do list and the crappy run-ins with Allison and her group of Barbie thugs. They do petty things, say things that they think will make me feel insecure, but I've thought long and hard about it and decided that I don't give a flying fudge about them.

One of Cole's friends pulls him away again, and I spend some time alone on the floor. The dance team at college is great, and the more I see them perform, the more I want to be brave enough to join. No one knows the old me here; Fatty Tessie never existed for them, so they won't see her and laugh at me when I audition. I've thought about it a lot; maybe if I join a club, I won't feel like such an outsider. While I'm having these motivational thoughts, I start hearing the voices.

"Hey! That's the girl from the flyers, isn't she?"

"Oh yeah, that blonde. Damn, she looks hotter in person."

I ignore them at first, but that's until one of them gets too close for comfort, and the hair at the back of my neck stands up.

"You want to test her out and see if she lives up to her promise?"

Their voices get louder and my heart begins to race. It's very possible that they aren't talking about me; it's plausible.

But then I feel someone place a hand on my butt and then

proceed to grope it roughly. That's all it takes for me to scream loud enough to be heard above the music. I've been in this position before; I've had unwanted hands on me. I still have nightmares about what happened in the bathroom with Hank at the start of my senior year of high school. I know what it feels like to have someone touch you without your consent, the revulsion that creeps into you. The sense of violation and of utter humiliation.

"Hey, baby girl, don't scream just yet. The ad said you'd show me a good time for one hundred dollars; I'll pay. Why don't we go somewhere private?"

I raise my elbow and hit him in the nose. He drops his hands from me and stumbles away, but then his buddy walks toward me swaying a little. I walk backward, the ravenous look on his face scaring the heck out of me. I look toward the bar area but the crowd is thick, so thick that that people aren't even noticing what's happening. I shake my head, this is surreal and stupid.

What's going on?

"You have the wrong girl. I don't know what you're talking about!"

"It was definitely you on the flyer." He leers at my chest and I start to shake.

I can defend myself, I'm not as helpless as I used to be, but…

"Tessie? Where the hell is she?" I hear him shout, and a few seconds later, he's tearing through the crowd with a furious look on his face. He sees the guys cornering me and nearly roars at them.

"What the fuck do you think you're doing?"

These guys aren't any match for Cole; he towers over them and has more muscle. One look at him and they're scurrying away. But Cole's expression doesn't lighten; he grabs my arm and pulls me toward the private room. The man in charge of security gives him a brief nod and lets us pass.

We enter a more private, softly lighted space with a huge beige sofa and thick carpeting. I wanted to sink into the carpet and disappear when Cole points his phone and, lo and behold, I see my face staring back at me, but very cleverly Photoshopped onto the body of a scantily clad, very curvy woman who's only covered by a tiny scrap of cloth over her lady parts.

"Who the hell did this?" he yells into my face, his face turning red.

"I…" I struggle to make a sound, "I don't know—"

"Bullshit! Tell me the truth."

He's making me angry with all the yelling. It's not my fault! If anything, it's his.

"Why don't you go ask the same thing from your study buddies? I'm sure they'll know exactly who did."

I try to shove past him and leave, but he grabs my wrists and pulls me into his chest.

"What do you mean? You think one of the girls did this?"

"Not just one, all of them, you idiot. I'm like a walking target for them and, stupidly enough, I've let them do things like this to me. I didn't want you to find out…I didn't want you to think that you had to start protecting poor old Tessie again."

His chest heaves at my back; he's furious, but I can't help but push his buttons.

"You should've told me."

"I was handling it."

"This? This is how you were handling it? Some guy just walks up to me and shows me a picture of my girl's face on some stripper's body? Asks me if it's true that you're really into…"

His body begins to tremble. "I'm going to kill them."

I begin struggling in his arms and he lets me go. Turning to him, I cup his cheek and pull his face to mine.

"Stop trying to be my hero, Cole; just be my boyfriend. I don't care about their immature pranks."

"This wasn't some stupid prank, Tessie; this was a shitty thing to do to a person. They crossed all kinds of lines here."

"And I'll talk to them about it; maybe you should come with me and give them something to look at while I threaten their academic careers."

His face breaks out in a tentative smile. "I'm still okay with mass murder but, damn, when did you get so grown up?"

"Just around the time you stole my virtue," I say pointedly and he laughs, pulling me under his chin.

"I know this is all my fault; I'm so sorry, baby."

"Yeah, I really wish you'd been uglier and a recluse, so completely your fault."

"Don't be cute."

"I'm always cute."

"Why can't you just throw a freaking hair dryer at me like a normal woman?"

"Nah, if I were to throw any electrical appliance at you, I'd go for my KitchenAid."

His heartbeat slows down just a little; he's distracted now. Mission accomplished.

CHAPTER TWENTY

It's Still Too Soon for Me to Be Thinking About Fat Suits

It's the kind of dream where you know you're dreaming, but that doesn't make the nightmare any better. I'm at the club; I'm back in the bathroom. I'm restrained, helpless and weak. I'm crying out; someone's hands are all over my body. I'm shaking, it's so cold. I need to run but I'm scared, there's a menacing face in the dark. I feel filthy, violated. He needs to stop touching me!

"Stop!" I cry out. I'm struggling in the dark. I reach for his face, gnaw at it. Arms go around me, pulling me back into a strong chest.

"Shh, wake up, Tessie. It's okay. I'm here; I've got you."

I know that voice; I know it's him holding me now and not any of them. I don't open my eyes, though; I know they're stinging, and if he sees me crying…

"Tessie?"

I fall deeper into his chest. "I'm okay." I sniff and I feel his arms tremble around me.

"You sure you don't…"

"I'd just like to sleep, please; it was a dream, nothing else."

I can feel his frustration but he doesn't fight me on it and wraps his arms protectively around me.

***

"Would you like me to wear one of those fat suits wrestlers wear?"

Before Cole gets the opportunity to reply, I think over my words a little. "Wait, forget I said that. It's still too soon for me to be thinking about fat suits."

His features contort into a scowl. "Do we need to have another talk about self-esteem? Because if I have to tie you to a chair and tell you how much I like big butts and I cannot lie, then…"

"My butt is not big!" Still, I twist my body to look at it, grateful that all the exercise has reduced its size significantly. "It used to be, but not anymore."

"And I like it in both sizes." He shrugs before throwing his sweatshirt at me. "Wear it, I think Eric has some friends coming over."

I glance down at my shirt and it's perfectly fine. Yes, it's a little tight, but Cami said that the red-colored jersey material made me glow. But that was only after I hit her with the bottle of fake tan she'd brought over. The day I decide to coat myself in orange goo is the day I become an honorary Kardashian.

I hold the soft fabric in my hand, tempted to bring it up to my nose and sniff Cole's delicious scent, but instead I glare at him.

"Are you telling me what to wear?"

"Shortcake, if it were up to me, you'd be wearing as little clothing as possible, not more of it. I just…these guys can be real meatheads, and you're wearing that…" He gestures to my shirt like it's offended him. "And I won't be responsible for my actions."

"I know what you're doing, mister, you're trying to change the topic, aren't you?"

He scratches the back of his neck. "What topic would that be?" He spins on his feet and heads back into his room. I follow quickly, determined to get to the root of his recent behavior.

"You've been acting like you're my bodyguard, not my boyfriend. Care to explain?"

Shrugging, he begins tossing a bunch of clothes in a duffel bag. I know he's trying to play cool, and that ever since he found out about his fangirls bullying me, especially the incident at the club, he's been going out of his way to protect me. Add to that my recurring nightmares, and he's willing to build a fort around me with skank-incinerating laser beams. He's outright refused to work with Allison and her cronies and has a permanent threatening look to his face, so no one's brought up the ad again. I shiver as I remember how violently angry he'd been when we returned from the club. After having dropped Cami off at the dorms, I stayed with him at the apartment just to make sure he didn't do anything stupid.

And while he's managed to keep his temper in check, he's also been treating me like I'm made of glass. More than anything, his guilt has created this huge barrier between us where he's hesitant to talk to me, and it's killing me. That's why I didn't want to tell him about what'd been happening; of course he's linking it to how Nicole bullied me because of Jay.

This is nothing like Nicole, and I've told him that repeatedly; if only he didn't have PBS, Protective Boyfriend Syndrome.

"Cole, please talk to me."

"Do you have everything you need? We're going to be stuck in traffic if we don't leave now."

He pushes past me and rummages through his drawers that I know for a fact have nothing but the extra pair of socks I bought for him.

"You have to know it's not your fault."

He drops down to his knees, and I see his knuckles strain, he's holding the edges of the open drawer so tightly.

"I'll bring our bags to the car; you should make some coffee to go."

I sigh, realizing that he'll push just as hard as I do. I'm not willing to fight with him, not when we're going home for Thanksgiving and getting the opportunity to be with our friends and families after quite a long while. Maybe he'll be more open to discussion during the two-hour journey; I can be very persuasive when I want to.

***

"Would you please stop playing that?"

"Would you please talk to me?"

"I am talking to you!" he cries before changing the track; too bad for him I've made a special playlist for this trip and it's one specifically designed to coerce him into not shutting me out anymore.

Taylor Swift's voice croons in the background and I'm reminded of the good old days, back when my favorite thing to do was to annoy the crap out of him.

"Look," he says gripping the steering wheel tightly, "my car, my music, and I'm begging you to stop playing that song. I can't take it anymore."

"Wait, did you mean this one?"

It's one of her older ones, back when she was a country music sensation.

There are few things in life Cole hates more than country music. Me singing alongside said music would be one of them.

"Okay, okay, stop! I'll talk; just make that thing stop."

I grin and quickly pause the music. Curling up in my seat, I look at either side of us. Because a lot of people are heading home for the four-day weekend and because we didn't leave in a timely manner, we're, as Cole predicted, stuck in traffic. Since he's not so fond of my taste in music, I may as well pass the time by making him fess up.

"You're angry," I tell him, "you're angry at yourself, and you're taking it out on us. You haven't been the same since that night."

"Oh, you mean the night when my girlfriend was nearly assaulted by a pair of assholes and who has been targeted and bullied because she's dating me? Jesus, why would I be angry?"

His jaw ticks and his body screams pent-up frustration. I wonder what he'd do to the guys from the other night if they were to come in front of him now.

"You need to remember that I've failed you once, Tessie; what good am I if I can't even protect you?"

There's a solemn silence between us as we remember Hank. I know we're both remembering different things; I picture being trapped in that bathroom and having a stranger's unwanted hands touch me all over, and he's remembering the aftermath.

"You went to jail for me," I say softly, "you fought for me; there's nothing else I'd ever ask or expect from you."

He sighs. "You shouldn't have to ask for anything; I should know and fix it…I'm fucking this up."

Anger starts to boil inside me. "What do you take me for, Stone? I'm not some damsel in distress, not anymore. You've always told me that I'm stronger than I'd ever considered myself to be. Then why don't you stop blaming yourself for not saving me from…I don't know, life!"

His lips curl into a smile and then eventually he grins. "If only you knew it's the other way around."

"What is?" I'm confused; the mood swings in this car are giving me whiplash.

"Who gets saved and who does the saving, yeah, you've got it all wrong."

I bite my lip and hide a smile of my own; this time I know he's not attempting to change the subject or charm his way into avoiding talking about the real thing. The fact that he actually believes the absurd thing that I saved him is written all over his face, and it makes me warm all over. I reach across the seat and kiss him quickly.

"Don't pull away from me; don't let them win."

***

Cole and I hold hands as we walk into his house. We dropped off my things at my house, which was empty since my dad's not supposed to back in town till tonight. Travis and Beth don't know that we ditched our Wednesday classes and are here a day earlier than planned, and I want to surprise them later. Megan and Alex don't get here till tomorrow evening, so it only made sense for me to agree when Cole asked me to have an early dinner with Cassandra and Sheriff Stone. Usually we don't spend a lot of time at his house, only because there's still a weird tension that exists between him and Jay.

Thinking about Jay, my former naive crush and current somewhat friend, makes me want to smack myself a good couple of times. If I'd confronted my feelings for Cole earlier and realized that Jay was never someone who deserved the amount of time I'd spent pining over him, then the two stepbrothers wouldn't have such a strain between them. I'm sure it doesn't make things any easier for the family.

As soon as we walk through the door and Cole drops his duffel on the ground, we hear a voice from the kitchen.

"Cole, that you?"

"Yeah, Mom! Unless you were waiting for the lesser child to show up!" he yells back, and I playfully glare at him. The holidays would go so much better were everyone not to make fun of poor Jay.

"Ah, Cole Grayson, you're livening up the place already."

"Someone has to; I'd rather it be the good-looking Stone."

Cassandra walks out from the kitchen looking a little flushed, an apron tied behind her back. Her face lights up when she sees the two of us, and I'm quickly engulfed in a hug. I hug her back tightly. "Hey, sweetheart, we've missed you around here."

The smell of Chanel No. 5 wafts up my nose, and she gives me a good, long hug. Cassandra has pretty much become a stand-in mom for me, ever since mine left in search of greener pastures and a richer husband. I still talk to my mom, but she hasn't really been a mother since before I started high school. Besides, this new mom is a neurosurgeon; how kick-ass is that?

"I've missed you, too; there's only so much of him I can stand." I shove Cole's side with my elbow.

"My baby boy," Cassandra coos as she plants a massive kiss on Cole's cheek, which he begins rubbing vigorously. "You've grown so much."

"Really? Are you really going to do this?"

"Are you really going to take away my one true chance to embarrass you in front of your girlfriend?"

"Yes, Mom, I am. We'll be in my room if you need anything."

"You won't even stay to taste the new recipe I'm testing?"

"If you can handle cutting open someone's head, I'm sure you can handle pastry."

"But it's a new filling," she singsongs as she begins retreating to the kitchen. "Someone might have told me that a person here has a slight Nutella addiction."

My mouth drops open, and in my enthusiasm for all things that include the chocolate-hazelnut goodness, I smack Cole's arm a little too harshly.

"No way."

Cassandra looks smug. "Now who'd you prefer to spend time with, the mother who offers you chocolate or the boyfriend who probably has a month's worth of laundry to catch up on?"

Cole shoots his duffel bag a dirty look. "Damn it."

"I suggest you better get started now before Jason shows up. I fear he'll be even worse than you." Cassandra shudders at the thought.

"She's got a point." I smile at him. "You may as well get started; I've got a pie to test out."

He shakes his head. "Who knew that damn plastic jar would be such a cock-blocker; talk about false advertising."

"Cole!" I gasp, feeling my face heat up as Cassandra just chuckles and goes back into the kitchen.

He gives me a mock military salute. "You know where to find me."

"Laundry room?"

"I'll be the one lying on the floor groaning in agony."

"I'll kiss it better, promise." I creep in closer and sneak in a kiss with just the right amount of tongue before leaving him for greener, more chocolatey pastures.

***

After having dinner with the Stones minus Jay, Cole and I decide to go into town for a while just for the sake of it. We start putting up our

Christmas lights pretty early, so I won't be surprised if some people won't even have waited for Thanksgiving.

It's cold out, and I press myself closer into Cole's side as we stroll past familiar shops and cafes; whatever the past may be, nothing feels better than being home for the holidays. I remind myself to go home and Skype with Sarah and Cami, both of whom are on campus for the break.

"Do you want to get a hot chocolate?" Cole nuzzles his face into my neck.

"Hmm, maybe."

"We could go back to your place later and then…"

His fingers press into my sides; they trail lower, lower until…

"Watch some movies, eat popcorn, catch up on some homework." He whispers all this so sexily that I almost, almost resist shoving him away from me, but in the end, I do. Laughing, I then fold myself back into his side; it's too cold not to snuggle.

"That was mean."

"And leaving me high and dry to hang out with my mother wasn't?"

"Let's call a truce, drink some hot chocolate, and then see where the night takes us. Shall we, Mr. Stone?"

"Such a dork." He kisses the top of my head.

***

We make it to our favorite little cafe and Cole gets us our drinks. I rummage through my bag to find my lipstick and nearly jump out of my skin when someone slides into the seat across from mine.

When I look up and see the last person I'd ever expected to meet while I'm home, I don't pretend to be anything but shocked.

"Close your mouth, Tessa; I think you're drooling," Nicole says in that half-bored way of hers that's not meant to sound snarky or cruel but in the end always does.

"Nicole." I'm a little dumbfounded. I haven't seen her since before graduation, back when we had a talk, and I was finally able to put her behind me. The way she'd put it, I didn't think she'd come back to this town once she got out.

But here she is, and I think she's trying to be nice to me; maybe she really is bored. You can't ever tell with Nicole.

"Tessa," she cocks her head to the side, "you look good, a little on the paler side, but you look good."

"Blame my Irish genetics, not me. So…" there's an awkward pause, "Home for Thanksgiving, huh?"

"It was either that or slumming it with my roommate and her boyfriend. You know how those things get."

"Actually, I have a great roommate, she's…."

"So," she cuts me off, "how are things with your soulmate?" She looks to where Cole must be standing in line placing our orders. Despite the fact that she's made it clear that she's no longer actively pursuing my boyfriend, I still bristle. Maybe it's too soon after the attack of the obsessed sorority cyborgs.

"They're great, how about you? Met someone?"

She's still looking at Cole; I would much rather she didn't.

"Not really, I haven't come across someone who gets me, you

know?"

"Have you considered working things out with Jay again?"

Never thought that sentence would be coming from my mouth but, oh well.

She gives me a long, withering stare. "That relationship was the most monotonous, soul-sucking thing I've ever been a part of. Why would I even consider that?"

"Oh."

"So, how's school?" She leans back in the booth. "I bet it's hard keeping girls away from him."

"Is it that obvious?"

"I had a hunch. But he's always going to be that guy that every girl wants for herself. There's no surprise there."

"But what do you do if you have him and want to keep him?"

There's a second in which she looks concerned, like she cares, but it disappears instantaneously. "I suggest you hold on tight and remind yourself that he's with you for a reason."

I look over my shoulder to see Cole staring in our direction. His eyebrows shoot up as he looks from Nicole to me, and I get that he's silently asking me if I'm okay. I reassure him with a smile and go back to Nicole.

"I guess I'm just really surprised to see you here. You could've gone anywhere you wanted; I know you're not into spending time with your parents. Why didn't you stay with your sister?"

"We had a fight, I called her a bitch, and she slammed the door in my face."

"Ouch, what happened?"

"Her boyfriend came onto me, and she thought I was throwing myself at him. Same old shit, I guess."

If it wouldn't make the situation a thousand times worse, I'd hug her just because she seems so sad and alone. But I don't. Instead I sit in my seat and watch her thrum her fingers on the table; it's a nervous habit I'm very familiar with.

"How…how are things at home?"

I meant to ask if her father's still got anger management problems, if he's tried to physically hurt her, but I bite my tongue.

"I just go there to sleep, haven't seen much of either of my mom or dad. It's kind of nice knowing that they don't have control over me any longer."

I nod.

Cole places steaming cups of hot chocolate in front of us, and it's just proof of how good a person he really is that he puts one in front of Nicole as well.

"Hey," he acknowledges her with a nod, and she smiles, just a little painfully.

I know how she feels; it's exactly how she made me feel time and time again when she was with Jay. It's difficult to understand why anybody would be happy making someone else that miserable; I haven't even done anything, yet I feel guilty seeing the pain in her eyes.

"Well, I'll leave you two lovebirds alone. Nice seeing you, Tessa." She gives me a pinched smile and begins to leave.

The words are out of my mouth before I can stop them. "Why don't you join my family for Thanksgiving?"

Cole's head whips toward me at the same time as Nicole says, "What?"

What the heck am I doing? Whatever it is, I continue doing it.

"Come to my house; my dad's hired some fancy caterers who're making a crap ton of food. Trust me; it's no big deal."

"Uh, you don't have to…"

"It'll be great!" I'm smiling so hard my cheeks hurt. "Plenty of food and wine to go around for everyone. Right, Cole?"

He's looking at me like anyone who's genuinely concerned for my well-being would look, like he's worried I may have brain damage.

"Yes, why not, we'll just have to keep the sharp objects away from Beth," he says in a low voice and then turns on the charm.

"But you're most welcome to join us. I'm sure it won't be that awkward; at least your ex won't be at the table, just a little overprotective best friend who sometimes needs to be physically restrained."

Nicole gulps. "I'm not scared of her."

Well, she should be.

And then I remember something my dad mentioned the other day and laugh a little nervously. "Speaking of exes, my dad did invite Jay. Well, actually, he invited your whole family, so there's that."

I quickly reach for my mug and gulp down the scalding liquid, burning my tongue. Cole's glaring in my direction, and Nicole stands there considering my invite.

"Look, if it saves me from listening to my parents tell me how I ruined their lives, then I'll be there. Thanks for the invite."

She gives us a strained smile and leaves while Cole and I sit there figuring out what just happened.

"Did you just do that?"

"I think I did."

"Huh, this will be interesting."

"I don't think she'll make it out alive but hey, at least I did the right thing."

Cole places his hand on mine, patting it. "When Beth attacks her with the butter knife, remind yourself that."

CHAPTER TWENTY-ONE
Nana Stone Is Going on About the Merits of Early Motherhood

"You keep an eye on Cole; I've got Beth," Travis whispers conspiratorially in my ear, and my eyes dart around the room to look for our significant others.

It's Thanksgiving Day and it hasn't gotten off to the best start, especially considering the fact that Beth's locked herself in my room, and Cole is destroying the flowers my father placed a special order for by mushing them in his hands. It wasn't my best idea to let him set the table.

"I don't get it; why are they so mad?"

"Gee, well, I don't know!" He slaps his hand on the kitchen counter. "Maybe it's because you invited someone whose face was pinned onto Beth's dartboard for a solid six months."

"Beth has a dartboard?"

"Why do you think she asked for our family photos before slamming the door on your face?"

"Huh."

"And then, because this family's idiocy doesn't stop there, Dad thought it was a brilliant idea to invite the guy you were obsessed with for a decade? And sit him next to the guy you're currently dating and the two just happen to be stepbrothers? You literally couldn't make this shit up."

"I can't tell Nicole not to come now; that'll be horrible!" I'm being trampled by my conscience, which surely isn't the size of a cricket, much more an elephant at this point.

"And Jay the giant Va-jay-jay?"

I imagine spitting out the drink in my mouth, were I drinking one.

"Make that Jay the unwaxed vajayjay," Cole grumbles, entering the kitchen, dragging his feet behind him. It's very cute, actually, to see him acting like a petulant child, as much as I hate seeing him like this. I'd tell Dad to call off his plans, but apparently there's going to be some press present later, and they want to do a piece on the mayor and his family being close with the sheriff's, thus painting the perfect picture of a tightknit community.

If only they knew…

Cole's still grumbling under his breath as he rests his forehead on my shoulder, coming up from behind me. "I feel your pain, man. Beth and I ran into my ex, Jenny, the other day, and I literally had to stop Beth from emptying a frying pan full of boiling hot oil onto her face."

Cole's chuckling into my shoulder and I gasp. "How did that even happen?"

"Beth's tight with the crew from Rusty's, she just waltzed into the back of the kitchen, and, the next thing I know, I'm throwing myself in front of Jenny to prevent a lawsuit."

I whistle lowly. "She must've been pissed."

"Let's just say I'm glad you're on the dartboard now."

"It's really nice to know my older brother's got my back." I scowl at him and Cole lifts his head.

"Don't worry, Tessie, I've got you."

"Kids! The rest of the Stones are here and look, they brought Nana Stone!" my dad shouts from the living room.

I whirl around to face Cole. "You did not tell me she was coming!"

He shrugs. "You didn't tell me Jay would be here, and you invited Nicole."

Travis scratches the back of his neck. "I thought you loved Nana Stone."

My face is quickly turning an alarming shade of red. "I do, but…"

Cole slings his arm across my shoulder. "Tessie adores my grandma; what she doesn't adore is the number of hints she drops about the next generation of Stones."

Travis bursts out laughing and I smack his shoulder. "Don't! She might be old. but the woman's got the hearing of a bat."

He continues laughing and soon Cole joins him. I leave them to be and go and greet the sheriff, Cassandra, and Jay, who surprisingly has brought a date. After an awkward introduction to both of them, we go sit at the table, and I excuse myself to go get my homicidal best friend.

A glance at my watch tells me that it's still quite a while to go before Megan and Alex get here after eating with their own families. I really need Megan on my side to go and confront Beth, but I also can't let her sit in my room and sulk all day. It's her first Thanksgiving without her mom and not in her old home; I don't want it to have bad memories for her.

I knock on the door.

"Go away, Brutus."

"What?"

"I'm reading *Julius Caesar* for one of my online classes. Now go away; I'm not having dinner with that soul-sucking succubus."

"Impressive use of alliteration there, now unlock the door, this is stupid."

"Oh, I'm stupid now? And what planet were you on when you asked the backstabbing bitch to share our pie?"

"If it makes things any better, Nicole doesn't eat carbs."

I hear her growling from the other side before the door flies open.

"She's bad news, whether in another state or not, any kind of interaction with that girl isn't good for you. How are you ever going to know any different from being bullied if you're hanging out with the one person who made your life miserable for years!"

I take a deep, calming breath; this is quickly getting out of control. If I don't get downstairs soon, they'll be sending up a search party. We have reporters coming soon, Jay's there with a date, and Nicole could arrive any moment.

Plus, I'm pretty sure Nana Stone is going on about the merits of early motherhood.

"Listen," something about my defeated voice makes her expression soften, "I really need you to come with me and be my best friend right now. This isn't going according to plan, and I've had a really shitty week. All I wanted was to come home and just have some peace of mind, but, clearly, that isn't happening. So, I'd really appreciate it if I have one person downstairs who is on my side."

She blinks a couple of times, and I'm more than prepared to give up, but Beth surprises me by throwing her arms around me and hugging me close.

"You're an idiot."

"Yup, that'd be me."

"But since I'm stuck with you," she sniffs, "let's go do this."

***

Nicole shows up sometime later, and, between the two of us, there's enough awkwardness and cringeworthy moments to last a lifetime. I'm sure it's not any more pleasant for her to be back in my house than it is for me to see her. There are a lot of memories for us that have been lived here, as is the case with best friends who literally used to live at each other's houses like Nicole used to live at mine.

"Hey," she says in a shaky voice, her eyes darting nervously around the room like she's waiting for something out of our past to come and attack her.

"How long did you sit in your car and think about going back home?"

She laughs nervously. "About an hour."

"Well, you're here now, so you might as well join us for dinner. My dad can't stop talking about his gourmet turkey."

"Isn't it weird?" she suddenly asks, and I wince at the thought of her bringing up the past. "This is your first Thanksgiving without your mom?"

Right, my mom's not here, and I hadn't given it a second thought until she brought it up.

"Not really, I think it's all about perspective. On one hand, you have someone like Beth, who can never have that with her mom again, and then there's me. I'm not going to feel sorry for myself; if anything, it's my mom's loss for giving up on her family."

"Wow, that sounded oddly mature coming from you."

"I've grown up, Nicole. You wouldn't be here if that weren't the case."

We're about to enter the dining room when I stop Nicole by placing a hand on her tanned arm. "Just a warning, Jay's here, and he's brought a date."

A perfectly shaped eyebrow goes up. "And I should care why?"

"Precisely." I grin.

Everyone goes deathly silent when we enter the room, well, everyone except Nana Stone, who's hitting Travis with her spoon and asking him to pass the gravy.

Nicole raises her hand and gives the room a meek wave. "Hey."

No one responds; in fact, the unreturned greeting makes things even more awkward. But then, god bless him, Cole gets up and pulls out a seat for her.

"Hey." He smiles and winks at me, but I swear Nicole blushes under his attention.

Control the bitch face, Tessa, control it.

As Nicole sits down, I feel a lot of eyes boring a hole into the side of my head, and when I look around the table, I notice Jay's date scowling at me. Oops? Maybe she knows Nicole's Jay's ex.

Things just keep getting better and better today.

"So, Tessa, Cole tells me you still haven't gotten off the pill. What did I tell you about the side effects?" Nana Stone cries out, and I almost contemplate face-planting into my plate of food.

On either side of me, Beth and Cole shake in silent laughter, and my dad starts coughing. Cassandra bites her lip to keep herself from laughing, and the sheriff clears his throat repeatedly.

"They're kids, Mother; I don't think now's the time to discuss these things," the sheriff chides her, and Nana Stone waves her fork in the air.

"I want to see my great-grandbabies before I go and that's it, damn it!"

My face continues to burn. "Well, there's time for both of those things to happen yet, so let's be patient."

She continues to mutter under her breath as we eat and keeps shooting me suggestive looks. I love Nana Stone, Nana Stone rocks my world, but right now I just really wish she'd choke on her turkey.

"Nicole," Cassandra says after some time, and Nicole's head shoots up so fast, it's almost funny. These two haven't had the best relationship in the past, so it's strange to see them interact. "You look well," she smiles gently, "I see New York's been good to you."

"It has; new beginnings always are." The corner of Nicole's mouth lifts in a small smile. "You were right."

There's a lull in conversation after that, and even though this dinner hasn't gone as smoothly as planned, I'm happy to be with the people I care about. Nana Stone continues to crack jokes about things that should definitely not be mentioned while my dad and brother are eating, Jay's date, Rose, continues scowling and twitching her nose at everything, and Cole's right there next to me, constantly telling me that everything will be okay.

***

After dinner, I take a few photographs with my family and Cole's. Later the adults go to the back of the house for coffee and drinks, leaving the rest of us in the living room watching mindless television after stuffing our stomachs.

"Let me get this straight; those girls actually put out an ad…" Megan has joined us, and there's enough rage on her face to match her flaming red hair.

"And two dicks actually approached you? What the hell!" Beth shouts, and I catch a glimpse of Travis's face, which is dark with anger. Cole's jaw is locked, he's fisting his hands and I can see him playing the events of the night in his head, seething with anger.

"It's done and over with; Cole's just overreacting." I try to make things a little less morbid, but that's tough to do when everyone's hell-bent on rehashing the past.

"I'm overreacting? You have nightmares, and I'm overreacting?"

I cringe at the hurt in his voice, at the hurt on everyone's faces. I didn't mean to bring up the night in the club, but Cole did anyway; apparently, I'm an open book, and the lack of a stellar college experience is very visible on my face.

"This was your dream school; I went because I wanted to be with you, not because I wanted you to continue living in high school."

At this everyone glares at Nicole, who's awkwardly sitting in a corner, holding on to her coffee cup for dear life.

"Knock it off," I tell him. I'm glad Jay's date forced him to leave because that just would've made the situation a hundred times worse.

"But he has a point," Alex chirps in from where he's holding a visibly upset Megan. "You didn't go to college to have to relive high school all over again, and Cole's only going to get more popular. The girls aren't going to go away; the real issue is how you are going to deal with it."

Travis has yet to speak, and his silence is scaring me. Because he was mentally absent during the worst phase of bullying I faced, he feels incredibly guilty. In turn, that makes him all the more protective now; add that to having an overly protective boyfriend and it's lucky that I get to step foot out of the house.

"Well, you could…" Nicole begins, and the way everyone looks at her makes her freeze. She raises her hands defensively. "What? If anything, the only person who knows what to do in these situations should be me, right?"

"Because of course you've only got her best interests at heart?" Beth says snidely, and Travis wraps an arm around her to hold her back.

"Suppose we were to actually listen to you, what would you say?"

"I'd say there's no way to get those girls off Tessa's back, not when they're so convinced that they're so much better for Cole than she is."

"That's reasonably stupid coming from your mouth. I expected something more diabolical and vile." Megan nearly snarls.

"Calm down, I'm getting there. What I'm trying to say is that nothing's going to convince them unless they convince themselves."

"I'm slightly confused…" I really am.

"What I think you should do is to fake a breakup. Not for long, just enough for the girls to realize that even single, Cole wouldn't be interested." She shrugs.

At her suggestion, everyone breaks out in protests quite vocally, especially Cole, before I can even process any of what she's said.

"No." Cole bites out, "That's not even an option."

Nicole rolls her eyes. "Jesus, you guys take everything way too seriously. It's only a pretend breakup, just until these girls get you out of their system."

"Would that have worked for you?" Travis asks.

She shrugs. "I wouldn't have wasted my time wondering about the what ifs if I knew for sure that he wouldn't be interested in me, even if he wasn't with anyone else."

I'm still processing and trying to understand how all of this makes sense, and the rest of them are weighing the pros and cons of the situation.

Well, everyone but Cole, who shoots up from his seat and storms out of the room. Nicole's looking a bit overwhelmed, so she quickly grabs her things and heads for the door, so I follow her.

"I shouldn't have interfered," she says to me quietly.

"We asked you to, so it's fine. I'm sorry they freaked out on you like that."

"You have a bunch of people that love you and care about you; that's not something to be sorry for."

"Still, you were only trying to help."

"I was, and I really think you might want to consider it."

She leaves quickly, and I have no idea when I'll see her again.

Next, I go to find my boyfriend, who's sitting alone in one of the deck chairs near the pool. I go and sit down next to him, placing my head on his shoulder.

"What're you thinking?"

"That Nicole's completely full of shit." He scoffs, muttering the word *breakup* under his breath.

"I know; I hate the idea as much as you do."

"But…" he begins, and my heart stops. That word is never good; if there's a *but*, then he might possibly see the merits of breaking up, fake or not. I can't even contemplate if there might be such a thing.

"Please don't tell me you're actually considering it." My voice is so low, I doubt he hears me, but he does. Cole frames my face and leans in close.

"I'll do whatever it takes to make you happy, even if that means…"

"We're not some star-crossed lovers in a romance film, Cole; don't play games with me. This is a real problem; we're real people. I don't need to hear these mindless plans and schemes; we work things out like normal people."

"Are you scared?" His expression is so tender, it's breaking my heart.

"Of what?"

"Of going back, of being seen with me, of what someone else might do, of what might happen if I'm not there?"

"The last part sounded the scariest."

He gives me a sad smile and kisses the top of my head. "Baby, I'm not going anywhere."

"But?"

"But I am going to protect you." He leans in and kisses me deeply.

"I'm not scared of those sorority psychopaths, trust me."

He laughs against my lips. "Who's to say that's what you need protection from?"

"Then what are we even talking about?"

He distracts me then, kissing me slowly, deeply, languidly until I forget my own name.

"I'll do whatever it takes to make sure you never regret for a second that I chose to spend these four years of our life together. I don't want you to wake up one day and hate me for ruining everything you worked so hard for. I didn't follow you because I was scared of what a long-distance relationship could do to us, I followed you because I wanted to get a head start on the rest of our lives and because I love you too much to be that selfless."

"Cole," I breathe, running a hand through his hair. "I'd never hate you, never regret my time with you, or even think about a future that you're not a part of. You don't have to prove anything to me."

He shakes his head, the sadness in his eyes is piercing me, and I'm terrified of what's to come.

"But I do, Shortcake, I do.

CHAPTER TWENTY-TWO
It'll Be Like an R-Rated Disney Land

Someone's placed a framed picture of Cole and me on my vanity table at home, and I want to hug whomever that person is. It's one from a trip we took to the beach this past summer; I'm grinning at the camera, Cole's standing behind me and holding me in his arms. His head's turned toward me and he's beaming at me; you can practically see the feelings that he has for me pouring out of the picture. Picking up the wooden, rustic-looking frame, I hug it to my chest and decide to take it back to my dorm.

"I had it in my phone and thought you'd like a blown-up version of it." Travis leans against my doorframe and smiles warmly at me. For old times' sake, he's crashing in his old room, though I imagine the memories it holds for him can't be too pleasant.

"I love it. It was a really good day."

"You're talking about it like there haven't been too many of those since then."

I don't want to mope during my time home because that's not

why I'm here. It's the holidays, and I'm supposed to be spending this time doing anything but unloading all my problems onto them. But they've already seen enough, heard enough, and my good intentions have gone to waste.

"You know how it is, Trav, college isn't always what you expect it to be. I'm just feeling a little lost right now, and Cole is, well…I think he's just suffering because of how confused I am."

"What's there to be confused about?" Travis walks into the room and sits on my bed, patting the space next to him, and I follow his directions.

"You've always known what you wanted from life, always more than I did. Hell, I never had any intentions of getting into politics or law school or any of the other stuff Dad had planned for me. I'm going back to school in a couple of months, and it scares the shit out of me because I still don't know what I want to do with my life. But you've always loved books and known you wanted to build a career around them. Are you going to let some entitled airheads get in the way of that?"

When he puts it that way, I feel incredibly stupid.

"It's not just the airheads; it's knowing that there's one thing that I've learned to feel the most secure about, and that same thing is being threatened over and over again. It took me a long time to feel comfortable in my relationship with Cole, to understand that we're equals and not ask myself why someone like him would be into someone like me."

He groans in frustration. "Are you even listening to yourself?

God, if Beth were here, she'd put you in your place. This isn't the Tess I know, and the more you put yourself down, the more I want to hurt someone."

"Well, it's a good thing Jay's in the neighborhood, right?"

"Can't get into trouble with the sheriff, he has to oversee all my community service paperwork, but I could always wear a ski mask," he muses.

"And jump Jay in a dark parking lot, oh, and Beth would totally have enough black outfits for both of you."

"I don't think she's aware of any other color existing. If she didn't look so hot in it, I'd say it was a little disturbing."

I laugh and he rolls his eyes. "That was a brilliant change of subject, but come on, we're not done talking about you."

"There's not much to talk about. I'm lacking in the confidence department, and that's a known fact. Those girls, well, *blood-sucking leeches* would be a better term, but they're aware of it, and they take advantage of the fact."

"They crossed a line, if I could ever fucking hit a girl…" Travis growls and I drop my head.

"Everyone keeps wanting to fight my battles for me, and I keep letting them. Maybe part of being confident is to stop doing that."

He's quiet for a while. "I miss your spirit; I hate that whatever's happening at school is taking that away from you. I might have missed out on the toughest part of your life, but what I did see showed me that you were brave, that you stood up to people who tried to hurt you, and, most of all, you were happy. Now you just look tired of everything, and it's killing me."

I'm speechless. My brother has never been one for making speeches. He's always there for me in his own quiet way, but he's never said something so touching before, and before I know it, my eyes are watering. I hug his side and he slings his arm around me.

"Be the fighter that you are Tess, come on."

***

The girls and I pack ourselves and our collective hoard of Black Friday loot into my car.

"That was so much fun!" Megan sighs as she pulls on her seat belt. "Victoria's Secret always has the best sales."

"Talk about yourself," Beth groans, "all that squealing, and the amount of pink in that room…" She shudders. "Why do you guys subject yourself to this torture every single year?"

"Hey, it's tradition, besides, it's not like you came out empty-handed." I point toward her own bags.

"I just bought some necessities. I do live in an apartment that requires me to actually shop for it."

"And under what kind of necessity would you classify La Perla?" I laugh but then immediately shut up at the sly look that comes across her face.

"Oh Tessa, dear old Tessa, you walked right into that one."

"No! Please, forget I said anything. I don't need to know why you needed that medieval-looking corset or any of the other…stuff."

"Your brother's quite adventurous," she goes on, ignoring everything I've said. "He especially requested that I look for these items. I might even wear them tonight; did you forget that I'm staying over? I really hope you have earplugs nearby."

"Stop, stop! For the love of god, I ask you to stop."

"I think she's going to have a panic attack, Beth, you should stop." Megan doesn't look up from her phone, typing furiously.

"She started it."

"I did no such thing! All I said was—"

"Tessa, don't be stupid, Beth isn't mad about the shopping thing. Isn't it obvious? We're still trying to understand why you think anything that comes out of Nicole's mouth is a good idea."

I hate traffic, I mean everyone hates it, but right now, it's making me feel claustrophobic. We're stuck in a long line of cars that don't look like they're going anywhere anytime soon. Maybe I could just leave the car running and jump out; it'd be less painful than the conversation we're about to have.

"I never said that it was a good idea."

"But you've been thinking about it. Ever since the she-devil left and you came back after brainwashing Cole, you've had that look on your face. You're actually thinking about the fake breakup, aren't you?" Beth looks ready to hit me.

"If I said that it's Cole who's considering it and not me, would you believe me?"

"No way," Megan scoffs, "he would never even think twice about it."

"You'd be surprised at the things that he could do when he deludes himself into thinking that he needs to protect me."

"Then stop acting like you need his goddamn help all the time."

"I don't." I'm starting to get annoyed now, really annoyed. "I didn't ask to be ridiculed in front of the entire student body, who've seen my underwear, by the way. I also didn't ask for photos of me to go around and advertise the fact that I'm nothing better than a prostitute." I hear my best friends' gasps but continue, "And I sure as hell didn't ask to see a girl wrapped around Cole every time I see him. I trust my boyfriend, and I love him to death for always trying to take care of me, but I don't purposely put myself into situations just to get his help or attention."

Both of them are quiet, and I think maybe I've come on a bit too strong. "I'm not angry; I just…I wish you guys understood that it's not easy for me. I'm not big on the idea of any kind of a breakup with Cole, it'd kill me, but then according to him, being together is doing the same thing."

"Just promise us you'll exhaust all other options before coming anywhere near Nicole's idea," Megan asks me.

"Of course," I promise, really hoping that I get to keep it.

***

Everyone sleeps in on Saturday, and the girls and I meet for a late lunch. Later in the day I go to have dinner with the Stones, which is awkward as heck, given that Jay's date is here and she's staring daggers at me. The moment I make the stupid mistake of excusing myself to go to the bathroom, Rose corners me and is standing outside the guest bathroom when I come out.

"Hi." She's got those crazy eyes going on, and I can't help but feel sorry for Jay. This is going to end badly for him, and he's probably never going to stop picking the wrong girls.

"Hey?"

"I've been meaning to ask you something." The way she's looking at me makes it look like if I don't answer her question, she'll plunge her hand down my throat and yank it out.

"Okay, and it is?"

"Is Jay cheating on me with you?"

I nearly start choking on air, well, it's either that or laugh until tears start streaming down my face, and naturally, I go for the latter.

"I'm sorry—what?" I can't stop laughing, and it makes her glare harder.

"I'm not stupid. I see the way he looks at you, the way he's always looking at you. Are you sleeping together?" She moves in as if to intimidate me, but Rose is as threatening as a sloth.

"I'm dating his brother."

"So?"

"Why would I date a Jason if I have a Cole?"

It's proof of how horrible of a girlfriend she's going to make that she accepts my point as being valid, but then her face morphs in anger.

"But you brought his ex to dinner yesterday. If that wasn't a move to sabotage my relationship, then what was it?"

At this I start laughing again, and I'm pretty sure we'll have an audience soon if I don't control myself.

"Nicole remembers Jay with the affection one has for an ingrown toenail. If you thought I'd brought her in for a passionate reunion, you'd be wrong."

"Well, then she isn't my problem anymore, you are! He's got photos of you on his phone and…and I had to force him to bring me home to see his parents. Just…just stay away from him."

I'm only just absorbing the fact that Jay's unrequited affections really need to be tamed when Cole appears by my side.

"I think she's heard enough of your shit, don't you?"

"Oh, I don't know, I do have some space left for some more BS, but only if she still thinks she's capable of spewing some more of it."

Cole looks at me with a mixture of surprise and amusement on his face. He understands that I don't really need him to step in for me right now. I see the virtual waving of a white flag as he steps back.

Rose's face is ironically turning red. "Leave him alone," she stutters and marches away, stumbling in her heels, and Cole and I burst out laughing even before she's out of earshot.

"What a piece of work." He shakes his head before grabbing my hand and hauling me to his chest.

"That was pretty sexy."

"What was?" I arch an eyebrow. It's nice to see him like this, all light and free and not brooding and distant.

"Seeing you like that, a woman in control." He settles his hands at the sides of my waist and teasingly begins bringing them up and down.

"Your parents are a couple of feet away," I squeak when his hands get a bit too close to trouble.

"Your overnight bag is in my room." He grins.

"What?"

"I thought we were stating facts."

"When did you…how did you? Am I staying over?"

He nuzzles his face in my neck. "Yes, and it's going to be fun."

"Fun." I'm beginning to lose my train of thought.

"Yeah it'll be like an R-Rated Disney Land."

"Oh my…"

"My parents are going to go drop off Nana and stay the night with some of their friends."

"And Jay?"

"Twenty bucks says that he'll check into a hotel the moment we close the door to our bedroom."

"That's not something I'm going to bet against."

"Smart choice, Shortcake, smart choice."

***

Before I know it, it's time to head back to school, but this time I leave knowing that winter break is just weeks away and that I'll be home for a good while the next time I come back. Megan, Beth, and I say a sappy goodbye to each other, and Beth promises to visit at least once in the coming month, ensuring that she'll bring Travis along.

Before we leave, my dad pulls me aside and hands me an envelope, which I know contains a big, fat check.

"What is it for this time?"

"She called it a pre-Christmas present present." He scratches the back of his neck.

"Well, you know what to do with this."

"Tessa…I can't keep pretending that I'm okay with you shutting out your mom like this. This is the only way she knows how to connect with people these days. I really think you should…"

"I don't need her money, literally. I really don't need it, Dad."

"And I'm proud of you, I'm proud that you're smart with your finances and that you keep a steady job. Don't use the money and see it for what it really is, a plea to get you to talk to her."

"I'll think about it; I'm not making any promises, but I'll think about it."

I hold my tongue from asking how her sugar daddy's doing, because that would just ruin the moment.

The drive back is oddly quiet; Cole seems detached again, and the sense of foreboding that creeps through me makes my skin crawl. When I can't take it anymore, I ask him to pull over.

"What?" He seems startled.

"Do it, or I'll jump out of the car."

"Tessie, what are you doing?" His eyes widen as I begin pulling off my seat belt.

"Being a sexy woman in control." I grin at him as he pulls the car to the side of the road, earning us honks and angry glares from other drivers.

Removing my seat belt, I move over to the driver's side and straddle Cole's lap.

"I think I'm getting my mojo back." I loop my arms around his neck.

"Your mojo?" His smile is a little bit cautious, like he's wondering if his girlfriend has gone batshit crazy, oh well.

"I'll try out for the dance team when I get back, and maybe the student newspaper."

His eyes dance with delight and mischief. "Really? I'll get to see you in that itty-bitty uniform?"

I laugh and kiss him. "You and probably every other guy on campus, mister."

This makes him scowl. "Why don't you just stick with the newspaper; I'm sure that'll keep you occupied enough."

"No way," we kiss again, "I'm going back and fitting in, and if that means getting over my stupid fears, then I will."

"And you," I clutch handfuls of his hair and pull his mouth to mine, "are going to stop acting like you're on a man period."

He starts to choke. "I don't act like…" I slap my hand over his mouth. "Shut up and make out with me."

His voice is muffled beneath my hands. "Kinda difficult to do when I can't even breathe." His lips tickle my fingers, and I remove my hand.

"Are you drunk?" His hands settle on my back, moving lower until he's palming my behind.

"Just a little liquid courage."

He shakes his head. "Drunk Tessie always tries taking advantage of my innocence."

I swat his shoulder. "You haven't been innocent since the day you discovered your first facial hair."

He gives me a disarming smile. "Now that, Shortcake, is the truth. What were you saying about making out again?"

***

Sarah's studying in our room when I get in, still feeling the after-effects of the beers I chugged down before leaving for school. I must look like a total mess with wild hair and swollen lips, and she gives me a sly look.

"In the car? Really, Tessa?" She shakes her head, her shoulders quaking with humor.

"Hey, it didn't get that far. Cole has a thing with not letting drunk girls maul him." I fall onto my bed.

"That I do." Cole walks in and drops my bag at the foot of the bed. "You need anything else, baby?"

"Just a really long nap."

"If you want to go out to eat when you wake up, call me. I just have to go home and do damage control. Eric really isn't into clean living spaces ever since his girlfriend left him…again."

"She'll be back by next week, right?" I mumble, fighting sleep and exhaustion.

"Give or take a few days. Sleep well, Tessie." I remember him taking off my shoes and pulling the blanket over me, kissing my forehead before he leaves.

I hear Sarah sigh, "You're so lucky."

I don't respond but silently agree, "I'm so lucky."

CHAPTER TWENTY-THREE
It's Like Finding Out McGonagall Wears Negligees to Bed

Coming out of the gym shower, I'm a little amused to see Cole and Bentley trying their best not to have a standoff. It's actually cute how hard they're trying, but the awkwardness is coming off in waves from their direction. Pulling my hair up in a bun, I walk toward them and try to get Cole away from my poor new friend before his newfound patience disappears.

"Hey, I'm all done. Should we go get some lunch?"

Cole looks relieved as the tension drains from his face. He grabs my hand and glowers at Bentley, who's shuffling his feet.

"See you tomorrow?" I smile at him, but his face just reddens in response.

"I can't…I mean I won't be here tomorrow." He scratches the back of his neck.

"Oh." I'm disappointed. He isn't just my trainer but has become a good friend in a place where I've struggled to find them. We don't get a lot of time to hang out, especially considering he's a senior and in all kinds of pain this semester.

"You're working in the evening, then?"

"No, I took the day off, I kinda have a date."

My eyes widen; this wasn't what I was expecting to hear.

"Really? You met someone?"

Next to me I can practically hear Cole rolling his eyes as he tugs at my hand. "That's how it works, Tessie. You meet someone, and if you don't hate their guts in the first fifteen minutes of getting to know them, then you invite them for dinner and a movie, and if you still don't feel like choking them, you go on another one."

He directs his question to Bentley. "This isn't your first date, is it? You look way too happy for it to be with someone you just met."

"No, her name's Amanda…I met her a couple of weeks ago, she, uh, she works at the campus bookstore and I've had a few classes with her before as well…"

His face lights up a little, and I realize that I'm truly happy for him, regardless of Cole's teasing.

"That's awesome, then! I hope you have a great time with her! Let me know if you'd be interested in going on a double date sometime soon."

It's almost comical how both boys have an eerily similar look of horror on their faces right now.

Okay, then, no to double dates.

***

"Double date with Bentley? Did you have this idea the same time as you decided to try out for the dance team mid-semester?"

Cami scowls at me as we stand outside the dorm room of the captain of said team in an attempt to talk her into letting me audition. Most girls on the team have applied for dance scholarships; others tried out in the beginning when the student-run clubs put up flyers. I, at the time, felt so overwhelmed and out of place that I decided not to become part of any of them. Hence, when I'm not studying, I've had a lot of spare time on my hands, and I realize that that's part of the reason why my thoughts have become so self-destructive, why I've been questioning pretty much everything in my life. So, to put an end to that, I've decided on a new beginning, one where the focal point of my existence isn't whether the vicious vultures will take Cole away from me or not.

"What's wrong with a double date? Cole's my boyfriend, Bentley's my friend, and if I want to hang out with both of them, then I should be able to."

"Am I the only one who notices Cole's urge to decapitate any guy who's even slightly interested in you?" I open my mouth to protest but she slaps her hand over it. "And don't even tell me that Bentley's not into you because he is."

"He's dating someone," I mumble petulantly. Cami withdraws her hands and sighs. "So was Kristen Stewart, didn't stop her, now did it?"

I blink a couple of times, trying to make a connection, but before I can point out that I'm not nearly as cool as the example she's just given, the door to Lindsey Owens's dorm room swings open, and

Cami and I have to jump back to avoid colliding with her.

She's a bit stunned to see us both. "Can I help you?"

"You can definitely help her by telling her that she's absolutely crazy for thinking she can join your team now." Cami scowls at her, clearly intimidating the older girl.

"Well," she stammers because obviously no one's ready for Cami this early in the morning. She turns to me and scrutinizes my body, obviously checking if I have the body for those sports bras and tiny shorts they like to wear.

"We do have an opening; one of the girls has a fractured ankle, so our routine is messed up. We weren't going to hold auditions, though, we have backups." She scrunches her nose and I see a glimmer of hope, something that might help this crazy plan of mine work.

"You don't think they're good, do you?"

"They're out of control, freshmen girls who think they don't look and dance like shit after an entire night out." She narrows her eyes at me. "You don't drink, do you?"

"I do occasionally, when I need some emergency courage and bravado." I think about our car ride back to campus and my cheeks heat up.

"Oh, what the heck, give me your number and I'll text you whenever we plan on holding auditions. Do you have any prior experience; have you competed before?"

"No, I just…I think I can do it, I'm a quick learner and I have no social life, so you won't have to worry about me throwing up during practice."

The corner of her mouth lifts up in a small smile. "We'll see."

Lindsey retreats back into her room and a wide grin breaks on my face; I squeal and hug Cami, who stands still.

"I cannot believe you're doing this!"

Stepping back, I don't let her less-than-enthusiastic attitude get me down. "I need to do this, okay? For me and for my peace of mind. If I don't, then all I'll ever do is sit in my dorm room and think about everything that's wrong with me. This is what I need, to know that…"

"You're just like every other girl who wants to be popular?"

Her comment hurts, but I do get where she's coming from. She thinks I'll change, that I'll become someone unrecognizable, because so far, she's only met Tessa the social hermit O'Connell, but what she doesn't know is that sometimes I'm not a recluse by choice but because I'm held back by my fears. Currently those fears are taking a toll on me and my relationship, and something needs to give.

"It's not about being popular; it's about being more comfortable in my own skin."

She blinks a couple of times and then rolls her eyes, slinging an arm around my shoulder. "I don't get you, but I support you because that's how good of a person I am. Now, on to the student newspaper office?"

I grin. "Yes, please, I know they're looking for an investigative reporter."

"Jesus, why don't you go for the nice, happy, fluffy things? The beauty section is desperately in need of a revamp."

"There's a beauty section?"

"See? That's my point! Hmm, maybe I'll go apply, too, God knows someone needs to tell the people that having your roots show isn't the cool thing to do anymore."

I snort as we head down to the offices where the editor in chief seats. Mentally I tick yet another thing off of my to-do list.

***

"You're going away?" I squeak as Cole begins throwing random clothes in his duffel bag. I sit at the edge of his bed, my textbook open in front of me currently being ignored. He's just sprung the news on me and it's extremely distracting.

He stops throwing the clothes in and leans in to kiss my forehead. "Just for over a week or so, baby, Coach wants us to attend some pro games and study their tapes. He's managed to book us into some training program, and apparently it's a big deal."

"Oh." Strangely enough, I try to remember the last time Cole and I were separated for more than a few days and nothing comes to mind.

"And you're leaving tomorrow?"

"Bright and early to Florida."

"Oh, it'll be a short flight then," I muse and begin playing with the end of my sweater.

"Hey," he tips my chin up, "If you're not okay with it, then..."

"No!" My eyes widen. "You're going; of course you're going. I guess I'm just not used to being here without you."

"I don't ever want you to get used to that." His eyes are intense, burning into mine as he sits down next to me and pulls me into his lap. The textbook is shut and pushed aside, of course. I wrap my arms around Cole's neck and nuzzle into his chest.

"I don't want to suffocate you," I tell him, somehow just starting to realize my worst fears. "I don't want to be that girlfriend that wants you to only spend time with her."

"Hey, where's this coming from? Why'd you ever think that I would want to spend any less time with you? Tessie, I'm here with you because that's all I want to do. In fact, it scares me sometimes that maybe you'll get sick of me."

He laughs, but it's forced. I have no idea how we ended up having this moment, but it's refreshing to know that he's got the same insecurities as I do. He might be completely wrong but hey, at least he gets it.

"Never," I whisper, "I'm going to miss you so much, but maybe this will be good for us."

"Trying to get rid of me already? I'm hurt." He jokes, but this time I know he's not taking anything to heart.

"More like I'm giving you room to not worry about your crazy girlfriend. It'll be a nice change."

"I kinda like my crazy girlfriend; I think I'll keep her," he says, tightening his arms around me. But then his eyes meet mine and his expression is serious.

"I'm happy that you're finally putting yourself out there. You deserve it, Tessie, don't let anyone tell you otherwise."

My eyes sting a little, there's a sudden crackle of tension in the air, and something shifts, something I can't put my finger on, and I'm not sure whether I like it.

"I love you." I kiss him swiftly, trying to find that reassurance that nothing has changed,

"I love you, too."

I pull back and study his face. "Are you still thinking about what Nicole said?"

His expression becomes stony. I don't know what has happened in the time between our conversation in the car to now but it's rattled him; something has, and he's not telling me.

"No," he says quickly and tucks a lock of my hair behind my ear. "But there are other things on my mind."

"And you don't want to tell me?"

This version of Cole is slightly scary because ever since the day we got together, he's been nothing but honest with me. Good or bad, he'll tell me, and right now I know it's killing him to have to hide something from me.

"I don't want you to worry, okay? I can handle it."

He doesn't let me bring up the topic again as he kisses me into oblivion.

***

I'm doodling when I'm supposed to be working on my ten-page essay for class, and Sarah notices that my thoughts are elsewhere. I'd holed myself up in the library while she Skyped with Grant, but when I came back to our room, I hadn't managed to even come up with an introduction. Cole's left this morning and after spending all of yesterday with him, I still can't figure out what's going on with him.

"How did things go at the paper?" she asks. I know she's trying to start a conversation that'll eventually get me to spill what it is that I'm obsessing over. What could I possibly tell her when I don't know much myself?

I shrug. "They're not looking for reporters, no spots left. But I sent one of the editors a piece I'd been working on and she really liked it, so I'm optimistic."

She smiles warmly. "I'm so glad you're pushing yourself to do these things."

She's involved in a bunch of societies for environmental protection, which explains her enthusiasm.

"So, what's wrong?" She frowns. "Why do you look so sad?"

I shake my head. "Nothing, it's just an off day. I can't seem to start this essay."

"Oh." She perks up. "Do you need some help? I could research something for you."

You know you've got the best roommate when they offer to help you despite being buried under a mountain of homework themselves.

"Thanks, I love you for offering, but I think I need to sleep on this. Maybe I'll have better luck tomorrow."

She gives me a knowing look. "It gets easier. you know. You'll miss him a lot in the beginning, but trust me, a little distance is always good."

She winks at me and my mouth nearly drops open. Wait, what? Sweet little Sarah surely isn't telling me about the merits of reunion sex?

Or is she?

Her face flushes a little after she's said this, and before I know it, I'm laughing like crazy, because who would've thought that my roommate had a kinky side to her?

It's like finding out McGonagall wears negligees to bed.

And then I'm laughing even harder at that particular image; from the other side, Sarah hits me with a cushion.

Once we're done acting like immature preteens, Sarah goes to sleep for the night as she has an eight a.m. class the next day. I keep checking my phone for any news from Cole because I don't want to be the one to reach out first. I remember promising myself to give Cole a few days to relax and just be his age with his friends. By being my boyfriend, he's automatically had to go into protector mode; I know he feels responsible for me, but that's not how it's supposed to be, right? I need a boyfriend, not a chaperone, and he needs someone he's not constantly looking out for.

But there's no contact from his side even though I know he landed quite some time ago. Maybe he's tired, I try to reason with myself. He probably needs to catch up on some sleep, or maybe he has commitments with his team, yeah, probably that. I pack up my books and try to get some sleep.

***

I'm up early the next morning and taking out all my frustration on the treadmill; I run and run till my heart's beating so fast, I can feel it in my mouth.

"Steady there or you'll wear yourself out too fast," Bentley chastises me but I ignore him. There's still no word from Cole, but I've seen the rest of his teammates post updates, and it's infuriating. Doesn't he know I'm worried? Whatever it is that's going through his head, the least he could do is tell me he's still alive.

"Okay, that's it." The treadmill comes to a gradual halt so that I'm not on my butt on the floor. "You're out of my gym until you come back without whatever the hell's going on in your head."

He literally pushes me off and shoves my jacket at me. I glare at him. "This isn't your gym, and I can't believe you did that."

"As your trainer, I don't want you to risk injuring yourself, and as your friend, I'm worried about you. Go take a walk, get some fresh air, listen to your sappy music. Then come back here, and if you still want to try that stunt, go for it."

My anger thaws a little, and suddenly I feel stupid for acting out like this. "I'm sorry, and yeah, let's go for a rain check on this session." My shoulders slump, and a pitying look flashes across Bentley's face that I hate.

"You haven't heard from Cole," he states, not even asking, and my head drops in shame. Yup, I've totally become that girl who bases her entire existence on one guy.

"I'm sure he's busy, but it'd be just nice to know that he's okay. He didn't really leave things in a good place."

Bentley looks uncomfortable, and I'm sure giving relationship advice isn't something on his daily to-do list, but I appreciate him trying.

"Well, I'm hanging out with Amanda later today, if you want to come with us…"

"No! Honestly, I'm fine. Don't ruin your date for me, but I do want to meet her sometime when I'm not acting like a raging beast with PMS."

To his credit, he laughs at this and doesn't turn any redder.

"Go home, Tessa, get some rest, and I'll see you tomorrow."

I shower and dress back up in my jeans and warm sweatshirt. Picking up my phone from my gym bag, I finally, finally see a text from Cole.

Cole: Sorry I haven't been able to call you, Shortcake. Coach is kicking our asses, but I'll call when I can, miss you.

I'm filled with a euphoric kind of a relief, but that ominous feeling is still nagging at me. This isn't like him, but maybe I'm reading too much into a text. Quickly replying, I make my way out of the gym and back to the dorms.

Outside my room I find Cami hovering and biting her nails; well, that's never good news. She looks deep in thought as she paces, and when she hears me approaching, her face drops and she rushes toward me.

"Are you okay?" She grips the tops of my arms.

"Why wouldn't I be?" I'm confused and half scared. "What's wrong?"

"Oh." She looks a little lost and then curses under her breath. "You haven't seen it?"

"Seen what? Cami, you're scaring me."

"Shit." She curses again and pulls out her phone from her pocket. It doesn't take her long to load whatever she's trying to show me.

"So, this is an interview." She bites her lip and hesitates before continuing. "Now, I don't think this is a big deal or anything, but some of the girls were talking in class. I shut them up, but I thought you should hear it from me before it gets blown out of proportion."

"I'm confused and freaking out, so you better tell me whatever the hell's going on."

I might be having a panic attack, who knows.

"It's Cole, okay? ESPN did a feature on him, and they asked him some personal questions. Everyone's making a big deal because…"

"Because what?"

"Because he said he isn't dating anyone, that he's not looking to be in a relationship and wants to focus on football," she says in a rush.

Okay, breathe, Tessa, just breathe. There's got to be an explanation, because there always is one. These things happen; people hide their personal lives from the press all the time. No big deal.

My chest rises and falls heavily, and I try not to have a full-blown panic attack now.

"And everyone's seen it?" I whisper.

She cringes. "Pretty much."

"And they're all taking it to mean that Cole and I have broken up?"

"Well, one particular breed of nasty bitch was spreading around lies that he was just using you for sex, but I think a punch in the face shut her up."

"You punched her?" I gasp.

Cami shrugs. "What can I say? It's been an interesting morning."

"Oh, okay, well, I think I need to sit down now." My legs feel like Jell-O; gingerly I let myself in the room and am glad that Sarah's in class. The poor girl has to tolerate more of my drama than I'd like her to witness.

"He didn't mention it to you?"

"We haven't talked since he left, so I had no idea." My voice shakes as I sit down on my bed and wrap my arms around myself. "But he texted me this morning and didn't say a word about the article."

"A little warning would've been nice."

"Yeah."

We're both quiet for a minute or two. "So what now?" Cami asks.

"I want to wait till he gets back before doing anything."

"That's wise, I guess."

"I also have a dance audition this evening." They didn't give me a long time to prepare anything; I have to learn a routine and repeat it. It'll be fine, I think.

"Are you sure you're up for it?"

"Of course. Like I said, I'm not going to react unless I talk to him, so there's no reason for me to screw up this opportunity."

"And what about everyone else who's chomping at the bit to make the most of the news?"

"I'll deal with it if it comes." Right now, I desperately need a routine, a methodical task, something menial to get over this sudden shock.

"Well then," she says enthusiastically as she walks on over to where my iPod is plugged in the dock. "Since we're here, why don't you show me these moves you speak of? I need to make a cheer for you and need some inspiration."

"Please don't."

"Oh, but I have to; I even got some pom-poms. Now, how does some S&M sound?"

CHAPTER TWENTY-FOUR
Friends Don't Let Friends Make Naked Mistakes

"I aced my routine," I tell Cami and Sarah while scooping a huge spoonful of ice cream into my mouth. Sitting cross-legged on my bed, I contemplate an extra couple of hours in the gym versus finishing the entire tub and, what the heck, I'll sweat it out. This is a complete ice cream emergency.

"Then would you mind telling us why you're putting more sugar inside you than all of Willy Wonka's factory?" Sarah pushes the bridge of her reading glasses further up her nose and gazes at me with concern written all over her face. She's aware of the situation with Cole; I'm sure Cami must've warned her of the crazy, possibly suicidal roommate, and she's been on Hurricane Tessa watch all weekend.

"Hmm, that was a nice book," I muse and reach for my ice cream again. I probably paint a pathetic picture. Ratty old pajamas with more holes than I'd like to count, hair unwashed for what's probably day three, and surrounded by heaps and heaps of sugar; sugar is good.

Sugar doesn't drop a Texas-sized bomb on you via the Internet.

Sugar doesn't avoid you and start screening your calls.

Sugar sure as heck doesn't take three days just to send an "I'm busy" text.

So, of course, I'd love to be left alone with sugar, but somehow, I've managed to find people who care about me and refused to let me streak around the campus naked on a sugar high.

Friends don't let friends make naked mistakes.

I'm pretty sure they've barricaded my door and are now trying some form of counseling; little do they know, my issues may not have only outsold *Vogue*, let's just say all of Condé Nast would have a tough time competing with my numbers.

"So, Lindsey actually said you have a shot at being on the team?"

I shrug, the audition and everything that followed is a little bit hazy. Cami did go with me for moral support, but I received the judgement in private. They didn't think that I sucked, and I sure as heck wasn't as flaky or prone to post-hangover tantrums like the rest of their freshman girls, so things were looking good for me. I'd receive an e-mail from them sometime this week, but some of the girls from the squad had already starting smiling at me, waving like they'd finally acknowledged me as one of their "people." I'd say it's a good start.

"I probably do, but then again, the rumor might just ruin everything."

It's funny, because back when people first found out that Cole and I were together, the frat and sorority crowd treated me like dirt, and now that they've started thinking that we're no longer together, the reaction's even worse.

How do I deal with these people?

Oddly enough, it's not the relationship I'm worried about, in my heart I know and am convinced that Cole would never break my heart like that, that he'd sooner kill himself than put me through that kind of pain.

Knowing all of this doesn't stop me from getting mad. I have an idea of what he's doing, and it makes me want to go all the way up to New York and practice my nonexistent ninja skills on Nicole because she's the one who started all of this. So much for trying to be a good person; it just came back to bite me in the butt.

Cami waves her hand, dismissing my worries. "Please, you'd be surprised by the kind of popularity you're getting right now. You're the mysterious girl that they know the freshman QB is absolutely batshit crazy about, but now they're all wondering why he's denying your relationship. The latest rumor is that you broke his heart, and now every guy on campus wants to hook up with you."

I think I might just throw up. The idea of rumors and speculations finally manages to kill my appetite and I pack the stuff up. The ice cream goes back into the minifridge and I take a moment to get a grip.

"This is just like high school, only worse, because at least then I had a hope of escaping anywhere, well, basically here, but now what? Do I think about the next big thing? Grad school? Do grad students like to gossip, too?"

"Honey, it's a good thing it's college; the semester is going to start kicking all our asses pretty soon, and no one's going to have time to be anything but the single reason why Starbucks stays in business."

Sarah snorts. “She’s got a point. How do people even have the spare time to think about these things when I’m struggling to breathe under all these books?” She gestures to the hundreds of dollars’ worth of textbooks strewn over our room, and she’s right. Between going regularly to classes, working part time, and studying late into the night, it’s not really convenient to be dissecting someone else’s life.

“They aren’t the real problem, Tessa; have you tried calling Cole again?”

I snuggle inside my blankets and pull them tighter around me because suddenly I’m shivering.

“He’s not answering my calls or texts. I know he’s on some kind of a heroic mission to protect me, but this is just…”

“Stupid?” Sarah offers.

“Absolutely moronic?” Cami chimes in.

“A dick move,” I end, and then for some reason, the three of us start laughing. Laughing feels good, I haven’t laughed in a while now, and somehow now, with these two around me, I’m able to forget about my idiot boyfriend’s idiotic plans for just a second.

***

On day six post Cole’s breakthrough interview on the ESPN website, I’m still fielding calls from my friends and family. Of course, Beth, Megan, and my brother are fuming. They’ve seen zombie Tessa at her best, so it freaks them out that I might possibly revert to that, but I assure them that everything’s fine. They know that Nicole’s words could’ve had a domino effect because Cole’s like a DIY addict when it comes to his perceptions of my safety; he always wants to find ways to make me feel more protected, safer, comfortable.

I think in the end he forgets that he's not supposed to be a winter coat, he's supposed to be my boyfriend, my more.

But it's exasperating to see how stubborn he is, and I'm not going to try forcing his hand when he's so far away. I push myself into focusing on my classes, taking copious notes that are far more detailed than necessary, and then knocking a good few hours in the library. I'm still waiting to hear from Lindsey, but she said they needed at least a week to sort all the details and decide which freshman girl's dreams to rip away from her.

With such pleasant thoughts, I make my way to Professor Flynn's office to collect a paper for my British Lit class. The usual butterflies-in-my-stomach feeling is absent because I know I worked my butt off for this paper and am really proud of what I submitted. Professor Flynn's class is one that I actually enjoy and don't need multiple cups of coffee to survive. Her lectures are interesting and make you want to participate; it's the only class where I speak up without the fear of being ridiculed or snickered at.

So, it comes as a definitely burning, hot steel rod in the chest when she places my paper in front of me and I see the letter "D-" encircled on the front.

For a couple of minutes, I think I refuse to blink or breathe. The other letters on the piece of paper in front of me start to jumble up, but that one letter glares at me, and I just can't seem to stop looking at it.

Wow, have I ever gotten a grade this low?

And did I really have to get it now, in my first semester of college, when my self-confidence is already plummeting faster than Juicy Couture's sales?

"B-but surely there must have been a mistake," I stutter as I push the paper back toward Professor Flynn, who's staring at me sympathetically. She knows how much work I've put into this, how many times I've been the only person coming to her during office hours to discuss it. I feel tears beginning to prick the backs of my eyes, but I refuse to be the wimp that cries in front of her teacher.

God, even I'm not that pathetic.

She sighs, "I'm afraid not, Tessa. I tried to point out what you were doing wrong all the times you came to see me, but you haven't seemed to pick up on it. I was really disappointed with your work, but only because I expect so much more from you."

And it just keeps getting worse.

My hands shake slightly as I skim through the paper that has more red ink on it than the printed black script. All those hours' worth of research and going over the material again and again, how the hell did I end up getting a D-?

This could potentially screw up my entire GPA; the dance team and the student newspaper begin to look like pipe dreams. Does anyone even get anything below an A in this place?

"Could you tell me specifically what I did wrong? Because, honestly? I did everything I possibly could for your paper."

Again, she looks at me pitifully. "You went about it the wrong way. As an introductory-level course, I wasn't looking for groundbreaking research on Austen; however, I will commend you for your effort. Not even my senior students put that amount of work into their resources, but what you missed was the point of the paper. I didn't want research, Tessa, I wanted spirit and originality. I wanted you to get your voice through to me in the paper, and all I received was you quoting and reiterating all that's been said and done before. Your paper lacked creativity."

Huh, good thing I'm choosing to becoming an English major. My noncreative self and I will surely flourish in the field.

I feel like the walls of her office are closing in on me. I want to argue more; actually, I want to throw a fit and call her out on her bullshit. Why did she not say these things when I was running draft after draft with her? Did she want to fail me and then shove all my hard work in my face, telling me that even my best isn't good enough?

With quivering legs, I grab my paper and make a beeline for the door. I'm sure when I'm in a better state, I'll reach out to her again and talk about a potential makeup paper, a redo or something I can do for extra credit, but right now, it's either leaving her office or dunking her head in her fishbowl.

I make the better decision to leave.

***

To say I've had a rough couple of days would be a really bad idea because I might shoot the next person who looks at me like my dog's recently been ran over. Sarah steers clear of me as I barrel through the door and begin changing into my workout clothes. I may have promised Bentley to not let my anger control me while working out, but it's either go running or lock myself in the room and cry for days.

The thought of my first-ever failing grade and Cole's distance looms over me as I change and head out the door. I don't even know where to go since Bentley's probably training someone right now and will probably kick me out the door, judging by my mood.

In the end, I just decide to drive around for a bit; who cares if it's Cole's car that I'm driving and that every moment I'm assaulted with his smell and the memories we have in this car. Switching my phone off, I throw it in the back seat and select a random playlist on my iPod just to keep my thoughts busy. Practically, I know that one bad grade isn't the end of the world, but someone should also have said that your first bad grade does seem like the end of your world.

I just failed my favorite class; do I even want to know how I've done in the others?

My grades were the one thing I thought I could rely on, that studying was something I totally had a handle on, and now even that security blanket's been taken away from me—I just feel lost.

Because it's November and we're just starting to get our first inch of snow, it's colder than I'd anticipated or dressed for. Cranking up the heating, I contemplate briefly about where my life's heading at this point, but when that proves to be more depressing than anything else, I turn up the volume of the music and sing at the top of my lungs.

It helps just a little.

I go through multiple playlists as I drive in circles, to nowhere and anywhere. There's a kind of peace associated with the freedom to lose yourself. I mean, if I've already hit rock bottom, I might as well enjoy it while I can. Tomorrow I go back to being good old Tessa, just going through the motions.

It's a little after midnight by the time I get back to my residence hall. I'm damn near freezing because I had to find a parking space for this damn car; Cole left it here for me so that I could use it and wouldn't have to walk all the way to his apartment for it. It's little things like that that tell me not to believe the things that are being said about us.

But it's still fudging infuriating that he won't talk to me.

My anger has thawed a little, and my meltdown over the bad grade has gotten a little better. I'll have to talk to Professor Flynn, beg her to give me another shot.

I'm lost in these thoughts, so when I step onto the stairs of my dorm, I miss the figure hunched down on the steps. But the sound of my footsteps alerts him, and there he is, standing right before me after straight-up ignoring me for a week.

"Thank Christ," he breathes before nearly racing down the stairs toward me and enveloping me in his arms. I'm absolutely still, the shock is definitely the most potent of my feelings right now. Cole's here and I'm in his arms, god, he's here.

His voice is muffled as he's buried his head into my shoulder. "Where were you? We've been trying to find you for ages. You took my car…I had no idea, Tessie…where'd you go?"

His breathing is heavy, and I can tell that he's really upset at the thought of my getting lost, but even as I put my arms around him, I'm hit with a surge of anger and utter exhaustion.

"I've had a shitty day," I mumble into his chest.

His pulls me farther into his chest and holds me like he's never going to let go.

"I know, Shortcake, come on, let me take care of you."

I don't even have the energy to protest at this point. Like a ragdoll, I let him drag me back to his car, and this time, he gets into the driver's seat.

What do I say to him?

"I can explain…" he begins, noticing how I'm more interested in staring out the window than catching up with him about his week-long disappearance.

"That's such a clichéd beginning, don't you think? I'd try to be more original if I were you."

He sighs and doesn't attempt to talk to me again. On reaching his building, we walk to his apartment in silence, not even attempting to hold hands. It's quiet enough to tell me that his roommate's not home. My eyes struggle to stay open as I trudge toward his room and into his closet. Here I'm comfortable, surrounded by all that's familiar.

I change into one of his T-shirts and get into bed.

We've still not spoken a word.

"Tomorrow, tomorrow we should talk," Cole says softly as he strips down to his boxers and gets into bed. He lies on his back and pulls me up so that my head rests on his chest, my arms go around his stomach, and my legs are tangled with his.

Maybe I nod, or maybe I just doze off.

CHAPTER TWENTY-FIVE
His Possessiveness Is as Uncontrollable as Kanye West

I love that moment between being asleep and waking up where just for that one moment you're stuck somewhere between a dream and reality. I mean yeah, it sucks that you've got to get up and deal with the general soul-sucking nature of life, but isn't it kind of awesome how two worlds collide? If you're lucky and the dream is a really good one, the kind that leaves you feeling warm and fuzzy, then that moment right before you wake up will extend to your whole day. There's something about having a fantastic dream that makes your outlook on the day that is to come really positive.

How I wish I'd had a good dream.

It takes me a little while to get my bearings. I must've been really exhausted the previous night to not remember falling asleep. I'm not the kind of person that falls asleep the second their head hits the pillow. It'll take at least five mini meltdowns before I realize that there's nothing much I can do about the fact that my stomach's getting a little too round again for my liking while I'm wearing my Scooby-Doo pajamas.

Yeah, Bentley better stop kicking me out of the gym.

But, getting back to more important issues, I may be slightly disoriented, but not enough to forget whose bed I'm in or whose shirt I'm wearing. I'm surrounded by Cole's scent and his arms that are usually wound tight around me but have loosened their hold in the night. The sun's streaming in through the windows and it must be late morning now, around ten a.m. if I were to guess. My mental calendar tells me that it's Saturday and that I shouldn't panic because I've got nowhere to be, but there's a sudden clawing at my chest. I feel a sudden panic grip me that makes me subtly struggle out of Cole's arms and out from the bed. He makes a sound when I get up but goes back to sleep, I guess last night must have been exhausting for him too, I didn't really know that he'd be back.

The thought fuels my actions and, on autopilot mode, I quickly change into my clothes from last night and grab my things; my phone's battery is dead, but I'm sure Cole must've let Sarah know that her roommate didn't wind up dead in the middle of the woods.

As noiselessly as I can manage, I sneak out of Cole's room, only to run into his roommate, Eric, in the kitchen. He's a nice guy, but we don't usually see each other because of our schedules, and it's a little embarrassing to meet him while I'm supposedly doing the walk of shame.

He's helping himself to a cup of coffee and offers me one when I greet him.

"No, thanks, I…I've got to hurry."

He raises a brow but doesn't ask more questions; I obviously look a little frazzled. "Do you want me to tell Cole something?"

"No, uh, I'll text him, but thanks." I give him a small smile and feel his gaze on the back of my head as I leave.

"He was freaking out last night when he came back. Is everything okay?"

I pause at the door and think about my answer, is everything okay? Turning toward him, I give Eric a reassuring smile.

"Yeah, we just had some miscommunication issues. It's all good now."

He doesn't look like he believes me. "Great, well, I don't know if he's gotten a chance to tell you, but my girlfriend wants us to have dinner with you two. Let me know whenever you're free so she can do the planning she loves to do so much."

He has such an adorable look on his face as he thinks about her that I smile despite my inner turmoil.

"Sure, we should be free sometime next week, before the professors start cracking the whips."

"It's essay season isn't it? Welcome to academic hell. How're you coping?"

I shrug, keeping my eye on Cole's door. I want to leave before he gets up and by the looks of it, Eric wants me to stay. He's a loyal roommate, I'll give him that.

"Speaking of, I've really got to run. I have a study group in an hour and I need to prep for that. I'll let you know about the dinner soon."

Giving him a quick wave, I rush out the door, exhaling heavily. Though it's when I'm outside the apartment building that I realize that Cole now has the keys to his car and that I'll have to walk back to campus in the freezing cold, and I'm not exactly dressed for it. Oh well, I trudge through the chill and grab myself a coffee from the Starbucks around the corner. The walk allows me to think clearly because I hadn't been doing so last night. I didn't even put up a fight before going home with Cole, should I have? He'd basically shut me out and refused to talk to me while I'd been dealing with a problem he'd created. Despite his previous record of being an exemplary boyfriend, this is definitely a strike against him. He should've known better than to go ahead with his stupid plan without even talking to me, heck, a last-minute warning would've been fine, too. I think about the looks I've been receiving on campus lately, and it just makes me angry because most people probably thought I was pathetic, heartbroken, a fool.

The beauty of college, though, is that you only get to be in the limelight for a millisecond, so I know the worst is over. People have bigger problems than my relationship status, and this is evident because by the time I make it back to campus, I'm a nobody again, and the biggest news is the party that one of the fraternities is hosting tonight.

Thankfully, I make it to the residence halls without being stopped. I look like I should after last night, tired and weary. My eyes are puffy and a little red, had I been crying in the halls? I take my bag of toiletries and take a hot shower in the bathrooms. Since it's Saturday, a lot of people are sleeping off a night of maybe drinking too much. Maybe I should've just gotten drunk too, who knows what adventures Drunk Tessa could've gotten up to. Oh well, maybe next time when my boyfriend decides to put me through the wringer.

Sarah is gone when I go into our room, knowing her, she's either at the library or running around for any one of her extracurriculars. I use the opportunity to once again stalk the ESPN website, which Cami and Sarah had tried to block. I go through the interview and the words never change, the comments, however, continue to get more and more interesting as the readers mention all the depraved things they'd like to do to my boyfriend. The only break I get is from reading a certain, "KickInYourNuts," who more than often has posted that the only depraved thing she'd like to do to Cole is one that'd leave him incapable of having children.

Oh Beth, how I miss you.

Thoughts of Professor Flynn's paper come to mind. There's still a chance that I'll be able to get a redo of some sort, so I need to start working on that. She wants me to be creative and spirited, well, now's as good a time as any. If heartbreak can make you win multiple Grammys, then a little stab in the heart may as well produce a good paper on Austen.

Scrolling through my laptop, I push aside the fact that I left Cole in bed, alone. Before I know it, all the stress from the past few days hits me hard, and my eyes begin to droop. For someone who loves sleep more than they love a limb, I haven't exactly been sleeping well, so it's no surprise that minutes into getting into bed, I'm asleep again.

***

Someone's banging on my skull, I think.

Or they could just be knocking at the door, it's hard to tell, but I'm woken up from a dreamless sleep too suddenly, which makes my heart start pounding. Shakily I get up and unlock the door, only to find Cole on the other side. I have no idea how long I fell asleep this time, but it must not have been long enough because Cole still looks dead tired. Beautiful as he is, he could use some rest because there are bruise-like shadows beneath his eyes that give away how he feels.

We stare at each for a while; I don't make a move to let him in, and he doesn't try to come into the room, which is very unlike him, but also goes to show that he realizes that he's messed up big-time.

"Who let you in this time?"

He lets out a breath of relief like he'd expected me to go all snapping turtle on him the moment he tried to reach out to me. We're close to that, Stone, pretty close.

"One of the girls on your floor, she, uh, recognized me."

"I'm sure your newly acquired single status must've been a pretty good incentive for her."

He flinches visibly and looks around; there's no one around yet, but pretty soon, people will start trickling down to the dining halls. I would worry, too, if I were him.

"Can we do this elsewhere?" He tries to step forward but I stop him with an outstretched hand. "Oh no, you don't. If you're okay with me becoming a laughingstock, then I'd like to subject you to some public humiliation, too."

His expression is tender, which, yeah, admittedly makes me want to pull him inside and wrap myself around him, but this is a fight where I can't let his brooding "come hither" looks break my resolve.

"Tessie, you have to know that everything I did—"

"Was for my sake? Was to protect me? Well, congratulations, Stone, because you did just that. Whatever imaginary creature it is that you're protecting me from by basically telling the whole world that you want nothing to do with me has been defeated. But guess what? The downside is that everyone thinks I'm just a quick fuck for you, the stupid, naive girl that you're embarrassed to be with. While you've been busy 'protecting' me and ignoring me, you actually failed to notice how your genius plan backfired."

His expression morphs into fury and despite me putting up a fight, he somehow forces himself into the room, slamming the door shut behind him. Cole grips me by the tops of my arms and pulls me into his chest.

"Who said that to you? You know I'd fucking kill anyone who even looked at you that way," he growls.

"You don't get to say that to me when you're the person who put me in that position in the first place. It hurt, Cole, it hurt when all of that came my way without any warning."

He blinks a couple of times and then drops his hands from my arms. He curses under his breath and then kicks the foot of my bed.

"You don't realize what the press is like, Tessie, if they found out about you or about us, you'd never have a moment of normalcy again.

Some of the guys I met…they told me about what their girlfriends had to go through, and I just…I didn't want you to have to face that."

I must really be out of tune with the world of college football because I didn't realize that the dating lives of the players were given such importance. I don't understand his world, and even as his college career is skyrocketing, with more and more attention from the media and pro scouts, I have never allowed myself to come to terms with the fact that our lives are changing.

"Why do you never ask me before you go off and do these things?" I cry out, feeling frustrated enough to want to bash my head against a wall. We've had this conversation so many times that I don't even see the point of having it again. "What part of being equals don't you get? Can you even imagine how embarrassing that interview was? And then, god, you shut me out so bad." My voice breaks and I have to sit down on my bed, just so that my knees don't give way.

I feel Cole hovering close by but he doesn't try to touch me. "I knew you'd be hurt, trust me, I heard an earful from your brother, but I knew that if I talked to you, I'd just call the interviewer up and beg them to change everything I'd said. I…I'm sorry, I know I could've handled it better."

I snort. "Yeah, you could've."

He gets down on his knees and cups my face, moving in to kiss me, but he sees the panic on my face, and the hurt in his eyes kills something inside me. "You don't want me to touch you."

"I'm confused and hurt. I don't understand where we're going, and every single time we take a step forward, it seems like you move us five steps back." I take a deep breath before continuing. "I'd do anything for you, anything to be with you. You mean more to me than all this drama, and I love you for helping me overcome so much this year, but now…now you're just making me feel like I'm a damn burden you have to carry."

He sucks in a breath. "No! That's so far from the truth." He lets out a bitter laugh. "Quite the opposite, actually. I'm waiting for the day you realize that you could do so much better than me and when I'd have to fall to your feet to convince you that even though you could, you'd still never find someone as desperate to have you in his life as I am."

Tears sting my eyes and I know this is the boy that I fell hopelessly in love with. The cocky, arrogant bad boy who's so vulnerable on the inside that it breaks your heart.

"It wasn't supposed to be this painful being together, was it?"

Cole drops his head into my lap and I feel him shake his head. I run my fingers through his hair, and it feels like the first moment of calmness we've had in a long time.

"Let's do this your way, let's keep this, us, away from the everyone who could possibly destroy us."

My breath hitches as I say this, and I know even as the words leave my mouth that it's a bad idea. But with the way things have been going since the moment we got here, I know that we need to give it our all and fight like hell to be the Cole and Tessa that fell in love slowly but oh so madly. Lots of little moments led us here, dances and dresses, fights and jokes, ice creams and chocolates, first kisses and hesitant confessions. If it took you that long to find each other, wouldn't you do anything in your power to keep that person?

And when Cole lifts his head from my lap and sits down next to me, gripping the back of my neck and kissing me with every ounce of love he has for me, I know I've made the right decision.

"I'm not ashamed of you or embarrassed. I love you, I'm in awe of you, you're the strongest person I've ever met, Shortcake." He looks me in the eye as he says this. "But I can't be the reason you're always doubting yourself or why other people look at you in a way that makes me want to become someone I haven't been in a long time. If this helps me make you happier, then I'll do it."

"And how you'll react when you won't be able to hold my hand in public or when someone tries to hit on me." I shouldn't be this short with him but I'm a girl; we tend to lack the male sort of tunnel vision. I'm preparing myself for the times when Cole's going to go apeshit and demand that I lock myself up in a room.

On cue, his eyes turn cold and he kisses me once more, a deep and admittedly dirty kiss that tells me that he's got no intentions of ever letting a guy get close enough to attempt anything of the sort.

"We'll still be friends, I'll just be that asshole guy friend that has no qualms about beating anyone who looks at you to pulp."

"Oh boy, you know you're going to regret this, right?"

"I already am, but if this means you'll still be around me when I'm eighty, then what's a few attempted murder charges here and there?"

"To be honest, I don't think you'd be able to pull off the orange."

He raises his brow sexily, and his hands began to roam over my sweater, which just happens to be a burnt orange, and when his fingers slip underneath it, he kisses the side of my neck and whispers in my ear. "You were saying?"

"I think you misunderstood me." My breathing picks up.

"Oh, I think I understood you perfectly." Cole gives me a wicked grin, but just as he's about to wander into seriously inappropriate territory, I have the good sense to think about Sarah.

"Oh no, you don't." I slip away from him. "I'm still mad at you."

His face drops comically and I know we're both trying to hang on to the last few moments of normalcy before we dive headfirst into something I know is a bad idea.

Because, Cole Stone? Yeah, if there's one thing I really, really know about my boyfriend, it's that his possessiveness is as uncontrollable as Kanye West. It tends to get the best of him at times, and I only have to count the number of times Jay's been punched in the face to cement that judgement.

He thinks he can handle the repercussions of letting people think we're not together because of some high and mighty ideals about making me feel happy?

Well, I think this is going to be something he learns the hard way.

About the Author

Blair Holden (@jessgirl93 on Wattpad) is a twenty-three-year-old college student by day and Wattpad author by night. Her hobbies include and are limited to obsessively scouring Goodreads and reading romance novels, with a preference for all things new adult. Her own work usually contains lots of romance, humor, angst, and brooding bad-boy heroes. Caffeine and late-night Gilmore Girls marathons help her find a balance between completing her degree and writing. She writes for herself and also to make readers swoon, laugh, and occasionally cry. Her book, The Bad Boy's Girl, has amassed nearly 170 million reads, which absolutely baffles her. Her dream is to see her readers holding a published copy of her books and remembering how far they've come together! Find her on Twitter as @blairholdenx and on Facebook and Instagram as @jessgirl93

Printed in Great Britain
by Amazon

67822062R00229